for the

Eleanore MacDonald

C000094799

All the
Little Graces

Eleanore MacDonald

All The Little Graces

Print version

Cover illustration - Wendy Spratt

Cover design - Lorraine Gervais

Photograph - Breelyn MacDonald

For Margarita

and all of the lost and abandoned ... the
misunderstood, the abused, the voiceless ones.
For my Damu.
And for the late, much beloved Djuna Cupcake.
In gratitude.

TABLE OF CONTENTS

ACKNOWLEDGEMENTS

All The Little Graces percolated and brewed and stewed for 10 years before it ever even whispered it's first words to me. There are many people to thank for it's 'becoming', those who contributed to the six years that followed in a blaze of words and pages - but I must first begin at the beginning and thank that mangy little brown mutt of a street dog, Margarita, for being the inspiration for it all. Though the story itself is a work of fiction, it is based in many truths - the first being that Margarita was indeed real. My family and I met her in 1990 at the beginning of six-weeks spent on a Greek island and she changed our lives forever. Though a victim of the streets she was quite a character, a pure little soul who captured our hearts and ultimately introduced us to the harsh reality of the life of a Greek stray. More truth ... Greece is enigmatic and magnificent, and for me, there is nothing that can match the magic and peace a Greek island can offer!

I must also thank Skiathos, an island of the archipelago Sporades in the Aegean Sea - a magnificent beauty and a deep well of inspiration, I thank her for our 26 year-long love affair and for being a throne for my Muse. My grateful thanks to her people, who over the many years have slowly helped me to better understand the Greek spirit and passion, and have given me some insight into their country's painful yet inspiring past. Skiathos is one of many islands and villages that served as a template for 'place' in the story, all of them responsible for the DNA that ultimately makes the 'Graces' island one of a kind and very much it's own character.

Grateful thanks also ... to my husband and partner, Paul Kamm, for encouraging me, humoring me, feeding me, letting me 'liberate' some of his words, and for being patient with my frustrations and the strange hours I had to keep to get the writing done - as well as for being an incredible help as a reader and an editor all along the path; to my darling and talented daughter, Breelyn MacDonald, for being a part of it all and always encouraging me along the way, and for the fantastic photograph that graces the 'About the Author' page; the late Reverend Djuna Cupcake, my dearest canine companion who always helped 'keep the space' for me as I wrote, and was a living, breathing conduit to the book's main protagonist, Margarita; to friends Wendy Spratt, for the lovely painting that became the cover, and Lorraine Gervais for the cover design; to Kip Harris, who was my English teacher when I was a junior in a remarkable high school neatly tucked away in the magical woods of in the Sierra Nevada Mountains ... an inspiring man who opened my world to Emerson and Thoreau, to Wordsworth, Keats, Hemingway and Shakespeare and therefore encouraged in me a passion for the colorful world of words; to my other readers - Cindi Buzzell, Maggie McKaig, Mike McKinney, Elena Powell, Kate Wall, Donna Natali and Tom MacDonald - for begging me for clarity, for weeping and giggling and ensuring that I wasn't writing *it's* when I should have been writing *its*, and essentially helping to make sense of it all; to Sands Hall for encouragement and tools that changed my writing life; Eleni 'Helen' Dumas, our darling Greek language teacher extraordinaire; Yvonne Ayoub, for her own unique perspective of an island we both deeply love; Kiria Koula, and Syrainoula Mathinou, for their loving kindness and true hospitality, and for the beautiful, inspiring spot on their veranda that hovers just above the Aegean, where the words flowed to me over the calm morning sea from the sun's rising ... and Dimitrios Mathinos, for sharing his tales of life on the seas and, and his knowledge of and glimpses into island life in days long past; Ioannis Tsikounas for his help, his friendship, and for being the source of boundless laughter, always; to Mike Voyatzis, for information about fish and fishing the waters of the Aegean, and most importantly for his warm and gracious hospitality in the quiet of several Skiathos winters - visits that truly enabled me to get my book finished; to the angels of the Skiathos Dog shelter, especially Helen Bozas, for making the shelter a reality and for caring so selflessly for the voiceless ones; Greek Animal Rescue, and Diane Aldan (Tails from Greece Rescue) for information, and for helping the animals of Greece's streets; and to my kind friend Giorgios Koumiotis ... and his beautiful old caique, 'ΘΥΜΙΟΣ' (THIMIOS) ... who both took away my fear of the sea and in doing so, encouraged me to listen to the poetry and music in the waters and the wind, and unknowingly always helped me to find the pure magic, that place where the words live and breathe.

Forever am I thankful to you all.

With a great love,

Eleanore

x

1990

margarita

Blinking in the early light, she raised her nose and drank in the scent of the morning and knew it was time.

She smelled the new summer's warmth, that briny mist that cloaked the early hours. She could scent the fishermen coming in with their night's catch, and the season's fresh coats of whitewash and in another note, the ladies' laundry, hung to dry in the balmy breeze. She stood and stretched, scratched hard behind her right ear and moved closer to the gathering excitement. There were loud voices on the paralia, and screaming gulls demanding their due of the returning fishermen … the arthritic rattle of awnings being unfurled for the first time since the last summer season's end, and while the flags of many nations were being raised, ropes clanged on flagpoles as though tolling a welcome to the morning ferry chugging past the old harbor.

All were sounds of the new season, coming quickly upon the island.

Margarita sighed and glanced back at her three pups.

Yes, it is time.

She was tired, bone tired. These pups were her sixth litter in five short years. She had spent much of her lifetime nurturing futile lives; nourishing them from within with her very bones and blood, birthing them, and then trying to nourish them from without on a diet of garbage and handouts. Year, after year, after year.

The winter past had taken its toll. Having spent it as she'd spent them all, moving, constantly moving, seeking shelter from the island's often vicious winter storms and refuge from the kicks and blows and rocks and bottles thrown by passing ruffians, she was past tired — and always, the strain of a brutal hunger competing with her sense of preservation was in itself a struggle of life and death.

She had learned long ago to mistrust food coming from the hand of most humans, especially the garbage men and the menacing grocer down in the village, as by their hand is how the others died. She had watched them eat the scraps of lamb or contents of cans, all that held a wicked something that made them scream in agony and then die a painful, prolonged death. She had learned quickly to sense, to smell the intentions of people and most smelled not of goodness, but of evil, rotten and filled with anger. There were those few, though, who smelled of good intention, of kindness and peace. They would set out a bowl of soup, or scraps of bone, a blanket to lie upon out of the rain or snow, and some would soothe her with the kindness in their voices. But it never was long before the pitiless ones, those with no mercy, would come along and she would have to be on her way again.

With the coming of the summer's people came the coming of the time the pitiless ones would take to cleanse the island of the all of the unwanted they could manage to find. There was little tolerance for a mangy mutt or a sad, thin cat begging at the shops or taverna tables. This cleansing meant that many of the pups and kits of the spring would simply disappear, and many of the mothers would be poisoned with baited meat — all so the village and beaches would look clean and inviting, and the island would wear a veil of purity, its illusion of a perfectly whitewashed world intact.

One of the oldest of the unwanted in this village, Margarita had survived the poisonings to live yet another year to bear her legacy, another brood of the unwanted likely to meet an untimely end. And behind her, further back in the culvert was yet another, a young bitch this one, pregnant — again — a petite white dog, lean and anxious.

Margarita lifted her nose once more and smelled the bread baking in the stone ovens. Mouth watering, she shuddered, and keened softly to the lightening sky. The warmth of the day was building, and in it, past the allure of the breads and stews, she could also scent the perils that lay ahead.

It was time.

She eased back into the hole, nuzzled her young pups into a warm, fat pile and then ran out into the light.

Hugging the alley walls she headed towards the water, trying her best to remain unseen. Instinct took her far from the heart of the village, over cobbled paths that traversed the hills it had been built upon, and down, down, down until she found the sea, sparkling and radiant in the morning's light. There on a low cliff, next to a forgotten stone bench stood a gnarled cypress.

She stopped. Sniffed the ripening air, scenting for any sign of warning, of danger and finding none, eyed the welcoming tree.

Good shelter. And quiet.

Nails clicking on worn cobbles, she trotted to the tree and sat upon the loamy earth at it's base, and scented again.

This smelled of good. Yes. And from here she could see the passersby, their comings and goings — and she could keep her pups safe. She had lost all of the others and would not let that happen again.

Kicking up needles and grass and sand and dust with her hind feet, she fluffed it all into a pile with her front, and with her small snout pushed the earthy mound close to the tree where it made a serviceable nest. When all was to her satisfaction, she set out to find Her.

Margarita adored Her, a kindly old widow who nurtured a penchant for the distressed and the unwanted as she weathered her own sadness. The one constant, a thread of kindness and goodness that ran the length of the little dog's life, she would have sweet words, a soft touch and some food to see Margarita through the work that lay ahead of her.

Some evenings, as the sun was dipping into the sea Margarita would sit, silent at Her side while the old woman stared out to the horizon, as though trying to pull her lost husband from the depths of that which took him so long ago ... always wearing the black of reverent mourning, little Margarita wearing her own very heavy cloak of despair. As the sun settled, Her gnarled hands would reach down to touch the dog, to rest on her, as if to let her know she understood her deep sorrow and hardship.

"Kala koritzi mou, kala, kala ... My good little girl..." she would murmur gently. It was a peaceful time for the dog, salvation, a deep breath and a moment away from the unrelenting worries of survival. The old woman would always leave her with a bone, a bit of bread or leftover lentils and a tin of water and then go back inside the cottage, alone, to await the blessing of the next sunset, the next connection to a vague memory of lost life, of love and of laughter.

But it was morning now, there was no time to idle and after a bit of a meal in the stoop of Her house Margarita snatched up a small, mealy bone and carried it back to the culvert, that dark and hidden place she and the pregnant one had both chosen as momentary respite from an uncertain future. She set the bone down in front of the other dog, the edgy bitch hungry and so weary from life on the run and the growing burden of her pregnancy.

The thin white dog had never known any kindness. People were to be feared and were useless to her. She had lost her first litter within their first days of life for she was discovered, and then betrayed, by children playing hide and seek in the rain culvert beneath their home where she lay in the quiet with her new brood of sightless, vulnerable pups. Under the customary spell of the island's traditional 'cleansing' time, those traitors of her treasured secret reported their find to their father and while the young mother was away in her quest for food, the pups were quickly and quietly washed to sea by torrents of water thrown in from buckets; a ritual purification, purging the house of its sins.

With a high-pitched plea Margarita urged the white one on ... come along now ... as she carried one of her own grumbling pups out from the darkness, but the tired young bitch just whimpered and hung back.

Three trips to the peninsula, with pup in mouth each time, took hours, hours dodging feet and legs and traffic, climbing the hill and sneaking unseen past the church and through the cobbled lanes and finally down to her tree by the water's edge. She would growl softly to each pup as she placed it in the new nest, a maternal command, *stay still*, and then off she'd go for the next.

When the moving was finished and all were accounted for, Margarita sat next to her brood facing the sea. Lifting her nose to the heavens she let out one thin, tired howl, perhaps a calling on some primeval blessing of the beasts, a blessing of the strays ... pulling an invisible veil of protection down around them there under the tree.

It was all she could do.

The weary little dog sniffed the air for safety, and satisfied, shook herself off, snorted and scraped and turned and turned, and then curled up around the small mound of pups and drifted off into a restless sleep.

ancient lands and timeless seas

It was a welcoming day on the vast blue, smooth as silk and quiet there between the bustle of the mainland and the step back in time of the islands that hovered, yet unseen, behind the sea mists. The tranquil Aegean widened ahead as the port grew smaller and smaller in their wake and the old ferry hummed and rattled as it picked up speed, cutting a trail of foam and spray through the sapphire sea; this same sea once witness to the passage of the ancient mariners, the home of Homer's great Odyssey. Here was the playground of Zeus, Poseidon and the alluring Sirens and the only other sign of the modern world now was the caique, the small fishing boat approaching the white ferry from the string of islands that lay ahead. It towed a smaller boat and in turn, one even smaller behind it and they passed by now, they and their mirror image afforded vividly by the clear, calm sea. Silently. Swiftly. The captain of the strange and lovely convoy smiled and raised his arm in greeting as he glided by.

Eleni leaned over the railing and, raising her arms, shouted out a greeting in return. *Ah damn, where's my camera...* She shaded her eyes and watched the boats slowly disappear into the salt mist, the shimmering reflections shattered by the ripples in their wake.

She stood with her hands on the old ship's wooden railing and bathed in the morning light, drawing in the bright scent of salt and sun and when she was full, turned to look at her family. Harry sat on a long blue bench, staring through sandy curls off to sea, his guitar cradled in his arms, while Lily swooped about the back of the open boat, ginger hair flying and arms outstretched like the wings of the gulls flirting with winds coursing overhead. The only other people out here in the sunshine and sea air were the lovers, entwined and whispering in the shade of the white canvas awning — and two older gentlemen embroiled in conversation awash in the music of foreign language, pontificating with dramatic gesture over small cups of coffee and a few packs of smokes.

She smiled and turned back to the sea.

Seagulls just hung on the wind now, motionless, wings outstretched, the babel of their ceaseless chatter rising above the sound of the old ferry as it began to rock and shudder in the open sea, rougher now that there was no land to shelter from the meltemi, the warm season's wind that blew in from the north. Eleni had her face to the wind and spray, eyes closed, quietly sensing a lightness rising within as each reminder of daily life in the States fell, one by one, behind her into the white-capped waters. She let them all go willingly and smiled as she noted that Lily and Harry both now seemed to be doing the same, facing the warm wind, still and silent and lost in the wonder.

They were on their way to that place where all of the elements draw together all at once and work their magic on one's sorry soul; where the fiery sun meets the earth and the waters and the balmy breeze and something about that pulls and tugs at one's being until one can just - let - go. Eventually, thoughts and worries simply go missing and a new sense of vitality and abundance takes their place.

There's magic here in these ancient lands and timeless seas.

It was such a specific peace, tangible, effortless. She and Harry knew it well, they had filled up with it once before, and then back at home, moving through the days and the responsibilities of life, Eleni had regularly called upon the peaceful calm, summoning that tranquility and quiet presence from deep in her core.

Turning around quietly, and facing her past trailing away now with the ferry's wake — Eleni thanked it, for leading her back to this magic.

Sheltered once again by land to the north, the blue waters calmed to smooth and the ferry's clumsy heaving mellowed, and poised on the horizon, the island rose from the sea to meet the cloudless sky. Eleni called out and the family pulled close, the three standing at the ship's railing from where they could begin to distinguish the red tiles from shale rock on the rooftops of white buildings as the ferry neared the harbor town. A charming tableau widened ahead, one of fishing boats and tavernas lining the quay, and clusters of whitewashed houses and churches draped over hills swelling behind.

Verdant cypress and pine stood out at water's edge, the calm, sapphire sea reflecting their brilliance, and emerging now through the shimmering Greek light, blue doorways and vivid purple vines began to take form, and huge white urns filled to spilling with red geranium

9

randomly punctuated the panorama of the island's petite but lively harbor. They heard laughter and even caught the scent of jasmine on the breeze.

"What *is* it about this place?" Harry asked, as if to the land and sea themselves. "How can we be so excited about a place, just a place, one we've been to only once before?" Eleni smiled. *Oh yeah, he's been captured by the magic too.*

With one arm around Lily, Eleni nestled into Harry's side. She fit right into that space under his arm as though it had always been meant just for her, and he reached over and took her hand, held it to his lips where he grazed her fingers, softly, softly. She could see in his eyes how pleased he was to be free. He had been looking forward to relief from responsibility, except of course for what was given to his family and to the Muse, his mistress of notes and words, and the languid days and the enchantment that one quickly became wrapped in here would encourage quite a partnership with his guitar, and many a song would be born of it all.

The lumbering ferry finally slowed and as it closed in on the island's sheltered harbor the captain initiated a slow come 'round, turning it 180° to align stern to quay where the vehicle ramp would be lowered. The old boat was the bridge from shore to shore for the summer's seemingly endless procession of humanity; afoot, on mopeds, in cars, trucks and even on carts drawn by horses, full of cases of wine, chickens or pigs, and this ritual migration was a parade of necessity, essential for some, opportunity for others.

The engines were loudly reversed, the upsurge of churning whitewater acting as brakes and buffer, keeping the boat from running into the cement dock and soon Eleni, Harry and Lily were standing harbor-side, the island firmly under their feet and four months of mystery spreading out before them.

"We're here, we're here, we're HERE", a delighted Lily squealed as she leapt about in her beautiful, unabashed abandon but the moment she caught a quick glance of a small brown dog darting through the busy-ness of the harbor, she stopped, mid-pirouette. *Oh! Good!* she hummed, beginning again to soar, *There are dogs here!*

As was the case with most Greek islands, here the daily excitement and much of the seasonal commerce takes place along the waterfront. Several times each day the mid sized trucks and horse drawn carts stack up side by side along the ferry dock, awaiting their turn to take on goods that come off the ferries and cargo boats from the mainland. The family stopped to pat the well-tended horses for a moment before moving on, snaking through the line of taxis awaiting fares and past the small crowd of locals who gathered for each boat's arrival to hawk spare rooms, calling out "domatia!" to those who may have come unprepared.

The waterfront was also the heartbeat, the pulse that measured the life force of the island, the place where eating and drinking and socializing all seemed to be woven together with a common thread. Here is where the old men wiled away days over backgammon, deals were made, and the fishermen told their tales of weeks at sea and talked about beautiful women while locals and tourists alike lingered over drink and a meal.

Harry led the way to the far end of the harbor, past the many tavernas lining the paralia that hugs the water's edge, past laid-back, modern cafes with their comfortable, thickly cushioned furniture, and fish tavernas that specialized in the fresh fish of the day. Past Ouzeries, the simple old style tavernas with wooden tables draped in colorful cloth and complemented by what Harry called the 'inquisition chairs', austere, straight-backed and which he was certain were designed, intentionally, to be impossibly uncomfortable, and where the menu of the day is in the pots on the stove in the kitchen and one ordered an ouzo and a meal by pointing to one's choices.

He stopped at a familiar traditional taverna sporting a new blue awning that sheltered a scatter of tables from the strengthening sun. The three looked at one another, nodded, dropped their packs and bags and settled in at a table with a perfect view of the gaily painted caiques moored along the quay, bobbing and swaying with the gentle swells that marked each breath of the sea.

And the lovely calm began its work.

It would take Eleni and Harry a few days, or a few moments, to step fully from one way of life, busy, driven and urgent, into this one where time moved slowly and concerns are finally, and very, very concisely pared down to a simple knowing of what really ... really ... really is important.

Lily had no transition to make, whatsoever. Unconcerned with the clutter caused by adulthood, she still possessed the child's gift of being able to live so effortlessly moment to moment, and this was just another perfect step along her way. Already absolutely at home she clucked sweetly to the wary-eyed cat, also seeking respite in the shade, before excitedly asking for a frappe, the frothy, creamy-sweet iced coffee drink that would perfectly cool the heat of her day. Her parents had told her of this nectar from the Gods that goes hand in hand with a Greek summer and she was dying to taste one.

Eleni and Harry each ordered tsipouro, a stronger and more esoteric drink than the more common ouzo. According to Greek intelligence, and custom, one must always consume food with any alcoholic beverage — drinking alcohol was not something generally done with the intention of getting drunk, and food countered that possibility with its sobering effect. Here the mezedes, the very civilized offering of tasty tidbits accompanying the tsipouro, consisted of one plateful of tiny fried fish so delicate that each one could be eaten whole, bones and all, in just a few small bites; another of a small helping of broad beans stewed to perfection in a tomato sauce with a lot of garlic, lemon and island herbs and yet another, piled high with a potato salad made with boiled eggs and olive oil and bits of the olives themselves. The perfect complement to these plates-full of island snacks was always a basket of bread, made fresh each morning at the bakery around the corner by the church.

After picking plates bare the weary travelers gathered up guitar and bags and ventured onward, to the end of the quay and up a long stretch of stone steps toward their pensione snuggled deep in the quietest part of the village's neighborhood. Tourists didn't usually find their way up there, as though it were just a bit too far from the familiar for their comfort, but it was here where one really felt embraced by the traditions that still ordered the island from the shadows.

As they wound through a maze of alleys only wide enough for a moped or the vegetable man's burro, the silence became intoxicating.

Silence …

Except for that annoying dog barking in the distance.

Very annoying.

Was that even the sound made by a dog?

It was more like screeching, a rusty, aching, grinding, like fingernails on a giant chalkboard. A growly, piercing Yiiii Yiiii Yiii. Yak Yak Yak Yaaak. The closer they got to their rooms, the louder it became, and at the top of the hill by the pensione gate they were standing motionless, heads cocked trying to figure out what this was that was disturbing the perfection of their day — when it suddenly stopped.

into the archipelago

Eleni and Harry had been here before.

With only a guitar and two backpacks they had roamed Europe with wild dreams of dipping into that same stream of inspiration that had washed over Michelangelo and Monet, Picasso and Puccini, with the hope of unearthing some of the secrets of those ethereal forces that also kept their own inner fires burning hot and clean. Those very forces nurtured their love, growing like a vine, branches intertwined yet separately reaching for the light, with roots running deep in earth and music and love and family — and in that rarefied atmosphere that only surrounds lovers they rediscovered one another as they touched history and feasted upon foreign culture, drinking in its music and its arts and then they landed here, on this small Greek island, quite by accident.

Lily spent that springtime at home, on the family's small farm with Harry's mother, her beloved grandma Nona. An artist and a dreamer herself, Nona had sent the 'children' off on a very belated honeymoon to feed their wanderlust and find their Muse, and now the postcards came regularly from Europe; Lily especially loved those from Greece, land of Myth and Minotaur, and kept her Nona busy with requests for the telling of some of its great tales as she traced the paths her parents took.

Before heading out into the archipelago in pursuit of a glimpse of island life, Eleni and Harry spent three days in the great, sprawling metropolis of Athens. The traffic was horrendous, the air was thick with the soot and grime of a city that was just now stepping into modern times, but there at their feet lay an undeniable history that they had to explore. Feeling as though they had stepped through a veil of mist that separated the loud, dirty Athens from its mystical past, they embarked upon a whirlwind tour down the thousands of years old path belonging to what was known as modern 'civilization'.

It began with exploration of the maze of beautiful back alleys of the Plaka, old Athens, with its quiet, pedestrian streets and crumbling facades and gardens and multitudes of tavernas all stacked one upon the other, up and over the hills. They were astonished to discover that at Plaka's outskirts one could still walk paths in the ancient Agora, the old Athenian marketplace, upon the very same stones Socrates and Plato and Aristotle had tread.

The hike from the Agora up to the Acropolis offered them a clearly schizophrenic vista, a view over a blurring of the lines that mark both the ancient and the modern urban worlds. On one hand, the quiet of the Agora: organic, its fallen marble pillars and statuary and fading buildings deferring to fragile edges where the reach of the unfathomably old blends easily into narrow alleyways and the sensuous, soft and whitewashed architecture of the marginally more modern Anafiotika. On the other hand, emerging from that calm was the spectacle of the vast, gritty scope of contemporary urban sprawl, all steel and cement and wearing a synthetic shroud of smoggy haze. Clamorous and palpable, it spread as far as the eye can see, far beyond the gentle certainty of antiquity.

Here, within their grasp was tangible evidence of the passage of the ages, as if one could actually see the great tangent of history in one brilliant moment, in just one glance, and that track of time could be traced back, from the transmission towers and satellite antennae and the high rise buildings, back through the ages and down the smooth, worn marble cobbles of the ancient Roman Road below.

Turning from the strangely evocative view to climb the hill of the Acropolis, towering above them, and garbed in the layers of its troubled past, the Parthenon stole what was left of their breath away. Though just a whisper of what was once Sacred Athens, its pillars of marble still stood, the timeless sentinels guarding the city's earliest, most treasured secrets.

They browsed the museums that house gold jewelry and pottery and sculpture dating from a time so distant it had never before quite seemed real to them — but the unfathomably old treasures <u>were</u> real and lay before them now, unearthed, telling their tale, like evidence from the scene of a crime.

They befriended the city's strays, the countless thin, hungry dogs and cats whose numbers shocked Eleni, who wept as she watched the desperate beggars in their play for survival in a big city, hovering in the shadows in hopes of a handout while pedestrians walked blithely by and deadly vehicles sped within inches of their giving flesh. But there were also those 'other' dogs, the big street dogs who knew just when to cross the busy streets with the pedestrians and where the best stoops were for a nap in the warm sun, those who often wore collars and were called by name. Friendly and self-assured, these dogs seemed to manifest from the shadows to accompany Harry and Eleni — and other willing tourists — as guides, or angels, on their adventures through the city's back alleys, in return for just a 'ham and cheese' and a scratch behind the ears. This perplexed Eleni, who couldn't understand how they thrived so in this place that appeared to so coldly ignore the multitudes of sick and starving animals. She loved that these wonder-dogs seemed to laugh in the face of her perception of Athens' arrogant disregard of any compassion for the creatures. She and Harry always made a point of sharing meals with all of the creatures who ventured by while they sat in the street-side cafes, watching the flow of tourists pass, listening to the mounting cacophony as the many different languages awkwardly melded and intertwined — it was the best they could do.

Their feet hurt from all of the walking, up and down and up and down the stairs and steps and cobbled ways. But they couldn't stop, lured on by a hunger for whatever newness would emerge at each bougainvillea-adorned, whitewashed bend and each night before retiring they sat together in the cooling air of their hotel's rooftop, recounting the day's graces and then, hushed and humbled, stared out at the one constant, that same sight that had met the eyes of humans in this land through all of the thousands of years before them - a massive, luminous full moon, floating lazily over the Acropolis.

Finally, after devouring Athens's offerings by day and by night, they were satiated and tired and it was time to move on.

It was late spring, just ahead of Pascha, Greek Orthodox Easter, a time when many of the people return to their families and the islands of their birth for ceremony and celebration. All of the ferries from Athens to islands that the two lovers had hoped to explore were already booked full of locals homeward bound, with room for not even one more migrating soul! One of the only choices left to them was this, a lesser-known island, but available, so they took the lucky chance.

They made passage on the slow boat, a delicious journey that traversed the calm, vast blue for hours, past a dolphin or two and fishermen heading further to sea. Once landed, unpacked and unwound they discovered — just beneath the island's veneer of newfound capitalism and tourism — a culture still living true to many of its old ways, a thread of connection still existing from past to present, and people still in close relationship to the water and the earth and the customs of their faith. The ritual and tradition of Pascha mesmerized Eleni and Harry, easily painting an indelible picture in their hearts; one of the land and its people, a portrait of their passion and the survival, through time, of their ways.

Usually harboring a visceral aversion to anything and everything religious, Eleni loved the drama of this ritual. She found a resemblance to the customs of the old earth religions thrilling, and this was not at all pretentious and exclusive, there was no fire and brimstone or Magic Jesus here. Instead, it was inclusive and earthy and celebratory and she loved it all.

Though most of the island's ancient ruins were long gone, victims of the wars, or of time and the elements, the island itself was quiet and beautiful, wild and green, the beaches pristine. Goatherds and shepherds still lived in the hills with their flocks and dogs, some riding on their burros to town over cobbled pathways built centuries ago. Tireless fishermen supplied their home village with its

19

need, and fresh vegetables came daily to market on the back of a sturdy donkey or in a cart pulled by a well-tended pony.

The one thing that confused and disturbed the tenor of harmony here, for Eleni in particular was that echo of Athens in the fearful, pleading eyes of countless hungry and apparently homeless dogs and cats. Whenever she bent to offer leftovers to the brave few that begged openly, more would always appear. She and Harry would care for those they could and then move on, and though this particular moral failing left a pain that gnawed away at both of their hearts, all paths in this place still led them back to the idyllic.

A delightful ritual, a play of many acts revealed itself here on the island as the winter was warmed away by approaching summertime; locals met each evening in the outdoor tavernas along the old harbor to relax and to eat and drink together after a long day of work, often socializing late into the night. The children ran wild and free like beasts, and parents rushed about tending to scraped knees or wrangling the toddlers who squealed and careened wildly about the quay like mad little drunks. And with the descending darkness came the promenade, mia volta; the walk along the quay in front of the open air tavernas, up from one end of the harbor, and back again, and again and again, men walking together, slowly, deep in conversation, each abstractedly fondling and flipping their komboloi, a string of beads, while the women strolled arm in arm laughing wildly at some shared secret.

Clusters of young teenagers spun about, barely in control of themselves, all inhabiting some parallel universe in orbits fueled by hormones and angst. The boys oozed heat and machismo as they swaggered about, pursuing the young women with hopeful eyes; the girls responded, casting their spells with shy smiles and an assured toss of hair, fragrant with desire. Circling, circling, like moons about the earth, planets around the sun, their trajectories were magnetic, bringing them ever closer. A deeply rooted sense of honor was the polarizing force, the only thing that kept them from crashing into one another. And those who followed this ritual from the benches scattered about in the shadows? They surely swooned in recognition and remembrance of the passion in this archetypical, age-old melodrama, now played out night after night here on the paralia.

Mothers — and Fathers — pushed strollers in which sat brave babies, fat little hostages warily resigned to the ticklers and kissers and cheek pinchers who would inevitably stop to pet them along the way. The Greeks love children, all children, any children. Old grandmothers and grandfathers, the yia yias and pa pous, sat with babies on their knees, the stoic faces of gruff old men, who wore the hard path of their lives in the lines etched there, would crumple and melt with joy at first goo and giggle.

Life moved slowly here and this, to Eleni and Harry, felt like Home.

the meeting

She stood, defiant under the tree by her sleeping pups, yelling at each of the humans walking through the dappled sunlight past her nest on their way to the rocks for a swim. She made it very, very clear that she would not stand for any lingering, for even a moment.

Yiiii Yiiii Yhhiii. Yak Yak Yak Yaaak.

The pups were round and tubby now, on their feet and eager to try them out in the pursuit of anything and everything, and keeping them in order was becoming quite the chore for her. The little mother was very thin, for dragging the wandering pups back from the brink of any moments' sure disaster and giving every last ounce of nourishment possible through what little milk she was able to provide had taken their toll and her efforts were using up what precious little energy she had left.

Trespassers scurried past, urged on by each of the wild dog's lunges that brought her teeth closer to their legs, and when they were safely away Margarita stood quietly, snout to the air, nose aquiver with all of the scents the day was offering up on the warm breeze. Amidst the smells of the summer people's sun lotions and anxiety, the salt sea smells and the earthy, green hint of the arrival of the man's donkey wove the delicious, warm scent of roasting meats riding the currents up the cliffside ... and then, above it all, the sweaty, acrid odors belonging to the pitiless ones, the odors that spoke of noise and peril. With a low whine she trotted nervously back to the tree and snuffling each warm body, counted her pups — again. Walking two full, brisk circles around them, purposefully, as though conjuring an auxiliary protection, she readied for a fresh assault. She was at war with these two-legged beasts. The battle lines drawn, she shook herself off, freeing some of the tension that made itself her constant companion, and sat. Waiting. She had to stay vigilant, for no one, it seemed, could resist a pup. Several of the people had already made attempts to take them from her, for good or bad.

She had left her mark on more than a few of them.

Yiiii Yiiii Yhhiii. Yak Yak Yak Yaaak. Yiiiiaaaak!

She was exhausted. Only when the pups were sleeping and the foot traffic to the water had quieted did she dare sleep at all but it was only then could she go off in search for food or seek out her gentle friend who would have a soft word for her weary soul and sustenance for her aching body. She was wearing thin.

One day there was a whisper, the echo of a gently beating heart and Margarita looked up to see a small person, a girl standing motionless before her and life began to change. The nervous little dog stopped her shouting just long enough to hear a sweet kindness in this girl's voice, a soothing, a healing. And it mesmerized her. But not for long. Margarita resumed her attack, the barking and growling out of habit, out of her need for

23

survival. But it had lost its fire. There was something about the way this person sat down so gently upon the cobbles and slowly brushed the wild flames of hair out of sea colored eyes, the way she extended her hand and the kindness in her soul out to her. As did Her, the girl smelled strongly of a calm ... and there was something here that cooled Margarita's desperation; a ghost of the familiar, hovering on the verge of her memory.

She quieted again, standing now just feet from this unknown but somehow comforting human who sat stilly, averting her gaze, soft sounds warm like the sun flowing from her throat. Margarita turned and walked over to the pile of sleeping pups and lay down, looking back steadily but softly at this small person. Rarely had she felt such safe peace in the presence of a human.

The girl continued to sit, ever so still, until her legs ached and her feet tingled — quite a lovely eternity for Margarita, who yawned and sighed deeply, the release of tension edging her further into comfort and away from constant worry and raging and terror.

The magic spell was broken when a loud group of summer people ventured by, intruding upon the delicious calm and reenergizing the dog's maternal vigil. Leaping back to attention, back to the defense of her babies, coughing and sputtering, her rusty, raspy bark sent the tourists scattering to the far side of the path.

Yiiii Yiiii Yhhiii. Yak Yak Yak Yaaak.Yiiiiaaaak!

The red haired girl rose, slowly, and backed off and away.

the (red haired) girl

Like most children, Lily would much rather be riding the Aegean's wind or exploring an ancient ruin than sitting within the confines of what it is that constitutes 'learning' in the eyes of the less adventurous. In this family, formal schooling was easily traded off, for both of her parents felt that there was nothing like travel to educate and to open one's heart and mind to the world of differences that only venturing beyond one's own borders can offer.

Now she was close to bursting with the excitement of this adventure unfolding before her.

"Puppies! That's what all the noise is about, Mama, it's puppies!"

Jettisoned about the room by a rapid fire of thought, the lively child went on and on in one long breath all about puppies she had found, and the brave mother protecting them, and the growling and the barking, and how cute they all were rolled up in a fleshy ball and how she wanted to help them ...

"… and can we please get them some food? And maybe I can make them a bed to protect them from the weather, and maybe we could even take them home with us when we leave. And …"

Eleni laughed.

"Why does this *not* surprise me?" She knew better than to doubt her daughter's mission to befriend some sad street creature, it happened everywhere they went, but here, on the other side of the world it was not just any dog. *Of course not.* It had to be the one and only unpleasantness of their trip so far, that belching, fire-breathing little dragon of a dog that cut through their tranquil rooftop evenings like a knife! Lily had inherited this particular compassion from Eleni, but being young, and secured by a childhood full of love and wonder, she was unfettered by any need for peace and solace. The loud little dog and her puppies were just a perfect piece of her Greek adventure.

Eleni herself was forever acting upon her own calling to help any four-legged in need, *But oh! Sweet peace!* she'd thought that she might have been able to leave some of that behind her, even if just for a moment.

Finished plaiting a two-foot-long braid in her own blushed hair, she reached through the laughter and excitement and placed her hands gently upon Lily's shoulders as if to bring her back to the earth, turning her around so she could set to brushing her fiery locks.

"Take them home with us? If it were up to you there would be no room left for even one more living thing there! Our home would be packed full to the rafters, with all of the animals that spill from the streets and into your heart. Lily! Stand still, please! We would be refugees in our own home, sleeping on bed corners or blankets on the floor! We would be the pets!"

Lily giggled and turned, her eyes wide. "I'm not the one who brings home horses — and goats, and cows!" and she went on, in her best small, pathetic, pleading voice, hands folded under her chin beneath eyelashes fluttering madly, "Oh Harry, look, oh please, please, it NEEDS a home, it NEEDS someone to love it. Oh how can it possibly live without us?" She stopped for a moment, waiting for a reaction, hoping that she might be softening her mother up a bit. Nothing. "Oh, come on, little Mama! What difference would these little tiny dogs make?"

Eleni laughed again. Lily always made her laugh, far better than the worrying some of her friends did over their own children. She deftly recaptured the girl, elusive as a butterfly, and after a hug turned her around again and set to finishing what she had started, Lily's hair reflecting the gold of the sun's own light.

"Hey Lil, let's just watch this dog for awhile. OK? We'll help her if she needs it — but first we can only hope that she might quiet down a bit! Up, braided, or wild and free, darlin'?"

"Wild … and FREEEEE!" Lily sang, dancing away, shaking any of Eleni's order right out of her mane. She always preferred that her hair be free to be blown about by the wind and loved to watch it spread and snake out around her in the water, like algae from a red tide or an otherworldly red inked octopus. So, left free it was.

In that one small moment Eleni caught a wondrous glimpse of two girls existing simultaneously within one pre-teenage body, or perhaps even in parallel but absolutely foreign worlds — the silly, gangly and uninhibited wild child, and the graceful, self possessed young woman-to-be, a sylph portending the future. They both seemed to dance about the small room together now, spinning, spinning — until they once again became one. She was staring after Lily when the girl turned, giggling again as the unmistakable strains of the little dog sliding into another of her persistent rants found them through the open window.

Eleni groaned.

That dog had barked her way through their whole first week on the island.

Most days the family was out and about. They spent quite a bit of their time hiking through madrone forests sure to harbor a nymph or two, or the olive groves, each with its own collared and belled herd of goats, tinkling and chiming through the grasses. Or they would hop an excursion boat headed to an untended offshore island, where the art of sitting under shade at a beach and staring out to sea so easily became a way of life. And there often were the days that, while the girls went off following their own inspirations, Harry took his guitar to a quiet taverna at the very top of the village and with a view of the Aegean spread wide before him, sat in the shade of a plane tree to work on a piece of music inspired by the reyvma, the mysterious, visible energy of the sea.

No matter what their daily agenda was, at some point in any lazy afternoon they could be all be found sitting at the waterfront, visiting with friends or watching people — Lily nursing a cold drink and a good book, her parents, a tsipouro while reading their newspaper to catch up on the war cry that had risen to a fever pitch back home in the States.

It was later, when they gathered on the rooftop of the pensione for their evening ritual, watching the sun lower itself into the shimmering sea, that the fierce little beast's barking came to them in unrelenting waves. The clamor would continue on throughout a good part of the night, at times even puncturing the air of calm that embraced their sleep.

Occasionally they were offered a glimpse of the dog as she darted stealthily between tables in the village and around the foot traffic of the quay. A skinny, nondescript brown bit of a thing with ponderous, swinging teats, her coat was rumpled and dirty and rough and she had a bark that sounded like it could bite you and do harm all on its own. Lily, of course, saw only the beauty in the beast and crooned sweetly to the little creature whenever she would see her in the town, and after several days Eleni thought she actually saw it respond to the child's Siren song … listening, hesitating, sad eyes lingering upon Lily with longing for just a moment before moving away and melting back into the shadows.

Lily was a precocious, self-assured child with red hair that framed her open face, newly graced by a cascade of freckles. The lifestyle here on the island suited her well. Lean, athletic and wildly imaginative, she loved to run and dance and swim and thrived on being so unencumbered and free. She was the jokester of the family, dutifully keeping her parents engaged in silly bits like hanging spoons from the ends of their noses or impulsive bouts of uninhibited dance, keeping them caught up on a very civilized quota of belly laughter and the importance of the beauty in the spontaneity of being childlike. But besides being a typical twelve-year-old — alternately goofy and serious, standing on that cusp between carefree innocence and an acute angst — gently balancing her wild side was the quietly thoughtful observer entrenched deep within, and that fragile, yet magical, transparency that accompanies those who are crossing the bridge from adolescence into womanhood.

Like her parents she was an artist, but preferred painting on paper or canvas to creating soundscape and stories with a musical instrument and words. She could spend hours alone with just a painter's tools. Always, she had been able to easily entertain herself — when she was five, or six, she could engineer castles from a few pieces of construction paper, or would stage plays with her placid menagerie of cats and dogs who sat strangely enthralled, cozily compliant for her despite being dressed to the nines in doll's clothing, or in her winter hats and scarves.

Very comfortable in the company of adults, Lily took an honest pleasure in the time spent with her parents on the beaches or hiking through the wilds of the island. Of course, they occasionally drove one another quite crazy, for there was no denying that chasm which always would exist between the realms of child and adult. Yet to be tamed by life herself, Lily could find them to be so predictable and so boring and so infuriating and in turn, the adults, who had long ago forgotten what it really was like to live within a child's unfettered sense of space and reality, could find her quite touchy and irritable, or exasperatingly perplexing, like a difficult puzzle. Thankfully, that chasm was easily bridged with just a bit of care. Patience, sensitivity and a touch of humor all worked the magic that brought their discordant wavelengths back to harmonious alliance.

The flame haired girl especially liked the quiet times that were easily found here. Walking alone, sitting on the rooftop or on the beach, there was always time that she could be within herself, time to grasp and decipher and organize all of the thoughts and the questions that sprouted and thrived like spring wildflowers in her head, fertilized by the excitement of being in a place so new, so foreign to her. When she wasn't alone or with her family, or off befriending the multitudes of four-legged wounded-in-spirit found at each turn, her time was spent running and playing with local children on the quay and the cobbled lanes in the heart of this safe and magical village, or in the inviting waters, pretending to be dolphin or mermaid for hours on end.

But now, the little brown dog and her babies seemed to have captured every bit of the girl's heart and about one week is all that it took for the feeling to go mutual, and grow towards common ground. The merciless barking was starting to fade.

With so much of her attention on the plight of the dog and her pups, Lily had begun to take notice of some of the other unfortunate animals around her, the dogs being chased off by waiters, cats kicked at under tables. Of course she would also see the occasional well-loved, and often too well-fed, pet sitting on a doorstep or by someone's side but mostly it was the hungry strays with no home but the streets who begged her attention.

"There are a lot of hungry, sad animals there, Lily." her mother had warned before they began their journey to Greece, "I'm not really sure why, but many people there feel differently about them than we do, and you probably won't like that. All we can really hope to do is take care of the strays that we meet along our path the best we can, always trying to remember that we are not at home. We are guests in another country."

Eleni and Lily did take care of those animals the best they could, forging a bit of time from each day to feed kibble or leftovers to the hungry who lived in nooks and crannies and other secret spots along their walk into the village. Lily, like her mother, so tender of heart, would never understand why anyone would not want to care for them.

She called now, from the balcony where she'd been watching a busy fisherman plying his lines in the water below. "Can I go and feed our kitties? They're probably waiting for me, Mama." Sweeping into the room, she grasped her mother's hands and swung her around in a happy circle. "That new bag of food ... can I take it? Oh yeah, and I probably will have to stop and see my dog and my puppies!"

"Your puppies, now? Oh, Lily, you be careful with that dog, please. I know she's probably just fine, but ... just pay attention. Let her take her own time to get to know you." She stopped, willing Lily to look her in the eye. "You know to be careful. Yes, yes, take the cat food with you, and we'll meet you down at Kosta's taverna ... in an hour, OK?"

The girl kissed her mother on the cheek and, snatching up the small bag of kibble, danced off into the clear, warming day, hip-hopping and humming her way down to the tree on the point where the dog was busy, loudly teaching passersby her rules of engagement. Lily sat for a moment in the distance, watching wide-eyed tourists moving quickly past the little brown tempest, all giving the maniacal dog wide berth. She hoped to catch sight of the babies but they were safely hidden away, snuggled in a covert pile there beneath the great tree, so she turned away to continue on her rounds.

Sliding down a gently sloping hill, a wake of dust marking her path, she headed for the lone neighborhood taverna, sitting right at the water's edge. Here there was always a crew of well-fed cats all lying about like sea lions run aground, dozing on the tiny sunlit beach.

"Kalimera my furry little friends!" she sang to the assembly, but each cat just looked up at the girl with a sort of a sly, contented feline smile, a dreamy, sloe-eyed salutation, and then went back to its dozing. There was no need here for her help, this group was already quite obviously well tended to by some other kind heart.

Lily danced on through dappled light, across the beach and up the thickly cobbled steps on the other side, taken two at a time of course. She was aimed for an overgrown plot where at least ten cats of various ages were secreted away, and stopping there she called out to them, the promise in her now-familiar voice invoking a deluge from the dense copse. Cats of all colors emerged, most of them purring and rubbing their greeting, a writhing mass of soft fur and expectant eyes. The thin creatures dove into the kibble Lily poured into piles, well placed along the plot of land's stone wall so that each cat could get their fill.

"Oh Mo, you're looking good, little man! Posy! Hey, wait! You're a piglet, let Emma have some!" When each hungry cat was sated she moved along to her next stop, where abandoned land on a hillside that hovered above the water was thick with elephant grass and fig trees and embraced by a low stone wall. These walls were everywhere on the island, old and densely wound with jasmine vines and moss. Missing stones here and there, they were sometimes all that remained as evidence of lives lived in times long gone on these lands, each plot that once housed a kalivi, a small stone cottage lived in by the fishermen or shepherds, all eventually shaken apart, kalivi, wall and lives, dashed into oblivion by the elements, or the earthquakes that frequented the islands of the Aegean.

"Kitties! Come on, come on kitties! Come on!" Young cats, some kittens, but all thin from not enough food to fill their growing needs, rushed out from bushes and stone nooks to greet her with their happy, hungry purrs and chirps.

Lily doled out heaps of kibble, but as she bent to pour even more was ambushed by an evocative scent, something warm and savory, rich rosemary and dill and garlic, and turning to trace the invisible trail, she saw the figure in the doorway.

Her face pinched and unpleasant, the bent old woman rushed from her kitchen stoop, a black scarved whirlwind waving a broom and waggling fingers, jabbing at the air in some form of reprimand. Screeching a litany of what could have been curses, she literally attempted to sweep Lily and the kitties away.

The astonished girl remained, unblinking, a brave and serious impediment standing between the harpy and the fledglings, now smartly hidden away in the rocks there. The woman did not relent, she rushed and pushed and pressed, sweeping and threatening, and as Lily tried to follow the furious dance, she grew angry. *What? What is with this woman? WHAT is her problem?*

It did not take much more of the old woman's bellowing and brandishing before the girl had enough of this nonsense — it affronted her good nature, and eventually overruled the respect she possessed for her elders. In disbelief that anyone would actually even attempt to harm kitties, she raised her arms, took one step forward and squealed, long and loud into the angry woman's face. "Excuse meeeee! Hey! Stop it, stop right there - NOOOW!" And then, in a huge voice befitting one of Artemis' very own protectors of the animals, "Hey you OLD BAT don't you DARE HURT THOSE KITTIES!"

The harsh little fury stopped dead. With eyes wide and eyebrows raised she backed away, and in dramatic gesture, with a breathy "po po po po!" and one more portentous glance towards Lily, she turned and slammed the door shut behind her. The warm aromas of the kitchen lingered in the unsettled air, but Lily's stomach only churned now beneath her chattering heart. She stood, motionless. And it was then that she began to see for herself that something was just not right with the relationships between people and the animals, here.

With heart pounding, she breathed her tension out, and into the quiet's return. Brushing away the one tear that had betrayed her fear, she turned back to her foundlings, pleading, and one by one they crept soundlessly back into the light.

the kindness and the goodness

Day after day the small, kind person came early in the morning to her lair.

The three pups were venturing further afield in their waking times and it wasn't long before they, too, discovered the girl as she sat so quietly. They took a great delight in biting on her toes with needle teeth, and grabbing and pulling the long strands of her hair and hearing her giggle in glee. Sometimes they took turns and, with a running start on tubby legs that sent them careening headlong towards her, would use her as a human springboard from which they could perform their joyful acrobatics. In return, the girl roughhoused and tickled them until they were squinty eyed and smiley with delight, and she rubbed their baby ears until they grunted their pleasure like happy little piglets. They had no reason to fear. Leaping over one another, growling and moaning in puppy play, they rolled along the dusty path in a bundle of absolute joy and ran about until they couldn't take another step and one day, rather than collapsing on their little pile of leaves, the three babes fell exhausted into the girl's lap for their nap.

Margarita fretted. She paced and whined. There they slept, where she could not easily touch them, or keep them safe from all of the many harms that could befall them. She kept her ears pricked, her radar up, nervously willing to watch and wait, but ready to rush in save her pups at any sign of trouble.

The girl, covered in fat babies, sat very, very still, drinking in the distinctive, delicious sweet smell of their puppy breath until she heard her own mother calling in the distance. Delicately she peeled the pups from her lap and with a kiss and a stroke, laid each one in the nest before she ran off into the day. With that, Margarita did rush in, touching each of the babies with her nose, moist and black, marking them with a lick and then curled around them, facing the path. She lay there quietly, her snout resting on her paws, alert, eyes and ears instinctively scanning for trouble.

But it never came.

When the small person next came to visit, Margarita just sat quietly and watched her, feeling, sensing as only dogs can. What she felt was calm and what she sensed was purity, and rather than the scent of anger, or of death here in this girl, as was in Her, was a kindness, a goodness and those things are home to a dog's heart.

It wasn't long before Margarita was trusting enough to leave her pups in the girl's care while she ventured off to visit Her or to find a morsel in the village. She felt an ease, a release, as though something was beginning to snap the chains that bound her to dread and fear.

She had her own girl.

One morning after she'd made her rounds the wee dog returned to the nursery to find the girl perched alone on the low wall by the tree — next to a rather large object that now sat right atop the nesting spot. There was nary a pup in sight.

Moaning, in a panic she rushed to where it was she had last seen her babes safe and asleep in a pile. After a long moment's anxiously sniffing about, she found them ... nestled on a thick bed of pine leaves and soft cloth, sleeping soundly, sheltered from the wind and anyone's sight by the cardboard box that now covered them.

Through an opening just large enough for her to squeeze through, Margarita crept cautiously into dark warmth, making anxious sounds as she sniffed each pup, scenting for signs of distress or danger, counting, sniffing ears, toes, under tails, counting again — and realizing that her babies were safe, licked them each furiously until she was absolutely free of all of her worries.

She backed out of the curious little refuge, turned toward the girl and sat down right in front of her, gazing shyly, deeply into her caring soul, searching for some reason to fear.

And she found none.

The girl slowly reached out, extending every ounce of gentleness she possessed in an open hand. The dog shivered while the girl gently stroked her chest, then her back, her chin, and she remembered, as only a dog can, this feeling, from long ago, the safety ... the other calm person who came into her life and poured kindness into her, the other calm person who fed her and touched her so gently, gave her a bed and a name and a dignity, that other person who had cared for her.

And she remembered, as only a dog can, how that person who had loved her so, suddenly one day, was gone.

Lily burst into the sunlit room as her mother was busy tidying the beds and gathering up what they might need for a day's adventure.

"Mama! Guess what? She finally let me touch her! I was really, really slow and really, really gentle and she liked it and I think the little dog trusts me now!"

Oh ... Eleni straightened and sighed, cupping her face with a hand, trying to remain passive, trying to seem unconcerned ... *she does know better, doesn't she? I did teach her properly, didn't I?*

"She's really sweet. And she doesn't bark at me anymore. Did you notice? The quiet? There's more of it now! And I made the puppies a warm bed underneath a big box I found just sitting out there in the alley." The girl, oblivious to her mother's slightly worried air, went on. "I used one of our knives to cut a little doorway, and then took one of my sheets ... will Haroula be really mad, Mama?" Eleni raised her eyebrows. Oh, yes, their landlady would be really mad.

"I don't need that one, the puppies need it more ... so I folded it up, and tucked it over a fat bed of pine needles and then I put the box on top and the puppies inside! I got a garbage bag from the closet and wrapped the box up with it and used Hair-ry's duck tape to stick it together and kind of wedged it between the tree and that wall. So they all can stay dry in the storm – and, not blow away!" The storm she spoke of was to come soon, within days according to Vassili, one of their boatmen friends in the harbor.

Eleni asked her daughter about the once-loud little dog's manner.

"She's really gentle, she's just shy, Mama. And scared. I think she's probably been hurt by people. And she is protecting her little babies, so she barks! And she is pretty skinny. Really, she is ski-ii-nny. I think she needs food. F-O-O-D!" The giddy child, spilling with pride in her architectural accomplishment, suddenly became quite serious as she looked up at her mother. "I think that instead of acting so tough all the time, she'd kind of rather be curled up in someone's lap. I feel really sorry for her."

"Oh, Lil. Well then, good job, lovie. Just keep going slowly with her. You know. And we will get F-O-O-D for her if it seems she really needs it."

She had great faith in Lily's intuition regarding the creatures. The girl knew the animals well, she seemed to speak their language and was careful and considerate of them, so Eleni was relieved to hear that this was a good dog. She had heard the rare story of a biting stray, though through what she had observed of their treatment by some, she realized that the biting most likely occurred for a very good reason.

Where's Hair-rrry?" Lily preferred to call her father by his name. She found it far more fun to say 'Harry', distinctively pronounced as "hairy', than to say 'Papa' or 'Dad'. "I need to tell him about my dog!" She'd grown breathlessly buoyant again, lit up like the sun.

"Upstairs, captured by the song faeries, I imagine. He took our towels up some time ago to hang them in the breeze, towels in one hand, guitar in the other and I haven't seen him since!"

Lily gave her mother a hug and ran out to spread her news.

Smiling, Eleni wondered what other tourist mothers might be thinking of her mothering skills as she allowed her pre-teenage daughter to run free to make friends with the unknown in this foreign country - which included this snarling, yapping little mutt. *At home I would*

*be branded ... a scarlet U on my forehead, U for Unfit, for letting
my child run with the wolves ...*

She threw a few books and her camera into a
yawning backpack. Parting the gossamer curtains she
stepped to the balcony where she could look out upon sea
and morning sky to see what they might foretell of the
day. *Clear and lovely, as usual.* As she gazed out over the
bluest of waters her thoughts strayed from the clear
Aegean morning to the freedoms she and Harry allowed
Lily on the island, simply because of people and place. *A
safe haven ... it's a 'PG' island, for heaven's sake, it oozes parental
guidance at every turn.* There was virtually no crime, and there
also was no way that a child could pass any window or
doorway without a mother knowing. ... *the women watch, they
see everything, they have a seventh sense about them, they just can't
help themselves ... skinned knees or toes studded with sea-urchin-
quills, that's about all that ever happens to the children here!*

The fact that most of these people cherished all
children set the attentive gaze of a whole island upon Lily.
All along the harbor, each taverna had its own family of
watchful eyes, the Grandpas with their jokes and candies
and Mamas with arms full of hugs and fresh bread, all
vigilant, all knowing. And the boatmen, their friend
Vassili and all of his fisher-kin who treated Lily like some
diminutive Queen, were honorable and fatherly, and
always at her service. Best of all there were always other
children to play with, and with this vast freedom at hand
and the village and harbor as their playground, they were
all safe. And Lily, free to explore, was never lonely. ... *an
incredible way to learn about other people, to learn about goodness...*

Eleni remembered that Harry and Lily were on the
roof, grabbed her hat and backpack and as she bent to fit
the old skeleton key into the door's lock, she heard the
little dog's braying in the distance. *Ah Lily*, she thought,

turning the key once, placing it in he pocket of her shorts and turning to climb the stairs to the rooftop, *what have you gotten us into here?*

Sprawled over the wall surround, Harry and Lily were pointing out to sea where Vassili could be seen in his small fishing caique, making way back towards the harbor.

"Oh, let's go!" Eleni called, "Let's see if we can beat Vassili to the quay!"

the long memory

Vassili could always be found on the quay in the mornings, mending his fishing nets or holding court with the other boatmen there. A kind yet somehow sad man, he knew the sea and the weather much like Eleni knew her own daughter's face; each gilded freckle, each sandy colored lash floating above blue, blue eyes; why it might be veiled with sadness one moment, lit with joy another; the contentment it took in the drowsiness that descended just before sleep came ...

Vassili knew when his sea would be wild, with the mirage of diamonds dancing on her waves, or calm like glass, and when the winds would part and make for good passage to the northernmost beaches. He knew just when the southerly wind would blow up hot and dry from the African deserts, the 'crazy wind' which drove people into fevered frenzy — or when the northern meltemi of summer would gust, cooling, but often making the sea impassable for the smaller craft. Vassili said even the fish could tell him the weather — while he sat out on the sea day after day, or night after night, reeling in his living, he had learned much from their activity. If he had found them swarming deep, or if they were swimming just below the surface, if they glanced his wake as they leaped for the moon, their behavior almost always would portend the weather in the days ahead. Most recently he had spoken of a wet and windy storm that would come in short time, only briefly lashing the island before moving on, leaving the sun's warmth and everything clean in its wake. This is the premonition that inspired Lily's flurry, the considerate creation of shelter for the puppies.

In his upper middle age, Vassili was an old, old man as far as Lily was concerned, old as the dirt and wise as the sea. She thought he was marvelous. So different was his existence from her own that she viewed his life — living on his beautiful, bright red caique and sailing the mythic waters with the dolphin — with the same awe with which she might view a life with the circus, or perhaps even life on another planet.

Eleni and Harry had met the captain when they'd first ventured to the island, boarding his beautiful boat, Hestia, for a daytrip to some of the island's more remote beaches. They stood out to him in the wash of boisterous tourists. As they absorbed the sky and sea around them he recognized a love for the magical Aegean in their far away looks and quiet smiles, and could sense their appreciation for his boat, how Hestia cut softly through the water and didn't bob about even in a roughening sea, and it was during the lunch stop at a primitive taverna, perched high above the sea and over plates of mouthwatering calamari seasoned to perfection by spirited conversation that the way to a deep and lasting friendship was paved by the captain and the two travelers.

Lily and her family loved to visit with Vassili on his boat, trying out their broken Greek on his studied English. They often took him a cup of the strong Greek coffee and sat while he sipped and shared local lore and told tales of the islanders, and of his travels to the far reaches of the world. For his knowledge and laughter, they traded their impressions of Greece — and their music for in his heart, second only to the sea, music was held in a place of highest reverence. Vassili also enjoyed singing and from deep, deep within his soul poured impossibly poetic love songs, and the haunting songs of grief and sorrow and rebellion, reybetiko, a Greek jazzy-blues borne of the heartbreak of occupation and wars. Whatever sprung from his vast well on any given day was dependent upon his moods, but was always accompanied by a bit of an education.

To Eleni it had appeared that the boatman sheltered some potent sadness — a testy melancholy lay just beneath the veneer of his good cheer, though recently she noticed it seemed to have softened with the addition of Lily to his mornings.

Vassili absolutely loved talking to the young girl with the red hair and dancing eyes, who told him of the small, brave, brown dog she had befriended as she stood before him now.

He listened to the child's tale, and looking up at her from his mending, smiled.

"Margarita is the little dog's name."

Lily looked desperately glum. Her usual ebullience had dimmed dramatically by the time she'd finished her telling of the hungry little dog and her adorable pups. At home the animals were as welcome on the furniture as she was — it was very hard for her to understand the lack of care or respect she was taking note of around her here, as evidenced by hungry cats begging for the kindness of a meal ... and little dogs who had to protect their babies.

"Margarita. Margarita ..." Lily rolled it around her mouth and over her tongue, "Margarita ..." tasting a name that was strong to her, and free, like the name of a wild Spanish dancer — an odd name for such a sad and tired little creature.

She gazed steadily down at Vassili, working methodically on a tear in his net. Resolute, yet with a virtue only those with one foot still planted firmly in childhood can possess, she suddenly asked,

"So, why don't people here take care of the hungry animals? What is their problem?"

Vassili took a deep draw from his smoke, lingering there as he thought for a moment. And then he chuckled, "They all are not so mean, little one! There are those here, as there are everywhere in the world, who have a great caring in their hearts for the beasts."

"Well, then why can't they *all* just be nice to them?"

"Ah, Kokinoula mou ... My Little Red, it is not so simple." He sighed. Realizing he was in for some serious business, he reeled his thoughts in from the deep and gathered them up carefully for the girl. "Lipon, ok then. It is true that many of the Greek people have been taught to believe ... some, by their church, yes ... that the animals, they have no souls. To have no soul is to perhaps, shall I say, embody the devil? Yes, the devil, or at least something one would not care to invite into one's life."

"The devil? A little, soft, furry animal, the devil? That is just stupid."

"Yes, it is stupid, you are right. But when the people, they do not know better, what can we do? You see, Koukla, those people, they are very fearful of the dogs and cats of the island and this great fear, it can cause them to treat the animals in ways you and I would not prefer. And those who do not know the animals, well, they only are able to see the begging, their rough and dirty coats, the sickness they may carry ... or their madness, as they nip and they scratch at the people who are not kind to them. And since the animals 'have no souls', or so some people think, they must not then feel pain or hunger, either."

"But Vassili ..." Lily interrupted, her blue eyes ice above lips pinched in protest.

"Darling, this is just what some of the people think. It is not what I am saying is truth. Hear me now. To some, the animals, they have no souls. And then, some people ..., they just do not care. So, to ignore any needs the animals might have? It is nothing — tipota. Because of this, hmmm, lack of knowledge, they are unable to see beyond their crazy fears or uncaring hearts to any goodness in the animals. And so, because of this it is very easy for them to forget that long, long ago it was us who made them tame! They forget that the humans, we made them to depend upon us when we took them in to help us work in the fields or as little companions! The animals, they are no longer meant to be wild beasts, because the people long ago took the real wildness out of them! So you see, I understand your frustration, Kokinoula, but it is a big and long story, something that is very broken and will probably take a big and long time to be fixed."

With a measure of sarcasm not lost on either Harry or Eleni, he added, "I do think this all started with the church, some old, wrinkly self righteous priest a long, long time ago interpreting the old teachings to his own liking, reinventing that word, 'dominion', yes? It meant 'caring for'. Caring for! But now? What does 'dominion' mean?"

He spat in contempt, and then boomed, "Domination! To the rich, to the powerful, to the ignorant, it means do-mi-NA-tion."

Lily had moved to Vassili's side, sitting cross-legged on a wooden toolbox where she could watch the antics of the seagulls that frequented the harbor in the mornings. A few were doing tricks now for Nontas, a small white haired man who, standing on the prow of his caique, was paying them in turn with the heads of the fish he had caught in the night. *Ok - so why will they feed those birds, but not other animals?* Lily wondered. Just then, as if on cue to utterly and completely confuse the girl, three cats sauntered out from the bushes lining the quay, blending into the queue of begging, squawking gulls. Nontas began tossing them fish bits as well. Her eyes went wide in surprise, and she watched the lovely if not noisy communion between man, bird and cat for a while before turning back towards Vassili.

"I know, those people, they are fearful because they have no mind for themselves, they believe only what they are told! And truly, a pious Greek, he had better not question the words of one's Priest!" Looking skyward Vassili mumbled, "Lipon, look, if there really is a God, please forgive me!"

He burst into a boisterous laughter, but sobered as he continued on, "Ah, but I must be fair, now. Many of these people here, they are poor. Life, it is hard for them and there is no time or not enough drachmae for them to spend on the animals. And then ... there are the others. Well, how can we really argue any of this with someone who has suffered feeding only crusts of bread to their hungry children, hiding in the night from a war that raged over their heads and through their lives?"

Vassili spoke now of those who had endured the hardships and inhumanity of the wars, World War II and the brutal Civil War that followed, pitting Greek against Greek and then, as if that were not enough, the dictatorship and harsh censorship of the Junta of the mid 1960's through to 1974. It seemed that the people of Greece were just now finally free — having made it to the illuminated top edge of a deep well of despair, after a long climb up from the depths of having tolerated so much darkness and abuse.

"They have the long memory, those people. It must be very difficult to undo habits they learned through the hardship of those times, no? Feeding a dog, a cat, it could seem very strange to many of them, to those people who cannot forget what it was like to be unable to feed their own babies. Sometimes they even had to steal from each other to stay alive." He looked up at Eleni, knowing that she needed this history lesson as much as her child did. She took in a sharp breath — it was almost too much for her, the thought of not being able to feed one's child, or keep her safe.

"During the war times not so long ago the animals that were not killed or stolen by the enemies, they had to earn their way in life. Some were used to help farm the small plots of land, and when they could no longer do the hard work, well, they became dinner for the people. The cats, they were tolerated only because they ate rats that carried sickness and stole what little there was of the people's food. But there came a time that, because of a desperate need, a hunger that would shake your soul, even some of them were eaten. So you see, keeping any of the animals for any other reason, especially as a pet, it is still seen by some of the people as outrageous!"

Eating a CAT? Lily's stomach grumbled and churned. Having only known comfort, a full belly and the animals as beloved pets, she could not find any rationalization for that even in the furthest reaches of her very lively imagination.

"Vassili, do you remember that time?"

"Ah, Koukla mou, I never ate a little cat, if this is what you ask of me!" He laughed. "But yes, I remember. I remember my mother and many other mothers taking all of the pedakia, us little children, to the mountains because the Germans, they bombed and burned this little town here on the sea. I remember it, all orange with the fire. But you see, life was not so hard for us here, on a little island, for all of the war times. The mountains here, they never were bombed ... only the town, the island's port. Yes, people were hurt and killed, they were hungry here, but in the mountains, we always had food, there were not so many of us. The sea and the fields, they could feed us and we did not have to starve." He stood and called out to Nontas as he left the harbor in his immaculate caique, most likely heading to an offshore island as was his habit, to collect up a meal's worth of ahkinos, the sea urchins, to share with a worthy tourist or two. Vassili took note of his leaving. The boatmen all watched out for one another. Sometimes, one did not return —and if not for others bearing witness, who would ever know?

"Ah, Nontas. Now, there is a gentle man who lived through the hardest of times. There are those whose memories of being starved and beaten have encouraged a deep sympathy, ah ... symponia, a deep sympathy for anyone and anything that is oppressed in any way. They have the unspeakable kindness. One of the old widows, in your neighborhood, she is that little Margarita's friend, everyone knows that she is generous to the little beast ... and she lost her two sons in the war and a young daughter when our town, it was bombed. She has the kindness. But, many people, they were made so, so toughened, made so sad that they now can be kind to no one, to nothing at all, even though the times they have changed and the war long ago made a way for peace. And people, many of those people who have lived through the hard times, they look to their church for solace, some comfort ... but then the Priest, well, what does he do? He does not help matters here by saying the animals have no souls! After all that the Greek peoples have been through, wouldn't he best be saying that some <u>humans</u> have no souls?"

Vassili spat a bit of tobacco from his lip and then grinned as he set his net down. He opened his arms wide to the heavens.

"Oh, but no no, no, one does not question the words of one's priest! Unless one is Vassilis Tsikakis! Ha ha!" He slapped his chest and then put a cigarette to his lips and lit it, taking in a deep and obviously satisfying drag. "Ah", he exhaled, "you see now, I sit here, with you beautiful people, in the beautiful sun and the fresh morning air, minding my Hestia, mending my nets ..." he swept the panorama of the harbor with a deliciously long flourish of his thick hand "... smoking my cigarettes, drinking my coffee, happy, very happy on the day those church bells they toll and summon the people to do their penance. I sit here, and I stay here! No worries, no problem! I will not be tortured by rules, or herded around by anyone's words! No priest will tell me what to do! But the whole rest of my village? They fill that church up there on the hill, like Mana fills her stuffed tomatoes at the taverna! Eklesia Evlogimenos yia Tamatas Yemistes, The Church of the Blessed Stuffed Tomato, ha ha ha HA!"

Bouncing from the marble rock of the wall behind them and back to the wooden boats in the water, his warm laughter soothed, like some beatific presence blessing them all with a bit of comfort.

He stood and shook out his legs and with his smoke perched at a right angle to his lips, grabbed an armful of mended netting and tossed it to the side. As he turned back to the family, he took another deep drag of his cigarette and exhaled, "Lipon. Seriously now, there are those people who still use the little burros for work in the field and those who use the ponies to haul the carts filled with bricks or the big boxes of wine from the harbor ... you've seen them, no?"

He turned then to Lily. She nodded cautiously.

"Those men, those women, in these times, now... they have grown to know the creatures in a different way than the people were able to before. And you see, they can take time to get to know the animals, so they do not fear them! Their bellies are full, there are not so many worries and they know that without those hard working beasts their lives would not be so good! So ... they take care of them and treat them as partners. All is not lost on the people of my land, agapi mou. Please, my love! Have some faith in us!"

She was listening. The buzzwords 'burro' and 'ponies' had served to bring the conversation into a more meaningful focus for her. Lily had noticed that the 'better' men (in her opinion) did fit their burros and ponies with bridles that looked comfortable on their little heads. They seemed well fed and cared for, and the harness' were well-fitted to their bodies and didn't look as though it pinched or rubbed their sensitive skin. Some of them even had macramé halters, woven of soft cotton and laced with dried flowers and colorful beads, and the small blue glass 'eyeballs' used as protection, to ward off envy, the evil spirits or the 'evil eye'. She wished that she could have a few of those beauties for her own ponies.

She took a moment to attend to the warm spanikopita that her mother had just set in her hand but before she could set anchor again in the deep of Vassili's discourse, she was distracted by daydreams of her sweet animal family back at home.

Lily's first memories were of the warmth of her mothers embrace and the promise in her father's laughter, but snuggled in between were also memories of the soft coats and the curious snuffles of her 'nannies' — the gentle clown of a dog named Macushla; Asha, the Siamese cat, who liked to play fetch like a dog, and her mother's small and ancient pony, Rosie. These sweet creatures had cuddled her, played with her and herded her about, keeping her out of their perception of harm's way. They had been a comfort, a source of laughter and in time were her great teachers of responsibility and unconditional love. Over the years it seemed Lily became fluent in the language of the animals, for all that she came in contact with calmed in her presence.

Carrot and Emily were old ladies too, once-pathetic creatures that had been starved and abandoned by previous owners. The ponies came to Lily's family like gifts on the wind, unexpected and unannounced one late summer's Sunday morning when Lily was nine years old. Her mother and a friend had gone to the local fairgrounds with the intention of buying fresh produce at the weekly Farmers' Market ... but as the fates would have it, they entered through the wrong gate that day and were deposited instead in the midst of a horse auction.

Rather than returning home from their Sunday pilgrimage as usual, with bags overflowing with melons and eggplant and peppers, the two women came home in an unusual sort of processional, followed by a friend's truck and trailer carrying two old and very thin ponies. Eleni had to quickly explain herself to her astonished family, "the sale was interesting, and most of the horses were fit and well trained and therefore could, and did, find fine homes", but then she and Molly discovered the small, dark pen in the back of the lot, overlooked like a dark and forgotten secret. This pen held two horses, each in such pitiful shape they'd been assumed to have no future, and would likely go to the highest bidder for a pittance.

It had been pointed out to the women that, at this caliber sale, the highest bidder for horses such as those two usually was what was known as the 'meat man' or 'kill buyer'. The meat man was something akin to a scavenger, attending horse auctions for the spoils, hovering hungrily for the weak, the cheap and the unwanted. These were the elderly that were being thrown away by owners who had lost interest in them because they were fraught with the infirmities of age and were just too much work, or those scarred and lame and therefore no longer of "use", the ones who had been so soured by their experiences with human unkindness and impatience that there was only the smallest hope of their ever finding a home that could rehabilitate them. And then there were those whose owners could simply no longer afford to feed them for one reason or another, and the only option to leaving their horses to starve, or to scraping up what savings they had that might enable them to afford humane euthanasia, was to bring them to auction and hope for the best. The meat man would bid his price, gather up his sad lot and take them to their end, the slaughterhouse, where he could sell them by the pound for a profit.

Sad stories here are kinda like sad stories at home, I guess. Lily took another bite of her spinach pie. Her eyes were anchored on the begging menagerie down the way, now in front of old Dimitrios' boat, but her thoughts raced like the flocks of swifts that screamed through the skies over the harbor. *My cute little old ladies... how could anyone ... Sheesh, what IS it with people? Do they just throw other people away, too? Is that the way they treat each other? Do people get put away when they are too old - or too lame? When they get to be too hard to take care of, are they left to starve, like the animals?*

Another bite, and then her mouth fell wide open ... she gasped, remembering hearing about 'old folks homes', places where grandmothers and grandfathers were left in the care of others — but also where some were abandoned by their families to wither and die out of sight and out of mind. She had heard of people in other places in the world, or even at home in the States, old people, children, little babies who were sick and without any medicine to help make them well, or starving because they didn't have enough food to eat ... *they DO just throw other people away! Oh my gosh. Why would anyone just let a baby starve? Or a grandma? Even if they are far away, somewhere else? How can anyone know they are starving and just not do anything about it? No wonder I like animals better than stupid people!"*

What Eleni hadn't told Lily back when she was nine, and wouldn't for a few more years, was that the 'end' for the unwanted horses at some auctions wasn't humane euthanasia, or even a swift bullet to the head. It came after a long and terrifying ride in a two level semi truck trailer really meant for transporting cattle. The horses would travel with little or no water and feed, packed so tightly into these cattle trucks far more suited to cattle's shorter stature, that if one panicked for any reason its fear could easily send them all into a frenzy — legs could tangle and break, or the small and the weak might fall and be trampled by the others. Their wounds or thirst or hunger would not be attended to, for they were simply going to be slaughtered soon anyway, destined for a can of dog food, or a dinner plate in Japan, or Belgium, or France. And then all that was left was to await the end, a brutal death which revealed itself to them over and over as they watched and smelled and heard those in line ahead of them meet theirs.

Many people didn't have any idea that this is what happened to America's unwanted, unneeded horses.

The two old ponies Carrot and Emily had been spared a fate that, according to Eleni, nothing living should have to bear. They were now fat and happy family members, especially well loved by Lily who brushed them until they glistened and carefully picked out their feet, checking for stones or signs of disease. She regularly inspected halters and tack to be sure that everything still fit the old pensioners properly with no tightness or worn parts that would cause any painful rubbing, and in the hot months, covered their faces with a mesh mask meant to keep the flies from bothering their eyes. She had been taught well and tended to them after school before she had to do her homework, choosing to do so instead of playing soccer or basketball with the other kids.

Lily sometimes spent hours in the barn with her best girlfriends, the lot of them working through any snarls and then plaiting flowers and ribbons into the ponies' manes and tails, singing and sharing secrets and laughter as they rubbed the tired, old bodies and gently cleaned out their ears and eyes and all the while the two old mares enjoyed this time with the girls, standing hip shot with one hind leg cocked in relaxation, eyelids at half mast and lower lips drooping and quivering in bliss, offering deep, deep sighs in return for the calm touch and soft words.

The ponies carried the girls confidently on their backs for rambling walks through the meadows that adjoined the small farm. If Lily was alone, she would ride one pony while the other just freely followed along, never far behind, catching grabs at the deep grass as they ambled. She would dismount by the quiet pond to let both ponies graze for a bit, and sometimes they would all just stand there together, silently at water's edge, watching the antics of the loud Canadian geese who called the pond home, or the stealthy deer and fox, passing quietly through like ghosts.

Lily looked up suddenly and realized that she'd gone a bit missing, meandering down her long trail of thought. "Chasing butterflies again, Lil?" her mother would ask her sometimes when she'd been caught adrift in her daydreams. Vassili was turned away from her, engaged in an animated discussion with her parents, so she took another bite and let her thoughts carry her away again. She thought of those times that she had cried into her ponies' manes, or into the sweet dog's furry neck when she had been sad or confused and she couldn't really tell anyone else what was bothering her. Maybe she didn't even know what it was herself, but the animals were always patient, and seemed to listen when her mother or father sometimes didn't. *Maybe people could be nicer to each other if they knew what it was like to be loved by the animals. And what if people were as happy to see each other as our dogs are to see us? Maybe there wouldn't be wars anymore! Yeah ...* She smiled. *How could anyone think that the animals DON'T have a soul? What doesn't have a spirit, anyway? Dumb humans.* As she took the last bite of her snack she looked up again and thought she saw Margarita in the distance, peering at them from the stone stairway beyond the quay.

Vassili sensed Lily's return, cleared his throat and looked directly at her. Softly, as though for her ears only he said, "And only if the people cast away their stupid fears can they truly know."

She stopped chewing, thinking that this crazy, wonderful man had been reading her mind.

He smiled then and twisting towards his boat, tossed what was left of his well smoked butt into a can sitting there, where it extinguished with a hiss. "I love the smoking," he had said once when Eleni carefully asked him about his habit, "it keeps me tied to the earth. Without it I would be flying with *ton glaron*, the gulls ... or lost in the clouds. And it is my friend, always with me!" He picked up his pipe and packed it quickly with a fragrant tobacco, lit it with three great puffs and as he gathered up his net again, he went on, slowly, addressing Eleni now.

"Darling Eleni, many Greeks, they do not believe in changing the course of nature, you know, so they will not sterilize the animals. But in all fairness I must say that the operation, it is not easily found here. So, what is it? They *will* not sterilize? Or they *can* not sterilize?"

"I could probably answer that for you, Vassili."

"Well now, darling Eleni, you do not know this. I do not know this! But what I do know is that these cats and dogs are left to do what comes naturally to them. Ba da boom! What else do we expect them to do? And so then, *tee na kanoume?* What can we do? Soon, the little island, it is filled with even more little cats and dogs, which also will have brood, after brood, after brood, after brood. You know, more babies!" He stopped briefly, took off his cap to wipe his brow, and as he set it back atop his full, dark head of hair, gestured towards the tavernas. "They have no homes, no people to care for them, so these creatures live where they can and make messes where the people walk and are all fighting through their hunger at the garbage bins, or even at the feet of the tourists in the tavernas, just for a little speck of food. Some of the tourists, they find this offensive and dirty ... so in the fear of losing business, certain people here, they feel entitled to scare off these pathetic creatures, or do away with them entirely. At this time, there is no acceptable remedy for this problem, my friends. It is like a snake eating its own tail, it just goes around and around in an endless circle."

Lily stopped chewing for a moment to allow Vassili's words to sink in, but finding that they had no friendly place to settle, in a manner bolder than her twelve short years might ordinarily reveal, she blurted out,

"So ... it IS following nature to STARVE them? To CHASE them or HURT them? Or just KILL them for no good reason? I don't get it! It's just not FAIR! It's NOT right! The poor animals just never EVEN have a chance to show how GOOD they are! How CAN they, when they are so scared and hungry ALL the time?" Tears welled up now, betraying all of the frustration brewing in her beautiful heart.

"Lily!" Eleni called, cautioning, surprised at her daughter's boldness but Vassili held his palm up to her and shook his head, eyes closed. He answered quietly, "No, no agapee mou ... it is not right. My love, my love, it is not right."

Lily's tears spilled over, trickling quietly down her cheeks. No one spoke. They just let the girl's feelings settle around them. Eleni came up behind her, quietly wrapping arms around her, holding her until she straightened and sniffled,

"OK Vassili. So then how come... the little dog... Margarita, how come she's still alive? And how did she even get a name?"

Vassili set down his net and pressed his large, calloused hands into the hard cement of the walkway, stretching out his cramping fingers and with a great sigh, as if the question was somehow a burden for him, he answered,

"Ah, Margarita. Well, I do not see her often, as I am sure she fears for her life too much to come out here by the boats! We might eat her for dinner, no? Ha ha ha!" He laughed weakly, reaching out to softly touch the girl's damp and reddened cheek. "Ah, I am only joking, my dear Kokinoula."

"Lipon, now then. I will tell you her story. You see, some years ago my own daughter ..." his voice trailed and then quieted. He caressed his thick moustache, tracing it with two fingers from under the tip of his nose down both sides of his wide frown and thought of how long it had been since he had seen his daughter, Kaiti. "Yes, five years now - she came in spring with her friends from University in Roma. They came for a long summer visit to the island. My Kaiti, a fiery and independent girl, she is much like you, Lily."

With a wide sweep of his arm towards the water, "She had a heart as big as the sea, a huge heart to fill up with the sad animals of the island. She fed little cats everywhere she went and one morning, on her rounds through the village, she found a man crouched down by the water, he was preparing to drown four puppies, their eyes barely even opened to the world. So, when Kaiti, she realized what she was about to witness, well ... she cried out to the man, 'No, no!' and tried to grab the little things from him. She only was able to come away with one of them. Margarita."

There was a pause in his telling. And then he cleared his throat, as though willing the words to come back to him. "Now before you get too horrified my friends, remember! There have been very few choices here, you know, about what to do about the unwanted puppies or little baby cats. OK? What do we do? This does not pardon that man, he was cruel, yes, but it simply is what it is. Lipon. Now, we go on. Lily, I do not know who the dog was named for, how she came by a name that is more appropriate for someone's old Aunt. That will all remain mystery. Toh mystiko! But Kaiti, and her friends, they watched over her."

Vassili jumped up and disappeared into the boat's wheelhouse. He could be heard rummaging about, muttering to himself, but returned quickly and as he sat again in front of Lily, tossed a worn photograph into her lap. "Oh! She was so cute!" Lily gasped as she poured over the picture of beautiful young women standing in front of Hestia, one holding the infant Margarita in her arms.

"Margarita, she sometimes rode the buses with the girls, or the caiques out to beaches on the little islands, and she would rest at Kaiti's feet while she and her friends ate in the tavernas here. A very independent one, Margarita, she started to learn her own way around the village as a pup, and I think because the people knew and loved Kaiti and the other girls everyone here came to know her too. And in coming to know the little dog, they were not afraid. But. Here is the great tragedy ..." He looked at each of them, Harry, Eleni and Lily, but lingered on the girls, "you must think well on this, and never forget it! ... This tragedy, it is that eventually my daughter and all of her friends, they had to leave the island, to go back to school, you know. It was not possible to take Margarita or any of the island's other mutts or cats along. Of course, my Kaiti, she had not thought of this. So, the little dog, she was left behind." Lily, sitting in a breathless silence, passed the photo to her mother.

"Oh, Vassili! You're breaking my heart." Eleni groaned. She lingered on the photograph, trying to imagine the weathered seaman a father. *Why doesn't he ever speak of his family?* "Didn't your daughter ever return?"

Vassili stood up and shook out his legs again, picked the nets he had mended and walked them to his boat, placing them carefully on the prow.

"No."

Returning to the pile of netting he had yet to patch he jabbed a finger into the air in dramatic response. "No! And with Kaiti's leaving also went any compassion or caring for Margarita. Poof, gone! You take the human protector away and the goodness of an animal will very easily be forgotten. The little dog, she became scared and mistrusting and of course, very, very hungry. She became one of the dirty beggars. I've heard the stories, the little dog, she is legend up there in the neighborhood. She has her friends ... and she has her enemies." He pursed his lips, nodding as he compared the weights of something unseen in his two hands.

"Oh, she has been able to care for herself it seems, with help from a friend or two over the long winters, but no matter, there is no sparing her the life of a female dog, pregnant what, one, maybe two times every year, no?

And then, having to survive through the raising of her babies and keeping them safe. She must be 5 years old now? Yes, and I believe she must have lost many puppies to death, one way or another. And now, she turns into a lioness, a wild mother bear, screaming and yelling and scratching when protecting her children! For good reason, no? Perhaps someone will want to drown her own babies! Does she remember what almost happened to her? How can we ever know?"

He pulled up an old wood chair, frosted with the patina the sea air lends to anything it touches for long, and sat down, now in front of Lily. "Her fury, it frightens the people here. I do not know if it keeps them from her babies but now I do know that they do not think so kindly of her. I am not so surprised that you have won her over, matakia mou, made a friend of her, for you have Kaiti's loving heart ... you nurture it my little darling, and it will serve you well."

Vassili stopped and gazed out over the water. Something had stirred. Something deep in his heart, feelings, frozen in time were being thawed, unearthed. He cleared his throat, took a deep breath and lit his pipe again and when he glanced back, his eyes were sad and serious and lingered on Lily for a moment that stretched to forever. But then he continued, his voice undulating, the melodic peaks and valleys making strong points of his words.

"You remember this: whatever you do for Margarita, whatever you do for her babies or any of the other strays here, they all must eventually carry on without you, take care of themselves. You cannot carry them all back to your homeland, can you? So, what becomes of them? You cannot save them all, my darlings. When you leave, they are back to nothing, a life of surviving, day by day by day. On and on. You can make friends with them, you can love them and you can give them some time when life does not have to be so hard, that is the best you can do, but remember this. They must continue on without you."

With that, he stopped. Suddenly softening, he reached out for Lily, "Now run, go, find that mangy little devil dog you like so much and leave me to my mending. Tha se dho meta, koukla. I will see you later, darling." And he patted her cheek and sent her off with a puff of his pipe and a grin.

safe haven

The storm Vassili had predicted came and went quickly. The island was buffeted by winds that rattled and shook the shutters on the buildings ... and electrified, the night shattered into pieces by a brilliant show of lightning, jagged shards splitting the sky from the heavens to the earth, each accompanied by thunder that seemed to announce Zeus himself, calling down his wrath from above. But the downpour itself was brief, just enough to quench the summer's crops and wash the dust away.

Margarita's little family stayed dry in their safe haven beneath the tree overlooking the sea.

Though the pups were nearing their seventh week, they were not yet fully weaned and Margarita's teats were raw and bloodied from their greedy clamor. She had lost even more weight, as the considerable amount of nourishment they took from her now came from her very bones. There just was not enough for her to eat.

She was tiring of their play. It was coming time to let them go.

Lily still visited the ramshackle nursery each day, perfectly content to run and tumble about with the pups but now when they ran out of energy and fell exhausted into their box, Margarita curled up confidently next to her gentle girl, and would allow her to trace the gaunt lines of her body. "Margarita ... Margarita ..." The child whispered the familiar, magic words, and with a deep sigh of relief the dog echoed each peaceful beat of the child's heart with a wag of her tail.

eleni

"Use your sunscreen. Please!" She tugged Lily's hat down around her head.

With a little fussing and plentiful kisses, she sent Harry and Lily off for a day of exploration of the wilder reaches of the island.

Ah, gentle peace!

A day of nothing! ... *perhaps a lazy walk through the village* ... Eleni poured another coffee and slipped into the filtered light of the balcony, both hands wrapped around the cup, seeking its warmth. Sitting there in the cool air she wandered in her thoughts along paths she might take, shooting photos at her leisure as she explored whitewashed alleys, accented startlingly by the purples and reds of bougainvillea and geranium and the blues and greens and oranges of laundry fluttering overhead on lines strung from one balcony to the next. She would stop wherever she wanted to along her vibrant path, to browse pottery shops or to talk with the old women embroidering under the plane tree in the platia. *Yes!* Or maybe she would have a coffee on the paralia with Vassili and then sneak a quick look at the Herald Tribune for news of the war build up in the Gulf.

Perhaps she would just sit here all day and write. *Bliss!*

A slight, fair woman with voluminous red hair, Eleni had been a dancer until age grew her body in all the wrong ways. She spun away from dance and into Harry's arms, and from that life shared with her beloved she now coaxed the voice of her Muse as a singer, a photographer and a writer, and of course, through her most cherished occupation, being Lily's mother. The Irish in her genes boldly trounced the Greek that hid far, far back in her lineage — adopted at birth, her family had named her Eleni in honor of that hidden bit of blood. No wonder she felt so at ease, so at home here in this land.

Something about the vast, primeval sea moved her deeply, and the elements here, the air and earth and sun, all in accord with the waters, tugged at her very being. They connected her to this place. She felt purity, divinity still prospering in the shadows and hoped to return again and again to tap into that well of holiness, to further nurture her artist's soul. *There's such wonder and comfort in anything so honest...*

In many of the island folk, so vital, still so connected to the elements, Eleni found a wealth to be gleaned from their zest for life, a zest perfectly tempered and seasoned by an extraordinary simplicity. Though quite a sensitive soul herself, without much sense of discipline it seemed that 'hotheaded' and 'opinionated' were the illustrative terms that trailed along behind her wherever she went. She just took the hard bits of life, and herself, far too seriously sometimes, but these people were not so complicated! Of course, they were just like people anywhere with warts and shadows and all, armed sometimes with gossip and secrets and even darker things, but still Eleni loved how so many of her friends here laughed deeply and loudly whenever the urge came about, and sometimes sang and danced for no reason other than that they were moved in the moment to do so. They — men and women alike — cried easily when touched by sorrow, yelled and stomped about in anger or frustration until the flames were finally spent and lucid words rose from their ash. And love was fiery, passionate, heartrending poetry.

To Eleni, it all came out as true beauty in the end. She looked from the balcony out over the water, smiling into the brightening morn, and breathed the gentle rhythms of the sea, the beating heart of their home away from home.

Behind her was their room, a small room with a bare marble floor and twin beds, draped with colorful cloths and embroideries she had found in a village shop, and pushed together so she and Harry could be close in the night. A lopsided wardrobe and a tiny desk with two drawers held only the essentials — they had long ago learned to travel lightly. On a nightstand, beside a candle and a pile of worn books and journals sat a delicate blue bowl filled with tiny seashells. She loved the shells, loved holding them, rolling them gently in her hands, always amazed at their detail and perfection, each one so marvelously unique. She could spend a whole day just walking the shores here, waves tickling her bare toes, searching for these, the jewels of the sea.

The guitar stood propped against the wall, a streak of light illuminating its graceful curves, seductive, mysterious, waiting for the Muse who often called upon

Harry here. Sunrise, midnight, they never knew when the calling would come, so the guitar just lay patiently in wait, though it never had to wait for long.

Just outside the innermost door there was a small, light filled room, more like a hallway but enclosed and big enough to hold the comfy little bed that Lily slept in. The walls of the tiny space were dressed with color, pictures the girl had painted of the seaside, of Margarita, Vassili on his red caique, and the animals at home. She had created a very cozy nest for herself.

The greatest feature was the narrow balcony that seemed to hover over the quiet walkway below, and just below that, the Aegean, which lulled them to sleep each night. The view was breathtaking, magic, a broad vista of the shimmering sea, and the small islands dotted about her surface in the distant haze sometimes looked as if they were just floating in thin air when the light of the morning or evening met the water at just the right moment. The balcony was a sweet spot for the family to sit together for breakfast, or with its offering of such vast peace, the perfect place to sit alone to rest one's weary eyes on the horizon. Occasionally a fisherman or two came 'round the peninsula in the mornings, gathering nets or hunting octopus just below the cliff in small, gaily painted caiques, singing all the while some tale of love or loss, at the top of their lungs as if they were the only ones alive in the dawning day.

Yet, it was so quiet here in the neighborhood. There were no loud American voices, no language they immediately understood for that matter, just the lilting singsong of language foreign to their ears, the mothers calling to their children at play and the cantor at the church on the hill, his tonal missive broadcast through a set of ancient, static plagued speakers. Or the soft patter of hooves and a gentle toning ... "Ehla, come!" ... the old man who would come through every few mornings on his burro to hawk his fresh vegetables and herbs to the neighborhood folk.

The sounds they did hear belonged here, they were a part of the island's magic.

White mosquito netting billowed silently in the balcony's doorway, the diaphanous clouds of fabric allowing the family to sleep in peace. There was no need to be shuttered away from voracious mosquitoes, sealing out the sounds of the night.

The sighing sea was their lullaby.

As the ease of her morning was drawing on at a leisurely pace, Eleni suddenly remembered that there was laundry that needed attending to. Now. *Oh, damn! So much for 'lost' time.* Kosta, the owner of the homey, blue-trimmed kafenion in the harbor where she and Harry enjoyed morning coffee and conversations, had warned of the day's pending strikes, actions launched by a segment of Greek workers protesting for better wage and better workday hours. The round, affable man told Eleni that these strikes would consist of electrical blackouts, coming at set times throughout the day and night, so she knew that she must rush to beat them if she hoped to get laundry done today. Knowing well how capable the Greeks were of getting their points across with their very well-organized protests, she gathered up the clothing and dashed out the door and up the marble stairs to the rooftop to snatch up the towels airing on the line there.

Many an afternoon had been spent on this roof tromping about in sudsy tubs of water filled with their well-worn clothes, the three of them taking turns churning shirts and shorts and skirts clean, laughing as they splashed one another cool in the afternoon's relentless heat. But once in awhile the clothes deserved a trip to the laundromat, and she was kneeling to stuff the still damp towels into her backpack when she heard Margarita.

Ayyy yiyiyiyiyiyiyiy ... yakyak yiiiiiyiiii.

Eleni raised herself to peer over the roof's wall to see what the commotion was about and chuckled, watching people scatter below. She knew that the little dog was just doing her job.

I would do the same, she mused. *I would do the same ...*

It was time to meet this mighty little being.

Each slap of her thongs echoed off the marble steps and hard walls as she ran down the two flights of stairs. Stepping through Haroula's garden into the sunlight, she saw the small, bent, very old woman walking up the path, a familiar sight swathed in black from head to toe in the traditional garb of the old or the widowed women.

Eleni and her family frequently saw the woman known as Yia Yia, Grandmother, sitting alone in the platia by the church, or under the plane tree with her cronies in the mornings. More often, as they made way at dusk into the village for dinner they saw her standing out upon her own balcony — motionless, always staring seaward. And quite often, little Margarita was there, sitting by her side.

She called out a respectful morning greeting now to the woman, "Kalimera sas! Pos iste, Yia Yia?" and the ancient, gnarled face lit up like the sun, a beaming smile cutting through all of the sadness that had veiled it.

"Kalimera, kalimera agapi mou!" Grandmother chirped in response, a fluttery, backward wave of her hand restating her welcome. She reached up to pat Eleni's cheek. "Poli kala Eleni, esei? I am good, Eleni. You? " Each small and seemingly insignificant attempt made to speak the Greek language with locals always brought with it a gift of sorts. This morning, it was an opening, an opening away from distant sadness, a face opening like a rose greeting the morning sun. The two women, facing one another from distinctly different worlds, exchanged their few words and warm smiles and continued on their separate ways.

Eleni walked toward the tree by the cliff's edge. She had only to follow the cacophony. Ayyyy yaakkk yiyiyiyiyiyiii ... throaty, raspy, rusty, such an enormous sound coming from one so small and desperate! And yes, there was Margarita, holding ground as people passed hurriedly by and when Eleni neared, the little dog turned and directed the mighty fury her way, the considerable effort put into each yelp and yip raising the wee dog's front legs up and off the ground. Quietly amused, Eleni stood back to observe this unlikely little warrior, who really was far smaller than she sounded! Speaking softly to the dog, almost a whisper, she knelt to make herself appear smaller, averting her gaze to seem even less of a threat.

Margarita kept up the charade though she was sensing something very familiar in this person, another with the kind eyes and giving voice. There was goodness here somehow, like there was in the small one, her girl — like there was in the kind one, in Her. The ferocious little dog stopped her yelling to sniff the air, warily, warily, around them and between them, and in it she smelled that calm she knew as safety.

After a long stretch of the stillness, Eleni left a piece of cheese on the ground, an offering of sorts, then stepped back to retrieve the backpack filled with ripening clothing and continue her way to the village.

Margarita smelled the food, her stomach rolling and churning and she almost snatched it up but the hollow gnawing of her mistrust was bigger than hunger, always there to remind her of how the poisonings come about. She wasn't ready, yet, to lose herself to comfort. She left the morsel where it lay and shrank back into the nesting box.

delicate wonder

The blackout did finally come, just as Eleni was folding the clean clothes, freshened now from time spent drying in the warm rooftop sun. She could tell that the power was off simply from the sound of the voices raised down at the harbor. Raised in frustration, they carried up the hill on the afternoon breeze and if she only had a better understanding of the language she'd have been able to discern exactly what curses were being flung about!

Eleni loved the blackouts, but especially when they came in the night for then the village crept out from behind the glamour, that veil of modernity and convenience that separated the visitors from its true magic. She was always joking about the feeling manifest amongst some of the taverna owners, that the tourists couldn't possibly enjoy themselves at all without the added ambiance of the glaring, bare bulbs that lit the tables from above, or the ubiquitous thump of techno music. What so profoundly enchanted Eleni about the nighttime strikes was that from the darkness and inevitable quiet a delicate wonder emerged, along with the gas lamps hung out for light and the candles placed at every table. People spoke more quietly, lovers lingered, reaching more deeply into the depths of one another's eyes ... the lack of ordinary light throughout the town just made everything that much more extraordinary, and the night view out to sea was simply wondrous. Without the usual distractions one noticed the lights, like sparkling jewels or light sprites, that spilled from land out across the water as the fishermen put out from shore for their night fishing, their old gas lamps ablaze and dancing in the darkening night.

Eventually, the old men who otherwise seemed to live their lives behind the tavli board and cups of thick Greek coffee — or bottles of ouzo — pulled out dusty old instruments and sat around the tables playing songs rich in the poetry of heart and love and sorrow and as the evening drew on and pitchers of drink were emptied and filled again and again, the music grew more lively. It was never long before everyone within its grasp was captivated by the spirits of dance and song.

The electricity would stay off for hours and when Harry, Eleni and Lily walked homeward, the lamps and candles burning in the windows of each of the houses along their way lit their passage up the winding steps and through the maze of alleys in the darkened neighborhood, all the way to Haroula's gate.

To make a strong point and hopefully institute change, the strikes were meant to disrupt the daily workings of the country. During the daylight strikes, far less romantic than those of the night, the electricity would be turned off for only a short while, though always during the times business was conducted. It was never during the early morning hours or the relative quiet of siesta times, much to the displeasure of the shop owners, and though the outages were to the detriment of all of the people, they did drive home how important electricity was to modern, daily commerce and therefore to the Greek economy, and that to have those workers well paid and well taken care of would undoubtedly be in everyone's best interest!

When the power finally did return, it came bubbling and percolating in fits and starts throughout the village, sputtering to life first in the harbor and from there heading up the hills through the tangles and bunches of ancient wires that hung haphazardly from old wooden poles, lighting up shops and homes in impossibly slow increments along its way. Inevitably it would shut off just as it reached the very top of the town, and the darkness and quiet would spread again, oozing slowly back down the hill to the harbor with the groans of village folk following in its wake. After several of these stuttering attempts, the power would remain 'on', much to the relief of the bankers and taverna owners and shopkeeps, leaving the ghosts of the dark, those extraordinarily quiet and magical moments, to wander about, only to descend upon the village again when called on by the next scheduled outage.

She was sitting under shade, taking advantage of every bit of breeze that found its way to the sweltering rooftop when Harry and Lily drifted in, hot and tired from their long day's adventure. Luring her with visions of a swim in the waters of the point, Lily took her mother by the hand and led the way to the salvation of the cooling blue.

But when they came to Margarita's lair, they stopped.

The quiet was curiously unsettling. So used to the war cry that warned trespassers away, they were struck now by a weighty silence.

"I just saw her here, not more than three or four hours ago! She certainly shrieked her warning at me then." Eleni said, peering over the wall to the water below for some sign of the dog.

"Oh, yay! You finally met her! Well. Margarita knows us now, Mama, and so I think that maybe she just doesn't need to yell at us anymore."

At the sound of Lily's voice, the pups' tiny champion popped out from their cardboard box. Armed now with only a coy dog-smile and a wag of her thin flag of a tail she sidled up to her girl for a shy greeting and after a good shake off and a yawn, sat squarely on her haunches to begin what seemed to be a thorough assessment. She stared long at Lily, then Eleni, and back to Lily as though reading the connection between this new woman and her comforting girl who had so carefully nurtured their growing trust. Neither Lily nor her mother spoke a word. After the long but apparently satisfying appraisal, Margarita gave a sneeze, stretched squeakily and shook again. A 'the end' or 'all is well' it seemed, for she then surprised them both by leaving her slumbering pups behind in their box and dashing off to lead the way to the rocks at land's end. Once there, she sat like a sentinel, keeping watch over Lily and Eleni them as they cooled in the silken water.

Eleni turned to her child, who surfaced next to her, a giggling dolphin-girl. "Poor thing, she is skinny, isn't she Lil?"

"I told you, Mama. So ... can we help her now?" She took in a great breath, closed her eyes tight and dove again.

Margarita had lost more condition, the weakening caused by nursing the growing babes through her own lack of nourishment. Bones were apparent under her dulling coat.

Remembering Vassili's cautionary words, they both knew that they shouldn't make her dependent upon them — but even if just to take a bit of the burden from the tired little dog, it was time to start feeding she and her pups.

"Well, we have to help her, don't we." Eleni stated to the passing winds. Lily swam up behind her mother, chirping happily and smothering her with kisses, and by the time they were cooled and dried and dressed they had formulated a plan and left in search of dog food, little Margarita still following closely at their heels.

None of the markets in the town carried such a thing as dog food. The shopkeeps were astonished, and looked at the two foreigners as though they had been asking after Caspian caviar or fine French perfume though they had in fact, very politely, asked for food for the dogs. Cat kibble was found easily, if only because the tourists enjoyed feeding the hungry masses in the island's many platias — like feeding the pigeons in Venice's great St. Mark's Square, it was a quaint custom, though most visitors here didn't really understand the gravity of the animals' hunger or what a difficult business simply staying alive really was for them.

But dog food? "Yia skeelos? Po po po! For a dog? No, no, you must go somewhere else."

Finally, a good supply was located in the tiny shop near the old cemetery at the top of the hill, the same shop where they bought their supplies for the street cats. The proprietor of the animal-friendly market was a dark, thin and elegant man who had previously introduced himself to the family as Takis Koutsinakis.

"Ehyete ena skeelo? Do you have a dog?" he asked.

"Neh, neh … Yes … well, actually it seems that the dog has us!" Eleni offered quietly.

With a kind, knowing smile Takis nodded as he placed the cans carefully in a bag, and Eleni knew that here, they had found a comrade.

"This dog is one of the lucky ones, you know." Takis spoke slowly, handing the bag over to Lily. "I see you here, getting the food for the cats. Efharisto poli, thank you for being the animals' angels."

"Oh, but they are our angels, aren't they?" Eleni replied. She took the man's hand in her own and thanked him ... *what kind eyes he has!* ... and as the girls and Margarita disappeared down the narrow lane, Takis called out that he hoped to see them again soon.

The three puppies greeted their return with squeals and growls, leaps and snarls, unable yet to define the differences between the sounds of their boundless happiness and those that normally signaled threat. Eleni opened a few cans of the food for Margarita who, as if she had come to some great epiphany, no longer hesitated at the promise of a meal from these people she had come to trust. She was very, very hungry. Trying to keep up with her appetite, Eleni added food to the plate as quickly as the dog could make it disappear and before long the pups stopped tugging on their mother with needle teeth and were following her lead, leaping in with great curiosity and a hunger that spoke to their souls, telling them that This Was The Stuff of Life.

The babies ended up with more on them than in their tummies, although plenty of the food did find its mark and in just minutes they were sated, full and round and sound asleep in a pile of distended bellies and pink paw pads. As Margarita cleaned up every last morsel that clung to their ears and their toes, licking and licking until each of the pups shone in the evening's rich light, she would glance up at the two gentle women with dreamy eyes, a look that said, quite clearly, "Oh yes, you are mine now."

And when she was finished, she joined her sleeping babies, curling around them for the first time in a long, long while with a full stomach that didn't groan or squeak or hurt from emptiness.

With just one good meal a day it wasn't long before Margarita started to fill out. The bony points rounded off and a layer of protective fat covered her ribs, and her coat soon lost much of its dull roughness to gain a bit of luster. She lost the gaunt look of the starved and abandoned.

She began to leave the pups alone more often, there at their tree by the sea. Sometimes they would attempt to follow her up the path, a tumbling ball of puppy energy rotating behind her, but Margarita would simply snarl the maternal canine equivalent of "stay put", and with whines and tucked tails, stay they did. She was slowly weaning them and the discipline had begun.

Margarita never begged or expected food from 'her' people. She seemed to want nothing but their company and, once she learned where they lived, the light of the morning found her laying in wait at their front door. When Eleni or Lily flung the big door open to the day, the dog leapt up from where she lay hidden behind a huge pot of flowers and with a dog's smile on her face she stood fast, eyes locked on theirs, her happy tail wagging so hard that it swung her whole hind end around to one side and then back again, the wildly waving flag almost reaching to touch her snout with each pass.

And in that delight, she made the strangest, strangled sounds, lyrical and melodic, almost beautiful, her inflections accented by such feeling that Lily just knew the little dog was doing her best to talk to them.

forever

The day itself was blameless, cool and clear, all to
be expected in a summer island's morn — it was the
puppies' leaving that came with no warning to Lily.

Sitting on the ground next to the now worn box,
she wrote in her journal, Margarita curled at her side with
her head resting on her leg. Two young women walked
quietly down the path towards them, but Margarita simply
couldn't find the impetus to get up and yell and chase
them off, as though all of the fierce bluster and fear had
been soothed out of her. She just lay still, watching their
approach.

Lily and Margarita both looked up as the women
stopped to greet them.

"We're wondering, are the puppies still here?
Have they found homes yet?"

Homes?

Lily nodded slowly, a bit wary at first. "Yes. They
are here." The women seemed gentle, and were nice

enough. She noted a slight accent, and that they both were very pretty and calm, with soft voices and kind eyes — and then one of them said that what they really wanted to do was to take the pups back to the Netherlands with them, to find them good homes with kind people who would love and care for them properly, forever.

Take them? MY puppies?

Lily panicked slightly in the face of this abrupt turn but really didn't need much time to see the good fortune nestled there. Though sudden and sad, it also meant a good life for these babies, surely one without the fear and hunger they would have to endure were they to stay here on the island. She knew this.

With one deep breath, her possessiveness dissolved.

She eased the fat puppies out of their box and waited while Margarita nosed around and licked them a bit, telling the dogs about this great good fortune that was upon them all and that Margarita should kiss her babies one last time — then took up each sleepy pup one at a time and, cradling it to her heart and kissing it softly, whispered its secret name ... Jovi ... then Moki ... and finally, Nina Cupenda ... and with sweet blessings that tripped and trembled under her breath, she handed them to the women, who cuddled them close and nodded and smiled kindly back at her.

Forever. Lily rolled the beautiful word around and around in her head.

With that, off Margarita's babies went, off to a life that every living thing on this planet deserves, a life of dignity and respect, forever.

Margarita seemed to sense this intention, this kindness. She sighed deeply, relieved and released, and drifted off into a full, deep sleep with her red haired girl's hand laying ever so gently upon her back.

here is happiness

They neared the bottom of the long steps to the paralia — air sharp and clear, with not even the slightest hint of breeze, the morning was as though cut from a rare glass. Vassili was an animated figure dancing about on the quay in the distance. He raised his arms and looking skyward yelled out,

"Filous mou! Simera! My friends! You must come today! No meltemi! No clouds!" As Harry neared, the fisherman held his hand out to him.

"Ah, Hari, my friend!"

"Kalimera, Vassili! What news is there from the Gods of the deep?" Harry took the fisherman's hand into both of his in warm greeting and Vassili, draping one arm around Harry's shoulder, lowered his voice for the rest of his proposal.

"Ah, lipon Hari ... you see, today the sea, she smiles on a journey to the north! You come with me ... on Hestia, we'll all go dancing through the waters." And louder, "Ok, Eleni, Lily, louloudia mou ... my flowers?

Endaxi!" He kissed them each on both cheeks as they nodded absolutely, yes, in unison, delighted to have Vassili be their captain and guide. There was no one better to reveal the magic that flourished out there upon the calm waters.

Vassili fluttered his fingers towards the town.

"So, now go ... go, go. Get some food, get your coffee but we must leave, soon." and with that, Harry was off to the market for food and drink while Eleni rushed back up to the pensione for the rest of the day's necessities.

"And my watercolors, please!" Lily called out, as her mother slipped into the shadows of the plane trees at far end of the paralia. She stayed on the quay, happy for a few moments to commune with her own kind, Stratos and Haris, the wild and cheery little kids with whom she'd become good friends. Little Haris caught up Lily's hand and danced her away, to the end of the quay where Stratos stood waiting, fishing poles in hand.

Like a dervish Eleni spun through the sunlit room gathering up their goods. Already laden with towels and hats and books, she slung Harry's guitar bag across her back, stacked two sun umbrellas under one arm and swooped up Lily's small bag of tricks with her free hand. In one fluid motion she kicked the door closed behind her, dropped the key that was held between her teeth into her hand, turned the lock and aimed for the pensione's slippery stairs, navigating with the grace of a pack mule picking her way carefully down a perilous mountain path.

She smiled as she stepped into the sunlight, met there by the lilting song that had come to be known as Margarita's morning greeting. The wee brown dog, waiting by the garden gate, was expectant as usual, dancing from foot to little foot.

"Well then, come on little one, walk with me."

Margarita celebrated with a high pitched 'rrroooo!' and a victory scoot down the cobbles and back, tail tucked, grinning madly, and then fell in at Eleni's side. All the while they walked the winding alleys back down into the village, the two shared a most exquisite conversation.

Pointing her snout upwards and looking straight at Eleni, Margarita crooned — a strange, lyrical refrain that rose in grunts and scratchy yeowls from deep within her great being — and when the little dog quieted, Eleni looked into her deep, soulful eyes. "Oh, what a smart and beautiful girl you are, Margarita. We all love you so much."

Margarita appeared to be listening quite intently, trotting alongside with ears pricked, staring quietly up at Eleni while she spoke, and in turn chimed back into the conversation with her own colorful chorus of woo wooos, throaty whines and sneeze-like snuffles. After many minutes of this enchanting tête-à-tête Eleni stopped, dropping her load mid-step to take the excited little dog into her arms.

"Come on, little waif. Oh ... we'll miss you today, yes, yes." She laughed as the dog lashed her face with a soft tongue. "What a good girl ... But we'll be back later, of course we will, we'll meet you on your rock. For our sunset!" Margarita went limp as Eleni scratched her ear. She closed her eyes and laid her head on the woman's shoulder, and Eleni just held her quietly, rocking back and forth, back and forth for some time before placing her back on the ground.

Kneeling, she tenderly cupped the dog's head in her hands.

"What a good girl you are, Margarita. We love you forever, you know. But, now you have to go! Have a good day, little one, go on now." The dog jumped away, dancing around Eleni.

"Oh no, you misunderstand! I am coming with you." was likely Margarita's reply. "I am with you always, wherever you go! You are mine!" It came out in her usual undulating, singsong squawk but as she leapt about, Eleni sensed the intention and the tremendous loyalty that poured from the happy little creature. She laughed. There was no missing the message.

Lily looked up from the fishing line she was baiting, again, for little Haris who had just reeled in an old sock from the harbor floor. She could hear laughter now, echoing and tumbling down the stairs at the far end of the quay and soon her mother, laden like a packhorse, reemerged from the shadows with Margarita prancing at her side. The dog scampered off down a side street when the pair reached Kostas' taverna and Lily turned back to her task, working the pieces of squid, slimy, spongy, creepy but thankfully already dead. Harry had taught Lily how to bait with worms, but it made her too sad to impale the squirming little things, still alive, upon a hook ... this was an infinitely easier job to stomach than the torturing of writhing little beasts.

She handed the pole back to the excited little girl and descended the three steep steps that led into the water to carefully rinse her hands. Looking down at her bare, brown feet, magnified by warm waters lapping at her toes, she wondered for just a fleeting moment what it was going to be like to be home again. *Well, my feet will hate it.*

Harry was back as well.

"Lily!"

Scrambling back up the steps, Lily called out to her friends "Avrio! Tomorrow!" and shaking her hands in the drying air, ran to see what mouthwatering treasures her father had found.

"Peaches, Papa?" Lily pushed sandy curls from her father's eyes.

"None today, lovie, but look, look at what I did find!"

His pack was filled with the makings of a feast, certainly one fit for a day's adventure at sea. He opened it, slowly, giving her just a peek, looking up with a sly grin spreading beneath raised eyebrows and smiling eyes.

"Oooooohhh! Hair-ry!" She spied the paper bag full of honeysweet, sticky loukomades, simply donut holes all dressed up in Greek finery. Harry pulled one carefully from the bag and set it in her open mouth and with a happy groan she turned again to his pack of treasures, began rummaging about. There was bread, still warm from the oven, and great hunks of kaseri, a sweet, buttery cheese made from sheep's milk ... a few of the first plump tomatoes of early summer, freshly harvested and perfect for slicing, and kalamata olives, not bagged, but wrapped up, as was custom on these islands, like a present in a thick, colorful butcher's paper. Harry had also secured a few liters of the local white wine, gone straight from the barrel into an ingenious plastic bag of sorts that had a small spigot at its top end, and of course, sodas and water enough for them all.

Finished with her sticky sweet, Lily pecked her father on both cheeks, put her fingers to her lips and made a dramatic kissing sound, just like Kostas over a steaming pot of Mana's stifado, and ran off towards the Hestia.

"Pahme! Let's go!" Vassili was calling from the boat.

Ready for the day that stretched before them, the family converged at Hestia's prow, Vassili clucking like a proud mother hen as he extended his well-worn hand to each, helping them aboard his beloved caique.

Built in the 1930s as a fishing vessel, Hestia was an elegant boat with a stable hull that sat deep in the water and bowed gracefully in the shape of a waxing crescent moon from bow to stern. She had a single mast, not often in use but when Vassili raised her sail she could cut quickly through the waves, in the running with the best of the more modern sailboats. With room enough aboard for close to forty people, she could also seat three or four passengers in her wheelhouse while Vassili stood at the wheel. This is where he slept, at Hestia's heart upon the cushioned structure that housed her engine, in a sort of comfort only a boatman could appreciate.

Vassili no longer fished solely for a living. Having bought into the fish market just steps away from the boats, he now enjoyed fishing only when his heart and soul directed him. He left the commerce of the market to his partner Babis who loved the people and the morning gossip and was as happy as Vassili was to not be beholden to the long days and nights of hard work, plying his trade from the sea.

Within the last few years Vassili had given the Hestia a beautiful new paint job, with a striking, very mysterious mermaid, 'i gorgona', decorating her hull. Beautiful, her golden hair spreading like the rays of the sun, she was a sylph in muted tones, swimming in a sea of red just under the brass lettering that spelled out the boat's name, ΕΣΤΙΑ. He also had covered Hestia's benches, each following the gentle outward curve of her wooden body, with brightly colored pillows and had taken to hiring her out in the season as a water taxi, ferrying small groups of people on tours around the island, or to neighboring islands for a taste of something different; new beaches to explore, new hills to climb, crumbling relics to discover. Vassili simply loved being on the water. Never were two days alike, and he took the greatest of pleasure in sharing the beauty of his sea with people who still seemed to be in possession of all of their senses, those who would relish spending hours aboard the caique just staring at the water playing it's tricks with the light, laughing as the salt spray washed over them or as the boat surged, surfing along a particularly large swell and sighing with delight as they drank in the life from the fresh air of the Aegean. Occasionally these journeys were gifted with the presence of dolphins, giggling as they danced in the bow spritz.

Taking opportunity in any of these exquisite moments sailing upon his beloved, calm blue, Vassili would slip in a cassette of one of the great Greek singers of the time, and the rich voice and haunting music would spill out of the speakers and drift endlessly across the sea.

He poked his head out of the wheelhouse.

"Today we will see the magic of my world!" He started up the old diesel engine, which billowed thick, black smoke as it coughed to life.

"There are not many days like this day! Look, look! A perfect sea, abandoned by the wind. Not even a whisper of the meltemi. It is as though the Gods, they have pried the waters and the wind from one another's embrace, allowing us to journey through to where not many ever go. Sketi magyia! Yes, it is pure magic."

But as Vassili began to back the caique out of the sheltered harbor, just above the clamor of her engine and the anchor chain being gathered came a high pitched screaming, a sound that makes a mothers blood run cold. Eleni flew to her feet — something terrible must have befallen a child on the quay? — but no, it was Margarita that she saw there, running frantically back and forth, back and forth along the waters edge, screaming as though her heart were being torn from her body.

"Mama! Vassili! " Lily wailed, her voice rising in a strained crescendo, "Stop! Please stop! We can't leave her ... oh, her heart is breaking! Can't we stop?" She stood on the prow facing the village and looked wildly from Margarita to her mother and Vassili, and back again to the little dog.

Lily's panic pierced the warming air, piercing Eleni's heart deep to her own sorrows concerning the dog's sad tale. *Oh* ... She understood Margarita's distress. They were leaving her. The little dog was watching comfort, kindness and love leave her behind, again.

Margarita was in the water swimming now, shrieking all the while. She swam frantically yet was pushed back by a slight current that she fought and fought with her short legs, her attempts only edging her further away. Turning back only when she couldn't fight it any longer, she took just a moment's rest and then made another futile run for the boat. Finally, her desperation surrendering to exhaustion, she swam to land where a crowd had gathered along the quay, curious about the commotion that shattered the usual quiet of their morning. As she heaved her weary body to the landing from the beach, defeated, still calling mournfully to the retreating boat, a waiter pulled off his neat white apron and flapped it about, trying to shush her away.

Aboard Hestia, on a bench now, Lily sat with her hands over her ears.

Eleni turned sharply to Vassili.

He simply closed his eyes and nodded, and set the boat back to shore.

The moment the caique touched the quay, Margarita leaped aboard and scrambled to Lily, curling up under the bench behind the safety of her legs, and without another word they set off.

The girl heaved a deep, shuddering sigh and wiped tears from her cheeks as Hestia backed out towards the anchor once again and then, leaning back into the comfort of the cushions, stared blankly at all of the indignant faces lining the quay. But the light soon returned to her own face with a smile that sprang from the great satisfaction of knowing that those people all had just witnessed the boat's hasty return to shore — for a dog. She glanced back; her parents were still standing with Vassili by the wheelhouse and once certain that they wouldn't be able to see, Lily turned again to the gathered crowd and stuck her tongue out at them all.

Vassili sailed Hestia north towards a sprinkling of uninhabited islands not marked on most maps and virtually impossible to get to when the meltemi was up. Not only was the sea mischievous and rough when those summer winds blew, making it difficult for anyone but the seasoned fishermen to make passage in the smaller boats, it also made it quite impossible for a boat to safely anchor, once there.

The shallow sea floor was rock in those isolated parts. In order to land its passengers, a boat had to pass just over the top edge of the rock and then be ever so gently run aground, up, onto the sand and pebbled beach, if only just long enough to let passengers disembark. This was no problem if the floor was sand, but here it was not and if the day was not blessed with a calm sea, a captain ran the risk of damaging his boat. If there were waves, just attempting to get close to shore was dangerous, for the sea would raise a boat up on the crest of each swell and then as the waves receded, scrape it over or even crash it down onto any rocks that might lurk below. There were sad tales around the island of the boats that had to make their final trip, a trip to the junkyard, far too soon for the years of scraping over the rocks had worn their hulls so thin that the they no longer were sound enough to safely set to sea.

As the cerulean Aegean spread wide before them Vassili explained that the small island they were sailing for had once been the site of an olive oil factory, its groves of twisted old trees providing the olive mash for the press to, in turn, produce a lustrous, rich oil. Donkeys had been used to drive the gears of the machine, walking round and round in endless circles, their harness hitched to the great arms of the mechanism that squeezed the mash, walking until the job was completed and the press offered up the last drops of its bounty; a thick oil the color of a mountain sage, or of a rich amber, depending upon how early or late in the season the olives were harvested. It all had been abandoned many years back as modern machinery and commerce, both dictating with a new hunger for speed, outdated the time worn ways on this desolate island. The old factory now stood derelict, crumbling back to the earth like one of Athena's forgotten temples.

A smoke waggled at the corner of his mouth as he spoke. It always amazed Eleni that embers from the ash didn't spread fires in his wake.

"All that lives on that land now is a tough herd of little goats. Their people, they go to the island every week, to take water because, you see, the island, it has no good water to offer in these dry months ... they go to be sure none of the goats are sick and to count all of the baby goats. You see, Lily mou? Some people, they do care. Sometimes these goat people, they will even milk the nannies, and with the milk they make a soft, salty cheese. Oh ... polee omorfi! Very lovely, it is heaven!" He feigned a swoon, rolling his eyes and holding the back of a hand to his head, which caused Lily to erupt in laughter.

"Soon now, they will take the little goat family to the north, to the mainland, there, across the water." He pointed to the faint outline of mountains on the horizon. "The promise of the brutal winter, with its cold winds and wild seas, it is coming."

But today, it was hot and the sea was like a glass reflecting the vivid blue of the sky, one of the many blues native only to the waters of the Aegean. Vassili cut the engine, letting the caique just drift so that they all could truly 'hear' the silence ...

Silence …

And within it, other than the faint sound of the silken sea licking lazily at the wooden sides of Hestia, there was nothing else, not the hint of a sigh, not even a breath. One could only imagine the sound of the sun, sizzling on the water. They all were still for quite some time, captured there by the magic, this quiet, adrift upon an endless sea. Even Margarita, perhaps curious about the enveloping calm, came quietly out from under the bench, hopped up and sat basking in the peace that captivated the humans so. They all sat, just staring out over the water — that moment and all that it held was surely one of the brilliant wonders of the world.

A large fish jumped. It broke the spell with a splash, and by virtue of the joy it seemed to take in its leaping it was decided that it was time the travelers tested these magic waters for themselves. Lily was the first to dive into the cool blue, followed soon after by her parents while Margarita stood with her paws resting on the railing, muttering to herself, nose working furiously and ears straight up, radar tracking her people who insisted upon disappearing under the water where she could not see them or keep them safe.

Slowly, slowly, the wonderfully refreshing water brought the travelers back from that dreamy place the sun and sea and absence of distraction had taken them, and after Vassili and Margarita accounted for all of their charges as they dripped about the deck, the captain started up Hestia's engine and set back on his course.

The island made its appearance like a mirage, undulating in the heat of the day. Quite small, it was shimmering with the olive and cypress and as Hestia came to safe harbor, thanks to the calm of the sea, the old abandoned buildings of the oil factory could be seen sitting long forgotten behind a scrim of trees. Vassili dropped anchor and lightly guided his caique right up onto the shore of a beach that stretched the whole length of the little island. A shaky, narrow gangplank was lowered, and Lily ran ahead with Margarita to inspect the beach.

"MOM! You have *got* to come *here*, you *won't* believe this!"

Eleni dropped her bundle in a pile and ran ahead to join Lily, now on her knees staring down at the sand.

"Look!" the girl gasped, holding out open hands for Eleni to see. In them was coarse, pebbled sand — full of shells, some the size of her littlest fingernail, some so small they were barely visible at all. After thoroughly inspecting the riches, the two continued walking the beach but didn't get far at all before they'd realized that the whole strand, end to end, was filled with the shells. There were shells under their feet, stuck between their toes and even clinging to the brown hairs of Margarita's little legs. Laughing, they grasped one another's hands and whooped and danced in circles to celebrate their discovery of this little El Dorado, a shell seekers dream. Margarita followed them around and around, yipping and growling at the edges of their delight.

When Harry caught up with his laughing girls the three took some moments to find the perfect place to settle on the beach, wide and flat and flanked by the perfect shade tree. They picked a spot close enough to the lapping waters that they could just roll over once and be in them when the heat became too much to bear, and the umbrellas were opened, towels were spread and soon each was lost in their own time, a book, or a nap. Harry sat cradling his guitar, gently coaxing her gifts, and Margarita wandered off to explore this new place full of fresh scent and to find a dog's perfect siesta.

She chose a sandy indent under a stand of wild beach grass, just beside a great olive tree, an old, gnarled sentry stationed at beach's edge. She rolled and rolled and sneezed and scratched her back upon the coarse yellow sand and suddenly was up and off, running madly with her tail tucked under her behind, a crazed grin plastered on her face, flying in circles, spraying sand, leaping, ducking and feigning in what looked like pure joy, her tongue lolling and flapping — Lily looked up just as Margarita skidded by, and laughed loudly.

"Zoomies! Oh my gosh, Mama! She's got the zoomies!" She squealed as the happy dog made another wild, sandy pass.

The animals don't feel? Well, that is pure joy! Eleni laughed. *When was it, that she last felt this free? Racing around in ecstasy, no fear, no troubles lurking in her shadows?*

As quickly as she had begun, Margarita stopped her happy dance and nonchalantly sauntered and sniffed her way back to the tree. And then she dug deeply, down to cool, damp earth and, turning 'round in circles several times to find just the right place to curl, she threw herself down with a grunt and settled in comfortably, nose on paws and keeping one eye on her family.

Vassili stayed behind on Hestia, set in deeper water and bobbing placidly about her anchor now. He preferred to stay aboard to read his newspaper, to think and doze in the music of the slight breeze that sighed through the shade of her canopy. Harry had left him with a wealth of food and a large jar full of the cool retsina wine, plenty enough to enjoy in the quiet of the day.

The family napped a bit, navigating dreams lightly colored with the faint sounds of lapping waters, before Eleni and Lily resumed their shell seeking. It was a strange dance, performed in half-saunter time — walk and bend, turn and crouch, inspect ... walk and bend, turn and crouch, inspect — and the heat further choreographed the curious minuet with random, staccato dashes to the sea, where waters cooled sun soaked skin. The shells were everywhere: tiny, iridescent, perfect, some no larger than a coarse grain of sand and they collected specimens of all shapes and colors, which Lily then carefully placed in a small, colorful treasure bag. These shells were among the few ancient treasures left to be found in this necklace of islands — most temples and statuary had been turned to ruin years ago, whether by the elements or the myriad of invaders that had wreaked their havoc through the eons. Abandoned by the various creatures that had called them home, the exquisitely crafted bits of mineral, evidence of nature's perfection and grace, had been tossed by the waters and thrown up as offering to the beach, to be recycled back to the sea by the wrath of winter's waves, or to return to the earth.

With the small bag brimming and their appetite for the precious gems sated, it was only a hunger for food that drew them on. Circling around a huge, beached driftwood tree, bleached white by wind and sea, they wandered back towards Harry and his glorious picnic where the three converged under the shade of the old olive, away from the blasting sun. The Aegean lapped at their feet while they ate and it wasn't long before spirits were raised even further, to the level of a pure contentment evidenced by happy eyes and dreamy smiles. Any speech was reduced to the monosyllabic, "yes." "water." "hot." "fine." "Oh.", punctuated only with scattered sighs. Margarita had wandered off on her own adventure, so other than the goats, and Vassili, whom they could now tell was sound asleep in the hammock by his snores, the loud, grating peals tolling in rhythmic waves across the water, there was not another soul around.

"Timeless.", Eleni managed, with great effort under this spell of sand and sea and antiquity, sublimely tranquilized by the calm and quiet.

Here were all of the elements in perfect combination — the crystal, cooling waters, and the air, so intense in its clarity that it magnified the colors and contrast of anything viewed through it. It felt electric and one could have thought that it was this air, and not the cicadas, that filled the atmosphere with a distant hum; the warm earth, with its fresh scent of the organic process, of scented pine and herbs, and the blazing sun, that set everything to shimmering. Water, Air, Earth, Fire. Like a potion, they all came together and worked Greek magic, an absolute, unequivocal peace.

Eventually — who knew how much time had passed? — Lily began to giggle. And giggle. The bracing energy and the quiet peace were conflicted within her, unable to occupy the same space, and they tickled her fiercely and quite suddenly, given to total abandon, she jumped up, threw her arms to the air and danced a wild jig along the beach and into the water. Startled from the calm by the splashing of their wild child, Eleni and Harry were swept up themselves, and stripping off clothing, raced shouting after her into the sea. Under and through and within the silent magic they all swam, until remembering that they still required air and surfacing, reduced now to pure delight they began to laugh, and laugh, and laugh until they couldn't laugh any longer.

Eleni pulled herself out of the water. *Place ... place is so profound. Look what* this *place does to us! I'm about to burst with love!* When the laughter subsided and she had regained some semblance of composure and could breathe easily again she shook the briny sea from her hair and slipped a shift over her head, rummaged her bag for the camera and began to walk towards the tree-covered hill that loomed over the far end of the beach.

"Come! Come on! To the other side!" she called as Lily and Harry crawled, laughing breathlessly, onto the shore. And up and over they went, scrambling over rocks and scratching their legs on heather until Harry found a sandy goat path that led the way to the crest of the hill, where a tiny stone church stood alone on the cliff overlooking the sea.

Peering through a window, weather-worn and clouded by time, they could see lit candles, and incense censors dangling from the wooden rafters and old icon paintings covering its whitewashed walls. Someone had been there. The church was unlocked. Harry pushed upon the heavy wooden door, which swung wide with an arthritic groan. "Should we go in?" They hesitated, but the odd, hallowed place seemed to beckon. The small room, already filled up with the divine, was hardly big enough for the three of them to stand in. Taking it all in through air thick with frankincense, Lily asked, "Who would come so far to light the candles and incense in such a lonely place?"

Eleni looked out the thickly trimmed glass, over the sea that suddenly seemed so empty. She shuddered, feeling suddenly claustrophobic in this place where God was confined to a box so small there wasn't even room for laughter. *Maybe distilling God down, from light and sea and trees and air, to something that can easily be kept within four walls enables other people to feel some peace? No distractions ...*

"Well ... maybe lighting these candles fills someone's loneliness with comfort and brings them closer to their God. Maybe just filling this little place here with light makes their loneliness disappear?" *People will go to these great lengths for their God, their place, crossing seas and climbing mountains, but won't see the animal begging at their feet!*

"Isn't God supposed to be everywhere, Mama? In everything?" Lily asked through the quiet as she came to stand with her mother at the window, and Eleni knew that they had just been sharing the same thought.

Vassili later explained to them all that it is quite typical the churches in the rural areas are left unlocked for the devoted, or for anyone in need of shelter. "If someone's soul needs a little saving, well, if this is what will save it, the churches, they are always open. The people, they will come to light candles for their dead, for a favor, for some prayer. And these places ... they will not be vandalized. Yes, I think there is still an honor and respect, it is etched deep in the soul of a Greek." he had said.

Honor and respect for all things human, maybe, Eleni murmured to herself.

Leaving the little church sitting its lonely vigil upon its clifftop they followed the path down a dry, rocky hillside sprinkled with rosemary and heather and passed through an olive grove to an astounding beach on the north side of the island. Rather than a strand of sand, this was a beach consisting solely of beautiful stone — smooth, round, white rocks of all different sizes, and where the water met the shore it appeared as though the incandescent white lit the sea from within and the sun, reflecting off the rocks that lined the bottom, turned it a color they couldn't quite name, for they had never seen it before.

"Lucent Blue! Is there already such a color, Lily? In your paint palette, maybe?"

"Don't know Mama, I've never seen it. It's crazy."

"Look, the water glows with light ... from these rocks! Let's call it lucent blue, then!" Eleni pulled out her camera and leaning in as close as she could, focused on the water. *Perhaps a photograph will be evidence enough that this color truly exists?* The shades the Aegean blue offered up, depending upon light, time and place were always unique, but this blue was astonishing, a clear blue with hues of greens and purples. When she had taken several photos of varying exposures and settings, she looked up at Harry with a smile. He had watched her collect the colors, the way one might collect sunsets or vistas, or an archaeologist might collect bones and he nodded now, acknowledging yet another great find.

They walked on as best they could, overcome with fits of laughter, Eleni and Lily holding tight to Harry's hands to stay afoot — it was as though they were walking on a loose footing of golf balls, or marbles of all sizes from peewees to shooters, the round rocks in constant movement beneath their shifting weight. At first it was almost impossible to navigate the earth at all as it rolled beneath their feet, but they soon adopted a curious shuffle, a bit like skating, that allowed them to move without landing unceremoniously on their bottoms.

Tall white cliffs that flanked the far end of the beach were the source of the mysterious rock, the grasping hands of the wild winter sea taking more to its own, year after year. Now, in gentle, rhythmic breaths, wavelets caressed the shore, the rocking and rolling composing a rather hollow, chattering symphony of shifting stone that echoed off the hard cliff face.

Lily fished goggles from her bag and while she and Harry used them to search for the perfect rock within the 'lucent blue', Eleni carefully crossed the shore, her eyes locked on the ground beneath her feet. These rocks had been tossed through the ages on the winters' waves, the fierce storms here in the north tumbling them over and over and over, to this smooth, luminous roundness. She picked one up and rolled it in her hands. *How old are they? Now, these ... these are the things of Myth! They can't possibly belong to this world.* She gathered just a small handful more, inspected them closely and then held them out to the sun in her palms, giving thanks to the Earth and Sea for each of the perfectly beautiful gifts before placing them in her camera bag.

As she walked, or staggered, or skated her way back down the undulating beach, looking up to catch her bearings she could see that Margarita had finally discovered them here and was sitting with her back to the shore. Silvery, from the angle the sun cast as it gained on the horizon, and shimmering with the caress of a breeze, the sea seemed to envelope Harry and Lily. Nearly indistinguishable, they were ethereal beings, sprites made of half water, half light, almost transparent. Eleni squinted, raised her hand to shade her eyes. Lily stood perched atop Harry's shoulders and with arms out for balance she stepped into his hands ... with the aid of her graceful crouch and spring, Harry was throwing Lily up, up, as high as he could into the air, and she fell back into the water with ecstatic shrieks.

"HAI-AI-AI-RY!" Her rolling laughter echoed, bouncing from water to sand.

Margarita made soft, strained sounds and slowly swept her tail to and fro. *That is a dog's pure delight.* Smiling, Eleni crouched to captured the moment with a click of the shutter — Margarita in silhouette, Harry with arms to the sky, Lily mid air, the diamonds sparkling in the forever sea. *Here is happiness ... HERE is God!*

As the sun started to weaken and fall towards the evening they all hiked back to the sand beach where Vassili awaited them aboard the radiant Hestia, her red hull ablaze in the deep blue and the softening sunlight. It had been a day they would not long forget, the day the veils had parted, affording a glimpse into Greece's very essential being, into her quiet, of Athena's olive trees, the herbed hillsides and the blue, lucent blue waters, the sun and stillness ... and the faith ... here, a lonely beacon at the top of a hill, but always within reach if one made the effort. Saturated with sun and quiet, they packed up their belongings and their trash and walked the shaky plank back to Vassili, and gliding through the sunset and the balmy whisper of a breeze, they would reach harbor just in time for dinner.

as only a dog knows

Margarita had resolved that the place for her night's slumber was no longer out in the leaves or junk piles, nor under abandoned cars. It was at the foot of Lily's bed. She slept there through the night with no fear or want, cradled in caring until the morning light came creeping through the window.

The little dog always awakened early. After yawning and stretching and scratching a bit, she ever so softly crept the length of the bed to look into the face of her sleeping girl, as though checking to see that she was still there. Satisfied, she would ask to be let out into the morn, pushing open the door to the bigger room and standing on her hind legs next to the bed, she reached up to paw at the gentle woman's arm. Eleni always greeted her kindly and, with the effort of one still half in the world of dreams, sleepily escorted her down the stairs to the front door and out into the new day.

There, Margarita would shake off the night and sit in the sliver of sunshine that warmed the stoop by the gate, scratch lazily, behind an ear, under an armpit with nose to the sky drinking up the fresh scents of the morning that took the long trail up from the water, past the fishermen's baskets filled with last night's catch, past the hunger and uncertainty of the unwanted lurking in the shadow, past a bakery and its delights, fresh from the ovens and the tavernas' daily stock brought to bubbling on the stoves. And after reading the morning's notes in the stew delivered by the breeze, she would shake and stretch one more time with a groan of pleasure and set off to follow her day.

When evening beckoned and her people sat for their dinner in the town, Margarita could always find them. Blessed with a mysterious radar that defied conventional intelligence, no matter where the meal was taken, whether on the beach over the hill and far from town or along the quay, the little dog was like clockwork. Harry had taken to pointing at the spot on his wrist, blessedly absent that device so telling of a life limited by time, claiming "it's Margarita time" and within moments, there she would be, prancing up to their table, speaking in that peculiar tongue, the smothered giggle that always hinted her pleasure and after greeting everyone she would settle, snuggled safely under Lily's chair. Occasionally Eleni or Lily held her in their lap and she hid her head beneath an elbow there, ignoring the disapproving looks and shaking heads of the waiters.

At evening's end, she followed the girl and her family back up to the pensione on the hill and digging and digging, turning and fluffing up the soft blankets until the perfect nest had been forged and the perfect position had been found, she would settle into her place on Lily's bed.

Eyes half open, she watched the child as she read her book and once Eleni had come in for a goodnight kiss and the light was turned, dog and girl drifted off together into a soundless sleep.

Margarita was drawn more and more to staying close to her people, and though she did not depend on them for food, she happily accepted when they offered a meal. There was no such thing as too much, for a town dog. Of course she still visited with Her, sniffing her way to the old woman's side wherever she might be to seek the comfort of their well-tended friendship. And she checked in often with her own tribe of lost spirits, the countless homeless dogs of the harbor, tavernas and beaches. But more often now, Margarita stayed in the company of her people, her new family, where she could watch over them and keep them safe.

She was even drawn to Vassili and now that a trust had been cultivated she would sometimes visit with him in the early mornings, jumping aboard Hestia for a pat and a bit of his conversation. The fisherman was kind to her. It was a poignant kinship, perhaps simply one of two sad creatures finding solace in the new friends they shared — whatever it was, the unlikely alliance made for safer passage through the harbor for Margarita, for it seemed that even Vassili's comrades had taken a liking to her. It was unusual for a town dog to find much of a welcome there along the waterfront, but once Vassili began to look out for her the other boatmen stopped throwing their net corks and harsh words to chase her on her way, the kindness spreading like a strange virus. Some even tried to tempt her with soft clucking sounds or a morsel of food, when they could be sure that none of the other men were looking, of course, but for now, she would have none of that.

"Ah Margarita, my little one," Vassili sighed, "are you still keeping the wind at your back?" The sympathetic man would give her a sardine or a slice of feta from his plate as he took a gulp from his small cup of strong, sweet coffee. Margarita sat at his feet, looking up at him all the while, intent, as if trying very hard to understand his sadness.

One day, as summer was drawing closer to its end, Margarita could not find Her. She spent the whole of that morning and more searching for the old woman who simply wasn't to be found; not at her kitchen door, on her balcony overlooking the sea, nor sitting upon the bench under the plane tree with her old cronies in the platia. Margarita could not feel Her anywhere her missing made the little dog very uneasy. Trotting from one end of the village to the far reaches of the other, she stopped at every kiosk, every market, at each pathway and crossroad seeking some fresh trace of Her scent, but found nothing. She raced up to the Acropolis, the top of the hill where the gypsy folk sold their fruits and rugs and the children chased her with sticks, where the old woman liked to sit in the shade and chat, but did not find Her there. Sitting at the highest point of the cliff, where the news of the village would sweep up from the sea on the airstream, Margarita faced the breeze and drank it in. But it was cold, without even a hint of Her familiar warmth. And with that, the empty cold, the worried little dog abandoned the search for her old friend and set off for the harbor.

Settling there under a cooler by a small, colorful kiosk where an old man whiled away his hours selling cold drinks and cigarettes, Margarita scratched and preened a bit, able to relax unseen with a clear view of the comings and goings of the harbor road. She knew the ebb and flow of life on the island, she sensed the rhythms, and sensed now that the island bus would soon deliver comfort, her people, to her. With that knowing only dogs possess, she could feel them coming, coming closer and she curled up to wait.

From the safety of that little place Margarita heard a yelp and a screech and glanced up to see a small, thin dog racing off down the quay. It was a town dog, probably kicked away by a taverna keep who didn't want the hungry mutt interfering with his business. Favoring one paw, she ran with her tail wrapped tightly between her legs, carrying herself low to the ground, a tactic known well by the unwanted of the island, an effort to be less of a target for someone's anger. Margarita moaned, and curled into a tight ball, her head under one paw as though hiding away from her own haunted memories. But when the bus arrived, depositing her people on the side of the quay as she knew it would, she wriggled from under the cooler, shook herself off with a happy snort and buoyed by love and courage, stood bravely in the open.

"Yia sou, Margarita!" Lily called, and ran to her little friend. They danced happily, Margarita up on her hind legs, white tipped front paws hardly reaching even past the girl's knees. Eleni kneeled to greet the dog, who responded with strange sighs and moans and warm, soft licks to her face. "Does she talk to you too, Lily?" Eleni asked, looking up at her child whose red hair, driven wild around her head by the beach wind, gave her the appearance of a slightly demented angel. "She does this most interesting thing, making her strange little sounds all the while she is looking deep into my eyes. No ... deep into my soul. I could swear she is talking to me."

Lily laughed and tickled Margarita behind her shoulder, causing the little dog to flail wildly in ecstasy with a hind leg. "She's singing! She loves you now, too, Mama. And she sings to us because she loves us."

Lily danced away with the dog, Eleni and Harry hanging back to stroll the new harbor where the yachts were moored, arms about each other's waist, stopping here and there to comment on the lines and colors of the beautiful boats tied there, each with someone aboard, tinkering, drinking wine, all enjoying the serenity of a calm island afternoon. They were watching a man swab the teak deck of a magnificent yawl when Lily and Margarita raced back to their sides, and as Eleni reached out for her laughing child she noticed the strange and somber procession moving slowly towards them down the narrow main street.

All of the people who had been sitting at the tavernas lining the way were now on their feet.

"A funeral, Harry." She tugged on his shirt.

As the cortege turned onto the paralia in front of them, they stepped back several feet to let it pass. "Someone has died ... this is the way of the island." Eleni whispered to Lily, standing silently now in front of her father. Just a bit unsure, the girl pulled his arms around her, a sheltering embrace, but any uncertainty was given to her curiosity as soon as the procession was upon them.

It was sorrowfully beautiful.

Walking in front of an old, battered truck singing a somber chant was the village Priest. Dressed in long, black finery, gray beard flowing down his front, he carried a large gold cross held close to his chest. The truck, flanked on both sides by several old men dressed in black, carried in its bed an open coffin that held the spent body of a woman, swathed in white cloth — her face, one that had seen many, many years, now in peaceful repose. And behind the truck walked a young man, holding the top of

111

her pine box casket in his arms, followed closely by a trail of women clothed in mourning, and a few young girls carrying flowers and candles.

Then, the most extraordinary thing happened as the procession made way past the tavernas along the waterfront.

Each one turned off its loud music.

The harbor was held in an absolute quiet, blessedly absent the usual discordance. All of the waiters and other folk in the harbor had moved out from the shadows to the edge of the narrow road and they stood there, somberly lining the promenade, a reverent tableau as the procession passed them by.

Margarita suddenly dashed across the road. Lily called out to her, but the dog raced on, intent upon following the sad cortege.

They continued to watch the funeral procession, straining to follow until it disappeared around a bend and up the hill to the town church. In just moments the bells of the church rang out over the silent village, as though reporting the sending of a spirit home.

The extraordinary then melted away — the ordinary returning with the loud and crazy melding of Sinatra, trance, Greek folk and rock and roll music, all clattering into one another and pouring from the tavernas as the workers fell back to their routines.

ebb and flow

Eleni and Lily walked through the dimming light of a sunset the same coppery wash as their hair. Their young friend Popi walked with them, laughing as she described the island's alter ego, the sleepy winter island — so serene, wood fire smoke instead of tourists snaking the alleyways, and snow sitting atop the boats by the pier, the harbor heavy with stillness.

To Lily, Popi quite simply was a Goddess. A short, animated woman who walked like a cat, she was sinewy and stealthy, with skin, clear like a fine honey and deep brown hair that flowed down her back. Not only was she beautiful and mysteriously Greek, she also was a painter. Her works were colorful, almost three dimensional renderings of the island, painted as though it were being viewed through a piece of glass — faithful studies, but distorted just a bit, in a way that made them even more interesting than the real thing. Lily wanted desperately to learn to paint like Popi and nearly fell in a faint whenever asked by the young artist to join her as she painted 'en plein air' at the harbor, or up by the church.

Theodorou, or Theo, was Popi's boyfriend, round and bespectacled with long, soft hands that obviously had never touched a fishing pole or a winch, or clutched greasy tools over a hot engine. Theo was a musician, a jazz clarinetist with roots deep in reybetyko, and as he walked now with Harry he was negotiating for another time they could collaborate, some late night, over a bottle or two of tsipouro — Harry and his six stringed beloved, Theo and his klarino, a reed instrument that produced, when handled knowingly, a snaking, melancholic sound.

One weekend, when the warm, playful winds first heralded the slide into the summer season, Lily was off on an adventure, entrusting her parents to the joys of doing things they might not ordinarily do. While she ran wild with Haris at her grandmother's small goat-filled farm in the countryside, Eleni left Harry to his Muse and journeyed to the mainland with Popi, to consult the Oracle at Delphi — spending a full day in photographers' heaven, surrounded by antiquity at Athena's feet while Popi painted the exquisite ruins — returning to the island on the ferry the next evening just in time to watch the promenade parade over a glass of wine.

She had washed the travels out of her long hair and stood on the pensione balcony, idly braiding an herb scented plait as she waited for Harry to show. Looking out over the sea, even more mysterious now that her head was saturated with myth and philosophy and images of iconic beauty, she heard it ... a perfect harmony, even through the discordant notes ... passionately wrong but somehow moving together, effortlessly, like familiar

114

dancers anticipating their partner's every step. She didn't recognize the song, it could have been Greek, it could have been in English. There really was no telling. She summoned her attentions from the sea, silvery under the moon, to focus on the dark of the alley below, trying to pick an image from the notes coming closer to her in it's shadows. Laughter, shuffling footsteps, notes more like a honking now and hoarse laughter coming again between the verses, and closer now she could hear it more clearly, a rousing chorus splotched with slur. She chuckled to herself. *Whoever this is, they're toasted!*

Then she heard the thick wooden front door of the pensione squeak and stutter open — and slam shut. She cracked her own door open to the song, words bumping into one another now, echoing off the solid walls and up the stairwell, voices warbling like those of two old ladies whose vibratos had grown larger and heavier than their ability to carry a pure note. *Wait! Who in the world?*

They emerged from the darkness at the top of the stairs, drunk as could be, Theo grasping his clarinet, Harry's beloved dangling precariously in her case from his one free hand. They each had an arm around one another's shoulders as they sang, tripping and staggering down the hall. *My God, it was Harry!* Eleni grabbed him by his shirt, hauling he and Theo inside where the two considerably inebriated young men collapsed in laughter, the notes all piling one on top of one another like a highway mashup. And after Eleni sent them each to a cold shower and had tucked Theo into the extra bed, she wrapped herself around Harry, listening to his teary babble about Apollo, the God of music, how he touched them and willed their notes and they had to honor his presence with many, many toasts, how "byoootiful ... so byoootiful." it all had been, until it all was exchanged for

115

snores, and she laughed and laughed until she laughed tears.

Theo and Harry both learned well that first delightfully drunken night, that initial expedition into their virgin alliance guided only by the grace of Apollo, to pay a bit more attention to the music and less to the tsipouro. Not only would they not awaken the following day to a raging hangover, they both knew that their collaboration might best be explored with at least some semblance of clarity — how unfortunate it would be to miss any of those doors that might appear to them, those portals to musical territories and magical fusions yet undiscovered!

With that maiden voyage a partnership was conceived and it continued to flourish here and there, with an hour or three over a bottle of spirits that always provided them opportunity for some inter-musical communication, cross cultural pollination as the foreign notes and keys and times sought ways to dance together in the ethers. To both Harry and Theo it seemed that their inspirations born of the same Muse likened them to belonging to the same Mother ... the music, their shared blood.

But the plan this night was for a simple gathering of friends over dinner at a small taverna set at the edge of a long, flat beach, just a bit of a walk from the village, a walk along cliffs that overlooked the darkening Aegean, restless now and somewhat foreboding. Vassili had warned of the approach of another storm and it was seen now in the churning waters, more like molten lead than the soft and seamless sea they knew so well.

Walking over the hill and past the island's acropolis they came to a narrow crossroad and there, where the road began its descent to the quiet beach below, stood the hallowed place the islanders laid their dead to rest — a small cemetery with a wide view over the Aegean. A most fitting location, as it was true that many of the people buried here were fishermen or their kin, the people of that very sea.

A glimpse of each of their stories was revealed in the framed portraits that marked every marble tomb. Adorned with urns filled with geraniums and censors spilling with the smoke of frankincense, the cemetery was colorful and beautiful, a sacred space with paths kept carefully swept, and stone benches where one might sit under a plane tree to contemplate death, or life, faced the sea that took many of these folk to her own.

Popi and Theo pointed out local dignitaries and other dearly departed as they all strolled the main path of the hallowed grounds, mindful of the care that kept the memory of these lives awakened for the grieving kin. It felt like a place of spirit, where life meets death, and earth meets sea. They spoke in a hush. After lingering over several of the tombs, each with its own beautiful sorrow, their hunger insisted, pulling them onward, out through the cemetery's tall gates and down the steep road towards the beach.

The narrow road was covered over by broad-leaved trees and through shade, spattered with the last of the day's sunlight, they passed the ghosts of the dusk. A few dogs skirted the shadows and the countless cats slunk about — one couldn't easily tell where one cat ended and another began. Escheresque, they seemed a writhing mass in the dimming light. They congregated at the bottom of the hill by an old boat works, where skeletons of caiques that plied these waters in years past were heaped about, like rare books, each with it's own story to tell. This is where the waste bins stood, brimming, in wait for the garbage collectors and cats were everywhere — tomcats on the prowl pursuing kittens in their first heat, cats in the garbage cans, on the ground outside of the cans, cats chasing rats, all hungry, thin and wary, ill looking creatures. Garbage was strewn about and the stench was overpowering.

Takis had recently educated Harry and Eleni about the poisonings, his country's age-old defense against the overpopulation problems. "So that the visitors never know of this dirty little secret, the atrocities are carried out at the beginning, and at the end of the summer season. In the dark of night. Places the animals gather to eat, the poison bait is left for them." He was bitter. The poisonings appalled him, embarrassed him, and he felt it cowardly of the local government to turn a blind eye and allow these executions rather than trying to implement a more modern thought. "They know it is wrong ... they must be ashamed. They should be ashamed!" he'd said. Often warned by one who knew the schedule of the deliberate killings, Takis and his wife placed notices in all of the neighborhoods, so that those with beloved pets of their own would know to keep them inside and away from harm.

Eleni stopped to watch the animals, covering her nose against the offensive stink of rotting rubbish.

The epiphany, making way from the stinking shadows, took its time to strike. But then, "Oh! Oh, no." She groaned, sinking to the ground. Just a part of the tragedy that spoke to the plight of the island's unwanted, this one scene told the whole tale — the fate of these unfortunate souls was undeniable. This is where the homeless, hungry, unwanted animals dined, this is where they eked out their survival, and it also was where many of them died.

Next to this beautiful old boatyard, with its untold stories ... they put the killing fields! Shit, it's like the gorgeous Goddess sites the world over ... someone has to put a church right next to them ... a place they box in their God, where someone has been burned, where Brigid is traded for Mary, where someone has been hung, drawn and quartered ... Of course, Takis had mentioned that the garbage bins had proven to be the ideal locations to leave the poison when the 'times' came.

Eleni stood abruptly, arms spread, the scene in front of them illuminated now by her concern, "Garbage, everywhere! Why don't they clean this up? Don't they hate this reeking mess? Of course the animals are going to get into it and spread it around, it smells like food to them! They're looking for a scrap, anything ... unless someone FEEDS them, they won't ever ignore the garbage! They'll never stop haunting the tavernas, the villas, the beaches - anywhere there might be some way to eat to stay alive. They're starving, for God's sake."

Harry and the others stood silently on the path watching Eleni pace and gesture like a madwoman, her long red hair like flame bursting from her head.

"What a torturous, vicious cycle! Leave the garbage out, it goes uncollected ... why, I have no idea. Lazy-ass people. It always seems to just sit forever, festering, stinking. Doesn't it?" She kicked at several cans being picked clean by busy meat bees. Cats scattered. "Or do they do this on purpose, to sabotage the animals? A self fulfilling prophecy, maybe? Yeah, leave the reeking crap lying around and then, of course there will be good reason to get perturbed ... exactly what they hate so much, the filthy, starving, sick, scary, hollow eyed cats. And dogs! Instead of being compassionate and sensible, people whine and demand ... the city sends in its henchmen, and the animals are massacred! Creeps. Fucking creeps."

119

Apathy, the bane of our existence. She turned to face the light, dimming now over the sea. "Some will survive ... but they'll breed, right? The whole cycle will just start all over again, on and on and on it goes! Don't humans even think, isn't our brain there for an actual reason?"

She went quiet and sat down again, frustrations and sorrows stewing up a cynical ire, well seasoned by human ignorance so obvious before her now in the form of starving cats. *Why won't people do something about this problem? Something other than killing, killing, killing? Why won't anyone speak out against such brutality? Good lord, this garbage stinks!* She knew that these sorry creatures might be being poisoned right then and there as they, and others, blithely passed by. For a moment her thoughts turned to the street kittens she and Lily fed.

In just days of regular meals they all had gone from wary, ghostly sylphs with weeping eyes to chirpy, bold and glossy little things. All it took was a bit of caring. Sweet cats, all of them and if sterilized and looked after they would be loving pets, most likely great mousers, easily picking off pests that regularly ransacked a family's storeroom of grains and goods. Already though, one female was coming into her first heat and being attacked daily by the neighborhood Lotharios, all fine cats themselves, simply following their natural urges. She would inevitably go on to bear a litter of kittens which, if not found and disposed of out of habit, would also live lives of desperation and hunger with the added promise of producing doomed litters of their own. There was no happy ending here.

Eleni had tried to find a way to have Margarita spayed, but faced the same inertia other animal lovers had found. For some reason it simply wasn't possible to have this done on the island. When asking around about how they might find out about having the dog sterilized, they were most often met with a wry "po po' po po", oh my gosh, you have got to be kidding!

Po po po right back to you all.

Popi came to Eleni's side and they sat, quietly watching the misery play out in front of them.

"Eleni mou. Ti na kanoume? What can we do? Theo and I have many cats of our own to feed, we do the best we can. What <u>more</u> can we do?"

Eleni looked up at Popi, who for the first time caught a glimpse of hopelessness on her friend's face. "I think we all must act somehow ... showing, telling, teaching."

"Pos? How? You tell me, how?"

"I don't know, Popi ... lobby your government, or strike, whatever the hell you all do here to get some action, let people know that this is wrong! It's just wrong and this is an embarrassment for your country and there are alternatives that MUST be made available! What was it that your Pythagoras said? "As long as man continues to be the ruthless destroyer of living beings, he will never know health and peace" ... I may be paraphrasing here ... " as long as men massacre animals, they will kill each other. He who sows seeds of murder and pain cannot reap joy and love." God, wasn't he a brilliant man? And he was Greek! Way back then, a vegetarian, he would not eat animals and was a great advocate for them! So, what happened?"

Popi shrugged, lifting an eyebrow. "It seems a goodness has failed us, Eleni."

"Ok ... listen to me, Popi." Her hands were open, cupped in front of her, as though holding the information she was about to disclose, and she went on, speaking directly from her own experience working with various animal shelters and rescue organizations at home. "One pair of breeding cats can be the source of at least two litters of kittens in one year, right? That translates to exponentially growing numbers of offspring that, in just four years, can add up to around twelve thousand cats! You do the math! TWELVE THOUSAND cats! So if those original two parents lived nine years, though I think that would be pretty unlikely here, the numbers of offspring through the generations could soar to around eleven million! All because of just two un-sterilized cats! It's mind boggling. And that doesn't even take into account that one tomcat can impregnate several females in heat per day! One tomcat can make up half of many, many pairs of breeding cats! And then, there are the dogs, Popi. One fertile dog like little Margarita can produce one, sometimes two litters of puppies a year. And then, if left to nature, her descendents, and their descendants, will number in the sixty-seven thousands in just six years. It's just astounding. These are real statistics, the numbers researched and made public by humane organizations back at home."

"No — you are kidding me! Oh my gosh, Eleni. Well, no wonder then the people think the animals are like rats. So, you tell me, what can we do about this, because, really, we have no choices here! If we do not believe in the murders we can only turn away. We keep our pet, our girl cat, inside our house when she comes into her breeding-time. No babies for her. One day, we will be able to afford to take her, and all of our wild cats, by boat, over to the city and get the operations. Until then, we must tolerate."

Eleni shrugged and turned back to her hands. She held them out flat now, waiting now for a brilliant solution to fall into them.

"You have to go to the mainland for that?"

"Yes. And even then we have to arrange it months ahead."

"Well, I said it, Popi. What you can do is show, tell and teach. Stop tolerating! Just stop it! I think that someone here needs to start loudly demanding that sterilization become an option. I'm sure that veterinarians come here from other countries. Don't any come here on holiday? Plumbers come, musicians come, why not vets?"

"I have no idea. How would I know this?"

"There must be some. And I would think that if they knew this nasty secret, they would help, however they could." She stopped and sifted through her thoughts.

"I wonder if anyone has ever thought of opening a shelter for the dogs and cats? Popi ... you're a native, maybe you could start working just to get the idea to ignite and then it would only spread, like a fire! There is so much educating to be done. Yes, you can start there, at least with the education. That is what you can do!"

"Oh, no, no, no Eleni! Po po, I am an artist, not a teacher, and not an animal activist! Oh no!"

"Look, Popi, this could be really simple. Your neighbors must ask you about your cats? Don't they?"

"Well. If you mean yelling at me because they think we are crazy to take care of them, well then, yes. "Oh, you will get disease!" they say! "Oh, when it looks you in the eye, it is stealing your spirit!" my old Auntie says!"

"You can start there, in your own garden ... show the people that they are not demons, tell them you are going to get them sterilized someday, and then you can tell them more! Tell them why! Besides statistics, besides all of those numbers and all of that math, you can mention the other facts, like they'll be less likely to wander, so

123

females no longer go looking for the boys, no more loud yowling and fighting at midnight! People would like that. And to those who already have pets, one could say that the risks of reproductive cancer and infections, big problems in un-sterilized pets, are essentially eliminated. Their pets will be much more likely to just lie around on someone's lap, or in front of the winter wood fire than roam the streets ... without their crazy sex hormones, they'll turn into sweet little couch potatoes! And, they can live twice as long as one that is unaltered. That means more rats and mice eaten in one lifetime, right?"

Popi smiled.

"You are very annoying, Eleni ... in a lovely, provocative way. I do want to help. I want to know more. First though, we need simple animal care here, even before all of the fixings and neuterment and sterilizing, is that how you say it? You see, even treatment of simple medical problems is very, very hard for us to find. We have to go to the mainland, by boat, to a clinic there for medications or supplies we can't find here at our chemist's shop. Oh, we used to have a wonderful woman on the island, your friend Vassili's wife, Maria ... she took care of all of the animals; the farm workers, the pets and the wild ones. Even she couldn't perform miracles and stop the births, but at least the animals could be treated."

There was silence. Eleni just stared at Popi.

"Maria? A wife, and she took care of the animals? That mysterious man! He's only just briefly mentioned a daughter to us ... Vassili's wife?"

"You didn't know? Oh. Yes, he *had* a wife. I will tell you another time, but now, you must finish my basic education ... I can almost hear those stomachs growling and grumbling from here, and I do not think that they will wait for us much longer!" She motioned to Harry, Lily

124

and Theo who were crouched now, doing their best to coax two small tortoiseshell kittens out of the shadows.

"You don't need more education, Popi. You have a caring heart, that is half the battle. And you know your people here, you are not foreigners with foreign ideas so you can really talk to them. I think the big obstacle, after the need for a doctor for the animals, is a change of viewpoint, which will not come easily. But, it will come. Vassili said that it will come."

The women stood and brushed off the pine needles and bits of earth. Eleni stretched, working to breathe through the thick stench of the garbage to exhale her angst, calming herself with visions of the meal that awaited them on the beach.

Of course Vassili had a wife. There's a child! But why hasn't he told us? She found no place for Popi's revelation to easily settle.

Unsuccessful in their attempts with the little kittens, Lily, Harry and Theo were walking towards the boatyard and swept Eleni and Popi up along their way.

Matoula served only the freshest of fish at her charming seaside taverna, fittingly called 'Psaria Fresca' - Fresh Fish. A carefully hand wrought wooden sign claiming the fact, ΡΣΑΡΙΑ ΦΡΕΣΚΑ, in bold blues and oranges swayed overhead under a single soft light that flickered on as the evening began to build. Her tables, each softly lit by dancing candlelight, sat seaside on the sand and she loved to enchant her customers even further by playing the music of Vangelis, the eerie, softly atonal notes caressing the spaces in between the quiet and drifting out over the water.

Dramatic and busy and, with bracelets a-jangle and her mass of wild bleached hair bouncing, caught up atop her head like an excited halo, Matoula ran out to greet her friends. She enchanted Lily, who quietly watched the dazzling older woman arrange their table and fill waters and wines and take their orders, speaking with Popi and Theo in Greek all the while. It sounded to her as though they were singing beautiful chords, triads of notes, melodious, their voices fluttering and dancing like brightly colored ribbons in a gentle wind. She closed her eyes, focusing only on the calming interlude.

Eleni did well. For a while.

She maintained a calm, even forgetting about the cats as she enjoyed the warmth flowing through the conversation and around their delicious meal, candles flickering in the building breeze and the darkening sea lapping at their toes. But just as Matoula rushed a plate of warm dessert out to the table, Lily pointed out a very pregnant dog they'd seen earlier in the town, the hungry bitch darting now through the shadows to circle their table. Everyone stared as Lily murmured softly, tossing the thin little thing the remnants of her own meal, and after devouring the precious bits, her wary eyes never leaving the people, the dog tucked her tail and ran off along the water.

That was it. The tears came. Eleni held her head in her hands.

"Oh ... Shit!" Weeping, she turned back to the hole in the darkness into which the frightened dog had disappeared. "I can't handle this any more! It just won't ever end, will it? Where in the world is that poor, scared little thing going? Where is she going to have her pups? In a bush, maybe under a heap of garbage?"

The table had gone quiet. Even Vangelis' atmospheric soundscape seemed to linger on one long, held note that floated out over the water before Eleni turned back to the group.

"Will she have any protection from this storm? Or from feet kicking at her, or the bottles that the kids throw at her? That little dog should be curled up in a box, in someone's cozy kitchen." She felt feverish, wiped her brow with her fingers. *God, I just feel too much, I think.* The well of tears dried up quickly; it was only rage that fueled her now.

"How will she ever even eat enough to be able to nurse her babies when she can barely nourish her own sorry, skinny body right now? She's worse off than Margarita was! And the pups, well, what is the point? They'll be tossed out like garbage before their eyes are even open."

"Eleni, come on ... let's finish eating." someone offered.

"And then that sad little bitch just will have to go on from there, on and on and on in the endless cycle all of these animals have to endure. Pregnant, starving, pregnant, starving ... Drowning. Poisoning. And this, this is just a fragment, a little preview of what happens everywhere, in every village, in every country, everywhere in the whole damn world, isn't it? When will human beings ever learn?" She was on her feet, pacing.

"Oh, Eleni, please stop, just stop for a moment. Just shut up! Jump up and down, do somersaults on the beach, something, anything to chase your demons away, just for a while. We're trying to enjoy a meal here, aren't we? So let's do. Jesus! Save the freaking world later. It, and all of the animals' troubles, will not go away any time soon. Not in the next hour. At every turn there will always be another pathetic creature that you will want to help, and you will, but can't you just chill out, at least now while we are trying to eat?"

Lily's eyes were big and round. Quite used to her mother's full-bodied feelings about the animals' troubles, she was not at all used to her father's annoyance betraying his honest calm.

And it was not difficult for Eleni to tell that Harry had simply had enough.

But it was the animal's suffering that was enough for her. She paused, and leaning on the table, stared frostily at her husband.

The candles were picking up the coming storm, dancing wildly inside their protective glass. Eleni gave Lily a reassuring kiss on the check and, turning to Harry, Popi and Theo, said only that she needed to walk, and disappeared down the beach.

Lily was staring down the beach, into the dark that had swallowed both the dog and her mother.

"Not to worry, she won't go far, Lil. She just needs time to feel all of this out."

"I'm not worried, Hair-ry. I know what she feels." was all Lily said, in chilly reply.

The sudden quiet was a bit grim, and growing heavier by the moment. But Theo laughed and the stillness was shaken. "She's so good, she has a good heart." he said to Harry. "I think it all is maybe just too much sadness for her sometimes. The Greek inside of her, it shows! So much passion!"

Harry smiled, shaking his head. "Yeah. I just wish that she didn't feel ALL of the animals' pain, at once, Theo. It tortures her sometimes. And us!"

Theo called to Matoula for the check.

"Ohi, ohi, ohi!" Singing her protest with arms waving and bracelets jingling, she bustled her way back to their table. "No, no. Don't insult me, Theo! You, you all, you are like family to me, so please ... let this be my happiness. You can pay me the next time, endax?"

"Efharisdoume, Kiria ... We all thank you for your hospitality, you are too good to us. Na'ste kala ... and the food, oh, so delicious!" Theo turned to Lily and clinked her glass. "Right, Lily? Yamas!"

Matoula ruffled his dark curls and, reaching out for Lily's hand, clasped it to her heart. Theo poured a glass for her and then held out his own glass to the darkening sky.

"One last toast. To all of the sad cats and dogs! And to you, Lily, and your parents, for helping them. May kindness overcome the fear!"

"Good, now go, go." Matoula glanced up the beach and then started whisking plates from the table. "It is already dark, you must go now and find the sad one. You tell her, make friends with her sorrows. Go!"

Calling out thanks to Matoula they set out along the beach, colder and windier now, and back towards the road where Eleni might be found.

They could hear the sound of frantic yapping in the distance.

"Margarita!" Lily said breathlessly, looking up at her father.

As they walked past the hungry, prowling cats they could see the cemetery sitting on its high point at the top of the hill — now, in the dark of the night, swathed in a glimmering light. Lily, pulled by the distress call that tumbled down the hill towards them, ran ahead. The others followed, drawn on more slowly by the ethereal vision in the distance, stopping short at the path that led through the tall cemetery gates.

Lily and Eleni sat together there, on a large rock, facing the light.

"Isn't it lovely?" Popi whispered as she turned to Harry, "Some of the older widows come up here to do this for several nights, usually just after a burial."

Hundreds of oil lamps and candles set in glass jars had been lit and each tomb shimmered with a light of its own. It was as if someone had thought of lighting the way through the night for those journeying souls who may not yet have found their way home. Here, no wandering ghost would need fear the dark.

Lily tried to hush Margarita who was patrolling the gate, harassing anyone trying to pass, as though protecting the burial ground. The dog eventually sidled over to the girl with a quivering lipped smile, one eye still resting suspiciously on strangers. "What is it, girl?" Lily whispered to the dog. After the quick greeting of a wag and a sharp shove of her snout she glanced back just once and with a decisive bark that seemed to invite them all to follow, disappeared into the cemetery.

Traversing paths illuminated softly by the airy light, they finally caught glimpse of her at the far side of the cemetery, sitting quietly on a fresh mound of earth at a marble tomb that faced a daily sunrise over the water. Surrounded by potted flowers, she wagged her tail, fanning dust and petals and pine needles and seemed quite pleased.

Margarita had found Her.

It was spelled out there on the grave, under glass by the vase of fresh flowers. Σεληνη Μαρκπουλου... Selene Markopoulou, read the placard under the portrait of the kind old woman they had seen so many evenings at sunset, on her sea watch with little Margarita sitting at her side. Next to her lay Διμιτριος Μαρκπουλος —

Dimitrios, the man she had been watching for, waiting for, all this time, the reason for her nightly vigil and perhaps all of the sadness that even her thick, black shawl could not disguise.

"What? She's DEAD?" Lily looked at her mother.

"When did this happen, didn't we just see her? Oh..." Harry caught his breath. "The funeral, the harbor... today. Was <u>that</u> why Margarita took off?"

"Oh my..." Eleni sighed and smiled. *Selene. So that's our old Yia Yia's name! Selene ... the Goddess of the moon, always mourning her lost Endymion.* After a stretch of quiet, the only sound, Margarita's tail scattering dust, she said,

"The sun will just have to set without her now, won't it? I think her long wait is finally over."

While Lily and Harry examined the flowers and pictures left in memorial, Eleni turned away. Looking through the wash of soft light she could almost see them in the distance, Selene and Dimitrios, dancing slowly together, finally together, in the flickering shadows.

clouds

The day dawned gray.

Slowly, slowly, it relieved the night of its place in the shadows, unveiling a sea of molten steel, clouds dark and heavy with promise. There was an unsettling sense in the vicious wind whipping in from the north.

Eleni, Harry and Lily, all bundled up for warmth in the few cool-weather clothes they had, were determined to enjoy it outside of the confines of their rooms. They set off down the narrow goat paths that stitched the orchards together, to the beach where the waves were busy pounding in and cleansing the shore, their retreat revealing a fresh deposit of shells.

Sitting on the cool sands, they watched the wild sea's storm dance for as long as they could bear, until the wind bit at their bones and, overtaken by the bitter cold, they laughed off their determination and traced their steps back into the village.

It was like a ghost town, eerily quiet, abandoned by tourists and townsfolk alike in their migration from the cold to a friendlier warmth. But there were signs of life. Vassili was sitting under shelter from the bluster at Kostas' taverna, holding court and drinking tsipouro with his harbor mates.

When the weather turned, or winter was upon the island every restaurant's outdoor seating area was transformed into an oasis, enshrouded in sheets of plastic that kept the elements to their place so taverna life could continue on as usual. With each threat of a real rain a momentary chaos stirred along the harbor as waiters and cooks scrambled about to unfurl these walls of plastic sheeting, like sails on the old caiques, anchoring them to moorings on the ground that kept them from cutting loose in the wind. And as soon as the sun returned to dry off the harbor, the flurry returned and back up the plastic went, into waiting for another rainy day.

Vassili waved his shivering friends into the warmth of the plastic womb and was quick to his feet, offering Lily his sweater. Kostas had set up a heater close to his kitchen, and not unlike a burn barrel or campfire on a chilly day it drew warmth seekers to it like insects to a flame. The place was packed.

Lily settled quickly, arms draped over Vassili's shoulders as she watched he and a small, wrinkly old man ponder the tavli board.

Eleni turned to Harry. "Can we talk, Harry? I really need to finish out those thoughts ... the ones that I assaulted you all with last evening. I'm so sorry. And I'm sorry that I just left. It all was rude of me, but I do have to say that I was just suddenly overwhelmed. And you deserve your say, so, can we sit here and talk?"

"Let's sit". Harry smiled. Turning to ask Mana for three cups of her velvety hot chocolate, he ushered Eleni to a table close to the heater. "You first."

She sat with elbows on the table, hands clasped, looking directly at Harry, her frustrations sweetened a bit now with regret. They sat in an uncomfortable hush that hovered just beneath the clamor of the winds and the heater's toil but the arrival of the chocolate seemed to unravel the disquiet, and Eleni began.

"My annoying habit of wanting everything now ... translating to 'I want to fix it all, now' ... certainly didn't add to the calm of our lovely dinner. I know. I'm so sorry. Really. I just think that the sight of that poor starving, pregnant dog pushed me right over the edge, Harry. She was just one too many. My love for the animals has no bounds, you know that ... but my ability to witness their suffering does."

She dipped into a warming sip of the creamy chocolate, surfacing with a whipped cream moustache that Harry leaned over and kissed from her face. "I know. I know you, my love." Light, filtered through the plastic appeared as though it was being blown in and around them on the wind, adding to the unease that already belonged to the day.

"I can't help but think of all of those damned calendars. I see them on the kiosk racks here. Everywhere! They're even in bookstores at home, too. You know, you've seen them, with beautiful, rich photographs of sweeping panoramas — the deep blue sea, a quaint, white washed wall overlooking the calderon on Santorini, or a view of the steps looking up at the Acropolis in Athens, the Parthenon glorious in the background. Pages and pages ... all featuring a cat! Or several, lounging in the sun, sleek and healthy ... and fat!

134

'The Cats of Greece', you know? Wow, what a great PR ploy by the Tourist Authority! Everyone's a sucker for something like that. If people only knew what many animals' lives are really like here. If they only knew."

Harry closed his eyes and nodded. "Wait ... let's get food." was all he said, turning to call out, "three orders of the small fishes, please, Mana?" The busy boss lady waved in reply to his halting Greek and tousled Lily's red hair as the girl slipped between the kitchen and the checkered clothed tables towards her parents. She had heard the magic words, mikros gavros, more than enough to pull her from Vassili's side. Eleni reached an arm around the girl's waist, gave a squeeze and smiled up at her. "Gavros are coming soon, too, Lil. Sit ... I just need to talk to your Pop for awhile."

"Talk on, Mama."

The wind battered the plastic siding now in building gusts and through the shuddering of the transparent walls and the heater's growling blast, Eleni continued,

"There is so much magic here. There are the Myths, blessed with a connection to all that is living, and there is the history, fertilized with the blood of Alexander's conquests and the many wars; and the knowledge of the great philosophers and the beauty of the ancient arts ... and the music, with roots that run so deep and wide. Amazing." She stopped for a moment, brushed her hand over the tablecloth. "And, it's a history blessed with a people in deep connection with all of the elements. Many of them still know when the rains will come or which direction the winds will blow, what moon to plant by! They just ... know. They get out and socialize, they visit and chat and they argue, but at least they are communicating, caring enough if even to argue! And it seems that most of them honor and care for their old ones and their children ... always the children. Yet Greece, to me, is still a very conflicted country with a lot of people who on one hand seem so in touch with the earth and their faith and each other, so civilized in many ways, yet on the other, have a flagrant disregard for any living thing that is not Human! How can this be?"

She cupped the huge mug of chocolate, thumbs and middle fingertips touching, her hands forming a triangle around it. It was still warm.

"Even though they are people who have sprung from connections to the earth and sea, there is an incredible disregard for this planet here! It just makes my heart so heavy, Harry. It makes me crazy! Look at Athens, the ruins and old buildings that should be treasured, they're being eaten away by what? Acid rot in the air, because nothing is being done about the pollution there! Nothing! Imagine what it does to the water, the trees and grasses, not to mention to the people and their babies. It's a poisoned, choking air. But those city folk just need to keep on driving their terribly polluting cars, no matter what, right? Actually, I don't even know why that surprises me. Isn't that just human nature? We want what we want, no matter what. Just like me, now!" She sipped the chocolate nectar and laughed. "Listen to me! Isn't that true everywhere? It's true at home, for sure. It's just the human condition ... yes, it's human nature."

"Oriste!" Mana set three plates of perfectly prepared fish before them. Eleni and Harry both smiled their thanks at the cheerful woman and after liberally salting her plate, Eleni went on, emphasizing her words with the half-eaten fish she held in her fingers.

"There are no air quality control standards here..."

136

"Wait, wait, where are you going with this, Eleni? We were talking about the animals. Are you taking us off on another long side trip now?"

"No, no, no! The earth, the air, the people, the animals ... they're all connected! You know that, Harry." She squeezed half a lemon over the pile of fish. "How the people treat the earth has everything to do with how they will treat the animals, and ultimately, one another. Isn't this just true? How long can people continue on with honor for one another, or for themselves for that matter, when they don't honor anything else that lives? Do you need lemon, Lily?" Mouth full and happy, Lily nodded and Eleni handed a fresh fistful of lemon quarters across the blue-checkered table.

"It's really just a young country, in the modern sense. Greece really was just freed from oppression in the '70s, but it's now that it must really work hard at doing the right things ... it doesn't have the luxuries of time and ignorance, like our country has had. The world is already extremely screwed up, our planet is already in peril. If they don't step into the problems that face them now, with that passion they are so innately blessed with, they'll soon be following us down the rabbit hole, down the path to becoming a polluted country of warmongering meddlers, with citizens who pit themselves against one another in their own wars of classes and belief systems. It all boils down to whether people care ... or not."

"OK. Now I can see that soapbox ... and you standing on it."

"Harry! Let me be, I need to get this all out! And then maybe I can stop inflicting it upon you and Lily, and our friends with my really bad timing! Like at dinner at sunset on an idyllic beach ..."

She laughed and looked over at Lily, still busy with her plate of fish, and back to Harry.

"Oh, where was I? The earth ... caring? Or not caring! OK, not caring, because every lovely cliff we look over here reveals at least a few old wrecks, a battery or two and always a refrigerator tossed over it to the sea for good measure! I just don't get it. This is 1990, not 1890! What is that going to do to the earth, and eventually, to the groundwater, and the water the people drink? Humans seem to have brains too feeble to think that far ahead."

She looked around the room and nodded towards Vassili.

"I know that it isn't all of the people here who hold this crappy, lazy attitude about the earth, the animals. Of course not. And it's not even only the people here, I know this! But it is something I see here in front of me on a daily basis. I am just so tired of seeing the animals suffer, with only a quiet few doing anything, anything at all, about it! And we can't even shield our daughter from it. She has seen the suffering, she's even been scolded for feeding the starving creatures, people threatening her for stepping in and doing something that THEY should be doing! I don't know, maybe it embarrasses them to see a child doing this? Well ... it should!"

Lily was staring at a fish she had just bitten in half. It's tiny face, frozen in miniature open mouthed and open-eyed surprise, just stared back at her. *It looks like it was yelling something when it was being fried. Ummm ... is this an animal? Aren't we talking about being kind to the animals? I don't know ... fish don't really have cute faces ... they don't nurse their babies? Do they? I mean, don't they just lay their eggs and then go away? But, it was alive. Once. Oh, I don't know.* She pondered this, a likely act of treason, just a moment more before finishing off the debatable half and looked back at her mother, who was just ending her monologue with an apologetic offering.

"I am so sorry … really, I am. I can be so reckless, and selfish, as you both well know. But, I will really, really try to think before I inflict myself upon others again. OK? I just get too full of feelings about all of this. How can I walk through my days here on this island I adore, without exploding in despair, or anger over all of the nasty little shadows almost everyone else seems to overlook?"

Now, Harry spoke out at any length only when he felt that he had something of substance to contribute. Far more at home navigating the depth of his own thoughts, he preferred to let the words of his songs speak in metaphor for him rather than joining in any idle conversation. But here, he needed to speak.

"We can't change the troubles overnight. You know that. And, they won't just go away. But, we can do all that we can to make sure that we see something positive and productive come of it all." He pushed his empty plate away and looked at Eleni. "Tsipouro, yes?"

She nodded and turned to Lily.

"Tea?" The girl agreed and Eleni sang to Mana in the kitchen, "Mana mou, parakalo … tsipouro, ke tsai?" and settled back to focus again on Harry.

"I suggest that you … well, that we just continue acting from our hearts, our conscience." he said. "Make our feelings about the animals obvious. You don't need to tell anyone what they should do, or what they should feel, but you shouldn't be afraid to be seen feeding and caring for the cats and dogs. It may not win you friends, but then again, you might be surprised. People will at least notice, and many will follow your example because good begets good, eventually. I just don't think you need to feel awkward about feeding the animals in front of the locals."

139

Lily fidgeted, her chin bouncing in 3/4 time atop her hands as she tap-danced her elbows upon the table. Adept at entertaining her bursts of youthful energy, here, it was just being wriggled away and yet, while slightly bored, she was still intently focused on the conversation. Eleni looked out through the plastic to the darkening sky and shivered a bit. The wind was still up.

"Talk to the people." Harry took a moment to pour the tsipouro Mana had brought to the table. Placing an ice cube in each glass and pushing the bottle of water towards Eleni, he was sensing her thoughts, like waves coursing through the silence, when she turned to him.

"But what good, really, can come of talking, Harry? I am a foreigner here and my Greek is pathetic. Wouldn't I just further muddy the already mucky waters that surround the animal issues?" She trickled water over the ice in her glass, turning the tsipouro an opaque white.

"Didn't it help you get clearer, just now? Gentle clarity can be very provocative, if not convincing. And even just a few words are better than none at all. Haven't you always said that it's important that we all, on this planet, do what we individually feel we can do, to make some difference? Well? Your passions are for the animals… and so, seeing that good comes to them is what you need to, and do, attend to however you can and no matter where you are. At any given moment, for any given individual, it could just as easily be children, the environment, recycling, hunger, homelessness, war, peace, justice, equality … the list is endless. It contains the whole human dilemma. The more those of us who have knowledge to pass along, DO so, the more we all speak up, the shorter that list could become."

He went on.

"So, yes, talk. Use your bits of Greek, but geez, Eleni, most of the people can speak English better than we do! Talk about why sterilization is the better choice over killing. Hold a cat or dog in your arms, like you do with Margarita at the tavernas. I've seen those guys there, their attitudes about her changing in front of our eyes over the weeks she's been hanging out with us at our table! You are able to show people that there is no need to fear, and that in itself can begin to replace inertia with action, negative with positive. That is how change can come about."

The growling heater and shivering plastic had become an awkward but ambient music by now. Eleni was pensive, floating in the quiet wake left by Harry's words, but when the heater cycled off and left a dazzling silence between gusts of wind, she laughed and leaned in towards Harry.

"Maybe when we are old, I will have finally learned to move my heart along with my feet and hands: feet, one step at a time and hands, one deed at a time ... rather than just jumping, heart first, all feelings, in one huge explosion! Thank you for being so patient with me, Harry."

Wrapping her arms around Lily, who cuddled in even closer for warmth, Eleni looked out once again through the plastic to the weather brewing beyond. *Too much wind*. It always unsettled her. She couldn't shake the sense of the day and was restless and cold. "And you, my darlin' Lily, thank you."

She stood and reached for Harry, bent to give him a gentle kiss and whispered "We're going to leave you to Vassili's mercy now. Watch out for that tsipouro ... I've heard it makes people sing in mysterious ways!" She winked, and scooping Lily under her arm, made way up the hill to the shelter of home.

While closing up their room's heavy wooden shutters against the wind, Eleni and Lily both noted the strange howling. Pushing them open again, they saw Margarita with her snout to the sky, just below their balcony. Lily set off to see if she might understand what the dog was trying to tell them and found her sitting there at cliffside, yipping and howling, barking frantically at any passersby – but this was a different bark, urgent and unsettling. Mournful. Something was wrong. A small white dog, a thin female with distended teats had joined Margarita in her strange vigil, and though wary of the small human who danced about trying to get Margarita's attention, stood off to the side adding a dissonant harmony to Margarita's unsettling song.

Margarita wouldn't be soothed. Nor could Lily figure out what it was that she wanted. Nothing was there, it seemed the dogs were just barking to spirits in the wind and as the cold began to grab at her through her layers, Lily left them for the warmth of the pensione.

"I don't know Mama ... something's wrong. But I don't know what it is." she said as she closed the door behind her. Eleni embraced her, trying to warm her, trying to warm herself. She had been pacing, the wind and the howling, together almost more than she could stand, but when they started again to close up the shutters, the sun suddenly broke the discord, shining brightly through the darkened clouds. It seemed to chase off the wind and the ensuing calm allowed Eleni to inhale, exhale — at the least, breathe the tension away.

Margarita and her wary friend took no notice and kept up their frantic barking and on into the evening they ran, up and down the walk leading along the cliff to the point, Margarita desperate, a pleading sorrow in her cry.

142

but without the darkness ...

    The night's crisp was perhaps the first real hint of the coming autumn.

    Lily, having eaten her fill of fish earlier, had chosen to stay behind, curled in her warm bed with a good book. After a simple dinner in the town, Harry and Eleni were walking back streets home, streets they usually didn't think to explore in the dark of night. On a quest for the sounds of the night's fall, Harry had a small tape recorder with him, one with tiny microphones he could wear on each side of his glasses, able to capture sound in true stereo. So they walked, and after a time, finely tuned into the fact that Harry was recording, each started to 'see' with their own sense of hearing — past the soft murmurs of lovers in the dark of a quiet taverna, and the thumping of the euro-techno in the teeming disco, bodies sweating and seeking, past the sound of water lapping the quay wall and the gentle bobbing and creaking of the caiques put up for the night.

    And they walked.

The strong night scent of jasmine, something so warm about it in the chill night air, almost derailed them, tempting their focus as it enveloped them, enchanting, almost paralyzing. They lingered, and all went quiet.

But then the sound of approaching footfall pulled them back on track, and chimes tickled the darkness, betraying a remnant of the day's wind ... a radio was broadcasting the news in Greek, the foreign tone lyrical, musical ... a couple argued in the night behind closed doors ... And there was music, in the distance, growing closer, taking form.

They stopped below the open window of a small home on the hill. The room glowed gold behind its lace curtain, filled with the light of just one oil lamp and laughing men, whose voices notched up a few decibels more with every swig of ouzo, or brandy. After a potent silence, a held, single note of a zourna, a wind instrument that moans and wails, took off, an eerie melody snaking through the void, bouncing off the walls of stone. Soon the zourna was joined by accordion, then violin and finally one clear, clean and mournful voice, singing the way one might imagine the movements of a languid dance would sound were its steps and gestures simply pure notes — slow and sensuous, passionate, rising to a quick turn, swirling, the baring of a soul.

Arm in arm, Eleni and Harry stood spellbound. But after just a few songs they looked at one another, lowered their heads and backed away, slinking off as though embarrassed to have witnessed something so intimate, so deeply touching, almost sacred, something they may have had no right to linger in the shadows for, and yet they had.

The music evaporated with distance, as though it had never been. And then, a church bell began to toll, a

144

lone incantation echoing off the walls of the emptied town, and cats, courting or fighting, one could never quite be sure, yowled in the dark. The rhythms of the shadows carried them onward.

And as they neared their pensione, there was the unmistakable sound of Margarita, still crying into the night. Harry turned off the recorder.

Haroula's husband, Mitsos, could be seen standing under a street light, clad only in undershirt and shorts and clutching a baseball bat tightly in one hand. Eleni chilled, knowing that the man harbored no fondness for the little brown dog that was now disrupting his night. *Standing there in his undies? In the cold? Drinking maybe? Not good ...* She glanced at Harry, who already sensed Mitsos' threat, and with a quick tilt of her head to signal intention she left him to walk a way around the building that would take her out of Mitsos' line of sight, and closer to Margarita.

Eleni found Lily in the shadows there. She grabbed the girl, held her close, her own heart beating wildly.

"Lily, what in the world!"

"I came down to see why she was still crying. HE was standing out there, under the light. He keeps walking away, walking around and then coming back, talking to himself. He's really creepy, Mama. I think he wants to hurt Margarita."

The two dogs were quieter now, though with her soulful eyes, Margarita still begged them to take notice of something yet unseen.

Mitsos neared, barking and growling in his own hardened, human tongue. Eleni peered around the side of the building and saw him scanning the night, looking for something out there in the dark.

He meant Margarita harm.

She snatched the little dog up and ran with her daughter, around the far side of the pension, away from Mitsos and his bat, through the iron gateway and up the stairs to safety.

In the darkness on the rooftop Margarita finally settled enough to take her place under Lily's chair, lying with her head upon outstretched paws, her worried eyes searching the night. Lily, bundled against the chill, wrote postcards to her friends by candlelight, while Harry and Eleni whispered together of man's inhumanity to man and beast, of a world at war with itself, of the seemingly unending cycles of humans' incomprehensible brutality through time.

"... brutality that often masquerades as God's right! It's a deceptive mask of righteous benevolence that God wears. How often ... throughout history and beyond, Harry ... has God's 'word' destroyed the fabric of people's lives?" Eleni sputtered. She was not friends with that God. Never had been.

They gazed skyward and spoke with sadness of the war as they watched the traces of light from military cargo planes, moving silently through the canopy of a million stars, shuttling supplies, troops, armored vehicles, from Germany to Saudi Arabia and beyond in the buildup to the coming war in the Persian Gulf. The stream of cargo planes cut highways in the heavens, their paths so obvious in the night sky.

As they rambled on though the labyrinth of esoteric deliberation, both began to notice a strange, eerie sound, a new sound, distant and muffled, a cry somewhat like that of a seagull weaving it's way though their words. Then Lily noticed, and Margarita perked her little ears and looked at each of them, cocking her head and softly whining, "I told you."

"A seagull, at night? That's not right." Harry said. Seagulls were not commonly known to be night birds. " Caught in a fishing line or a net, maybe?"

The strange sound came and went on the breeze that lingered with the night. Harry finally decided to go down below to see if he could find what it was.

There was nothing but the quiet and the small white dog, like a ghost, hovering at the edge of the darkness.

The family headed off to bed, a slumber most welcome after the long day spent trying to stay warm. Margarita reluctantly followed along.

As always, she woke Eleni before dawn.

Eleni tried to ignore the little dog after giving her a soothing scratch on the chest. Her night had been fraught with a fitful sleep, the mystery sound winding it's way to her through fleeting dreams.

... Something alive, calling to her from the borders of the land of the dead ...

But each time she started to drift back into sleep Margarita's insistent paw brought her back from the brink. Eventually she arose, let the dog out into the dark of the early morning and after checking on Lily, deeply asleep, snuggled back under the blanket and into the warmth of Harry's skin.

Margarita resumed her raspy barking under the window, but Eleni's need for the comfort of warmth and sleep won over her curiosity and she drifted away.

"Eleni! Eleni!" She heard Harry, far off, as though calling through a long tunnel in her dreams ... and then again in her waking. He was not beside her. As she pulled herself from the depths she heard him again, "Eleni! You have to come down here!" His voice was strained, anguished, and in one seamless movement she leapt up, threw open the shutters and leaned out over the balcony to see where he was.

"Eleni! You have to come here, NOW."

Barefoot and barely dressed she flew down the steps and out the door and into the cold grey of dawn, down the cobbles to where he stood by the sea cliff.

Margarita was at his side, looking up at him as he held out a plastic bag toward Eleni.

"It was puppies." he said. "I had to get up to see what Margarita was still raging on about. She brought me here. She lead me all the way down this cliff." He pointed to the bottom. "Down there, I heard that sound we were hearing last night, from the roof ... she looked up, so I looked up ... hanging from a tree branch there was this bag! It took me a while to get it down. Shit, Eleni, it's a bag of puppies."

Eleni took the bag from him and opened it cautiously — and there inside the plastic tomb were two shivering, newborn pups, still wet from birth and steaming in the chill. "Ohhhh!" She took the cold little things out of the bag and held them to her heart, close to her own warmth and asked him to please go to the room and get a few towels.

Who would do such a thing? What are we going to do with them, what can we possibly do, here, with newborn pups?

Eleni looked over the cliff, presuming that whoever was responsible must have meant to throw these 'unwanted' off the cliff and into the water to their deaths, a common way to do away with the byproducts of the island's un-neutered pets and strays.

The bag must have caught there. Oh, Margarita. What a smart girl.

Eleni felt the wee things stir and warm a bit as she held them closer still. As they thawed, their whining grew louder.

Harry returned with Lily and the girl immediately took a pup from her mother. They both set to rubbing the newborns gently but vigorously with the towels to stimulate and warm and dry them, wondering aloud all the while what they could do with them.

Eleni exploded, her shock rising now to fury. "WHY would anyone DO this? Throw them off the cliff like trash? Living, breathing, newly born beings tossed to the sea to die? Why? For convenience? Why were these puppies even born to begin with?" She kept rubbing, less briskly now, occasionally blowing her warm breath over the tiny body.

"This end wouldn't even have to be a thought in someone's head, if only people would figure out how to get these poor animals sterilized! We are NOT still in the dark ages here." *Oh yes, we are ... yes we are.* She held her breath trying to still herself.

There was only the silence as they continued to work on the pups, though the sounds of the thoughts racing through each of their heads were deafening.

"Margarita!" Lily exclaimed suddenly, lit up with her distinctive certainty. The girl was gifted, as were most children — through innocence and belief in goodness — with a pure optimism.

Margarita heard her name. The knowing little thing looked from Lily to the pups, and then back to Lily with an 'Oh NO you don't!' wariness in her eyes.

"Margarita will take them! She probably still has some milk, don't you think, Mama? She had her own babies ... I'll bet she'll do it, she'll take the puppies!"

Eleni noted that the dog's teats still hung with a bit of heaviness. *Maybe she does still have milk, or at least the ability to make some?* She was quiet for a moment, staring at the shivering pup in her hands as though it might offer up the answers to this hard and desperate situation.

"Maybe the kindest thing really would have been for them to end up in the sea." She sighed and shook her head, but then looked right at Lily. "But you're right, Lil, we should give it a try. There's no way we can bottle-feed them here."

All three looked at Margarita and knew that either she would accept the newborns or she wouldn't, and there wasn't much more that could be done. They didn't think at all of what they might have to do if she were to reject them. Eleni handed her pup to Lily, who walked both babies, warm and dry now and whimpering with hunger, down the stone path to the old nest still there by the old tree, the box still lined with pine and cloth ... and set them deep inside.

"Ok, girl, it's up to you, whatever you decide, it's OK." Lily said, as she caressed the little dog who was very quiet now. But without any hesitation Margarita stepped into the nest, curled around the pups and set to cleaning them. Squeaking their pleasure, they rooted around for nourishment and latched on to life.

The sound heard all night long had been the weak cries of those babies, clinging to life, calling out for life from the bag hanging on the branch.

Eleni could take no more, and with the crisis passed she started to weep, quietly pouring out her sorrow for the animals of the island as the sun rose behind her to greet another beautiful day.

the foundling

Lily practically flew down the curved marble stairs. It was early and she was eager to get to Takis' grocery for the makings of their morning's meal. She could already taste the rich, creamy Greek yogurt and juicy peaches, infused with sunlight, all topped with drizzles of fragrant flower honey.

Skipping the last two steps, she leapt light as air to the door and threw it open to the morning and there, as usual, sitting next to a large flower urn in the strengthening sun, was Margarita. The little brown dog, after nights spent tending to her adopted babies, could be counted on to be there in the mornings now, waiting patiently in Haroula's tidy garden for contact with her human friends.

But she didn't rush to greet Lily and smother her with kisses, or grunt and squeak her usual morning hello. She just sat quietly, smiling with her deep, brown eyes, tail beating a steady and insistent rhythm.

"Yia sou, Margarita ... HEY! What have you got there?" Lily asked the dog, crouching to get a better view.

Sitting beneath Margarita's chest and between her delicate, white tipped paws was a tiny kitten. More like a bit of grey and white fluff with large ears than a kitten, she didn't sound any more like one than she looked. The little thing stared up at the girl with wide, round eyes, and opened her mouth. "ACK", was the sound she made. "AAAACCCCKK"... a very loud sound, not unlike two pieces of metal rubbing together came out of the mouth opened so big and wide Lily could no longer even see the kittens head, just wide rows of sharp, little teeth, and the tips of her mule-like ears. She seemed to take great strength from Margarita's protection, for she held fast and bellowed out her demands.

"Ohhhhh. My. Gosh! Margarita! What a good girl! Come on, hurry, let's get upstairs before Haroula comes." Lily scooped the skinny little kitten up with one hand and ran back inside, Margarita close at her heels.

She gently deposited the scrawny little bag of fur and bones with ears onto her mother's bed. Eleni looked at the kitten sitting there like a baby bird, all hungry mouth, and then up at Lily's hungry grin in weak protest. But protest quickly lost its footing and soon Lily, Eleni and the dog were all curled on the bed around the grumbling cat, a warm and embracing mass of protective, maternal instinct. Chattering on about what to call her, where to keep her and how to best hide her from Haroula and what to feed her, Lily suddenly sat upright, remembering breakfast and her abandoned trip to Takis' store. She left mother to the task of cuddling and tickling the foundling kitten and ran off with Margarita to complete her errand.

152

Takis was a very kind man with small children of his own. He'd taken a fatherly liking to the redhaired American girl; he treasured her visits and always prompted her for snippets of her life at home in rural America, and in return, helped her to learn how to ask, in Greek, for almost anything she was looking for in his shop.

"Yiassoooo, Kirie Taki! Ti kanete? OK. Ummmm ... Kriazome treez ... um, darn ... no, tezzura ... yoortow, kay treez YUMMY rodakina ... um, and, some malia!" she said, fearlessly to him now.

Takis tried to keep a straight face. "Good morning to you, my Lily! And how are you and the lovely Margarita doing on this fine day? Your parents? Lipon, now then, Lily. You want four ... tessera, not tezzura ... yogurts, which is yia oor tee ... yiaortee, Lily, not yoortow! And, wouldn't you rather have some melie, dear one ... not malia? Not hair! Hair! Ha ha ha ha! My little friend, you want honey, not HAIR, no?"

"Oh, geez, Mr. Takis ... "

"And, here they are, three ... treece ... three. Not beautiful, green 'treez', Lily mou! Treece, three, perfectly ripe, juicy peaches. Bravo, good job though! You are very brave! To just speak, mistakes and all, is how you get better at it and you do get better and better! Very soon, you will BE Greek! Now then, how are the island's waifs and strays, Lily? Are you keeping them all well-fed?" They spoke briefly about Margarita's little foundling.

"She will thrive if you give her a name, you know."

A good friend to the animals himself, Takis did his part by keeping a good stock of food available in his shop for those who were kind enough to look after them, and left bowls, filled with kibble and water, in wait for any of the needy who crept by his own stoop. Always, just as Lily was about to leave he would hold his finger to his lips in a "sshhh", look both ways as if to be certain no one was watching and then, with a warm, knowing smile, pass her his complimentary secret — a can of food for the waifs she cared for in the alleys and empty fields.

With her goods dangling in a bag from each hand, Lily thanked Takis and ran all the way from his shop to the room. Still catching her breath, she sputtered on excitedly as she told Eleni "today instead of just one can of food, Mama, Takis gave me another one, one for the kitten!"

Lily had asked him how to say 'kitten'.

"Well ... ghataki is the word for cute little cat." He had not been sure that there even was a word in Greek for kitten.

"But then he said "Minou", Mama, and he thought maybe it was a French word for kitten. I like it. I think it's pretty." She set a few peaches and a jar of honey on the table and handed the yogurt over to her mother who immediately opened one of the small containers and set it on the floor for Margarita. As she finished preparing Lily's breakfast — Harry was already lost to his Muse on the rooftop — she handed a spoon to the girl.

"You know, yogurt would probably be good for her little empty stomach! Probiotics and all. Try a bit, Lil." Lily dabbed a spoonful of the yogurt onto a jar lid and set it in front of the ravenous kitten who dove into it with a squeaky "yumm umm umm yumm", alternately swapping happy purrs for protective growls over what may have been the first food she'd had in days.

"Minou ..." It would do just fine.

Minou finished up her meal, played at bathing herself a bit and then assumed a sternal pose on the edge of the bed, on her belly with paws tucked under her chest. Closing her huge eyes she set to purring herself to sleep,

154

purring so loudly that contentment echoed off of the bare walls and marble floor of the simple room, rumbling like a distant thunder. Lily, Eleni and Margarita all sat fascinated, Margarita peering over the side of the bed with her eyes fixed upon such a small thing making so great a noise. Drunken with comfort the kitten drifted off easily, her purr coming in staccato bursts now and her head bobbing and wavering just above the bed, like a boozer who's about to go down for the count — but when a child's shout echoed from the alley, bouncing through the neighborhood and in through the open doors, her eyes flew wide and she came to with a start. ACK AAACCKKK, the kitten complained, but with the quiet's rapid return she repositioned herself comfortably and, closing her eyes, continued her rumbling lullaby. Her head wavered awkwardly again ... back and forth, up and down, back and forth and soon the teeny Minou was fast asleep. With a muffled thump her head fell heavily onto the blanket, a large dollop of yogurt still on her nose. The purring ceased.

"Who needs television, anyway?" Eleni laughed.

Within days, the kitten had gained a bit of weight and energy and was more mobile, underfoot all of the time. She had taken to exercising her gymnastic skills by swinging from the mosquito netting, ambushing ankles from beneath the bed with a tuck and roll, climbing Eleni's legs like they were trees growing up under her flowing dress, and tumbling down the length of the stairs to beat them to the door. She was so vigorous that they felt sure it was fine to put her outside during the daylight hours. The kitten already knew to run and hide at the sound of an approaching moped or to run from unfamiliar humans and stay hidden, an understanding surely passed to her from her mother before they lost one another.

The town dogs wouldn't bother her. They rarely were seen bothering the cats. it was as if there was an unspoken truce between the species, a strike of sorts against the constellation of humans who secretly hoped that the hungry dogs might naturally eliminate the unwanted felines.

The sight of the elfin cat, exhausted by her Olympian efforts, attempting to suckle on a bewildered but willing Margarita only reinforced the notion of an interspecies truce.

Minou spent her nights inside with Lily, who let her sleep curled in warmth in the crook of an arm or behind bent knees ... there was more room on the little bed now, with Margarita off sleeping with her two waifs.

Initially Minou slept with Eleni, but rather than under a chin or in the crook of an elbow, she nestled in the woman's hair. On those first few mornings of 'life with kitten' Eleni had awakened oddly anchored to her pillow. She labored to sit up in bed, her head held back by the mystifying weight, and just when it seemed she could rise no further her long hair would unfurl and out of the mass of red fell the little cat, onto the pillow with a 'plop', mewling her displeasure at being so unceremoniously tossed from her deep kitten sleep.

The untangling of the kitten's nesting materials was not easy, nor was it a pleasant task — so, much to her delight and with her own hair safely plaited away from the reaches of busy, kneading purr paws, the title of Keeper of the Kitten was passed on to Lily. At bedtime Eleni took to tucking the foundling under the girl's covers, where kitten and girl both dreamed in safe, soft warmth 'til the coming of the morning light.

a fragile hope

The island cats were savvy.

Survival had been born into them and most could do quite well on their own, dining on mice and bugs and scrounging for taverna scraps. If they could stay away from the garbage, and as long as they stayed healthy, they could survive. Many of the softer- hearted tourists would feed them kibble and leftovers through the season — those who didn't know of the country's sad little secret just thought that the cats were all part of the natural ambiance of the islands, but whatever bits of food the cats received, for whatever the reason, it all helped them to carry on through the leaner times in better health.

Dogs were another story, naturally being far more dependent upon people for survival. The fact that they were known in the western world as 'man's best friend' spoke strongly of the connection, but life for a Greek dog was more complicated than it was for a cat. Being trusting, dependent souls they were more easily and more cruelly dominated by lesser men, and being a bigger and sometimes more frightening problem than the cats, they were dealt with more aggressively. It did not help that finding food for them in the markets was close to impossible.

The troubles never really started for any of the animals until just before the season's start in the spring, or much later, in the autumn when there were no longer tourists around to look after them. Without foreign witnesses to the killing times, the dark secret could be kept.

But there were witnesses.

Eleni and Harry arose early one morn for a sunrise walk to the site of one of the island's only remaining ancient ruins, a crumbling Temple to the Goddess Athena.

Now just a few columns were left standing, the rest strewn about as though one of the mythological giants had tossed them about in a game of 'pick up sticks'. It was a particularly peaceful place that this temple had stood sentry for so long, high upon a hill above an olive field that trickled it's way to a remote beach below — the ruin itself, a reminder of those times when the peoples of the Earth recognized the Goddess, respecting the feminine in and our connectedness to all things living on this planet, before domination and war became the rote remedies for all conflict.

Athena was a virgin Goddess, impervious to the pull of Aphrodite, the Goddess of Love. She was strong, fair and merciful, the patron of poetry, music, the arts, the Goddess of wisdom, of reason, of agriculture and civilized life. In the annals of mythology, she was also known as the creator of the olive tree, having struck the bare soil with her spear, from which sprung forth the Olive. She had provided the people with the tree, and here her sanctuary had overlooked their fields.

Harry half joked that her temples in such scattered disarray were proof that she had vacated the premises, and perhaps some of the country's current problems existed because of this — bereft the Goddess of Civilization, she who breathed soul into man, the growth of civilization was stunted.

The less traveled fork in the path to the ruins was a longer trek, but it led past ancient cisterns and old homesteads, alongside stone walls and meandering streams that now were scarcely shadows of their ample springtime glory. A goatherd tending his flock from the shade of a great plane tree waved, calling out a greeting and they waved back, shouting "Kalimera!"

They were walking in flickering light through an enchanted stand of cypress when the heady bouquet of the graceful trees yielded, abruptly, to the unmistakable stench of death. Just a few steps further on, the terrible smell betrayed its source. A pile of carcasses had been cast behind a screen of late blooming heather — a few cats and older kittens, several dogs, some they recognized from the village including the pregnant bitch, the one seen running on the beach, all wearing the grimace of a torturous death, frozen in time and discarded here, in the shadows, by someone's guilt. Mortified, Eleni and Harry stood hand in hand, staring silently at the carnage.

Now that the summer season was settling into the fall, and the ferries took away more tourists than they delivered to the island, the culling had resumed.

Takis had been the one to explain it all to Harry and Eleni. He'd said that at first word from a town director, the killers would have fanned out across the village in the dark of night, leaving food laced with rat poison sitting out on the open ground by the garbage bins. The poison found its mark easily in those less wary and its victims would die fairly quickly, though not mercifully. Some of the killers played more willingly into evil's hand, and laced the food with ground glass — much cheaper than poison — which took its time to do the dirty work, usually causing it's prey to run off in agony to bleed to death, slowly, far from the scene of the crime.

Yes, it was a dark, dark secret.

There was a crew of men who would move soundlessly through the streets before first sunlight, removing any evidence of the horror that had snaked its way through the night. The dead usually were deposited at the island dump, far from the town, but sometimes the sad heaps would be left scattered throughout the countryside by the lazy, someone who gave with little or no thought to what might become of the carrion crow or the seagulls swooping in to do their bone cleaning.

Eleni pulled away from Harry's side and walked to the mound of carcasses, her hand covering her nose. "Sons of bitches," she muttered, "those evil, pathetic sons of bitches." Crouching, she scanned each face while trying to banish any thought of the fear and pain the animals must have felt.

After her breakdown at Matoula's taverna Eleni had spent much time carefully reconsidering the issues of neglect and the poisonings. Vassili and Popi both had attempted to enlighten her regarding any rationale behind the gruesome customs; simply being that until sterilization surgeries were more easily obtainable, the animals would continue to breed, and the better choices could not always be made. Though that hadn't changed her feelings about cowardly acts of cruelty, a bit of regret had begun to seep in, a discomfort over having allowed her own cultural mores, her emotions and personal ethics to prevail over those of the people who had lived here with this particular enigma for generations. They were simply doing as they had always done.

But why did it have to be done like this?

She had tried to be hopeful. She wanted to believe that intolerance and hardness would give way sooner than later, and that with some encouragement the people would make the needed changes; both in their belief systems and in the accessibility of alternatives to the killings.

But in this moment, there was no hope. Any remorse that she may have been nurturing fled quickly as she stared at the reeking pile of abandoned possibilities, and all that filled that space was sadness.

Harry found a flat rock and started scraping the ground around him, gathering dirt and fallen leaves enough to lightly cover the mound of bodies, an attempt to keep the stench from so easily advertising a free meal to the wild things. Fearful that the poison might harm them in turn, he covered the dirt with what rocks he could find while Eleni carried over an armful of the pungent rosemary she had found growing in the sun. She spread the sprigs over the makeshift grave and was saying a silent blessing for the betrayed when she straightened with a gasp.

"Oh, Harry — what about Margarita?"

The poisonings had reached out from the shadows to touch them personally.

"She's survived it all in the past, Eleni. And for several years, according to Vassili." Harry said this evenly, sensing her dancing on the edge of panic.

"But how can we be sure she will again? We can't, can we? We can't just leave her to this. God, and what about Minou? Lily's kitties ..."

Their plan for quiet hours at the temple ruins had turned instead to one of urgency.

They sat at the foot of an ancient Doric column, under a weakened sun finding its way into another season. The breeze was comforting, blowing over the warm Aegean from some other timeless place, the ruin and the elements all impervious to the disorder triggered in humans by these incidents of death, just a part of the ebb and flow that marked the path of all existence through the dawning and the dusking of the eons, the ebb and flow that would continue still.

They talked through the disorder and their horror, there at Athena's compassionate feet, until it all was tempered to a fine worry and they had come up with the roadmap that would help them find the way to take Margarita home. It was a start. Shortening time and a fragile hope was all that was left to them.

... that's just the way it is

Minou lay curled upon her lap as she wrote.
The Muse surely lives here.

For Eleni, it was in these exquisite moments that all felt well with the world. She stopped writing and looked up, sensing energy coursing in the light all around her.

There was nothing quite like the light in Greece, a light with a particular quality that seemed to infuse everything with more life, making it all more dimensional, more tangible somehow. At this particular time of the day the far hills sheltering the cove that lay curled before her – – and the rocks along the water's edge, and the trees, standing tall along the cliffs, they all seemed to emanate this light, as though they had absorbed it throughout the long day until they could take in no more and out it seeped at its dimming. The energy they now cast off as a soft orange glow upon the coming evening blanketed the land and sea with an otherworldly sheen for the whole hour preceding the sunset.

She breathed in the color with the cooling air and as she slowly exhaled could hear tapping in the distance, the men at the boatyard far below the cemetery working their magic upon the old fishing caiques there, a magic born of generations of experience passed from father to son. Those men kept the old boats seaworthy, able to carry the new generations on in their own discovery of that bounty hidden deep within the waters.

Every sound here had a story behind it, some meaning, and every sound that came to her now was calming, for they helped to mask the decibels of frustration found in her quest to save Margarita, which had not been going well.

For Eleni, this place was her own holy trinity — one of earth, sea and sun. And it was a place of great history, of discovery, divination and inspiration that she could share with her daughter and husband, a relief from a weary and conflicted world. Somehow, outside the confines of time and unencumbered by life's predictable burdens, here was a freedom into which she and her mate could fall into love, again, and yet again. Certainly, for her, it had not been a place of struggle or survival, and for this she was eternally grateful.

It had not been a place of struggle and survival until the unpleasant bits about the animals came into focus. Now, a new chaos filtered through her refuge of peace. At times she felt she was spinning around in an alternate reality utterly discordant to the peaceful world that usually surrounded her, here and now. She willed the old ways, such as those regarding the animals, to change – – and yet she mourned the inexorable chipping away of other old ways, the deeply rooted customs of the people here.

I am so tired of people saying 'that's just the way it is'. Why not work towards something that can be mutually beneficial? Why not just want better? A new paradigm ...

She wrote these thoughts in her journal, adding to the well-worn pages filled with reflection and hope, frustrations and sorrow, smeared here and there with tears or the essence of a pressed flower. Minou growled in her sleep and Eleni looked up and out, into the feelings she found coursing over the ancient waters in the distance.

Eleni deeply mistrusted the changes, inevitable perhaps, that were occurring around this island, 'her' island. Why it was that they couldn't simply coexist with, concede to, and most importantly to her, honor the old ways of life, rather than pushing them further into obsolescence? These weren't the changes that would ease life for the abandoned animals, or for the local folk who offered the beauties of a well-worn island life to those who came to Greece seeking refuge from the cacophony of progress.

Why does the new usually seem to have the need to feed off the best of the old, suck it dry to enable the quickening of it's own growth? That's just the way it is, that's just the way it is ... Jesus, Mary and Joseph, I grew SO tired of hearing that from adults when I was a kid! The tides of change, blah blah blah! BLAH! Is this kind of change really for the better?

On most of the touristed islands, locals didn't necessarily work in their home villages any more. Many of the seasonal tavernas and tat shops in the towns were now owned by large companies or the urban wealthy who not only had plentiful buyers for their mediocre fare but also found cheap labor in the young, eager foreigners that flocked to the islands for a good time in the summer. Or they brought in polished waiters from Athens. There was

165

really nothing local about them, other than the fish they served at an extortionist's prices. These businesses were enslaved by companies that really cared nothing for the wellbeing of an island, and proved this in taking their profits away, to the mainland or even out of the country at the season's end. The Greek government, which apparently had no desire to look out for its own people, just let them do so.

Yeah well, the government probably pockets some change. Those muckity-mucks in high places have to have some way to buy the Mercedes limos they love to drive around ... they're probably bankrupting the generations to come ...

This island, like most of those that lay scattered over the Ionian and Aegean seas, was easy prey for the development contractors who lined the pockets of its Mayor in return for his favors. He far too easily forgave their building mistakes and code violations, overlooked the unregulated developments built too close to the waters edge that spewed their sewage to the sea, and often allowed covert, highly illegal and in-the-dark-of-the-night demolitions of hallowed old buildings — making way for new development which, though disputed emotionally by neighbors, would easily move ahead if the pockets were again filled with drachmae. In return for his turning a blind eye, besides the offers of expensive dinners and elegant yacht parties the developers and business owners brought in their cheap and 'pretty' labor force that the Mayor thought made the island look more cosmopolitan, and therefore more desirable.

He paved a gilded way for the big travel agencies that brought in masses of tourists who didn't come for the experience of the ethos of a culture, or to immerse themselves in the magic of Myth and Greece's other varied beauties — more often than not they were there for the magic of Metaxa, and for an easy, well-deserved and inexpensive holiday. They bought their flight, hotel accommodation with all of the luxuries of home, meals and excursions all inclusive, and their tour organizers encouraged them to flock en masse to the larger boats moored in the harbor that were owned by the hotels themselves, rather than to the colorful smaller caiques owned by local men. There were also the pre-designated eateries upon which those same flocks would descend for uncomplicated food and perhaps the odd, quaint 'Greek Night', all with the security of nothing unexpected. These establishments certainly were not the small, local eateries and fish tavernas in the harbor, or the ouzeries, where old men got into yelling matches over politics and dancing and singing might erupt spontaneously, the local fishermen pulling out their worn instruments while friends gathered around for the telling of the tales.

The sheer numbers of this type of tourist, of course, made the Mayor look good to the prefecture's governing officials, and the National tourist authority — though they were not necessarily good for the nurturance of the whole of the island and her people. Some of the more resourceful, and even the poorer of the islanders were able to sustain themselves and keep the island's heart beating, by staying on to make their living in the fishing trade, selling their home farmed vegetables and goats milk in the markets or by making bread from wheat borne of hard labor in their own fields for the restaurants. Some made wines, and some grew enough olives to be able to market the freshly pressed oil, or the soaps and candles that could be made from it. Some tended herds of sheep or goats while others taught the children in the schools. Mechanics kept trucks and buses running, painters and plumbers stayed busy and the boat yards were busy keeping the excursion and fishing caiques afloat. And there were those who operated lovely, small hotels or who opened their homes to travelers, generally people who came to the island with respect for the pace of life, the people and their culture. Several of the town tavernas, some having been passed down through the generations, were open the year round and continued to tend to the social and gastronomical needs of the island. These constants helped to sustain the local economy, somehow able to bypass the Mayors' hungry pockets while keeping locals employed the year long, taking all the provisions they could from the local farmers and fishermen and in turn keeping everyone well fed.

In winter, when the tourists fled the cooling seas and wild winds, many of the locals were able to count their blessings and relax a bit with their families, take a small vacation to the city or another island or unwind in the cafes with the time to spend lingering over coffee or ouzo with friends — some found joy in walking for hours in the hills collecting horta and herbs, some in cutting firewood or tending to their boats in drydock. Some spent too many hours in gaming rooms, gambling away the boredom the dark of winter can call up, as well as any ease the season may have provided — but then, many banked their earnings and banished boredom by continuing to work.

The old ways continued on as they could, and the people thrived on community, together celebrating births and mourning deaths, attending weddings, sharing the solemnity of the orthodox holidays and the pageantry and gaiety of the various paniyera, the Saint's Day feasts. The island, with it's echoes of the real Greece, was still alive, just getting by as it always had ... with the seasons' ebb and flow, like the tide ... and likely always would. Those who

168

were able to see the richness in this way of life were content, they easily found happiness. Those who needed more and more drachmae in their bank accounts in order to feel rich and safe became suspicious of others, angry even, and they remained unfulfilled.

It was tourism that drove the National economy. While it boosted the local economy some and put tax monies in the coffers, it challenged the island ecologically, it overburdened the local landfill and changed the landscape forever. What some considered to be a virulent plague — the spread of vacation villas and huge new hotels, and the hulking gray hulls left unfinished and empty because funding for building had expired — made it's march further and further across the island with the passing of each year. Water, once plentiful and clean, was in shorter supply because of the influx, and now more often it was brackish, contaminated by seawater breaching the bore-holes as the natural forceful flow was diminished by an ever bigger demand. Or it was being slowly poisoned, thanks to the continued indiscriminate disposal of truck batteries and building supplies.

With tourism booming, prices on the islands soared up and up, but this was mostly to the benefit of the bigger companies that took earnings away with them when their tavernas were closed up, the canopies were put away for the season and the winter storms backed up along the length of the Aegean. They conducted winter business elsewhere, and had no problem paying leases on their emptied buildings until the next season saw their return to the island. The locals, without the benefit of much profitable winter trade, were left to struggle with having to pay the same huge rents to ensure they would still even have a business with which to take on the competition of the next season. Fishermen found that they had to begin to compete with the lower market prices in Athens and Thessalonika, making it more difficult to make a living at home and keep up with the inflated economy. Yet many of the restaurants that bought the local men's fish at Vassili's market boldly turned around and offered it to tourists at ridiculously inflated prices, essentially pocketing the profit that rightly belonged to the hard working seamen themselves. The smaller ferry lines had to give way to the larger ones; and the local teamsters, along with their hard working ponies, were finding less and less work carrying goods from the barges anchored in the harbor, for the expanse of construction on the island called for far more materials than the teamsters could handle and large trucks were being brought in from the mainland to haul the materials.

In such a close-coupled society, one so interdependent, so tightly knit, any shift or change surely caused upset in its order.

Eleni had come to her education in these matters over many a lengthy, ouzo fueled conversation with Vassili and Nontas and had just recently learned further that fewer and fewer local youngsters aspired to become fishermen, or to captain the small boats in the season, taking tourists on magical mystery Aegean journeys around the islands in search of perfect beaches and dolphins.

"They want money, big money! They want things! And there is not enough glamour in that life, no, the boats, they are not new enough, they are not fast enough!" Vassili moaned. Instead, many sought to be grounded in the modern world, surrounded by wealth and the newest of toys, a way of life not afforded by the long hours of hard work put in by those plying their trade from the water. Even the ways of the boatmen would eventually disappear.

"And many of the people here, they have found it necessary to leave the island, to go to the cities or to the big ships for the work, just to be able to keep their children and their old mother or father fed. You know, the inflation, it is hard." And so, over the years, bit by bit in these ways and along with the natural exodus of the young and the adventurous, the community lost some of it's soul.

Vassili had ended his discourse by saying, with sorrow, that many of the islanders — especially the elders — would much prefer the old ways of life. But the government had decreed, years ago, that the island must be touristed in order to bring in more revenue for the country. And touristed it was. A great tension still existed because of this.

Greed ... it leaves no room for compassion towards anything... people, animals, nor the island herself...

A gentle balm blew up in the evening's breeze, bringing the last sounds of the day to the balcony. Eleni stared through transparent thoughts to the vast blue. When she closed her eyes and breathed in the sea and earth and cooling sun and set to pondering how she might navigate the strange new and turbulent eddy moving so swiftly within her normally peaceful sea, she heard him, in full voice, as he came around the point. Vassili was in the smaller of his two caiques, the one that he used for hunting octopus or shore fish.

She sat forward and squinted for a better view.

A caricature of a figurehead, he was standing on the prow bellowing his heart out in song. He directed the little boat with a stretch of yellow twine wrapped around his ankle and tied back to the tiller, and would occasionally break into a sort of crafty jig when he wished to change its course, feet flailing, the yellow twine dancing and jumping in its efforts. How beautiful!

Suddenly quiet, he held up a long spear, a trident that he would use to stab the poor creatures in the shallows. *Oh ...!* Eleni cringed, and then laughed at herself, her romantic notion of 'holy trinity' momentarily shattered. She set Minou down on the marble floor and went off in search of her clan and the little dog, up to the rooftop where they all awaited the glory of the setting sun.

vassilis tsikakis

Vassili left Greece as a young man.

He had studied in England and was far better educated than most of the tourists who now came to his island, but he turned higher schooling's prospects away for his love of the sea. Choosing instead the life of a merchant marine, the hard work aboard enormous cargo ships and oil tankers earned him entrance to many of the great ports of the world and through these years of toil and travel he learned several languages, and wisely gleaned the beauty that lay deep within peoples' differences, and in those customs foreign to his own.

Vassili believed that if everyone had the opportunity to travel, the world would be a far better place. Not the sort of travel many people made in these modern times, that which showed them only the famous tourist spots and housed them in hotels offering all of the comforts of home and not much more, but a journey that really brought one in touch with the people of other cultures, with their lives, their passions and consequently, in touch with one's own soul. He felt that the real experience of differences, and of seeing how others lived, banished fear and built tolerance and understanding, patience and caring. A better world.

He liked his work and treasured his many adventures and the friends he made along the way, but in time longed deeply for the land of his birth. He eventually made his way around the world, landing back in Piraeus rich enough to buy a seaworthy boat, and sailed it homeward to his island to make a humble living in the fishing trade.

Hestia was originally named 'Eudora'. One of the ancient Nereides, mythological sea nymphs or Goddesses of the sea who watched over sailors, Eudora was a Nereid of good gifts — good sailing or good catch — and her name was perfect for Vassili's caique for many years.

But then he fell in love with Maria.

A girl with a quick wit and dancing eyes who blossomed into a woman never afraid to speak her mind or stand up against any cruelties or oppression, Maria enchanted Vassili with her deep passions for life and anything living. She in turn was drawn by the pull of his warm laughter and gentle hand and when the Fates had braided together their desires, Maria and Vassili were wed in the island church on the hill, their traditional ceremony followed by a great feast of roasted lamb and goat, a celebration that brought all of the locals together, singing and dancing far into the night.

They lived in a small house just outside the village, surrounded by a fruitful olive orchard that provided them with a bounty of sweet oil every other year, and a fertile garden in which Maria patiently grew the vegetables and herbs she sold in the local markets. Fig and mandarin and lemon trees further added a delicious grace to her garden, and jasmine grew up and over the arbor that covered the outdoor kitchen, filling the house with its heavenly scent through the late autumn months. Bougainvillea cascaded in great washes of purples and reds over fences and sheds, and the music ... of the goats' bells, and wind chimes made of glass and shells ... floated over their land, enveloping it in a haunting, lyrical song that defined the place as one of peace and harmony.

Maria's mother, Melina, was quick with her hand and had taught her to create beautiful handiwork. Together they made the pieces for Maria's dowry that filled the box, lovingly crafted and painted by her father, which eventually found its home at the foot of the bed she shared with Vassili. She had learned well, and was easily able to trade her exquisitely handcrafted woven shawls and embroidered tablecloths for furnishings, or rugs, or for the fruits that came into the port on the weekly barges.

Maria, though honest and sometimes sharp of tongue, and with no patience for those not kind or who were heavy handed with the weak or needy, truly had a gentle, giving heart. Not only was it full of caring for the people, it had an especially tender spot for the animals of the island. Her milking goats had all been lovingly christened with names that they knew to be their own, and each nanny would calmly wait her turn to be near her mistress, bleating softly with first touch of her hand. She had saved the lives of a good many animals that had not taken in a fatal dose of poison and also took a multitude of cats and dogs into her heart and into their home, animals she either had found roaming on the quay or sickened from the rotting food they were forced to live on. Neighbors would bring their own sick farm animals to Maria for care — she had a way with her herbs, and a touch that no veterinarian could claim. ("...were one ever around to be of any use!" It was no secret that she held those "useless, well paid men" in great disdain.) Happy chickens ran freely around the yard, gossiping and eating bugs and delighting in their dust baths ... cats were draped over anything that lay in line with the sun and Maria always had several contented dogs curled at her feet, watching over and keeping her company while Vassili was at sea working his trade.

Vassili's heart, hardened early on by an inherited disregard for the animals, eventually softened, out of necessity. It was the only way Maria would have him. She knew in her heart that the animals themselves, like children, were the true innocents, the embodiment of pure love, of joy and grace, life and truth, and she needed them in her life as much as they needed her care and nurturing. And Vassili knew that if he did not like the idea of a dog curled by the hearth or a cat on the bed, he would be the one sleeping out under the stars, alone! Their home was a place of peace, and many an afternoon that Vassili did not spend on his boat, he could be found napping in the hammock with a cat or two happily curled in the crook of his arm.

He loved his life with the beautiful Maria and it wasn't long before he felt he should change the name of his red caique from Eudora, the one who watched over a wanderer, to that of Hestia, Goddess of the hearth and home. The new name would be their talisman, ensuring that he would stay safe at sea, always returning to his Maria, to his heart.

Maria and Vassili's fertile ground and great passion bore them one daughter. Kaiti was surrounded by love, raised in such happiness and with a great respect and honor for all life, the land, the animals, all cultivating within her the mirror image of Maria's own caring heart.

But she also had inherited Vassili's wandering spirit and eventually went off in search of the world, drifting from city to city, country to country like a vagabond before landing at the University in Rome to further pursue interests in the Arts. Higher schooling was the means to finding a path to the fulfillment of her dreams, and eventually the seeds of those dreams took root when something propelled her to distant America, where she fell in love with New York City and was able to make her way as an artist.

She hadn't been home since.

While Kaiti was still at school in Italy, Maria fell gravely ill with a sickness that sapped her of her essence before Vassili's eyes. She grew sad and thin, eventually too weary to take any more joy in this earthly plane and it wasn't long before Vassili was burying his beloved Maria there on the very property where they had shared so much love and life.

She died a fairly young woman, well before her time, and Vassili could not bear the thought of having to carry on without her. He refused to stay on in their home with its shroud of sorrow, abandoning it for Hestia and a life of too much drink in an effort to numb his pain. Neighbors, out of their respect and love for Maria, took in most of her beloved animals while her mother boarded up the house and tried in vain to console Vassili who, like a ghost himself, wandered in the darkness of his grief. Visiting him weekly aboard his boat, she plied him with home-cooked meals, trying in vain to get him to talk, to come back to the world of the living, his community and his church. In the end, she simply sat with him in an overwhelming silence.

For a few years he reached out to no one, never spoke of Maria — not even to his own daughter. He pushed his Kaiti away, perhaps she reminded him too much of all that was lost and so, in his wretched sorrow, he lost her too. His mistress was the sea, only the sea, and he filled his existence with hard work on her waters, fishing day or night depending upon what fish were running, mending his nets and helping his mates with work on their own boats. There was nothing else.

He eventually stopped drinking so hard. After an endless stream of too much ouzo and too little food, he fell down in the darkness of a drunken night aboard Hestia, hit his head, and when old Nontas came to fetch him for work the next morning he found Vassili lying in a great pool of stale blood and feared his friend had been murdered. Vassili came to consciousness with Nontas weeping over his bloodied body, and nearly scared the old man to death when he finally spoke.

Perhaps it was the accident that knocked some sense into him. Vassili realized that if he truly wished to be dead, he would have been by now — and if he kept up the wretched life of the harbor drunk, perhaps he soon would be. He wasn't ready to die. Something within him still fought for life and he knew that he had to slow down, straighten up and let some light in to burn off the fog that enveloped his soul. When this epiphany brought his missing years into focus, he finally began to come to terms with the overwhelming grief and let himself begin to feel and cry, and laugh, once again.

Buying into a partnership in the fish market there on the waterfront gave him the time and some ease with which he might try to reclaim himself. He had his boat and the Aegean, his harbor friends and fishing mates to share philosophy, argument and drink with — he had all that he needed.

... Until the red haired child came skipping down the quay and into his life on a lazy springtime day.

Something about her seemed to thrust Vassili back towards the land of the living. He sputtered to life, not unlike Hestia sputtering and coughing in weak complaint after a long winter's rest.

In Lily he recognized that same hopeful and caring spirit he had, not so many years ago, laid to rest on his land. So much like his Maria, he saw in this child the deep love she'd had for the animals, that heart wrenching honesty and resolve to set things right and to speak out against the wrongs she saw in the world around her. No longer like a spear to his heart, a reminder of Maria had become like a sweet blossoming, an opening.

He loved the bold way this young girl had marched into his life, lending it caring and color again, dimensions that had been flattened by his loss. She made him laugh, bouncing belly laughter which echoed from the depths of his being, from the depths of a distant memory, laughter which began to heal the gaping wound in his heart.

In asking him questions about his fishing nets and the boat he loved so dearly, asking him for his songs and help with her own attempts to learn to play his bouzouki, how she listened so intently to his stories of the sea and told him so passionately of her sadness for the animals, she unknowingly pulled him up from the bottoms of his sorrow to where he could see clearly again, to where he could care. Once surfaced, as he took great gulps of life giving hope he could see that, despite his pain, he still had a heart and a worth — and that he must use them.

Vassili was alive again.

wine from lemons

After a bit of rain in the night, the morning broke, hot and clear.

Eleni sensed something different about the day — the air, thick and still, seemed dense, hard to move through. She let the notion pass as she and Lily made plans to take a girl's day together at the beach, time for long swims and a picnic and a talk about Margarita's future. Harry would stay behind, for the Muse had found him again. It was proving difficult to pry him from his guitar and was best, in these moments of illumination, to leave him to his craft as something lovely and telling always came of it. He was already up on the rooftop, taking advantage of the last cool of what promised to be a hot day.

After breakfast Lily sat on the bed tying her shoe, waiting for Eleni as she flit about embroiled in a private battle — a stupid battle particular only to grown women, it seemed to Lily, over whether to wear this dress or those shorts.

The girl's image echoed from the glass door to the mirror and as Eleni fussed she could see her in reflection, reaching out to stroke the little cat laying next to her, sound asleep, flat on her back with legs askew. Margarita sat at the open balcony doors, sniffing through the notes in the sultry morning air, the light pouring in around her. Eleni smiled, her battle defused.

They both heard it at the same time, the rhythmic whoosh, whoosh, swoosh of Haroula's broom just outside the door. She was early this morning. Eleni caught another reflection on her next round back from the dresser, this just of the kitten, belly round and full, on the bed, innocent enough ... but on the bed ... in the room ... exactly where she should not be at this moment!

And Margarita! She gasped and whirled around.

"Lily!" but the girl must have been reading Eleni's mind for now she was sitting upright, her mouth forming a perfectly startled 'O'.

"Oh ... Oh oh!"

And just then Haroula erupted, a maniacal dervish on the other side of the door, her pitch and volume undulating in wild rhythm. Her tone was unmistakable.

"da da da DA da da DA da da DA DA DA- ohi! OHHEEE — ELENI!"

Ohi — NO — and her name was all that Eleni understood of Haroula's words, as the rest came too fast and furious, harsh sentiment roiling through her native tongue and echoing off the naked walls.

In a moment she was pounding on their door.

Lily shoved the comatose kitten under the covers, clucked to Margarita — who moved immediately to her side — and gently pushed the little dog down onto the floor on the far side of the bed, all in one seamless motion. An anxious smile was frozen upon her face. She looked up at her mother.

They both hoped that Margarita would not bark.

Eleni finally moved to the door, opened it a crack and peered out. Haroula, though small, was all hell and fury, lips tight and eyes ablaze, and dangling from her fingers in front of Eleni's nose was the evidence.

An empty tin of dog food.

Again, the lilting war cry. In her own territory, someone was feeding the pests.

"Ohi! Ti ine AFTO? What is THIS?"

"Herete, Haroula! Kalimera sas!" Greeting the angry woman with her most soothing voice, and most beatific smile, Eleni tried to sweeten her temper a bit.

Though she deeply loved her little American family, Haroula had always seemed disapproving of their contact with the creatures of the island. She would stand shaking her head with the back of a hand pressed to her forehead, a rather stern but maternal "po po po po", Oh my gosh, rushing through her deep sighs when she saw them feeding the hungry cats, or offering belly rubs to one of the island's lonely mutts. But here, now, this can found in the trash was trespass, a betrayal — in her own territory someone was feeding the pests.

"Of course, Haroula. Absolutely. No more!"

They truly loved their landlady, always so welcoming and generous. She regularly waylaid them on their way into the town, herding them into her own cozy home for an aperitif and a bit of a game of pantomime. She spoke less English than they even spoke Greek, but hospitality has no need for common language. They were always welcomed in the best of the tradition, often with a plate of fresh dolmades wrapped up in leaves picked from

182

the grape arbor that sheltered her courtyard, or home made cake, warm from the oven, and rich, lemony bowls of her very special rock fish 'psarosoupa'.

But, she didn't like her boarders bringing the islands' strays into her clean rooms. Most certainly she wouldn't like any of those creatures being as close to her pensione as this empty can in her furiously waving hand was right now! Haroula was forever shooshing Margarita out of the garden with her broom, and now, with the evidence in hand, she knew why.

Eleni politely endured the tirade, all the while the furious woman tried to peer around the door and push past her and into the room. She dodged and weaved, doing her best to keep Haroula out, and finally when the woman had cooled, assuring her with a sympathetic nod and a smile and uttering a weak "yia sas, Haroula mou." Eleni bid her a good day and quickly closed the door. With disaster only narrowly averted, she turned to Lily in the sudden quiet, leaning her weight against the door as if trying to hold any further discovery of their betrayal at bay. A long, stunned silence passed before they both burst into riotous laughter.

The little kitten was still sound asleep under the covers.

Margarita peeked over the side of the bed and sensing the relief she jumped up, turned about a few times, fluffing the covers to her satisfaction and settled heavily with a groan. She lay with her head on her paws and heaved a great sigh as she looked up at both Lily and Eleni with sad, nervous eyes.

Margarita knows ...

Just recently the dog had become moody, fretful, following just a bit too closely at their heels and rarely letting them out of her sight. It was with that great knowing all animals possess, a deep insight that humans seemed to have misplaced long, long ago, that Margarita seemed to know that the time here had turned, and that her people would be leaving her.

Oh, she knows ... Eleni sat on the bed and laid her hand gently on Margarita. Stroking her slowly down the length of her back, over and over, she murmured sweetness as she sought to somehow soothe the little dog's angst.

"I'll keep her close to me, today." Harry, back now from the roof assured the girls, knowing that keeping Margarita with him would not only help the dog feel more secure, it would make it much easier for Eleni and Lily to get to the village bus.

Easier, because Margarita didn't like to let them wander beyond her reach at all now and they'd had to take to sneaking into the village, hiding from her all the way in an attempt to keep her from following along. Hide and Seek had become a familiar game in recent days.

Scurrying silently along the winding, jasmine-adorned back alleys they passed old yia yias and gnarled fishermen sunning themselves, taking their ease upon a chair in their stoop or seated around tables set in small, immaculate gardens as they chatted about old days and shared the latest gossip. After several days' observance of the Americans' antics as they hid from the busy dog, these elders had begun to follow the daily expedition with mirthful, toothless grins, elbowing one another in hushed, crinkle eyed laughter.

"Great." Eleni whispered. "Now they think we're nuts."

Harry would sometimes send Lily ahead, their scout, peering around corners and down the long, open lanes to be sure that Margarita was not there laying in wait.

If the dog was nowhere to be seen, Lily, always the artiste, especially with such an audience waved her parents onward with great, dramatic flair, stork-hopping, arms flying and head nodding a soundless COME on NOW, and as they scurried ahead and past the gallery of assorted fishermen's caps and head scarves, they heard the elders' giggles cutting through the quiet.

Occasionally the dog would be spotted some distance down a cross street, nose to the ground, scenting on her mark. They would stop then as one being, silent and still, together holding their collective breath so as to not make a sound and give themselves away, a moveable tableau daring to stir only when Margarita had moved on and out of sight. But more often than not, as they turned a corner certain that they had thrown the dog off their trail, there she would be, waggy and smiley, singing them her praises, surely pleased that she had finally found her lost tribe and saved them from harm.

It hurt to leave their little friend behind, but she had been quite unreasonable lately, often putting herself in harm's way. Most recently, Lily, invited to spend a day in the country with little Haris' family, was followed into the village by Margarita as she made her way to the bus. Determined to stay by Lily's side, the dog jumped aboard and tried to stow away under the girl's seat but the bus driver would have none of a dog hitching a ride on his bus.

He ordered her off.

Lily fumed. He always offered a helping hand and a seat to the old woman who was often accompanied by a lamb, or had a live hen slung under each arm. *But he won't let Margarita get on the bus?*

"Get it off. Tora! Now!" he had said, gruffly to the girl, the smoldering butt stuffed between his lips flinging ashes about as he spoke. Lily glared at him through narrowed eyes — and then looked pointedly up at the sign above his head, the image swimming in his gray smoke, a picture of a cigarette within a red circle with a thick slash running through it. No Smoking. *Ass.* She looked back at him, her jaw set and her fierce gaze, biting.

"Tora." He said again and turned away from the clever girl before he felt he must give in. He tossed his cigarette out the open door.

Lily had to drag Margarita, screeching in protest, from under the seat and off the bus, and then perch on its steps to keep her from leaping back aboard. She watched over the frantic little dog, trying to soothe with her voice, with all of her love, until the driver yelled "Pahme" and the bus finally started to move. Once the doors began to close Lily raced to the rear window where she watched as Margarita, yelping her protest, or her sadness, ran after the bus as fast as she could on her short little legs, dodging vehicles in the middle of the busy street for several blocks before giving up. Tearful and furious, the girl whirled about and threw herself onto the seat and, with arms crossed as though trying to keep her pounding heart within her chest, spent the whole of the fifteen minutes of her journey trying to bore a hole into the back of the busman's head with her glare, hot as fiery coals.

To Lily, all of the sneaking about was a terrible betrayal of Margarita's love — and of her deep loyalty to them. She felt that they were casting her adrift, that it was awful of them to deny the dog what she wanted and needed most, to be close to her people, to watch over them, to keep them safe from harm. *How can she know why we're doing this? It just makes her get so worried.* Her mother had tried to help her to understand that weaning Margarita from them, now, would prove to be for the best for her in the long run if their plan to adopt her did not work out as they hoped.

She hated this.

Every night before sleep she closed her eyes tightly and said a little prayer for Margarita, envisioning her safe, fat, and curled comfortably upon her very own soft bed at their house in California.

They left Harry and his furry companions behind and headed to the village along the long path above the town beach with its wonderful, wide view of the sea, past the old, ruined stone houses and overgrown plots that were now lived in only by blooming jasmine and the feral cats. Eenie, Miney, Mo and the rest were all there, basking in the early sun on a pile of rock as Eleni and Lily neared, but came to, jumping up to greet them with tails straight in the air, winding between their legs, rubbing and purring with great pleasure as Lily doled out their meal. Each had a greasy nose, an indication that someone had been by in the night with the remnants of a fish dinner for them. The oil from the fish, mixed with the dirt that they ate from left the street urchins with dark, dirty looking noses, all pointing up at Lily now. *Dickens-esque*, Eleni mused.

Satisfied that the cats were doing well and fattening up for the bleak winter to come, they continued on down the long sweep of steps that led to the quay — sixty steps, exactly, Lily had counted many times. At the last wide stone step, the view of the harbor opened before them and they saw Vassili sitting in his usual spot by Hestia, mending his nets. They stopped in at Kosta and Mana's taverna.

"Ah ha ha ha, Eleni, Lily, my flowers!" Mana called to them, through her thick, deep laughter.

"Kalimera sas, Mana! Ah... Boroume na... ehome... dio kafedes ellinikous, ke... ena frappe! Parakalo'?" Eleni stuttered back to the matron who stood with hands set upon ample hips, her head cocked in a focused determination to make sense of whatever issued forth from Eleni's attempts. "Hmmm. Po po! Agapi mou!" Mana sang, "Oh my goodness! My love! You get better, better every day, every day! Two Greek coffees and a frappe! Endax! Ah ha ha ha!" and turned to prepare the drinks that Eleni and Lily carried out to Hestia, their excuse to sit aboard the caique and share a few moments with Vassili, laughing in the strengthening sun about their early morning encounter with Haroula.

Vassili clarified what the day's oddly interesting weather indicated.

"When we get this heavy, hot air, poli zesti, and that chop in the sea ... it seems to come from nowhere, for no reason ... look, you can see it there, beyond the harbor," he said, pointing to the south, where in the distance small, chaotic waves could be seen churning the usually calm sea into a white froth, "it is telling me that the African wind, it is coming. Tonight." Still looking out to sea Vassili lifted his black cap with one hand and raked the fingers of his other, like a thick comb, through his hair. Thinking. He carefully rearranged the hat and turned back to his friends, a wide, mischievous grin revealing a few gold capped teeth, sparkling in the sunlight.

"You watch out, that crazy wind, it will shake your soul! It will make you crazy! Malista — yes, tonight it is a good night to stay inside the house." He stood and stretched, yawning loudly and then, inspired suddenly by the unseen, extended his arms out to his sides, head cocked over one shoulder, and snapped his fingers as he shuffled in a circle, causing the Hestia to pitch lightly in weak protest. Lily giggled.

"Close up your house, your shutters tightly, light your candles, yes. Drink ouzo ... yes! But not too much! And dance? Yes!" With a wink he began to tone a haunting, wordless melody, and gently took each of their hands and helped them off the boat. Then he led them down the quay, hips swaying, three steps forward, hop ... two back, leg crossing over, three steps ... a dip and a slap to the ground, and with a tip of his cap, a bit of a bow to any woman they happened upon along the way.

"Yia hara!" With joy!

Several innocent bystanders were swept up, unable to resist Vassili's flair for the dramatic, and joined the spontaneous flow. Five, ten, twelve dancers trailed in his wake, locals and sunburned tourists alike, eyes closed, all snapping, swaying and singing their way down the gauntlet; on one side, waiters standing with arms crossed over their chests, looking on in sober scrutiny, on the other, the row of colorful caiques in the water, tied to the quay and bobbing their approval.

As Eleni and Lily neared their waiting bus, a laughing Vassili danced them out of the queue, blew them a kiss and floated away, off into the distance followed by a train of laughter.

The rest of the morning was spent as close as possible to the softly lapping water of their favorite beach. When not actually in the water, they were both under shade of their umbrella and while her mother read a book Lily painted a picture of the pile of seashells she had stolen from the sand. Here the sand was fine, white and translucent like alabaster, and the clear turquoise sea gave no indication that just days earlier it had been a roiling mass of dark froth, spitting shells up from the depths and depositing them upon the shore. Nor did it indicate any certainty to Vassili's prediction of the coming of the 'crazy wind'. The still heat, stifling by mid day, called for yet another long, cooling swim and as Eleni and Lily dried off in the thick air, nibbling on feta, fresh bread and the divine local olives, they finally started to talk about Margarita.

A few days before Eleni had spoken at length on the telephone with people in Athens who run a shelter devoted to caring for and working to home the city's strays. She was told that their mission to take Margarita to America was essentially hopeless.

"We can be of no help to you, I'm afraid." a caregiver there had said. "The vaccinations needed for a Greek dog's papers for passage to America are very, very hard to obtain ... and to make matters worse, we have a problem with the vets who service our shelter, vets who do their jobs only when they feel like it rather than when they're needed by the animals. Even when they do show up to do their work, they don't arrive when they are expected. Actually, quite often they are up to a month late! I am sorry." It would have done Eleni and Harry no good to rush Margarita to the city shelter for her shots. Nor would they have been able to leave her there to wait out a vet's arrival or any quarantine, for the Athens shelter was terribly overcrowded and rife with illness. There were far too many dogs in the city that needed help, with little enough that could even be done for them. "The dog has apparently survived several winters on that island. This sounds quite harsh to you, I'm sure, but you're going to have to just leave her there and hope for the best."

She and Harry further researched what help they might get there on the island, or in the mainland clinic that Manolis took his cats to. There was none.

And so Eleni began the wretched task of telling her child that they would not be able take Margarita home with them. Distressed by her own very profound frustration, she fought to seek composure from which she could explain, clearly, why their hopes had crumbled around them. She didn't want Lily to think they'd not tried hard enough.

Eleni looked over the water, as though she would find the words there, somewhere. And then back to Lily. Feeling as though she were stepping off of a cliff, she hoped for wings to break her fall as she began.

"Your dad and I have come to the realization that it is just impossible to take a dog, from here, home with us. It is so much more difficult than we could ever have imagined, Lily, heartbreakingly difficult. If we lived in Italy, in France, or any other European country, it would be easier. But to transport an animal to the U.S. is a different story. We've spoken to a lot of people about what we would need to do to take Margarita away with us." She handed a bottle of water and a tube of sunscreen to Lily before continuing.

"What we first learned was that we need to get her vaccinated for various things. No problem, right? Why should there be? There have got to be vets here ... somewhere! I believed, silly me whatwasIthinking, that we would easily find one to take care of those few shots. But then we were told that, were we even able to get her the vaccinations, something very difficult in itself, Margarita would then have to wait, confined someplace safe, here, for thirty days. Then, she would need a blood test to prove her health for her travel papers, and the results of that alone could take at least another week. Probably much more."

Lily sighed impatiently as she drew doodles in the sand, wishing this conversation were over already. It was starting to hurt. *Get to the point, Mama.* She stopped drawing to look up, searching her mother's face for some sign of hope. Her own was full of questions. She turned back to the sand.

"Our greatest obstacles have simply turned out to be to find the vaccines and a vet to do the work. And there is no vet. And ... there isn't any vaccine to be had." Eleni went on to explain that the veterinarian who services the animals of this island lives on the mainland, and is scheduled to make his routine rounds here every three months.

"Three months! But really, it seems that he only comes if, and when, he feels like making the journey. Vassili knows the man, he actually was due here last week to care for an old farmer's donkey, but he never showed up. He decided he had to go on holiday instead! Vassili very kindly contacted him for me, to see if he would do a great favor and come to the island now. He explained that not only did the donkey need a doctor, there are people here who want to take one of the town dogs away to a loving home in America. But the man simply refused."

She turned and murmured the next words to the sea. "The bastard ... probably relaxing on a yacht somewhere ... floating around on the pay he gets from the government for being a so-called veterinarian to the animals that he does absolutely nothing for!"

Glancing back at her sad-faced girl, Eleni took another breath and went on.

"If it were somehow possible for us to get these things done ..." She saw the hope lingering in Lily's eyes and knew she could not skirt the hard truth, if only for her daughter's sake.

"We can't take her home with us, Lily. I am so sorry. It's just not possible! Friends offered to help us with quarantine and a crate and transport, but they have to be back in London within the month. We don't even know when, or even if, we can get Margarita vaccinated, because there is no damn vet! And if we even could, well, the whole process would certainly take longer than a month." She snuggled close to Lily who was now weeping quietly. "We tried ... we did the best we could."

"All we want to do is give a little dog a home. Why is that so hard?"

"I don't know, darlin'. I just don't know. It's really very simple ... to us. But, we have to remember that we're not at home, and here, some things just don't work in ways we think that they should. There's a lesson here for us, I guess. A lesson in patience. That's a really hard one ... a lesson we'd rather not have to endure because the animals suffer in the meantime, but we must, just because we love the them, and we love this place. It all seems stupid and wrong right now, but with patience we'll watch our hopes for the animals finally come alive. We will. But now, we just need to continue to do the best we can for them with what is within our control. Sadly, getting Margarita home is not within our control."

Eleni reached to gently wipe away the wild strands of red hair that were sticking to the skin around the girl's damp eyes.

"That vet is an idiot!" Lily fumed. " I just don't get it. Aren't vets supposed to help the animals, isn't that why they <u>are</u> vets? Aren't they supposed to <u>care</u>?" Her voice wavered as it fell from fury into her deepening sadness. "If they just don't care, then why can't we just take Margarita with us when we go? What would it matter to anyone?"

"We hope that a person would become a veterinarian out of love for the animals. I suppose that to some, it is just a job, a way to make money. We don't know why the vets here are so complacent. Is it because even they, too, believe that the animals have no souls? Is it because the government doesn't strictly regulate its Vets, and people are simply taking advantage of a bad system? We just don't know. We do know that there are those who care, Popi told us of the one on the mainland. We were going to take Margarita there to her but she, too, would have difficulty finding the vaccines in time to meet our deadline. And to make it all worse, for some stupid reason this Mayor here says that he must sign a release form before any local stray can have passage on a ferry to the mainland! We could have, and would have, snuck her over on Vassili's boat ... but right now, there is no vaccine."

"I don't get it, Mama."

Eleni was becoming impatient. Not with Lily, but with the situation that loomed so miserably over them there. It made the already thick air almost too thick to breathe. She was ready to run, to dive into the Aegean's balmy embrace but the sight of her daughter in tears in front of her pulled her on to some conclusion. She started jamming things into her pack.

"Margarita just can't leave here without proof of the shots — and the blood test. That is true, whether the vets care or they don't! There is no system in place here that can help us. There's only the broken system that is stopping us. Without our being at her side through the whole process, there is no sure way to see her through and then onto an airplane ... but this is something that could take months. Our time here is up, Lil. We can't change our plane tickets and we simply don't have the money to stay on and wait ... or to buy new tickets. You have to get back for school and your father and I have to get back to work! God, if ever I wished we were rich, in time and money, it is now. I would stay here on for as long as it took. But I can't. We'll do the very best we can for Margarita, Lily. You know that. We'll see her into the winter months as safe as she can be."

Lily sat facing the water, idly pouring the fine, white sand over her feet. Eleni moved close, wrapped her arms around her and spoke quietly.

"I am so sorry. I know how sad you must be. I know. My heart breaks, too." She softly traced the tear sliding down her daughter's reddened cheek. Then she remembered something that Vassili had mentioned to her one quiet morning as they shared an early coffee.

"Vassili told me about collars, Lil ... that a collar on a dog is a sign of its belonging to someone. He said it might help a dog stay more safe ... at least people would probably leave it alone. I'm thinking that a collar would be a good thing for Margarita."

After a long silence, the girl quietly said, "Well ... we should find her a collar, then. And a name tag, too."

When is it, that we lose this ability to have such hope? Eleni smiled.

"Oh, Lily. You have such a gift, always able to make sweet, sweet wine from lemons. You can grow hope from ground that looks as though nothing could grow in it! You are incredible, my brave girl."

She stood to shake sand from a damp towel but stopping suddenly, turned back to Lily.

"You know, I do know of a coppersmith. He has a shop just up from the harbor! You've probably seen it at the top of the steps. Why don't we see if he would make a name tag?" She had admired his work, looking in on him many a morning as she walked to the village to take photographs. He had a small, dark workshop at the head of the stone steps and always seemed very pleased to have visitors wander in through his ever-open door.

Eleni gently pulled the sad girl close to her heart and held her tight. "Let's go. We'll ask Vassili to speak to him for us."

Rather than trek through the hot orchard, back up and over the hill, to catch the long bus ride back to town, they walked along the beach to beg a ride with the captain of the lovely blue caique tied there to a mooring set deep in the sand. The man was just starting to pull his gangplank but he recognized the two as Vassili's friends and kindly ushered them aboard his boat for a cooler ride home over the water.

Eleni noted the wind, dry and hot, yet sensuous, tickling her neck and teasing her sun soaked skin. It picked up as they headed round the sheltered peninsula into open sea. She and Lily leaned back against the railing under shade of the canopy, Lily dozing and Eleni watching the chaotic movements of the building waves. The sturdy little boat rocked and pitched on the white-capped swells.

"Crazy wind." was all that the captain said.

In just twenty minutes they were setting anchor in the harbor, beginning now to toss about itself with the unaccustomed wind from the south. Hestia was battened down and anchored away from the quay for the coming storm, her nets heaped in a pile. There was no sign of Vassili.

"Efharisto para poli" both chimed to the kind man as they stepped carefully from the swaying caique to the solid quay. They stopped in at Kosta's and found their fisherman sitting in his customary spot, nursing an ouzo as he read the newspaper. He listened thoughtfully as Lily told him of her idea for a nametag for Margarita.

"Ah. Neh, neh. Yes, you find just the right words for your little tag, and I will ask Yiannis to make it for you." he assured the girl. He noticed that she was minus her usual share of mirth and playful words and questioned Eleni over the tops of his reading glasses. She shrugged back at the gentle man and tapped her fingers over her heart. "Margarita", she mouthed. He nodded soundlessly, pursed his lips and looked quickly back to the girl.

"We will help the little dog be safe from harm, koukla mou. We will do the best we can."

Lily gave him a kiss on the cheek as he reached to pat her hand, and then the sun bleached duo waved to him and wandered off, wondering aloud what the Muse may have brought to Harry.

He was not on the balcony, nor was he on the roof. The sun was already dimming, so they thought to look for him out on the peninsula of flat rocks that jutted out of the water, facing the West, the perfect spot to take in the sunset, and he often played his guitar there in the evenings. Many times they had all gone down to the rocks to swim, and sit out the evening show only to find Margarita already there, curled quietly in the golden light. They'd taken to calling it 'Margarita's Point'.

Stopping along the way to check on Margarita's fat little adoptees, they found the pups alone, cuddled together and fast asleep. The only stirrings came from puppy dreams, ancestral memory, whimpers and growls drifting in whispers from the furry pile atop the bed of pine needles. In recent days their eyes had opened up to the world and with that they had started to crawl about and explore — spastic, jiggly, still wobbly on their little

197

feet. One was black and white, the other a bay pup, brown with black ears and feet, both round and healthy since Margarita had been able to regenerate an adequate milk supply.

As Eleni and Lily continued on to Margarita's point, the sound of a guitar came drifting on the strengthening wind, shimmering, dancing through the pine trees. Drawn by the music, they carefully navigated the rocky end of the pathway, stopping at the head of the frail wooden stairs that led to the rocks on the point below.

The path overlooked a taverna that sat at the water's edge. Manolis, a troubled, sensitive soul carried away by the ills and injustices of the world, owned the old, worn restaurant. He caught his own fish from aboard the ancient rowboat he kept moored just off the shore, and served it up fresh daily. The man was known for a lovely meal, but as each night wore on he always managed to get caught up in a wild argument with someone, and sometimes with no one but his own demons. He would shout about God, the universe, the state of the human soul, capitalist greed versus communism and the injustice of life in this world and ultimately his ranting and ravings scared off of most of his customers.

While Manolis' mind was torn, he had a gentle heart and he loved the stray cats. One of the few islanders who extended a great deal of caring to them, he had a passel of feline misfits crowding about his place and they all adored him in return.

A few years earlier he crated them all up and took them for the long journey in his small boat to the mainland, and from there on an even longer drive in a beaten old truck over treacherous, winding roads, to a vet clinic in the nearest large town. He insisted they all be spayed or neutered and vaccinated.

Of course, this gave the village folk even more reason to think that the man was mad as a hatter. But Manolis knew that this effort would ensure that his cats would produce no more unwanted kittens to endure the winter's wraths and fates, or wander or fight in the waxing and waning of their hormonal tides. That epic journey became an annual springtime event for him, as each year brought new additions to his little herd. His cats, all soft coated and fat, were obviously very healthy and most of the time were seen lazing about the taverna's brightly painted wooden terrace, bellies full of fish heads or rats, and plenty of the kibble Manolis always left out for them. One of them was missing a whole hind leg, another had only one good eye and one sleek, black kitten was missing a part of his upper lip which left his face locked into a perpetual, toothy smile, like Alice in Wonderland's Cheshire Cat. A most delightfully happy kitty, he always lay in wait to ambush passersby there on the cliffside stairs, leaping out of nowhere and chirping his greeting.

And there he was now, grinning up as he pounced and embraced Lily's tanned leg gently, with claws considerately sheathed.

"Yia sou, Toonses!" Lily sang softly to the smirking cat as she scooped him up and hugged him close. His eyes half closed, a purr of gratitude echoed from the deep as he drooled happily in the girl's arms.

Standing there on the cliff they could see Harry below. And Margarita. The little brown dog lay upon the craggy rock, facing the sunset, her head up, eyes squinting in the blaze of last light with what looked like a smile upon her face.

Harry, sitting cross legged next to her, gently played the sun to sleep.

litany of sorrows

The wind came hot and strong, just as Vassili had predicted. It painted a haze over the water that glistened with Saharan sand, and whipped up dust and leaves and howled around corners of the old buildings while the harbor waters churned and danced, splashing over the wall onto the promenade. With the building winds, the caiques had all been moved around to the ferry port for safety from the storm and the harbor was gray and sullen now without its colorful little boats ... it seemed to be missing its heart.

Shutters that had been left open at Haroula's pensione rattled and banged noisily upon the sides of the building in the wind and Harry and Eleni rushed around to unoccupied rooms, closing those they could. What couldn't be shut tight clattered on endlessly through the long night.

Lily was snuggled easily in her own little den, away from the noise and able to sleep peacefully, but Eleni lay in her bed as if with fever, drenched with perspiration in a half sleep filled with visions of dervishes and deities whirling around the room in a taunting dance.

Crazy wind.

She came out of the fevered twilight sleep restless and wildly awake. To her, their room, now shuttered off from the world, from the air, from life, was a stifling prison — she felt like a caged animal, walls closing in, no escape, no breath. As Harry snored softly next to her, blissfully oblivious to the dissonant energies and static air, she was about to get up to find a book to read when she heard Margarita barking frantically in the distance.

She didn't sound right.

Eleni went to the doors and pried open the shutters, listening hard through the clamor of the wind as though it would afford her some sight into the swirling night. She was sure she heard a women's voice too, somewhere out there with the moaning wind and Margarita's call.

Distinctly, and suddenly, she heard a loud and brittle "No! NO!" followed by a man's raised voice. It sounded to Eleni like a woman in trouble. Perhaps someone was being assaulted? She called to Harry, who scarcely stirred from his deep sleep, when she heard it again ... and then Theo's voice in the distance.

Theo!

She finally shook Harry, who awoke to see her hurriedly pulling on one of his big shirts as she told him a woman was in trouble out there in the night, maybe it was Popi and she was going out to see what the problem was.

When she stopped speaking, they both heard the stifled cry. "Eleni! Harry! Oh shit!" Then there was another man's voice, and a bitter clash of angry Greek words, tossed about by the wind.

Eleni's blood froze.

She navigated her child's room as calmly and quietly as she could, flew down the stairs and out the door, down the cobbled walk through the dim, hot night, barefoot and nearly naked over the pine needles strewn about the path, until she came to Margarita. The dog was barking frantically, throwing a high-pitched distress call furiously into the shadowy night. She was standing on the spot where her sweet puppies' nest used to lay.

Used to lay. There was nothing there now.

A streetlamp cast it's soft light towards Margarita's point and Eleni continued through it until she could see Theo and Popi standing on the steps, in heated conversation with two young men who appeared to be drunk and quite agitated.

"Popi! Popi!" she cried into the roaring wind. "Are you alright?"

As Eleni arrived, Theo — pale in the ethereal light swimming with specs of dust and salt air — reached out for her and explained breathlessly that these boys, local boys, had come along as he and Popi were sitting away from the wind on the stone wall by the pups, talking. Belligerent, obviously drunk and itching for a fight, without warning they had snatched away the box and grabbed the pups, and as one put them in the box and held it over the cliffside, the other carried on incoherently about foreigners not minding their own business, foreigners daring to think they know what is best for this island, foreigners, arrogant foreigners.

"And when Popi asked them to please, please just put the little dogs down and to talk about whatever was bothering them, we live here, talk to us, one of them turned away ... but the other just looked back at us, blankly ... he had death in his eyes, Eleni." And then, with what Theo said felt to be a perverse sense of entitlement, the boy threw the box, pups and all, over the cliff, into the night, and into the water below.

The boys stood swaying in front of them now, boasting, faces contorted with a strange mixture of fright and the belligerence of too much drink. As one stepped forward, filled with a fearful bravado, adrenaline and alcohol coursing through his veins, he shouted in a very schooled, British accented English as he pointed his finger at Eleni, "YOU don't know! You don't know! Why can't you arrogant tourists all just leave us alone?"

"Where is your heart?" she screamed.

A handsome boy, he strutted about, drunkenly accenting his words with a lift of his chin and a very strong tone.

"You! You bitch, you bring with you, what? Your fucking world, your mighty ideas, you think you can come here and tell us what to do? You think you know better ... than us?" He jabbed at his own chest. Fierce and agitated, he seemed to Eleni engaged in some private battle, one the visitors may never fully understand.

"What do you know? What do you know? You do not know us! You have no fucking respect for us, you do not know what it is like to be one of us. We live here ... you do not." He became more threatening and as he staggered toward Eleni, Theo moved in to protect her.

"No Theo, this is my fight. " she said to her friend, gently holding her palms out towards him. She tried hard to find peace in her heart for this boy, but it just wasn't there. One hand fluttered back to her face, to cover her mouth as though to hide that shock — and her fear.

"This is MY island, and these animals are not your business!" the drunken boy-child slurred. "They are our problem ... This is OUR way. Why should it matter to you if they live or they die? Aren't the people ... the people! ... more important than those dirty little beggars? They are better off where the seagulls can pick at their bones." He gestured to the sea behind him, churning in the darkness. And then he spit at her.

With that, and the thought of the young pups surely drowned in the waters below, Eleni flew at the boy, all mother, fury and grief, her hands aiming for his neck. The small and usually gentle pacifist had simply had enough of unnecessary cruelty and the human race's general want of compassion, and she just broke.

She was ready to throw that callous, boorish boy himself off that cliff, when Harry stepped from the shadows and pulled her back, and to his chest. Wrapping his arms around her, he held her close, kept her from shattering further. Instead of blows, words flew; furiously, back and forth, heated and pained and passionate. Eventually the boys stumbled off into the night, leaving Theo, Popi, Eleni and Harry standing there in disbelief, the crazy wind still swirling and taunting at the edge of the shadows.

Eleni pulled away from Harry and sat down on a step, her head in her hands. *It's true. I don't know what the reality of this world here really is. We're just visitors. Here long enough to savor the beauty and wonder, mystery, then we go home. We take care of the animals ... and then we go home! And we leave them here when we go, we leave all of the problems behind us. How stupid of me ...* But in her heart she knew there was no excuse for the manner in which the lives and the deaths of these animals were dealt with.

"Eleni, Eleni." Theo said softly. "Those boys are shamed by your caring for the animals, for those puppies. They are embarrassed that they do not do the same, they want to be in control, but they don't know how ... they sit back and do nothing, while you — you act. And so, this becomes their control. A very strange way of showing it. They take their control of the situation by making the little dogs disappear. No more problem. It is a pride that really has no place in this world anymore."

Dear Theo tried to make sense of it all for her but the frenzied wind seemed to spin Eleni's fragile thoughts further out of control.

Sweet little things. Killed, for what? A point? For drunken boys' macho posturing ... just to show that they are still in control of what happens in their world? Cowardly, sneaking in, in the middle of the night ... to purge some fear and frustration masked so neatly by their macho attitudes. The bastards.

She sat there, unable to move, a monument to sorrow.

Greece was no longer the poor little sister of the European Community. No longer was she terribly disadvantaged, under siege, or even a developing nation. Greece was now cosmopolitan, worldly, growing into her own wealth and her own independence and she hoped to enter the European Union one day, with the respect and regard of her neighbors. Eleni just couldn't understand how this lovely place could allow her children to believe that it was all right to behave so dreadfully.

So, shouldn't she act grown up? Shouldn't she stand accountable in these times? Shouldn't she teach her children how to behave in a way that might show that she is worthy of respect, and regard? This one thing is so simple ... Don't Murder Defenseless Beasts! Pfff ... She doesn't deserve anyone's respect.

Eleni didn't see a thing. She only felt far too much. Fury, sadness, outrage.

"What is it, exactly, that makes a human life more relevant, more worthy than any other? It's all life, isn't it? The cats, the dogs? We walk this earth together, we live and breathe and feel pain and suffer, we share the need for food and shelter, we all have a beating heart."

We all mother our young.

The wind picked up in great gusts and seemed to beg Eleni's presence as it swirled around her, blasting her with sand and pine needles. Surfacing from her private depths, she came up gasping for air, lightheaded, exhausted. She had to stand and bend over to catch her breath and she thought she might be sick.

They all stood in a quiet, stifling and void like the eye of a storm. There were no words left. Eleni and Harry bid Theo and Popi goodnight with tired eyes and went off to gather up Margarita, who was howling softly by the bench under the pine tree. Harry swept the little dog into his arms, and he and Eleni walked on to their room where all three barely slept, only dreaming fitfully of the swirling demons as the wind seemed to try to get to them, clamoring until dawn at the shuttered doors.

Margarita asked to be let out quite early in the morning.

Soon after, Eleni and Harry could hear her howling somewhere below their window. She was joined by a second voice and Eleni peered out over the balcony to see Margarita and the dog Lily had named Spike, the thin little white dog who they thought might have been the pups' mother. Spike had been there with Margarita that night they all sat on the rooftop straining to identify the eerie sounds calling for life from within a plastic bag left hanging from a tree.

Eleni crawled back into bed, snuggled next to Harry, and listened to the two small dogs sing their mournful song together.

Later that morning they found a path near Margarita's Point that led down to the water. One pup's lifeless body was found floating by the shore, the other was nowhere to be seen. Harry buried the one in the dry earth and while a sad Lily decorated the tiny grave with rosemary sprigs and seashells, they all listened to Margarita and Spike's litany, the two still sitting together, keening softly in the distance.

queen of the heavens

An offering, arms outstretched, held in suspension by the velvet sea, she lay open to the moon. She could smell the salt, that magic element that allowed her small frame to float effortlessly in the warm water, clear and smooth tonight, without a ripple. There was no sound other than that specific hush ... hush ... almost a whisper, a sound made only by calm waters — calm on the surface but teeming with life beneath.

The full moon lay at her side, Selene the Goddess, Queen of the Heavens in reflection on the glassy plane, so bright she surely cast a warmth. Selene, bringing light to the darkness, holding peace and space.

Eleni sighed deeply and sank below the surface.

All of her thoughts went quiet. Deep within a momentary absence of ego, a thoroughly emptied vessel, she was sinking, sinking ...

As she broke through the silvery calm to the air above, she could hear Harry's guitar, and drifted closer to the shore. He was playing just what she imagined the moonlight would sound like were it able to be heard as it danced on the water, sparkling, shimmering, chiming, soft.

She lay back, floating again, staring at the heavens, given totally to the water's embrace. In that effortless moment Eleni knew that her thoroughly sated being was an emptied vessel, able now to start again to fill.

Lily had already climbed out of the water, onto the rocks where she sat under the full moon, faithful little Margarita at her side. Eleni pulled herself to the rock, gazed up at her daughter — and was startled. It was as though the moon had suddenly illuminated a Lily previously concealed from her.

Oh ... my baby ... she's grown up.

The girl looked older, exhibiting a new poise. Angles had changed, baby fat was gone. Eleni couldn't stop staring. She knew that as Lily had stretched and grown in body, her spirit must have also gained a great depth. The girl had weathered her share of emotional storms, had laughed with more mirth than a thousand Gods or Goddesses could provide, but also had sadly learned about broken hearts and the world's want of human compassion far more quickly than Eleni would have preferred.

The girl had grown up before Eleni's eyes.

Where have I been? How could I miss this?

Margarita sat very still next to Lily. She was wearing her new collar, the sturdy, olive green strap of flax and cotton made for her by Popi. A buckle and a ring had been woven into it, the ring to hold the nametag they were to retrieve tomorrow from Yiannis, the coppersmith.

Popi had been waiting for them in her small brick courtyard, sitting barefoot in front of a canvas streaked with the spectrum of color, her dark hair unruly, tamed only slightly by the piece of bright red fabric that she had wound loosely about it, a mountain perched indelicately atop her head. Several cats hovering over a bowl of milk scattered madly when Lily and Eleni pushed open the gate, a string of goat bells clattering their arrival.

"Yia sas, my beautiful friends!" Popi stood up, the green collar dangling from an outstretched hand. As they gathered around what Eleni considered to be a small miracle, knowing that this bit of green could be the thing that would save Margarita's life, Popi told them of the other collars she had started to make in her spare time and planned to give to friends who had pets of their own.

Eleni asked Popi where her amazing talents had come to her from.

"Oh, Eleni, these things, the painting and weaving, I've been doing since I was a small girl. You are too kind." She put the collar down on a table and looked back at her friend.

"Oh ... now I remember! I was going to tell you about your Vassili, his wife! And now is a good time." Popi rushed about collecting colorful cushions and, placing them on a bench, invited Eleni and Lily to sit. She eased cross-legged upon the ground herself, gathering up a fat calico cat to caress as she spoke.

"Maria. Her name was Maria. A beautiful woman. She was the sky and the moon to Vassili, and it was Maria who taught me to paint. You see, I lost my mother when I was just a child. Maria and her own mother, Melina, both became the mother I had lost and I will never forget the weekends I spent at the cottage there, up on the hill ... Baba, my father, often traveled to Athens for his work, and my Yia Yia Niki was so busy with her life so I would stay with Vassili and Maria's daughter, Kaiti. I went to school, always, with Kaiti. We never strayed far from one another. She and I were the best of friends, like sisters, joined together, here, you know?" Popi gently placed a hand over her heart.

"At the cottage there was always bread baking in the stone oven that sat outside on the great stone terrace ... and hugs! Oh, there were so many arms for hugging! A lost child never forgets these things. Maria was an artist, and when she wasn't busy baking or tending to her animals, or creating the beautiful, beautiful things that she sold in town, she taught me, alongside her Kaiti, about the world of color. I don't know how she found the time! In winter we would all sit to paint in warmth by the fire, under rows and rows of herbs that had been left hanging to dry from the wooden beams above our heads. They filled that house with such a heavenly smell, I will never forget it! But in the warmer weather we would paint outside on the terrace. It overlooked what I thought was the whole world then, those hills covered in olive groves and the sea not too far in the distance. We were serenaded by the sounds of wind chimes and goat bells ... and the cicadas. I still love the sounds of the cicadas. I also remember that there always were a few fat nanny goats laying around with the dogs and cats that sprawled on the cobblestone!" She laughed. Eleni and Lily were spellbound.

"I loved it there. It was a magical world ... color, puppies, laughter ... Maria was so loving, oh, so loving. And not only to people, because she was always tending to a hurt animal, or two! It seemed that neighbors always were bringing an injured donkey, or a cow who couldn't milk to Maria for her to doctor, and somehow she always made them better. And the lost ones always found their way to her heart. When Vassili wasn't out fishing on the sea, he was there too, laughing, always laughing and singing and playing jokes on Kaiti and I! He was very kind to me. Maria's mother, she was always around, as Greek mothers often are, and it is she who taught me the finer arts of embroidery and weaving. Maria was good, but Melina was better."

"Popi. What happened? What happened to Maria? Why hasn't Vassili ever told us about her?" asked Eleni, still surprised that Vassili had never made any mention of this woman he had apparently loved so deeply.

"Maria became ill about five, six years ago ... a cancer, in her womb, they said. She went to Athens for tests and treatment, but it wasn't long before Vassili brought her back home, back to the place that she loved so much. She didn't linger, death was kind to her, but it wasn't to him. The man was devastated. His poor heart broke and it seemed that he then just shrunk away. Poof, the Vassili we had known was gone. I didn't see him much after that, but my father told me that he just gave up, he just didn't want to live without Maria. And then, well, he started to drink too much. I don't know what became of that beautiful world they created, the cottage. I walked by it a few times, but it was too sad to see it standing empty and lifeless and I haven't been back. I see dear Melina in the town, but to that sweet cottage, I've never been back."

Popi put the cat down on the stone and reached for a cushion to sit upon. As her arms flashed in the broken light Lily thought that even the paint smudges on her hands looked like a beautiful painting. She loved everything about Popi, and listened intently to her every word as she continued on.

"He lived on his boat and would talk to no one. Actually, I have heard from Nontas, his old fisherman friend that he simply didn't speak at all. Old Nontas said he sometimes heard Vassili moaning, crying in the dark of the night, on his boat like the wind. Grief, you know? And he wouldn't even speak to his own daughter, for some reason. I don't know why, but I think that because of all of that, Kaiti moved on. She went to America. We haven't seen her here since the summer of the year they put Maria into the ground. I have missed her. It was tragic, Eleni. All of it."

A modern Greek tragedy! Eleni glanced at Lily, who looked like a 6 year old girl, beguiled, deeply engrossed in the telling of a fairytale.

"A few years later, it seems that Vassili came around a bit. He bought his fishmarket, he stopped the heavy drinking ... oh, he still drinks, he is Greek, what can I say, but he does not disappear into the alcohol much anymore! Truly though, it hasn't been until this very summer that we've seen him laugh. I mean, really laughing. So, that is that! A sad story, but with a happy ending, so it seems, because our Vassili is now a happy man! Lipon, let us hope that this can give our little one a happier ending too!"

She leaned forward to fasten the band of green around Margarita's neck, and as she stroked the dog's head, she said, "There, now, little one, you go with Maria's blessings."

As her eyes moved slowly from her daughter to the dog, sitting together there on the rock, Eleni noted that Margarita had also undergone a change. She was healthy now, with a softly blooming coat, her ribs and hipbones no longer protruding from tight, thin skin. She held herself differently. No longer was she the slinking, wary stray they had first encountered here, in what now seemed lifetimes ago.   Rather, she looked as if she belonged.

Eleni sighed, anxious, knowing that soon they not only had to face leaving this beautiful place, but they also had to say goodbye to Minou and dear little Margarita, leaving them both to the Fates.

Pushing off from the rocks, careful to avoid the prickly, spiny urchins that clung to life there, she drifted again with her arms out as though about to embrace the moon.   She let her thoughts just ebb and flow, like the breath of the sea.

Eleni knew that she and her family would go home restored and replenished, ready to face life there with new vigor.   There were months' worth of photographs to process and pages of journal musings to sort out for the book she would be writing about the strays of Greece. Lily would carry potent memories and a bounty of life's lessons home with her — so much to reflect on, harvested from experiences provided by the whole of an island that had embraced her as one of it's own. Both had been deeply touched by the misfortunes of the animals. Seeing firsthand the power of action, they had promised one another to continue to work to help and care for the forgotten animals back at home in their own land.

That is the least we can do, Eleni thought as she watched Lily place an arm over Margarita's back and pull her closer. She looked over at Harry, her love, playing guitar as he stared unseeing out into the darkening night. *Or is he just feeling — seeing with different eyes?* She laughed as he mouthed the syllables and vowels he had found hiding in the notes and chords, but she knew that these silly sounds would magically transform, sometimes quickly in just minutes, sometimes over a period of weeks, eventually to reveal the marriage of melody and words in a newly formed song. This was how Harry's Muse worked her magic. He had written several new pieces and was eager to get home, eager to ease them into whatever shape they would take there, eager to get into the recording studio to commit them to perpetuity, gifts from the Muse to the mortal world. His anticipation pulled at him, so he would be the one to drag his reluctant family along through their last few days on the island, and onward to their return home.

The island, it's vivid heart, the people, the animals, the water, everything would remain close as they all clung as best they could to the peace and calm it had so freely offered them. And with as much certainty as they could possess, they knew that they would return.

But Margarita and Minou ... they face a less certain future.

With that, Eleni expelled all of her air and quickly forced herself into the dark deeps, sinking down to where the notes didn't reach her and the moonlight was just a shadow on the surface above, and deeper still, until she was certain that lack of air would freeze the trail of her thoughts, right there — and then shot back up towards the heavens.

When dried and clothed, they all climbed back up the wooden stairs, and in the patches of moonlight along under the scented pines, Margarita followed Lily very closely, very quietly.

The only thing that was certain for Margarita, was that she had been through this before.

In the candlelit room that hovered so gracefully over the quiet sea, Eleni tucked her child in for a restful sleep and before leaving, knelt to face Margarita. She cupped the dog's small, brown head in her hands and whispered thanks into her ear, thanks for the great honor of knowing her, for being chosen by her and for giving them all the opportunity to care so much ...

So many little graces.

She pressed her forehead to the dog's. *We'll find you, Margarita.* She gently kissed the top of her head. Margarita's eyes were shut tight, she was deep inside herself, focused intently, listening, feeling. But she opened them to hold Eleni in a long, steady gaze before settling back down into the comfort of Lily's chest. Minou, curled by the dog's heart, erupted in a cascade of purrs.

A quick shower rinsed the salts away, and Eleni stood out on the balcony braiding her hair, time to linger on the full moon Goddess dancing on the water. So beautiful. So quiet.

She took in a deep breath, drawing nourishment from the silence, and with a deep sigh, stepped back into the shadows, slipped into the bed next to Harry and fell, into a dreamless sleep.

the belonging

Instead of asking to go out into the day Margarita had jumped up to linger awhile next to Harry and Eleni and was still snoring, curled against the warmth of the woman's stomach. Lily sat next to her, patiently, holding Minou in her arms. The kitten lay on her back, absolutely relaxed, four legs pointing straight up in the air, still purring furiously.

With her mother's first stirring, Lily took in a great breath and leapt up with the kitten still belly up in her arms.

"Mama, I know what we'll do with Minou! It's perfect! Let's take her down to Vassili! He needs a friend, and he would take very good care of her. Wouldn't he? She would be safe on the boat ... well, as long as she didn't jump off ... she wouldn't, would she? And no one would bother a cat that was Vassili's. Would they?" Harry, feigning sleep, tried to keep the bed from shaking with his laughter. "I think they would be perfect together! PURRrrfect! Wouldn't they?" She stopped to catch her breath and scratch the kitten's belly and stared steadily at her mother. "Well ... what do you think?"

Eleni rubbed the sleep from her eyes and met Lily's eager gaze in drowsy wonder at the girl's ever-boundless capacity for hope.

They all enjoyed a leisurely last family breakfast on their rooftop oasis, committing to memory every detail in the priceless view of the sea and her islands before Lily and Eleni wandered one more time to Takis' store on the hill. They intended to buy all of the dog and cat food they could afford with their dwindling cache of drachmae.

The shopkeep was sorry to hear that they were leaving for home.

"Already? Oh, I will miss you Kiria, and you Miss Lily. And what of your cats, your dogs? Surely you are not buying this food because you are taking them all home with you?"

As he bagged up far more food than they had paid for, Eleni explained that Popi would watch out for Margarita while Arianna, the owner of a villa along the cliffs where Lily fed her little herds of foundlings, had offered to take on the cats.

Takis nodded, smiling, "Well, good then. None of them will go hungry. I will keep an eye out for the little dog as well, but I do think that she must have some sort of divine protection ... she really needs little help from any of us mere humans." He turned to Lily and with a wink, continued, "And you, my friend, you keep working hard on your language skills! And when you come back to our land, you can work for me here in my store since you will know well all that I have taught you!"

He held out his hands to them both. "My regards to Harry, please. Kalo taxidee, have a good trip, and God willing, we shall meet again."

"Bye, Mr. Takis! Thank you for loving the animals!" Lily called to the kindly man as she and Eleni waved and turned down the alley towards the village, off to deliver the bags and cans of food to Popi and Arianna, and to say some sad goodbyes.

And as Lily cuddled her cats and whispered sweet, secret blessings over each one of them, she tried not to cry, but the tears still found their way.

"Cry, cry, cry." Eleni said to her daughter as she kissed her forehead and stroked Mo, the sinewy gray tabby sprawled in the girl's arms. He stretched, one long leg up, gently touching the girl's face with the tips of his toes.

"Learn now to let it out, to cry ... out of respect for, and in honesty with yourself, my sweet. Never hold it in, Lily. I think that if we hold our sorrows in, then surely, by the time we are old women we are all filled up with sadness and regret. It's good to cry, Lily."

To feel her daughter's sadness was pure torture. There was no way to make it go away and it was certainly nothing a band-aid or a mother's kisses could make all better, so Eleni just sat close, trying not to show her own misery while Lily grieved. But when the tears were dry the girl set Mo back down on the wall and walked the row of happy cats, scratching chins and stroking heads just one more time, turned to her mother with a little bit of a smile, and they moved on.

Their first delivery was to Arianna.

Arianna offered rooms to rent in an old villa, the lumbering giant that stood over the sea on one side and the overgrown lot, home to one of Lily's feline families, on the other. She not only had agreed to look after the cats there, she offered to set kibble out from time to time along her walk into the village for all of the other strays in the neighborhood. This was a happy turn, for it was very obvious just six weeks earlier that Arianna didn't think kindly of any of the hungry cats. Like many on the island, she had seen them only as a nuisance as they pestered the patrons of her establishment for handouts, always hungry and hovering at a distance, staring.

Their silent desperation had made her shiver.

When Lily first began to feed the cats there, Arianna watched from the shadows of her terraced gardens. She was mystified, unable to understand why the child would bother with the cats, and was not at all pleased when she realized that the child was actually encouraging them to stay, with her offers of food and comfort.

"Oh! No, no! Ohi!"

She made many vain attempts, with crossed arms and sour stares, gruff "tsk tsk tsk's" and "po po po's", to scare the girl off. Even the occasional stomp, with a flourish of waving arms, elicited only a sideways glance and wary smile from Lily.

To Lily, this was nothing. Arianna's attempts paled next to the screeching fury of the broom wielding old woman who had been her very cold initiation to the world of the animals' adversaries.

But Arianna watched, and in time grew fond of the red-haired girl and her antics as she noted the horrible, hungry cats blossoming with her attentions. They started looking healthy and bright. She watched them emerge from the thicket by the pile of rock and brick at the first sound of the Lily's happy voice, rub on her legs and stand on hind paws to reach up and gently tap her if she wasn't paying them enough attention. Arianna could hear their happy purrs, even from a distance. Eventually taken by her own curiosity, she was drawn closer, and then closer still, and when she finally found herself standing next to the girl she was astonished to find an obvious intelligence in the cats' soft eyes and regal, independent bearing.

Arianna let Lily take her hand and lay it upon Mo's soft back.

Lily could feel the woman's anxiety, tangible, almost electric — the almost imperceptible shiver of apprehension — and also felt her relax as soon as the cat turned, his open, kind eyes bathing her in obvious gratitude, responding with his gentlemanly "meow-meow".

That was all it took.

Arianna's fears melted away, she was taken by the little beasts and from the magical perspective only someone still close to childhood could have, Lily went on to teach her all about the nature of cats.

Eventually, Arianna promised her that they would be cared for through the winter.

Their next stop was Popi's cottage, deep in the heart of the village.

Popi loved all of the little foundlings that her new friends had introduced her to, and by now had won over even the most skeptical amongst them. While she and Theo always had cared for several cats, now in the mornings her stoop resembled a soup kitchen, a gathering of countless of the furred homeless and cast offs of the village, all eager for their morning meal. The gentle artist had declared her allegiance to the dogs as well and assured her friends that she would leave food and water out for Margarita and any other strays in need.

With their task accomplished, Lily and Eleni took the long way home. A track that led from the north side of the sheltered bay, through the groves and fields above the back of the village, it led to the cemetery and from there it forked; one way led back towards the town, the other continued all the way to the westernmost point of the small island. An ancient path of cobbles, worn smooth through time, it was bordered on either side by short rock walls and fields turned golden by the autumn now enveloping the land. A route once used to move the goat herds from one feeding ground to another, in the years before the main roads were constructed the folk would also travel it, on foot or aboard surefooted donkeys, to get from the town to the far end of the island.

Winding through the olive groves that clung to the side of the hill, the path blessed Eleni and Lily with an expansive view of the silvery sea and the neighboring islands, the fishing boats, and the ferries' comings and goings.

Margarita, with the great joy only a dog can possess, bounded around them in circles, around and around and then ahead, scooting and leaping, crooning in her strained, airy voice all the while. She stopped occasionally to sniff, scenting deeply and carefully, her long, deep in-breaths punctuated by staccato snuffles, perhaps to better read messages left here and there by other four-footed travelers — and after adding her own notes to the mix, would double back to check on her two charges. Eleni and Lily chatted with Margarita and sang silly songs, stopping only to identify various herbs and the early autumn flowers and when they passed through a herd of curious nanny goats whose bells tinkled and chimed as they turned to follow along close behind, the nibbles and bleats and tickles caused Lily bubble over with laughter.

Oh, I've missed that laughter. Eleni turned to her daughter with a smile.

Lily pointed to a large kalivi sitting above them on the hill amidst a vast, overgrown garden, a place that looked as though it may have once been loved and lived in, but now sat derelict. They had never really taken much notice of it before. But now, wondering ... *Vassili's cottage?...* Eleni imagined children running and playing, a great tide of laughter spilling down the hillside with the tinkle of goats' bells.

"Nya, nya ... nya, nya ..." A monotonous growling met them where they closed in on the main path that would take them back to the village. "Nya, nya ..." Lilly laughed as she collected up flowers, a parting gift for Haroula. "Ma, I bet it's Mr. Vegetables and Rosa!"

It was the distinctive patter of clip clops accompanying the strange groanings that gave them away, and sure enough, in just moments from around the bend trotted the vegetable man, sitting sideways upon his donkey, Rosa — her wooden saddle minus its customary load of the late summer's fresh herbs and vegetables, for it had been a prosperous day in the village. He rode towards them, "nya, nya, nya", grunting nasally to the very assured looking little gray ass as he tapped her on the shoulder with a stick, the look on the man's face one of knowing that the creature was far more in control than he. But as he was whooshed past, his face brightened and he raised his stick and called out a toothless "Kalimera sas!" to the two, recognized from his rounds of the neighborhood in the village. But there was no stopping Rosa.

Lily stopped her gathering to watch the old man ride away.

"I can't believe we have to leave already." she whined to her mother who was still watching the donkey tap dance into the distance. Crouching, she clucked and Margarita ran to huddle close between her knees.

"Home seems like a movie, or a book to me now, so far away, or maybe not even real! This feels like home. If I didn't miss our pet furries so much, I think I would want to just stay here ... with Popi, or Vassili ... and Margarita. Our friends at home would just have to come here to see us."

"Yes. I know ... there's just too much to leave behind. It's very hard to go. But we do have a lot to look forward to, Lily. And we will be coming back. We will." Eleni responded, almost as though trying to convince herself.

At the cemetery gate they left the goat trail for the narrow alleys where whitewashed walls enclosing the quaint townhouses were heavy now with the last of the season's jasmine. Stopping often to take in the scent, eyes closed and inhaling deeply, both willed the heady, intoxicating aroma to embed itself in their memory. They walked on, past wooden doorways painted the varying deep blues of the sea, bordered by the deep greens and bright reds and purples of richly blossoming bougainvillea creeping up and over, and windows veiled in tatted lace, down hidden, spiraling stone steps and right through the backstreet tavernas that sprawled across sidewalks and spilled into the street, where waiters were setting up their tables in anticipation of the afternoon's business.

The enchanted way eventually deposited them at waterside, where Margarita gave a great sigh — moving through the maze of inland tavernas still held memories that were not comfortable for her. She sat on the quay to sniff the familiar salt air and scratch and preen in her ease before leaping up and off, with Lily dancing along in pursuit. They ran ahead like two pups in play, pausing only at Kostas' taverna where Margarita lay down before a bowl of water and lapped her fill. Eleni, strolling lazily behind her daughter and the little dog, could hear Mana's rich, resonant laughter rumble over the din of the harbor.

"Ahhh ha ha ha, yia sou little Margarita! Lily, kardia mou!"

Mana had recently taken to leaving the big bowl of fresh water out for the strays, something that did not go unnoticed by Eleni, who had watched in amusement as Mana and Kostas argued over this new challenge for several days. Kostas would remove the bowl with great fanfare and pointed gesture with his thick, soft hands, making certain that everyone in the taverna bore witness to the drama of the dumping of the water — and then, Mana immediately replaced it, full of course, in her motherly, dictatorial tone. Finally on day three, tired of the game and towering menacingly over her short, round son with hands on her heavy hips, her substantial bosom bouncing up and down in rhythm with her booming voice, Mana won out. The bowl for the dogs would stay and now it sat, ever full.

By the time Eleni reached the taverna to pluck her daughter from the matron's embrace, Margarita had completely drained the water bowl and sat with drooping, dripping tongue and nose to the sky in eye-squinted pleasure as she scratched lazily under an armpit.

There, in a taverna … in comfort.

"She's a good skeelaki!" Mana said proudly. "You see, Kosta, the good little dog?" Eleni had to pull out her camera and get this moment on film, big Mana smiling, standing with a towel draped over one shoulder and a hand on her hip on one side of the bowl, little Margarita sprawled smug and sure on the other.

Here was change, in real time.

Fully quenched and with all itches scratched, the dog skipped ahead again with Lily, past the long line of colorful wooden boats and up the marble steps that led away from harbor life and into the fluttery, laundry-lined and children's laughter-filled world of the neighborhood, until finally at the pensione she stopped, drippy tongue lolling through her crooked smile, and stood on her hinds, resting her tiny white forepaws upon the black metal of the gate.

"Oh Ma, look, she thinks she's home." was all Lily quietly said as she pushed it open, and the little stray ran up the stairs, her nails clattering as she scrambled on the marble.

Harry had finished with his writing and stepped out of the shower just as the three came into the room. The old guitar sat in a ray of sun by the open balcony doors, caressed by diaphanous curtains riffling in the afternoon's breeze, and Harry's easy smile whispered to Eleni that he and the guitar had again together found success. She loved it when he found his Muse — or his Muse found him.

Toweling off his overgrown mass of curling hair, Harry turned to Lily.

"Hey Lil. I talked to Vassili today. You know, about your little 'plan' for Minou?"

"Oh? ... Papa! Papa! And?"

"Well ... our captain is waiting now aboard his boat for her arrival."

"My HAIR-ry Hairy, thank you, thank you! Woo hoo! Mama!" The girl squealed as she leaped and danced through the room, shaking and shimmying in her relief. Eleni smiled.

"Oh my gosh! Harry! That's incredible! Good job, darlin! You too, Lily! Now there's one less kitten left to the streets ... one you've saved!

Throwing happy arms around her fathers neck, Lily planted loud, wet kisses on the softness of his freshly shaven cheek.

"Was he happy? Papa, do you think it'll work?"

Harry had spent a good bit of the morning helping Vassili create an order of his nets, and alerted him then to Lily's wild hopes. He had thought it kindest to give their friend the opportunity to think on it all for a few hours. He didn't want to risk Vassili feeling put upon or that he must politely accept the kitten just for the sake of the bright eyed girl, springing the idea to him on the spot.

But Vassili was honestly touched that Lily would think him worthy of being the guardian of the special little cat.

"Oh yes, it will work." He pulled on a shirt and reached for his daughter, madly tousling her hair. "He's excited, actually. It has been awhile now since he's had any live-in company on the boat! So ... let's not keep him, get your bag, let's go!"

Eleni settled Minou atop a parcel of what was left of the cat food wrapped in a comfy sweater in Lily's canvas tote, and by the time they all set off for the quay the kitten was already napping, nestled comfortably with only a pair of paws pointing up, toepads tipped together as if in prayer, a resounding purr and the tips of her huge ears giving away her whereabouts.

Vassili was indeed waiting and greeted them with his usual wide armed élan.

"Oh! Po po po!" He reached into the bag to tickle the soft white of the sleeping kitten's belly. Minou's humming intensified with the fisherman's surprisingly tender touch. He looked up at Lily and laughed. "What do they say, she is 'sawing logs'? Listen to her, she is so loud, I will lose my beauty sleep! Nontas, he will make me move Hestia away, to deeper waters!"

When they were all standing upon Hestia's deck, he took the kitten from Lily, gave her a kiss on the nose, tucked her under one arm and then with a great groan he bent over, reached down and wrestled for awhile with something unseen. Finally he pulled a well-worn nest made of matted wool and fabric out from under one of the boat's elegantly curved benches.

"A ha!" He held it up to show them all before setting it carefully upon the bow. "Now, this? This, it was made many years ago, by a beautiful person, a woman who loved the animals of this land as much as you do, my little Kokinoula. But! It has not provided comfort to any needy creature for a long, long time - because why? Because Vassili, he has been a stupid old man with a very shrunken heart." He accented "stupid", slapping his head with the butt of his palm, and then shrugged and stroked the kitten gently.

"But now, the ghataki, the little kitten, she changes all of that, thanks to you. And, once again, this old bed, it will be of good use ... yes ... and I will carry on with the approval of it's maker!" he said, pointing towards the cloud washed sky.

Lily looked over to her mother who gave a slight nod. They both were thinking ... *Maria.*

With the pliant kitten snuggled in the crook of one arm Vassili reached out to shake Lily's hand, crouching down to look her in the eye.

228

"I, Vassilis Tsikakis, I am honored, my little one. I will take good care of your Minou, and you will not worry."

There is nothing Vassili could say that Lily would not believe, for despite her most recent introductions to the coarseness of the world, she still trusted in goodness with the whole of her heart. When the fisherman straightened, she took the kitten from him and placed her in the ragged nest that Maria had made so long ago. Smiling back at her friend, she whispered, "I know. Thank you."

Vassili winked at her in return. "That little dog, too. I will watch out for her. If she was not such a free spirit, Koukla, I could take her too. But no, this whole town, it is her home. She will be OK. Endaxi!" He spread his arms and boomed "Tha sas doume meta! We will see you later!" as Lily turned quickly to her family, and to Margarita. Then they were off, up to the top of the sixty steps at the end of the quay to meet Yiannis, who had earlier sent word that he had finished making Margarita's nametag.

The coppersmith brought the metal tag out from the cavernous depths of his shop. It glittered in the sun as Lily held it up, and they all inspected the words the craftsman had inscribed on its rather large surface ... in Greek on one side:

ΜΑΡΓΑΡΙΤΑ
Ανηκω σε ολους
Σε παρακαλω, προσεξτε

and in English on the other ...

MARGARITA
I belong to everyone
Please, care for me

"This is really nice." A very stoic Lily handed the talisman back to Yiannis who fastened it tightly to Margarita's new collar. They all stood back to admire the little dog, making quite a fuss and telling her how beautiful she looked as she sat facing them, the big, sparkling medal of belonging now hanging from her neck. She sat quietly, looking from one face to the next, from one heart, to the next until, with a goofy, lip lifted grin turned suddenly and scampered away, disappearing down the narrow lane, the tinkling of her tag echoing off the hard stone walls.

It was the first time in a week she had left their sides.

redemption

There was a stirring from within the red boat there between the whites and the greens, and from its small wheelhouse Vassili stepped into the morning. The sun peered sleepily over the hill, and through a salt air lens cast the colors of its new light upon the calm waters of the harbor.

He stooped through the short doorway, stood a moment then groaned as he slowly stretched, holding his back with his hands. Stepping over tangled piles of red netting to the table by the bench that ran the graceful curves of the caique's hull, Vassili sat ... he caressed a cigarette rescued from the pack of Gauloises left crumpled beside the full ashtray, and lit it, took a deep, satisfying drag, and regarding the two empty bottles of ouzo he vaguely recalled being full sometime last evening, smiled sheepishly and shook his head. A haunted melody, the one that probably had danced alongside the ouzo, escaped with his exhale as he pulled the heavy black cap from his head and ran thick, calloused fingers through his graying, morning hair. Squinting into the warming sun, the man searched the quay for signs of life.

Walking back into the wheelhouse he mumbled sweetness to the kitten curled up on his blankets there. He'd awakened to find that she had forsaken the old, tattered nest for the warmth just under his chin.

Vassili sighed deeply as he poured kibble and topped up the water bowl.

"Ah, Maria, matia mou, can you see me now?" he asked of the unseen presence that still always hovered so close to his heart.

As he headed back into the still light of the dawn he closed the wheelhouse door behind him, locking the kitten in for safety.

"Not for long, little Minou. Your captain will soon be back."

Drifting over the water now, the warm aroma of freshly baked bread reached the boat. The harbor was awakening. With a smoke dangling precariously from his lips, Vassili grabbed the heavy rope, the umbilical link that kept he and his boat tethered to life, and pulled himself closer to his first thick, sweet cup of morning coffee.

He needed to find Eleni.

Their last full day on the island was upon them and they were already glassy-eyed from the attempts at solving the packing puzzle, the 'hows' of filling very small bags with the large heaps of stuff that lay scattered on the beds beside them. Besides clothing and other practical bits and pieces, now there were also the collections of beautiful round rocks and seashells, and colorful pottery made from local soil and thrown by local hands; collars for their own dogs at home, made by Popi of course; and cassettes of the passionate and haunting Greek music they

232

had grown so fond of; bits of local art, the weavings and tablecloths and of course, bottles of tsipouro and special ouzo, which would always aid Harry and Eleni in instant recall should the scent and feel of this land ever stray too far. It all had to fit. One by one, each conquered their own puzzle and it wasn't long before there wasn't a thing left on the beds and three bags all sat neatly by the wall in waiting.

Eleni kissed Harry and Lily and made her way to the harbor to take some last pictures of the water.

She sat on the edge of the quay, legs dangling and toes just inches from the silken sea. Her hair, windblown and wild, kept finding its way in front of her lens and she brushed it away, annoyed. The light would change soon – – at this time of morning, its dance on the gentle swells turned the water yet another magical hue, yet another otherworldly blue she wouldn't be able to convince anyone of were there not pictures as proof. She had to capture it before it melted back to the ordinary and into just another beautiful blue.

"Eleni! Eleni mou!" The urgent call echoed down the long, colorful row of boats moored there at water's edge.

Not now, please Vassili!

She turned, brushing the errant hair again from her face, and squinted. He was coming quickly, but without the usual dance in his step.

The fisherman crouched in front of her now, his eyes heavy with the weight of something troubling. "Ah, Eleni, darling. May I take your time? Please. There is something that I must tell you. My heart, it is weeping and I must heal these sorrows."

Worried now, Eleni focused her attention on the deep blue of his eyes.

"You know I always have time for you! Are you all right, Vassili? Please ... what is it?" She set the camera down, and reached her hand out to her anxious friend.

He sat. "I do not know ... how to start."

There was silence but for the rhythmic clanging of the mast lines.

Vassili sat staring at the ground, as though somewhere there he would find the words he needed. He looked back up, pressing his palms together, stretching the morning from his stiff joints and then tossed his cigarette into the butt can sitting by the mooring. He gazed steadily at Eleni as he lit another.

"Do you remember, the story I told ... of the little puppy Margarita, Eleni? Just a new little baby puppy, rescued from the man who was caught throwing her to the sea?"

"Yes, Vassili. Of course I remember."

"Well, I must tell you now, the truth about that sad and pitiless man." He paused, shaking his head, a heavy scorn written into the lines in his brow.

Eleni smiled, uneasy now, took a deep breath as she settled into this unlikely confessional, and waited for Vassili to continue.

"I lost my wife, Eleni, my beautiful Maria, some years ago ... as many years ago as that dog has been alive. I have not told you, for I could not speak of it, myself. I was haunted, my heart, it was torn from my body and just now, I have found it again! Your Lily ... she is like my Maria. She is like my daughter, Kaiti. But, she is here, now, and she is so alive. How could I stay dead, myself, with so much life around me?"

"Vassili. I am so sorry. Are you sure you want to talk about this now?"

"Yes, I must! I must, Eleni. There was time when I did not, I spoke to no one. I could not. I was too angry, I was tortured, I wanted only to feel nothing at all. Too much of a coward to leave this life, to join my Maria, I drank myself dead within it, instead. No, no more being so stupid now, but the demons in the drink, sometimes they do still find me and I am tired of it. So weary. Finished! But now, yes, I must talk about this. Tora! I must. I am pulled back and forth, back and forth, from bitterness, from that sad man who maybe was not always so good ... to the beautiful happiness of my life now, to this Vassili, with a song in his heart and a dance in his feet. My heart, it is mostly peaceful. But I get pulled, from one life to the other! Sometimes, the drink, it helps to keep that stretching of my soul from hurting so badly, you know? But now, I am ready to step away, for good, from the dark, I must leave it behind me so I can find myself the light of a future. So, please forgive me my darling, but I must talk."

He lit yet another cigarette, and he left it to dance wildly between his lips as he paced in front of Eleni, gesturing as though conducting these matters of the heart with his hands as he continued.

"Maria, she had a way with the animals, Eleni. She could fix them! Yes, she could and she cared so much for them, she even taught me to open my hard old heart to them. When she died, I just went crazy. And the animals, they all were reminders of my Maria. Most, they went away to live with friends, the neighbors. But there was one, Gigi, Maria's favorite dog, still waiting there. Ah, you know, the kitten's little old bed? That was Gigi's bed, my Maria made it for her. So, Gigi, she was pregnant, you see.

235

And what did she do? She had her babies, after Maria's funeral, on the day that I would leave my beautiful house forever. I could not bear to stay there, where my life, my love, had been extinguished. Poof! But even gone from this life, Maria, she was everywhere around me there. Everywhere. But I could not hold her. It made me crazy. She was in Gigi, in those puppies. And what of them, where would they go? Who would care for them now? I lost my head, I lost my soul, I forgot everything my Maria had taught me, but what could I do? I took up the puppies and I carried them down to the sea. They were just one more reminder of my Maria that I could not bear. So I took them to the sea to drown them."

"Oh. Vassili."

'No, Eleni! I must tell you! But only you! Please, my little Lily, she must not know of this, not now! I can not bear for matakia mou, my little darling to see me as an evil man, just another one of those monsters she hates. Oh, Eleni." He moaned.

"No, she sees truth, as all children do. She knows you are good Vassili. She would never ..."

"Well, I hope to never know. I had no excuse for what I did to those little puppies. Oh, I could say that there no longer was a Maria to care for the animals, and so I was doing the puppies, and our island a favor, blah blah blah. But really, I was striking out in anger, trying to banish the reminders of all of the goodness that I once had — and all that I lost."

Vassili stopped pacing and crouched down in front of Eleni. Lowering his voice he spoke through his anguish, thin tears streaming down his tired, worn face.

"I was standing by the water, Eleni ... I was weeping, with those four puppies in my hands ... when I heard the voice of my Kaiti. What? What? I could not believe it! And what was she doing there, at that very moment? She had been swimming there, I suppose. I may never know how she came to be there, just then. Perhaps it was the angels. Or Maria herself. But I can tell you that I nearly died when I turned to see her standing there."

There was a stretch of a profound quiet before Vassili took up a gasping breath, as though he had just surfaced for air, and then went on with the purging of the sorrows he had held for so long.

"My Kaiti, she yelled at me. No, no, Baba! No, no, she said! Her cry, it cut me," he sliced at his arm with his free hand, "like a knife and I will never forget the pain. That cut may be the last time in many years that I felt anything, before I made myself go dead. My daughter, she tried to take all the pups from my hands and ended up with just one, and she ran away with it. The others, well, now you know what became of them. But that pup that was saved? Margarita."

He went quiet. *Oh* ... Eleni turned away and dangled her legs over the water again, unable to keep the trace of a sad smile from spreading across her lips. *How ironic is this?* She was feeling such deep love for this dear man, this man who had done the one thing that she despised most about some of the people of this land.

And redemption? It is perfect! All is, as it must be.

"You know, Eleni, I could not speak to my Kaiti. I spoke to no one after Maria died, not even Kaiti — but after this? I could not ever face her, I was so embarrassed." Vassili was quiet again, reaching deeply into that place now so full of feeling. Standing, he paced a bit, tossed what was left of his cigarette down onto the quay and stomped on it before turning back to Eleni. Sitting at her side, he continued in a strained hush.

"But of course, in her own sadness my daughter, she wanted to talk to me about her mother! That is all she wanted, and I could not. I would not, all I could think of was myself ... po po, a drunk man's pride ... And then, she finds me, killing her dead mother's puppies! Pride and pain, they both struck me dumb, I was blind, deaf, without speech! The stupid ass that I am, not only acting like a beast with the very things Maria loved so much, but then allowing the drink to take me over." He paused, looking as though he wanted to crawl into the concrete of the quay, into the ground, and disappear. "So, Kaiti, she stayed on our island for that long, sad summer — I think to heal from her mother's dying. You know, I saw her everywhere with that little dog, but we did not speak. It killed me to see her, it reminded me, always, of the fool that I was. And then, when the summer ended — she left me. Yes, I was such a fool, Eleni. I kept my child from being able to get close to her mother's memory, ah ... my little Kaiti."

He sobbed, his face hidden in his large, giving hands, his body shaking with the sorrow. When there were no more tears he looked at Eleni.

"I have seen her, Margarita, like a ghost, every year since then. A ghost, like me. Silent, sneaking in the shadows! We were both the pathetic sadness, all that remained of a tragedy. I watched her from a distance, barely surviving, and me, barely surviving. But now ... now, we both are alive again. Love! Yes, I think this. Love makes us real again, not ghosts. Ah, Eleni, the little dog, she comes to me now, she jumps onto Hestia and shares my meals, sometimes we even take naps together. How do you say that ... it is irony? I don't know if she remembers – – ah, my memory, it is enough for both of us. But, that dog? Not only through our friendship are you, Harry, I connected. Now we are connected through the dog as well! The dog, she found Lily! And you ... you brought Lily to me."

Vassili raised his arms to the brightening sky, his hands outstretched. He took a deep breath.

"Air, light ... life, i zoi. Ah Eleni, yes, my Maria she is everywhere, like she never died. What is she? She is goodness. She is ... everywhere. And you know? Now, it is OK. Endax!"

He heaved to his feet with a groan and nodded as he lit another smoke. He just stood there looking out past the row of boats toward the distant horizon. Quiet. And then he turned to Eleni, winked and spread his arms like wings, snapped his fingers and with his face to the sun, danced his way back down the quay towards Hestia.

Her laughing eyes damp, Eleni snapped pictures of her friend as he danced his way out of his old life and into his new.

go with good ...

      With Eleni off capturing the elusive colors and Harry sitting on the roof with his guitar, taking just one more moment with his Muse, Lily went in search of the village vendor whose old wooden cart overflowed with Greek herbs and nuts and sweets. She was hoping to buy some of his freshly roasted pistachios and several bars of sesame candy — they would be of comfort and consolation throughout the long flight home. He was a moveable feast, there was never any knowing where he might be located but today she found him stationed at a busy crossroads in the pedestrian-only part of town. She made her purchases wisely and when she had she tucked the treasures safely away into her pack, she turned to take in the familiar sight of the long main street one last time.

      There, not but a half of a block down the way was Margarita. Lily could see a glint, the nametag reflecting coppery sunlight as the little brown sprite trotted at the heels of Takis' wife and two small children. She started to call out ... but placed a hand tightly over her mouth instead, as though her voice might change Margarita's good fortune were it to escape. Lily watched the little parade fade into the sea of people coursing the street and then ran off as fast as she could, taking the winding steps two at a time into the neighborhood to tell her family this breaking news.

"Ah, well, maybe it's really not that Takis and his clan have decided to take care of Margarita, but that Margarita has decided to take care of Takis and his clan!" Harry said with a chuckle after Lily told of her sighting.

Eleni was on the bed counting their remaining drachmae. She looked up.

"Can you remember, how scared and sad she was when you first met her, Lil? And how thin? Your love and caring really are the magic potion, you know. She is so different now, a changed little dog. And really, I think that there are a lot of people here who are starting to feel a little differently about the animals now, leaving food out for the cats. And look at Mana, leaving a water bowl out for the dogs! By just being true to yourself, by showing your kind heart, Lily, you've made a difference."

"I'm going to miss her so much. I just can't believe we have to leave her here."

"I know, darlin'. I know. But at least you've seen with your own eyes that she has other people she can trust now, someone to care for her. Takis and his Eleni will see to it. As will our captain. Vassili will keep an eye on her."

Eleni handed the colorful foreign bills to Harry. It was time to settle up rent with Haroula and then walk to the sea ... a bittersweet but delicious linger over a last sunset awaited them there. She emptied the tiny, tired refrigerator of its store of food and they set off.

"This is for you, Kiria Haroula." The bouquet that Lily handed to her, the wildflowers picked from the late season's hillsides, sent their treasured landlady all aflutter; she threw up her hands and broke into a singsong chatter that defied them any translation. Eleni and Harry presented her the rent money and a bottle of a fine brandy, perfect for the cold winters' nights that lay ahead and when the hugs went round, Eleni mustered the best Greek she could to tell Haroula that they would be returning to this home away from home.

"Oh, agapi mou! Neh, neh, prota o Deos.", Haroula managed through her dramatic snifflings. My love, yes, yes, God willing. She clutched them each one by one to her breast, depositing loud kisses, both cheeks, and waved them on until they disappeared down the path that led towards the sea.

Popi waited for them on the beach, almost empty now, adorned only here and there by prone figures. The afternoon was as perfect as it could be, with a searing, early autumn's warmth cutting through the vivid Greek light, the water, gentle and luxurious under a cloudless, deep blue sky. There was no more brilliant way to say goodbye to this place they loved so well.

The sun made its slow, final slide into the sea, a ball of red through a palette of bright orange haze streaked with hues of green and purple. Eleni was quick to photograph the harlequin waters, still as a mirror, and remarked that it seemed the sunsets there lent one the eye and the feel for the sky that an impressionist painter might have.

"They see magenta skies with clouds of purple and green, with splatters of orange and pink! Who else sees the sky lit up like that? No one! If you do ... unless you are a

Monet or a Munch, Renoir or a McSwane ... you'd have to be sitting here, looking at this very sky! It's no wonder that artists flock here to paint."

Popi turned to Eleni and remarked that never before had she noticed so many colors in just one sunset. "This? It's a gift, just for you my friends. Our island knows that you are leaving her."

As the colors faded off they wandered down the beach, drawn now by the vibrant hues of the brightly painted taverna that sat upon the sand. Ducking under the gruesome, dangling tentacles of squid left hanging to season from the wooden beams, they found a table with an unobstructed view of the water. The owner was happy to have patrons on such a quiet afternoon and offered up a few generous plates of the fresh calamari, perfectly cooked and seasoned and smothered in lemon, and it was savored as though it might be the last supper itself.

Eleni ventured into the sea, followed by Lily and then Popi, all carrying bits of bread for the 'begging fish'. The small minnows that could sense a treat coming from fathoms deep descended quickly like a flock of tiny sharks, swimming through legs, gathering all around in a ravenous assembly. Up to her waist in the water, Popi bounced from foot to foot as the fish tickled her thighs, hands up by her ears framing an anxious smile. Lily laughed out through her friend's squealing,

"Popi! Be STILL, shush you'll scare them! Stop, you have to see this! Stop it, Popi!" And then, as though on cue each little fish sat up on end, like a dog sitting to beg, thrusting tiny heads up and out of the water an inch or so, stopping Popi's fuss and prompting gales of laughter from them all. Fifty, seventy-five, one hundred little heads were stuck up into the air, with bug-eyes wide and little mouths agape in perfect little o's.

"See, see! The begging fish!" Lily flung a handful of bread and the festivities began, water churning and bubbling as fish writhed around and over one another in the quest for their grail.

Filled with sea and sun and laughter, it was a lovely day's end, the perfect bookend to a journey through four months of stories, peace and beauty, the bits of sadness and frustration twining through like the fish, begging for attention. The only one missing from these beautiful last moments was their little friend, Margarita.

"Lily. Now. We have to go."

The sun was barely up when Eleni, Harry and a very sullen Lily filed solemnly through the iron gate, into alleys still damp with the cool night's final kiss. Margarita had come back to spend the night on Lily's bed and sang sweetly now as she scampered at their sides. Knowing what was to come, they all found her joy torturous.

Eleni had her camera out and was making a last chronicle of the light, shooting photos as they moved quietly through the still sleeping neighborhood. When they passed Selene's small, familiar house — where they would see old widow standing in the evenings with her eyes to the sea in search of her past — Margarita dashed down the steps and squeezed through the gate, partly off its hinges now and woven through with runaway vines. Eleni captured the dog in silhouette, sitting alone now on the balcony, with the gold glow of the morning sparkling off the sea in front of her.

"A good way to keep her in our thoughts." she said, her voice hushed.

"I hope someone will love her for us." was all Lily had to say.

Nearing Hestia, they could see Minou sitting on the prow. It was apparent that all would be well for the kitten and Vassili, for Minou looked right at home after just a few days on the red boat. Lily ran with her bags, noisily and unsteadily like an overburdened donkey, towards Hestia to see the little cat.

"I had to climb up!" Vassili was animated, flapping his arms about. "To get her, I had to climb up the mast, Lily mou! She's crazy! Like a crazy little monkey, she went up the lines after a dove! All the way to the top! And then what did she do? Get down? No! Mew, mew ... she cried and she cried is what she did, and everyone was gathered here! So what is an old man to do? I had to go up and get her! Po po po ... I knew that you would be coming, Kokinoula, I could not leave her up there, to weep and to wail. All up and down the harbor, they would say "oh, what a mean man, that Vassilis Tsikakis!" Ha ha, oh yes, she is a crazy one, the little demon! She will drive <u>me</u> crazy!" He tickled Lily's cheek and laughed as he turned to help her parents board but Lily just stood there, looking twenty feet straight up the length of the mast, imagining little Minou at the very top hanging on for dear life with her front paws, the rest of her body fluttering like the flag in the morning's breeze.

"Ah, but Lily, I love her! Do not worry, I love her! She will make me crazy, yes, but she will do this old man's heart good! And, she will remind me of you."

Vassili was ready for them, waiting with fresh cups of thick coffee and sweet tea. He passed around a plate of feta and bread, and sang a mournful song of leaving, an island song he had learned from his father who always sang it as he set to sea. The time passed them by far too quickly though, they had hardly had a bite to eat or enjoyed the familiar comfort of the morning's conversation before Popi was there to see them to their boat, and they were all swept up in a whirlwind as they said their goodbyes.

Lily burst into tears.

"Oh, now - Minou and I will be here, on my Hestia, waiting for you to return, Koukla mou."

"But I don't want to GO." Lily wailed, as the sad little girl within her finally took back command from the confident young woman she was becoming. Harry picked up her bag as Eleni wrapped calming arms around her and, looking sadly from the shuddering girl to Vassili, kissed her fingers and laid them on their treasured friend's cheek.

"Efharitsto para poli, Vassili. Thank you so much, dear friend. We will see you soon."

"Prota o Deos, my darling."

"Yes, Vassili. God willing."

As they were walking with Popi the three travelers glanced back one last time to see him standing in front of his beloved red caique, kitten in the crook of one elbow and his other hand held up high.

"Me to kalo." he boomed. "Me to kalo ... with the goodness, my friends! Go, with good!"

They were not taking the slow boat back to Athens.

Eleni and Harry felt it best to leave it all behind as quickly as one could at the end of a journey so they were taking the hydrofoil, a bug-like hulk that raised up on skis and skimmed quickly across the water. It would get them to Athens in half the time the lovely old ferry would take, but now there were only moments to say goodbyes to Popi and Margarita — the boat was loading up as they stepped onto the dock.

The girls gave Popi hugs and kisses while Harry bent to stroke Margarita, nestling his face briefly in the soft fur of her neck. Eleni and Lily took turns taking up the little dog, holding her next to their hearts and pouring the warmth of their love all around her. Lily tearfully begged her to stay safe and Eleni whispered that they would love her, forever, they could never, ever forget her as she would live in their hearts.

"We will be back, someday. We will find you, Margarita. Dear little Margarita."

Both choking back a desperate sadness, they followed Harry onboard ... and then Margarita's mournful cry pierced the morning's still, a heart wrenching, blood chilling shrill that turned them to ice. They could see the little dog make a vain attempt to leap aboard after them but Popi caught her and crouched with her there, big tears filling her eyes as she held the frantic little dog back. Helpless, Lily had to turn away and cover her ears for fear her own heart might break right there, shatter in a million pieces of sadness if she looked for one more moment — and her mother held her close, for fear the girl herself might just leap back out after the little dog.

The metal door slammed shut.

They moved to the open back of the hydrofoil as it left port, from where they could see Margarita still struggling in Popi's arms, the both of them blessedly growing smaller and smaller as the boat pulled farther away from shore.

"Me to kalo, Margarita", Eleni whispered into her daughters' hair, the depth of her sorrow in its cold stillness deafening, drowning out the roar of the vessels' engines.

MARGARITA

margarita

Margarita could smell the snow in the wind that drove in fiercely from the south, and she could sense the hunger and fear, the coming days on the run. Already the gales had nearly taken her life. The old and crumbling wall she lay hidden behind finally lost its battle with the winds, exploding in pieces of tiles and chunks of cement. Her right paw was useless to her now, bleeding, hot, and the pain drove her on.

She had to seek safety but nowhere near the water was safe. Running through the usually peaceful harbor she had seen the boats, in splinters now, washing up and over the paralia by the storm driven sea, and had barely escaped.

The little dog shivered violently as she held the one paw out in front of her and tried to lick the pain away. With a long, anxious whine, she pointed her snout to the heavens and searched again in the scents on the wind. They were not there.

Since they left her, Margarita had held daily vigil while the boats came and went. She knew the times well and she watched from under shelter of an overturned rowboat ... waiting ... waiting ... but her people had not yet come.

Now all that met her at the ferry dock were churning waters and a frigid sky.

She sat bravely there in her pain and cold and fear when a great wave found her and threatened to take her to the sea. With a yelp she leaped quickly from its grasp, turned, and ran.

And ran. Up the hill and through the familiar alleys, past all of the places the comfort had lingered until their scent was gone and there was nothing left ... past the puppy tree ... she ran on and on into the hills, through the brutal winds, under fences that grabbed and clawed at her until they finally caught the green collar and held her fast, until she slipped free and ran on, leaving the talisman of belonging behind, swinging empty on the wire. She kept running until she fell exhausted under an abandoned car.

Several pairs of eyes stared at her from the sheltered depths there, other cats and dogs taking refuge from the winter's fury, all drawing closer for warmth and comfort as the wind roared and the cold rains came, pounding down upon their refuge like angry hands upon a metal drum.

In time, she slept.

And when she awoke to a gnawing hunger — and to pain, her paw hot and angry — she found the ground blanketed with white, a heavy snow falling all around. The sad little gathering drew in even closer, warming, waiting for the storm to break.

Eventually Margarita was driven to continue on, to that unknown place, that somewhere, something that existed away from fear and sadness and pain. She shook off a numbing inertia and digging and digging from under the car through the deepening snow, as best she could with one paw, she found herself at its surface. But there was nowhere to go. She sank back into snow far deeper than her short legs could possibly navigate.

The grounded cast offs continued to huddle in their timeless vacuum, silent, curled closely for warmth, life suspended in this dark, damp haven. For days and days they waited, until the day the crusted snow was hard and passable, and the sun had taken its rightful place in the icy sky.

They all were hungry, so hungry, scattering to the four directions in search of food. A keening escaped from deep within Margarita's wounded soul while she ran, running until she could run no more, her energy gone. She was finished with fighting and running, finished with searching and starving and pain and she found a friendly tree amidst a grove of many, a kind and sheltered place for a lasting sleep.

She collapsed there and thought of kind touch and relief from fear, and then, of nothing, as her eyes dimmed … and in sleep she was released.

19 MONTHS LATER
SPRING

myth

Eleni and Harry stood atop the highest mountain.

Before them lay the stretch of the island that catches the first of the morning, where the Aegean draped herself upon the shoreline like a translucent slip of silk, and through the soft light, tendrils of milky sea mists stretched to bridge the mélange of water and sky ... they seeped up, up, deep into the valleys. It all seemed a mirage, giving the appearance that the island had been cleaved into many smaller islets, hovering now in the thick air before them.

The winter had been kind to the island, the green late spring grasses waist high and awash with wildflowers brilliant as precious jewels, glittering and swaying in the cool breeze. Pungent, earthy, filled with moisture and light, the scent of wild herbs was all around them.

They were home again.

The overnight ferry from Brindisi, sitting on the heel of Italy's boot, to Patras, Greece was not the quickest way to reach their destination, but it was a beautiful trip and a gentle means to cast off the busy world. When not watching the grand panorama of the Ionian Sea and her lush islands, or playing cards over a beer or two, they each looked silently to the intrigue of whatever it was the ancient land held for them. There was plenty of time for shedding layers, the layers of intensity, impatience, busyness, all peeling off like layers of clothing, a symbolic shedding that in the end literally left them both down to naked skin and deposited on a sun swept beach.

From Patras, they continued on a ferry that traversed the Aegean, and they had arrived late in the night, the island greeting them sleepily and seductively, like old lovers lost, their anticipation and her familiar warmth, together eliciting a sharp degree of mystery.

On a brief tour, performing music in small clubs from London down through the Continent, Eleni and Harry had easily decided to steal away several more days with the intention of making a quick sweep of their Greek isle to find Margarita. Living with the limited funds that define the lives of many artists, they had not been able to make it back before now.

Lily had gone wild when first news of 'project Margarita' was leaked. She and Grandma Nona had been following the parents' progress from home on an old map upon which they had drawn lines through England and France, and a few criss-crossed lines in Spain — and now with the addition of the new mission, they appended a long trail through Italy and across the Ionian Sea. A big X marked Athens, with bold arrows pointing East, seaward, and once time had landed the parents on their Aegean isle, Lily and Nona would just finger that tiny spot on the map, wondering aloud what might be uncovered there. Always the optimist, Lily had even drawn a picture of Margarita sitting happily in the waters right next to that hallowed little spot in the sea just beyond Athens.

Vassili had stayed in touch with his American friends, his newsy letters and colorful postcards always assuring Lily that the kitten Minou was well, the Queen of the harbor who got exactly what she wanted; the personable cat was becoming a wee bit chubby due to having made slaves of the fishermen and their wives, all well trained now to bring her fish heads and soured milk and other feline delights.

He sent along pictures, proof of what magic a Greek winter can offer. The colorful boats all covered in snow was not the usual scene that elicited fantasies of weeks spent on an exotic Greek island, but it was a beautiful scene and a thoroughly enchanted Lily stole away the photos. There was one of old Nontas standing aboard his little caique in two feet of snow, shovel in hand and a grin on his wizened face, another of a vista of the usually colorful waterfront rendered monochrome by the wash of winter white, and one particularly precious shot of Minou peering out from a cave carved into snow piled aboard Hestia's deck. Lily placed them near her bed on a small table decorated tenderly with candles and pictures of Margarita, of her cat families and some of Popi, along with sprigs of dried island herbs and wildflowers and her collection of shells and round, white rocks. It was her little altar of hope and remembrance.

"There have been stirrings on the island!" Vassili had also written.

An earnest band of women, all foreigners, had come together in their concern for the stray dogs, with plans to build a sanctuary for them. One of the women was married to a Greek, the owner of property enough to accommodate a shelter that could grow in time, and with the help of various animal rescue organizations and generous donations, progress was well underway. Already, it housed rescues from the streets and had been the means for the homing of several of the strays to other countries.

This wondrous news had given some confidence that, were Margarita still alive, they surely would be able to find a way to bring her home.

But that was the last news they'd had from Vassili.

So now, up with the dawn, Eleni and Harry were eager to begin searching for their little brown friend. Inhaling the cool freshness in the mist, turned golden now by the sun's rising, they welcomed the new day and then headed back down the mountain into the village.

The locals seemed in good spirits, busy arranging tables and chairs, washing streets and whitewashing walks and walls in anticipation of Pascha, the Greek Orthodox Easter. With all of this also came the final preparations for the unfolding of the summer season, for when everything was well in order for that most cherished of all Greek Holy-days, the season could begin. Eleni and Harry would miss the rituals and feast of the celebration by just days, but already were talking of a trip back with Lily with the experience of Pascha in mind.

Passing through the town, greeted warmly by busy folk at every turn, they saw a few of their other old friends, familiar island dogs at work begging the tavernas, survivors still. But, they didn't see Margarita.

Over morning coffee aboard Hestia — wearing a fresh coat of paint now, a brilliant crimson with an eccentric trim of blues and greens — Vassili told them that he lost track of her sometime in the recent winter.

"A storm, a freak storm, it blew in late one night following a clear, blue day. What do they say, "out of the blue"? Yes, out of the blue, a big wind, from the south and indifferent to the shelter this little harbor provides. We were all caught in the surprise. The wind, it pushed huge waves over our quay, and it piled up many of the smaller boats into broken heaps, over there by the tavernas. Like old, forgotten toys."

He shook his head sadly.

"Yes," he said with a deep sigh, "some of my friends, they did not make it down here in time that night. And those that did, well, they almost lost their lives trying to save their boats. My Hestia, she remained safe only because I had taken her out of the water! In winter, I take the room, there, over the market. That is why Minou, she is so fat! She worked at the market with all of the other cats and ate fish heads all winter! You see, I take Hestia out of the water so she can rest, and I can get work done. A little here, a little there, fixing her engine, giving her new paint if she needs it. Thank the Gods, she was resting for the winter. But the fishermen? When weather permits, many of them, they must work. Those who do not take the winter off, or those who do not go to Norway to fish on the big boats, well, they must stay and work on the island. So their little boats, most of them were in the water, right here."

He stopped to boil more coffee and offer Eleni and Harry neat slices of spanikopita, fresh from the ovens of the harbor bakery and still warm to the touch.

"That storm, it blew off many tiles from the roofs, it ruined the road and pushed over huge trees. To go from one end of the island to the other? It was impossible, for many days. And then! Very soon after the big winds and waves, the island, it was covered in a deep freeze! The snow came, and a thick white shawl held the whole island in stillness for one frozen week."

258

Vassili reached out quickly and tapped Eleni with the back of his hand.

"Eleni, you should have seen Manolis, who likes to wear his little shorty shorts and his hairy feet bare, all winter long! Ha, ha, crazy little man! But, you know, he took all of those cats of his inside his house! Inside! Out of the cold snow, he kept them safe and warm by his wood fire!"

His laughter, echoing down the still morning-quiet quay hardly soothed the hollow, empty feeling Eleni had sensed spreading in her chest.

"Ah, yes, and when his time comes? Just for that I know that my Maria will be giving the crazy little man a personal escort on the golden pathway!"

Vassili assured his friends that, before the storm, he had always welcomed Margarita onto the Hestia for some conversation and a bite to eat whenever she happened through the harbor.

"Of course she is welcome. She is my comrade."

"But how did she look, Vassili? Was she healthy? Did she still wear the collar?" Eleni asked, quietly.

"She looked good, our little brown friend. Not thin like the poor beggars you see now over there by Kosta's place, Eleni. The collar, yes, I remember seeing that tag hanging from her neck, shining like a diamond, like sun on the water.

And sometimes, in the town I would even see her following Takis Koutsinakis, or his wife Eleni and their cute little kids. And Popi too, maybe once or twice. But after the big storm? I never saw the little Margarita again after that. Eleni, darling ... I am sorry."

Eleni sighed, lips tensely pursed. *Of course. What in the world are we doing here? We shouldn't have bothered, we should have just gone home instead.*

"Vassili. Will you give me one, please? One of your cigarettes? Now would be a good time for a smoke." She had never been a big smoker. She had quit long ago but there still were moments when the simple ritual itself, the lighting, the tipping of the building ash, the breathing in of alien atmosphere and the searching for illumination though rising tendrils of diaphanous white, all seemed to clear the debris in her head and give her thoughts focus and an open place to land. ... *ah, screw the born again non-smokers!* She needed a relief, something to still her dismay.

Vassili feigned shock, but handed her one of his strong French cigarettes and patted her hand. Harry locked eyes with her over the scattered landscape of coffee cups, oilcans and ashtrays. He could sense her starting to flounder.

"Let's just start looking." he said.

She turned back to the captain.

"Vassili. You didn't tell us! Why didn't you tell us?"

"My darling, I did not have the heart to tell you before, " said Vassili, shrugging as he pushed an ashtray under the long ash drooping from her still fingers, "you know I have no wishes to cause my Lily any heartache! And what could you do from America? Nothing, but to worry!"

"I know, you're right, Vassili. Thank you. I guess we just need to get on with it now. See what we can find." *What did we expect?* Taking one more shallow puff before stubbing the cigarette out, she looked up, over the calm spring sea, the subtle contours constantly changing - *oh, how stupid to think a street dog would still be alive here after so much time has passed.* "Shall we, Harry?"

"Wait, wait I have to tell you this, Eleni. There is something that happened, before the big storm. This, it is very important. You see, before the storm, there was a little girl ... she was playing too close to the sea and she almost drowned. How do I know this? It was in the winter, but there were some tourists here on the island, they were in the cemetery that day, and they told this story to the police. The cemetery, it is up above the rocky beach, you know ... that beach where people, they sometimes go to collect the ahkinos from the rocks, the urchins, for good eating. This little girl, she was there that day, there were waves and she must have slipped into them. She fell in there where it is deep water. Those people, they heard someone yelling and looked over the wall to the sea below and saw a child struggling in the cold water. They were high above, there is no fast way down that cliff to the sea. They were afraid the girl, she would drown. But then, what did they see? A dog. A little brown dog, it ran over the rocks and into the water, it swam out there to that girl and it took her into its little mouth and pulled her to the land! It saved that child! Those people, they yelled and yelled to anyone they could see and then, they ran down to the beach. They found the child, wet and very cold, but she was alive. But the brown dog, it was gone."

"Margarita?" *Oh my god ...*

"Yes, it is thought that the hero is that loud, ugly little dog of yours. She changed many minds that day, I think — when the story, it was told by those tourists, no one could believe it but the little girl, when she was in her mother's arms, she also said it, yes. That a little dog pulled her out of the water. A little dog, with a green collar around its neck. She thought the beast was going to eat her! Ha ha! But no, that little beast was her little tiny angel! So the people, they spread the story and it has become a Myth. Yes, a myth of sorts, because no one ever found this dog! The big storm, it came, and we have not seen Margarita since then. This, you needed to know, Eleni mou. The little dog, she is missing, she might be gone — but what she did that one day maybe changed many, many years of many people's thinking. The dogs, they are not so worthless now. This, you must know. I could not tell you before, but I tell you now."

They found Takis at his shop, singing cheerily as he tidied his storefront, sweeping the cobbled walkway around the freshly painted oil urns filled with huge, newly budding rose geraniums.

"Yia sas! My friends, it is so good to see you again! Welcome!"

The gracious man invited them to sit and then disappeared into his store, returning with a tray piled with pastries and cookies, and small shots of ouzo and coffee to wash it all down with. When they'd all settled around his table in the morning sun and had caught up on news, he told them what he knew about Margarita.

"The little dog was always welcomed by my family, of course! But as you know, she is a free spirit and moves about as she pleases. She came and went, like the wind."

"She looked good, Takis? Not thin and hungry?"

"Yes. Good. I knew that others here must have been watching out for her, she looked well fed. But the big storm, the snow ... they were hard on everyone, on everything. Do you see my flowers there? Twenty five years old, they have survived many cold winters, through my father's care, and now mine. But if I had not covered them carefully, they would not have made it through the long freeze. So it must have been very hard on the animals. She's a good, smart dog, my friends. There are stories now about her now ..."

"Yes, we heard, Takis. Saint Margarita!"

"Ha ha ha! Ah, yes! Well, I hope that you do find her, for her own good ... and for your sweet Lily's."

With the arrival of a boisterous gang, the old men of the mornings making their rounds for coffee and a measured dose of politics, Eleni and Harry thanked Takis and left him to his work to begin their search of the village neighborhoods.   For hours they walked the maze of alleyways, calling for the dog, showing her picture to anyone they met along the way — "ohee, ohee " was always the reply though there seemed to be some light of recognition, a catch of breath as people glanced at the photo. "Po po, ee skeelaki yia nisi!" one old man said as he pointed to her image, "the island's little dog!"

They didn't stop searching until late in the afternoon and only then to meet with Popi over a tsipouro with mezedes for some sustenance. The artist floated into the harbor Ouzerie in a dress of flowing deep pink, her mass of hair wound through and held atop her head with cloth of purple and sparkles. In this world of whites and blues she stood out like the vivid bougainvillea, or a fuchsia flower, eccentric and self possessed. A bright ray of happiness, Eleni said.

"Your mother should have named you Eleftheria, Popi!" Eleni laughed as she greeted their friend. "You bring such beauty and happiness with you wherever you go." They settled into Popi's entertaining telling of the island gossip, and of course shared news of Lily and Theo before the subject turned. "So when was it that you last saw our little lost friend, Popi?"

The big storm blew through in the last December, Popi said. Until then, Margarita had visited her stoop several times a week, joining the others in her courtyard for a meal and frequently was seen napping under a sheltering bench, curled with one of the cats for warmth.

"But to be honest, through the winter I was often in Athens with Theo, or in Brussels, for weeks at a time. I've had some gallery showings and had to hang my art and attend openings ... Yia Yia Niki took over the feedings for me. Eleni, it really wasn't long ago that I realized Margarita was not among my little friends. I could only be hopeful ... I had heard of the new dog shelter and was encouraged to think that she might have found her way there. My flock here seems to be getting smaller and smaller and I know that the poisonings may have some to do with that, but ..."

"Oh, well ... shit! She's probably dead. She's gone. No one has seen her. So what will I say to Lily? What can I possibly say?"

"... but so must the dog shelter. Oh, Eleni! She's not necessarily dead!" Popi said, pointedly trying to put a stop to Eleni's fretting. "Those women from the shelter come through the town like a band of Amazon invaders, and they sweep up any homeless dog they find in their path. They are relentless. But it is a good thing! I must tell you though, they leave the dogs who wear collars behind, they know that the collars mean belonging. And all of the little ones here, you know, they all wore my collars. I don't know what to say, Eleni. Some of those dogs are missing. Maybe the collars broke somehow, that is possible ... maybe Margarita lost hers and is at the shelter? Go up there and see. The dog had made it through many years, why should this year be any different?"

"You don't ever check at the shelter to see if your dogs are there?"

"Eleni! First, they are not <u>my</u> dogs! They come to me, I feed them, I give them collars, I do what I can to care for them and when they leave me, I must let it be! Second, I do not have a car or a scooter to get myself all of the way up to that shelter. And, I could spend my life worrying about all of the animals — like you do — but I do not, I cannot, that is not me. I don't have the time for that, but I do what I can. The best any of us can do is to do what we can." She raised her hand to order three more tsipouro.

"Well ... you know, I don't have the time, either, Popi. But you are right, we do what we can. At home we say that we "choose our battles". But the poisonings, don't you ever say anything to anyone about them? The mayor, the town council, anyone? How, HOW can you just watch as the dogs disappear, one by one, knowing that it is most likely because some of your fellow citizens are killing them?"

"Those people, those killers ... they are not human. To kill defenseless creatures? They are not human and they will find their judgment in the end, if not before! It worries me, Eleni, of course it does." Eleni thought of Vassili. *Does Popi know that story?* "But no, I have not spoken to the mayor about this. When I do see him, we talk about cultural events, how the island can support the local arts. Keeping the local culture alive is my path here, and I do what I must to make sure that the mayor pays attention to these things." She rummaged around in her purse, and pulled out a pack of cigarettes. After tapping one gently on the table, she lit it and with her exhale, continued.

"But it is hard to get that man to see much other than how much BIGGER he can make everything here. What is it with men, eh? Bigger, bigger, bigger! Sorry, Harry! But this mayor, with him it is all about a bigger airport, bigger hotels, bigger boats, bigger tourism, more, more, more ... he gives no thought to supporting small pensiones run by widows or families who have known nothing else, the small tavernas that are open all year round and run by people we have known all of our lives. The guys like Vassili with the smaller boats, the little excursion boats? No, no, no. No thought to any of that, it's just build and build and bigger rents, and tax, tax, tax, more, more, more. Bigger!" She spoke louder, more quickly now. "Those big companies can handle the taxes, the local boatmen or the small pensiones? Ohee! No! They cannot. They need all of the drachmae they can get, just to live! Oh my gosh, don't get me started here. Where is that tsipouro?" Popi rolled her eyes and fanned herself with both of her hands.

Mana set the drinks on the table, "Oriste!", and with a brow-raised nod she threw her glance to the two women, then back to Harry. A low whistle escaped her lips, a whispered "po po po po." She shook her head and reached out, patting him gently on the cheek. He was leaned far back in his chair, hands clasped over his chest, content to quietly observe Eleni and Popi as they maneuvered their distinct differences toward some path of unity. But he loved that they both were strong and opinionated, yet maintained a respect for one another. "Efharisto poli, Kiria". He smiled at Mana as she turned back to her busy-ness.

"See, to me, Popi, the animals deserve the same attentions as art ... and as people! What have they done to NOT deserve that? I understand, I do, that the arts can bring money to the island, through tourists interested in such things and of course, straggly, hungry stray dogs can't. Everyone wants only the happy times, right? They're on holiday! The dark secrets of the animals can't really compete with glamour, and color and social events. But ... that new shelter could. What well heeled art lover wants to see hollow, hungry eyes staring at them from under a

266

taverna table? Or run into a pile of poisoned kitties on a stroll though the alleys? That shelter, as a symbol of an island known to care for the animals, could attract the attentions of animal lovers from far and wide. What a name that wretched mayor <u>could</u> make for himself, eh? I can see it, in all of the magazines, in all of the travel guides, "The ONE Greek island that cares!" The people would flock here! And isn't it just possible that, were we a kinder species and we didn't think twice about taking care of anyone or anything weaker than us, those with no voice, maybe then there would be less of this greed you speak of?" Eleni poured her tsipouro into a glass over two ice cubes, topping it with a bit of cold water before she went on.

"Margarita is important to us. She is one of the reasons we've come to be so close to you, Popi! She's the main reason for Lily's deep, deep bond with Vassili, and she introduced us to so much of the culture here ... island life, people, all for good or bad. She made us all laugh, and cry ... that damn mayor, it seems all he does is make people cry! Shit, now it sounds like Margarita saved one of the children here! Where is the island's loyalty to her for that? Why should the possibility of Margarita, or ANY of those dogs and cats we've known, having been poisoned to death for no good reason not be important to us? Or to you, Popi?"

Though their voices had both reached a fuller timbre, a bit louder and higher in pitch — Eleni, tapping her finger on the table percussively as she spoke while Popi conducted her feelings by gesticulating to the air — the friendship that the two women had nurtured insisted that each listen as the other's views were being voiced. *A lost art, that.* Harry sipped at his tsipouro.

"The animals? They are important to me! They are! I take care of those in need, you know I do, but I am just not an activist in this way, Eleni. I will protest in the streets of Athens for better health care and better pay for the people, I will march against any stupid, stupid war that your idiot Mr. Bush is concocting, but the welfare of the animals, that is your path, my friend. Of course! I understand why little Margarita is so important to you all, to your kind hearts! She is purity. She is love, she personifies ALL of those animals out there! You see, from you, I am learning <u>not</u> to turn my eyes away, to pay attention and do what I can! For that, I thank you. But, the mayor? I will talk to him about my worries! You go and talk to him about yours!" She waved her hand dismissively, as though brushing an annoying fly from the air before her, effectively ending the conversation as only a strong Greek woman can.

But then Popi reached out to pinch Eleni's cheek.

"Tora, tora, tora ... you want everyone to be concerned, the same way you are, now, now, now! But, your worries are your worries, my friend. Mine, they are my worries! Mine! I cannot fix anything, in your way, for you. Po po po. Do what you can for yourself, for the animals, but do not expect me to feel the same way you do. Oh Eleni mou, maybe let your concern go a bit, do us all a favor and laugh a little!"

"Please, do not tell me what to do, Popi! I have to be concerned ... always ... because I know that there are too many who are not. I cannot turn a blind eye. You may be able to, but I cannot. As hard as it may be for you to comprehend, I simply do not understand how anyone can! Yes, that can make me a difficult and cranky person sometimes and if that bothers you, I am sorry."

There was quiet, filled with electricity, a snapping tension — but then Eleni attempted a laugh. "Harry, we need to go ... because Popi's going to order more tsipouro and then we'll all be sorry and you will have to carry me out of here!"

"I would carry you anywhere, my love. But I'm having a wonderful time here, just a little fly on the wall ... watching ... all of this fire and heart, this luscious womanness! Amazing! But if you wish ..." He smiled at them both, waved to Kostas for the bill and then picked Eleni up, draping her over his shoulder as if she were light as a small spring lamb. He started to trot off with her, and only when the laughter came easily to both women did he set her back to earth. They turned to say goodbye to Popi, and the colorful artist leaned in to her friend.

"Then *pirazi.*" she said softly, "It does not matter. You are difficult but you are beautifully difficult, my friend! I see it Eleni. When we voice our passions, when we paint them, write them, sing them, speak them, act them, whatever they are, we make change. In our own ways, we make change. It is happening here, and I think we can say that we are beginning to see it. You, just look around you ... all of the kindness, the food, and the doctoring you and Lily did when you were here? Well, if you stop looking only at your own worries and look around you, then you will see change. Bravo."

She kissed Eleni sweetly on both cheeks, gave Harry a big hug, and fluttered off.

In the still of each morning after coffee in the harbor with Vassili, Eleni and Harry would part, each to comb a new bit of the small island in their mission to find the missing dog. Taking bus or boat taxi to the more remote places, they searched through the small villages and their farmlands, to no avail. They saw her kin everywhere though, and any time Eleni saw a small brown dog, she would gasp with a fragile hope, holding her breath until she could get a closer look. Many of the dogs had Margarita's foxy little ears and white tipped toes – perhaps they were her children, her children's children. But they were not Margarita.

Eleni had a brief meeting with the Mayor, calmly voicing her concerns for the animals, but was met only with defiance.

"What do you mean, how can you say these things? Please, do not insult me! Poisoning? Here? Never!" He pounded a soft, plump fist onto his barren desk and stood up, rearranging the few papers that lay scattered there. He never met her gaze. "I am sorry, but this just does not happen here on our island, Kiria, please, you must trust me on this. Do not worry yourself over it any longer." She then watched him brush his hands together, as if to brush her prying out of his life. "Now if you will excuse me I have more important matters to attend to ..."

... *Than to stay here and listen to you insult me*, is what Eleni thought he forgot to add at the end of their rather terse conversation.

aethna

The weather was lovely and they needed a break. After several fruitless days Harry and Eleni hired a scooter — there was no better way to easily explore the more remote northern farmsteads and beaches, and to take in the magic of the spring, to watch and feel it stream by was just the ease they needed. No effort.

But there also was a box of veterinary supplies that needed to be taken up to the new dog shelter. They had come well prepared.

Once it had been decided that their way home from Europe would be via Greece, Eleni made an urgent call home to Nona, asking her to please retrieve the box from their veterinarian and send it on immediately. The box held a variety of veterinary medicines and other necessities, all initially destined to travel back to the island with the whole family.

With first news from Vassili of plans for the new dog shelter, Eleni and Lily had been eager to help however they could from across the sea. Eleni spoke to her own veterinarian about the plight of the Greek strays, and without hesitation the kind doctor started to collect up whatever he was unable to use any longer — a box marked 'Greece, donations' sat on a shelf in the back room of his clinic, and filled quickly with various outdated, but still viable medications, packages of ear mite and worming pills. The kind man also provided old surgical instruments, new syringes, bags of intravenous saline solution, antibiotic creams, eye and pain medications and most importantly, one precious bottle of euthanasia solution, stealthily disguised by a new label marking it a benign antibiotic.

"This is contraband, my dear ... I cannot help you if you are caught!" He spoke very seriously of the one thing Eleni had begged him to include, the one thing that could get her into trouble should Greek customs actually make an attempt to do their job on the day she were to pass through. They were old friends. She had worked as the man's occasional assistant for years, and in turn, he had doctored almost every small animal she had ever had in her care. She understood him well enough to know that his kind heart had broken when he had done animal rescue and veterinary work for the strays of Mexico. And so, she knew that he agreed to send this precious means of humane euthanasia along with her if only because he understood how desperately it must be needed.

Lily had started up her own collections as well. Gathering up used collars and leashes donated by friends, she had hoped to take them to the shelter herself one day. But now she placed them gently in the box, alongside a few cartons of dog cookies and several tennis balls — things she had purchased with her allowance money — and then she and Nona wrapped it all up securely and with great fanfare, sent it off for the animals in need.

272

The precious cargo made it to Theo who in turn handed it over to Eleni and Harry in Piraeus, the port of Athens, where they awaited passage to the island.

At the least, if they could not find Margarita, their trip would not be in vain.

Eleni climbed aboard and sandwiched herself between Harry and the box, which had been bungeed securely to the back end of the asthmatic old scooter. The road that led to the shelter was another idyllic path they'd somehow not yet managed to discover, and on the flats they scooted past fields rich with young tomato vines planted hopefully under tall, conical bamboo trellis, and musical herds of belled goats, each nanny with a suckling kid or two at her side. Wrapping her arms tightly around Harry's waist, Eleni closed her eyes and tipped her face to the warm sun, taking in the scent of damp, fertile earth, the organic process working its magic all around them. The wind blew her hair about, and it reached out like arms to wrap around the precious cargo behind her.

What do dogs smell in the wind? she wondered as Margarita came to mind. *Is she there? Can she smell us now, can she smell us coming to her?*

Old cisterns and forgotten kalivis dotted the countryside, as did the little shrines built in someone's memory that one found all over Greece in the platias and alongside roads. They stopped at a few of the white shrouded huts along the way, like tiny churches, decorated with photos and icons and an oil lamp that was always lit behind a glass window. Often one would see old ladies and old men and occasionally a grieving youth keeping these shrines, talking to their dead loved one as they tidied and trimmed wicks, working to keep the memory of a lost one alive.

The road began to twist up and up the island's largest mountain and the hills grew so steep that Eleni often had to dismount and walk, leaving Harry to sweet talk the poor old scooter and its priceless payload to the top on his own. By the time they'd made it to the last of the hills and the old thing sputtered and coughed in complaint and pooped out yet again, both were barely able to walk at all because they were laughing so hard.

Ironically, it was near the dump, where countless animal carcasses had been secreted over the years that they found the fledgling shelter newly sprouted up. Behind a long, tall stand of narrow Italian cypress, two framed buildings stood separated by a large fenced enclosure where dozens and dozens of dogs of every size and shape sprawled in the sun, at rest, bellies full. Kibble was heaped in piles everywhere — obviously, not one of the shelter's denizens would ever face hunger while living there. They all jumped to attention as Eleni and Harry neared, braying and barking their alarm at the sight of human strangers.

Kneeling at the wire fence they both murmured their kindness to the frenzied assembly and soon the dogs quieted and came, one by one, eventually crowding the fence in their curiosity, for a touch, for a sniff. Their faces were soft and open, tails wagging in greeting. It amazed Eleni that dogs who had most likely been terribly mistreated could so easily forgive the human species ... though a surly few stayed back, glaring with a wariness that was seared into their souls, a mistrust that might never leave them.

As they were scanning the pack for a glimpse of a certain homely little brown dog, a woman stepped through the door of the shelter's office and the racket resumed, joyous now, the dogs rushing the fence towards her as one body. After quickly introducing both she and Harry, Eleni presented her with the precious, well-traveled box.

Aethna was the small, cheery Irishwoman's name. "Ah, you're both angels, you are! Truly, a Godsend!" she said, laughing as she riffled through the bottles and packets and collars. "Just when we think we're done for, we've run out of everythin', the angels provide. And here you are, then! Thank you, from the bottom of my heart."

Aethna invited them to sit in the shade of a sprawling mulberry, gently scooting an old dog off one of the few chairs there. Pete was a 'lifer', she said, and had the run of the place. Old and sick, he didn't have much time left, but it was important to Aethna that he live out his days in as much comfort as possible. So he napped in the shade of the tree by day and slept in the office at night, curled in the warmth of a plush bed, brought just for him by a kindly visitor.

As she began the long telling of the shelter's tale, Aethna first spoke with great respect of the abundance of kindness from the complete strangers who provided weekly shipments of food, enough for all of the incarcerated creatures there. But that was where the ease left off.

"Aye, strangers will dig deep into their pockets for the dogs, they will, but the government vet has yet to make an appearance! Can you believe it? We must depend upon the kindness of veterinarians here on holiday from other countries, who donate their time and what supplies they can carry here with 'em! These lifesavers not only perform the sterilizations, they also mend the wounds and broken bones that have been borne of abuse."

But only time, and the caring of the volunteers could mend the broken spirits.

Aethna chirped a "Pipe down now, Georgie" to a noisy inmate and then went on in her beautiful, melodic brogue.

"With the advent of the shelters sproutin' up throughout Greece, now there has also come a new protocol for the homin' of the beasts, you know — reams and reams of paperwork, which of course needs to be handled to the government's satisfaction. Doesn't it, now? And the government is never satisfied, it seems. But, nor do they ever look to have anyone available who knows anythin' at all about paperwork!"

She got up yet again to clap her hands and growl a bit at noisy Georgie, and as she came back to sit even closer, Eleni noticed her blue eyes, kind eyes, set deeply in a face hardened by the sun.

"Any sort of paperwork! Jesus, Mary and Joseph, it's "You forgot this and oh, by the way, you forgot that..." Oh ... now don't even let me get started up about the government! They just make balls of it all. Really now, it can't ever get anythin' done! So, the paperwork we belabor is usually ignored. Isn't that just the way? Here, where the animals obviously matter so little, you would think that the government simply wouldn't bother us for paperwork. Ah, but, oh no!" Aethna shook her head and glanced at Eleni and Harry with a playful look, proof that her sense of humor was still intact.

"With so many problems, how do you get anything taken care of here? How can anyone ever even get a dog off of the island?" Harry asked the tiny woman.

"Ah, a good question, Harry. There is a good, good network that exists between our foreign vets here and the larger city dog shelters. This wasn't always the case and it is a bridge that has been built quickly, and therefore is very fragile. But now dogs with possibility of findin' homes in other countries can indeed be sure to get what they need for their passport — the proper vaccinations and the blood work and such. But! All of this work is clandestine! It's all cloak and daggers and has to be conducted very, very carefully, sometimes with names forged and papers doctored ... it's like we're still in a war here! You see, Greek government doesn't like foreigners takin' it upon themselves to do work meant for its own employees, even though the government won't always hold its own employees to the job they are paid to do! Pfff! How they ever get anythin' done, I'll never know. It's really just a convoluted matter of false pride, isn't it now? I just want to tear out what little hair I have left on my head, sometimes! And then to top it off, sadly ... no, infuriatingly! ... far too many of the native vets rarely seem to care enough to even visit this island, or any island for that matter, let alone get any travel papers in order in a timely manner. And it's their carelessness that has cost many a dog a chance at a home."

Aethna went on, explaining that the hastily built shelter itself was fraught with problems, from leaking roofs, to a lack of sanitation, and finally, to the island's present mayor who would love nothing more than to see these buildings razed to the ground, the property used instead for some form of revenue gain. She took a sip of water and dusted a bit of hair from her eyes.

"The man's off his nut, he is. He just wants another hotel, another bloody hotel! This is my husband's property, mind you! And my husband is a local boy! What's the mayor thinkin' now?" She laughed but then quieted quickly. "I'll tell you though, just months ago, a wee, much needed new wing was added on to the shelter, here. It was primitive at best, had a dirt floor and all, but it included a small infirmary and a room where surgeries could be done in a bit cleaner environment for a change. But, wouldn't you know, that infernal little man ... he caught wind of the doin's and he proclaimed the work illegal, done without the proper permits, he said! Built with undocumented foreign money, he said! Never mind that we HAD the permits, if you can call them such ... a bloody indecipherable bunch of nonsense that took us months to get in order. Well now then, what did he do? Try to work it out with us? No. Not the *right* permits, he said! And late one night, well, a handful a'thugs tore the wee structure to the ground. His thugs? We'll never know, will we, but one can only imagine."

Oh my gosh, that little bastard! So self-righteous, pretending to be so concerned and compassionate, and right to my face! Eleni was disgusted.

Aethna said that if he had torn the heart from her very chest instead, it surely would have hurt her no more than this barbaric, unnecessary show of bravado did.

She went on then to tell of another disturbing problem the shelter had encountered from time to time. "There's a wee handful of the townspeople, perhaps offended by ... oh, or maybe shamed by the substantial efforts of foreigners that goes into the welfare of the animals. Meddlers, they say! These locals have been met, face on, by a growin' dissatisfaction with old practices that are considered by many to be barbaric ... the poisonin' for one ... but rather than acquiescin' to the growin' sentiment, they blunder ahead with their hurt pride..."

... And continue to poison the animals. Some of the disgruntled few came to the shelter occasionally, she said, but late in the night, under their shroud of frustration to toss poison laden meat over the fence. And then, the shelter volunteers would come to work the next morning to yet more heartbreak. But there were the other mornings that they would arrive to find a dog, perhaps a hunting dog who had outlived his usefulness, tied to the fence, or a pregnant bitch about to burst with new pups, left in a crate by the gate.

"At least those people were thinkin' of bringin' the creatures to us, though, rather than starvin' them, or dumpin' them off of a cliff! There is hope!" Aethna laughed.

She told of a devastating illness that had recently swept through the shelter, claiming the lives of almost half of its population. "We were impotent, we were. There was really little that we could do, it was impossible to keep the buildings sterile, and therefore keep the disease from spreadin' and anyway, there were very few medications available to treat so many sick dogs."

She sighed.

"I do wonder occasionally, what would be worse. Being taken by dreadful illness, or barely livin' through, to this meager existence behind bars?"

A potent silence followed. They all knew what it held. It transcended the animals, the island, even life behind bars, it was an eternal conundrum, a condition of existence that had no special regard for any species. Suffering was suffering, and it knew no boundaries. But Aethna snapped them right back, to the dogs there behind the wire, to the mulberry tree and the Aegean breeze.

"Sometimes we have so little here, a meager existence is all that it is. The best we can hope for is that people continue to care, and support the creatures through their donations. Ah that, and then fall in love with one of the wee dears and take it home with 'em, away to a better life!" She laughed then, a lovely tinkling bell of levity ringing through the weight of it all.

"Ah, but then some of our inmates here are former pets, you know. The locals, some of 'em, just don't yet know how best to care for a pet. They neglect to give their dogs the trainin' that helps them to grow into good citizens, and so, when they are no longer cute, wee puppies, but are still poopin' in the house, or leapin' up on people, they became bother and burden ... often cast to the streets to find their own way. They just turn 'em out. And well, then, there they are." She pointed to the row of curious faces, quiet now and begging for attention at the fence.

"Some of them were abandoned when owners went off on holiday and couldn't be bothered to get anyone to care for 'em. Found runnin' on streets, on beaches, hungry and scared. And many of those had originally come at a dear price, being 'purebreds', you know. People still have that notion, don't they, that rescue-shelter dogs are useless, diseased curs? They refuse to even consider that they could be wonderful pets. And, as everywhere, there an this odd, misplaced status in owning a purebreed animal. Ah, but once the dogs are considered to be a problem, for whatever reason and no matter their cost– off to the streets they go! Purebreed or no."

Most often they were cast off to the streets un-sterilized, ready and willing to multiply the problems.

Many of the dogs at the shelter belonged to no one at all, and never had. They had been born in the bushes and under homes, and if they survived would breed and give birth to their own. They learned from their mothers how to beg in the tavernas and raid the garbage, to live in the streets. These dogs had learned to be warily kind to those who might offer them food, and this made it easy for them to be caught and rescued. Some of them were the victims of abuse, or starvation, and many were pups that had been found left in boxes or garbage bins along the side of a remote dirt road.

Eleni, never one to hold back her lowly regard for a great percentage of her fellow human beings, spoke up in her empathy with the compassionate seraph of the shelter.

"You know, Aethna, this happens in the states too. I am just not sure that humans, generally speaking, really have the capacity to understand how important it is that we be responsible with these lives that depend on us so much. We domesticated them, long, long ago, so how is it that we don't think it is still our job to care for them? We don't seem to have the sense yet, do we, to realize that the creatures feel, they bleed and mourn and they mother their young, many suckle their young like we do. Why shouldn't they be treated with dignity and kindness? Are we simply too stupid to understand?"

"Aye, I know, bloody arrogant humans. When will we learn? Ever, will we ever learn?"

Aethna threw light on the fact that there were no tough sentences for abandonment, abuse, or poisoning of the animals in Greece, so the problems just rolled on and on in an effortless, endless cycle.

"If there are any penalties against the abuses, we surely don't know about them." Aethna said as she pointed again to the main enclosure, filled with the homeless dogs.

"This municipality does nothin', nothin' at all to protect the animals. I should be fair now, and say that none of the municipalities throughout Greece does anythin', not one thing, to protect the animals. It is not just this one here."

With no formally sanctioned welfare programs to protect them, the cast off animals depended upon the kindness of shelters such as hers, all operating on a wing and a prayer. The future of these somewhat clandestine sanctuaries was always tentative at best, dependent upon the moods of those who wielded local power since not only were they always controversial, they were also funded in great part by foreign money.

The lack of any legal recourse for the animals and the hardships under which the shelters had to survive were inexcusable to Eleni and Harry, but what surprised them the most was the dearth of euthanasia solution, an entirely humane means of ending the pain and suffering wracking many of the lives that found their way to Aethna and Mary's sheltering arms. It was something that in 1992 should be readily available, but wasn't.

"We have so little, ever, because the damned veterinarian never seems to care to come callin'. It's controlled, you know, it must be provided by a doctor. Yet, what there ever is of it here at the shelter is generally brought in by our visiting vets! Not Greek, but the foreigners! It always gets used first on the most dire of cases and there is never enough of the stuff."

Shaking her head, she told of dogs there who had survived poisoning only to now be dying of kidney failure, one of poisoning's very painful after effects. And some of the older dogs, like Pete, who had cancer or other terminal maladies, were sadly suffering at the end of their days.

"There are few functioning guns here on the island, really. People just don't find a need for them. Isn't that refreshin', actually? You see, they don't often shoot their food animals, they bleed 'em. What guns there are usually are only used by the young men to, quite loudly now, announce the arrival of the New Year, or Easter, their shotguns blastin' away to the sky! Ah, that and the hunt, a new sport here. But as repulsive as a gun is to many people as a means of bringin' death, used properly it really can provide a very humane end. 'Tis better than nothin', that is for sure!" She saw the look of horror creeping into the gentle calm of Eleni's face. "Oh dear, not a big old shotgun of course, but a small, neat instrument! There are the times that my partner Mary and myself have longed for the use of one to help dogs in agony find a quick relief. We do have a few friends in the town, our "Angels of Mercy" we call them, they will answer our frantic calls — at all hours mind you — and will come to the aid of the shelter to put an agonized dog out of it's misery in the more primitive ways. Ah, but always, always with a kind touch and a gentle prayer."

The shelter was not equipped to care for cats, yet a handful sprawled on wooden tables or took their siesta in the shelter of the great tree limbs, legs askew and dangling from overhead.

"These characters are the lucky ones, they are." Aethna said as she ran her hand the length of the soft calico lying there.

"There simply is not room, nor is there food enough for any more cats here. The rest must be left to survive on their own. They are hardy creatures though, the cats. At least they know how to feed themselves. Right? One day perhaps we can better help them, but now, no." She picked up the sleepy calico and touched her nose to its own moist, black triangle. "Oh, believe me, it breaks my heart ... if it can break any more than it already does! Sometimes in the springtime, boxes of kittens'll appear overnight, just left at the door here. We try to find homes for what we can, even takin' some of them home ourselves. Mary's angel of a husband only half jokingly threatens divorce, should she bring any more strays to their home! But sometimes, there are just too many leftovers."

"Do your visiting vets ever neuter any of the males, Aethna?" Harry asked. "It seems that even just a few less tomcats in the town could really help the population problems. There'd be less fighting, for sure. And less wailing in the night!"

"And less sick and hungry kittens." Eleni offered. "But we all know that story."

"Our darlin' vets are just too busy with the dogs, you know. We can sterilize only a very, very few cats, the ones that end up here when the vets are on the premises. And then, we well know about men and their balls now, don't we! Many men won't let their animals part with 'em, for Christ's sake! What is that all about now, Harry?" Aethna laughed and patted Harry warmly on the knee. "Oh, I'm just kiddin' you, dear. But the people here do seem to take more kindly to us leavin' the males intact, so that's what we'll usually do, to gain whatever favor we can! So then, less of the males get done up, even though it's a far easier procedure than the sterilization of a female. But after they've had their surgeries we'll take the cats over to the Monastery there, where they live in a happy little colony, eatin' rats and mice, fed whatever else the nice caretaker can feed 'em, certainly plates of milk from all of her goats. There are some intact females there still, but they all live happily together, no matter. No toms to get 'em all riled up! What males are there'll be eunuchs by now! Oh, occasionally though, a tom'll find his way in, as they always do, and I'm sure it's like he thought he'd died and gone to heaven with all of those girls traipsin' about ... well, at least 'til he finds out there's very little business for him there! We'll eventually get him trapped and fixed up.

But until we have more space here, and can afford to really care for them, these cats here and those at the Monastery are all we can help."

"What about the rest, Aethna, the kitties you can't give a home to?" Eleni asked, with the fertile clans of town cats she and Lily had fed daily in mind. Undoubtedly they had all bred. *Do I really want to know?*

"Ah. We'll take what the Monastery can bear to the caretaker there, and the rest, well, we regretfully hand them over to our "angels", Eleni. At least there's the promise of a gentle end to a life that most likely would have been fraught with the sufferin'. And then, well, we cry and we cry at what seems like no end to the misery."

Aethna dug into the box now, deeply touched by the generosity of the American veterinarian she had never met. She held up a few of the vials and a larger bottle and looked up at the shelter's newest angels.

"These here? These drugs and supplies your dear doctor sent along will see the shelter through the problems of the springtime. And, you see, they'll enable many dogs to have their homing process initiated. And this, this liquid gold ..." she recognized the bottle of euthanasia solution, even with its false label marked 'sulfadimethoxine', gave it a kiss and held it up in front of her, "well, ye know you coulda had your arses put in the slammer if this one had been figured out! I think if you can get the 'blue juice' past customs, you can probably get anythin' into the country! Oh, no, not really, but this is one time we can be quite glad that they do not do their jobs, right?"

"Our vet is a very good, kind man. His own experience with the broken animals of Mexico just destroyed him. He knows what you face here, that this is something you must need."

"Well then, the Gods will ever bless that kind soul, they will", Aethna sighed.

Harry was very impressed by the small woman, full of such big caring for the animals.

"Jesus, what a big job, Aethna. And so important, even though many people might not understand your passion. To them, the animals just don't count. Humans haven't yet discovered that there will never be any peace on this earth until we can tend to it, in all seriousness, with dignity and intelligence. To all of it ... the people, the creatures and the earth itself. And if we can't figure out how to treat the animals with compassion, how can we ever expect to come to any real peace with our fellow human, to an end to violence? We just never seem to get it."

"Yes, Harry," Aethna sighed, "it seems we just do go on, round and round, without ever really getting' too much farther down the road, doesn't it?"

A cool wind rushed through a moment of silence. It swirled about and as it left, kicked up leaves and dust in its wake. "Well, the Gods agree!" Harry laughed. When the air was still again, Eleni cleared her throat and shook her head, looking over at him.

"I don't think people really want an end to the violence, Harry. It's so much easier to act out in fear and anger than it is to think a problem through ... and then actually act responsibly. That takes work, commitment. You know, Aethna, we face these same troubles at home! People refuse to spay or neuter their pets, too many babies are born, animals are abused, abandoned, and there are pets who end up in 'prison' for no crime other than that they're no longer cute. We should know better! You would think, right? It just drives me crazy. There have been educational programs and low-cost spay and neuter clinics across the country for <u>years</u> now. But the problems just persist. Machismo, laziness, lack of education, whatever is the cause of the persistent misery, none of it should be excused, or tolerated any longer!" She reached for one of the ginger tabbies sprawled across the table and took it into her arms. The cat lay still, purring quietly, absorbing every bit of attention Eleni was willing to give her, eyes closed to just golden slits, a cat-smile of contentment on her upturned face.

"The saddest thing of all, to me, are those who don't seem to see the correlation between someone beating a dog and then abusing a child ... or their wife! They won't see how closely connected the thoughtless abandonment of a pet — old and gray, feeble, and suddenly with more difficult needs, but a family member no less — is to their eventual ability to thoughtlessly discard a human elder. Grandma, or Grandpa, neatly put away from sight in some god awful home filled with bored, underpaid nurses and screeching, overmedicated old folks. It's all connected! If only we could make it a priority to teach about this in schools, teach children how to care, how to be compassionate and kind to everyone, everything."

"Aye then, what's it gonna take, for all of us to come to the kindness? Sometimes I do think that's it all just futile attempts that we make. But I tell you, no matter, I just can't bear to see an animal sufferin'."

Eleni shifted in her chair as though it might make her more comfortable. Her spirit was aching, she just wanted to flee, soaring over the treetops to the sea, away from the sadness. The plight of suffering animals always did this to her. The cat opened her eyes and reached out with her front paws, toes spread and claws slightly unsheathed, resting them on Eleni's chest as though to

287

hold her there in place. Eleni laughed softly into the serenity that gazed up at her. "This one is certainly not suffering, Aethna!"

There was the quiet again ... the only sound, the muted humming of the wind.

Easing the limp cat to the tabletop, Eleni stood to steal ripe mulberries dangling from the tree overhead, awakening the cicadas slumbering there. Under the swell of the eccentric symphonics she passed handfuls of the sweet, plump berries to Aethna and Harry, the sweet nectar spilling down her own chin as she sat again in an attempt to make new order of her thoughts, to keep them pacified, to prevent them buzzing and shrilling again like the creatures now stirring in the tree.

"I am starting to really get that Greece is just now coming into some important realizations about so many issues. It's at the beginning of a difficult educational process. In a way, this place is like a blank slate, Aethna, and you are a part of the writing of the "new rules". Don't you think?"

"Aye, I suppose, but I thought we all were taught 'do unto others' and all that, so to speak, long ago! Isn't that what our parents taught us when we were wee children? It shouldn't be this hard."

"A few years back, our friend Vassili ... he's one of the boatmen, a kind and honest soul ... he gave us a bit of an education about Greece's more recent history. A turbulent one at that. Freedom from oppression is never easily won, it seems. We were pretty clueless, I'm embarrassed to say. But we found that Greece is newly emerging from a dark past into these modern times. It was only what, fifteen or twenty years ago, the 70's he said, that the country was in the grips of a dictatorship? And that insult, after suffering through so many brutal wars!

Now, so much is new; modern convenience, a place in Europe's Community, freedom even. All that is new, although the country and its long path are so ancient. It's like it is being reborn now. Hopefully Greece can pass through the birthing woes with the best of itself left intact."

"Is any of this any excuse for abhorrent behavior towards the animals, Eleni?" Aethna asked, wearily. The weight of her caring, those unremitting efforts she made for the beasts, were evident in the lines etched around her sad, kind eyes.

"Never! But you know, Aethna, Vassili's history lesson at the least gave us a few answers to the 'whys' of some of the attitudes, here. It helps us to know a bit more of a culture that has had a much harder path than we — at least we Americans — have. You know it all well, Aethna, you're married to a Greek. You live here. You know the history, the people, all of the goodness ... but you also have to deal with the daily miseries, the worst of it all. You have to deal with the cause, and then mop up the mess. We knew SO little! Vassili offered us more of an understanding, and with that, certainly some humility. Really, how dare we, coming from a fairly fortunate existence ... well, specifically I mean me ... how can I really expect anyone here to feel or do as I do, regarding the animals? I can't. I shouldn't. I can hope, though. And I must always expect kindness, of course! How could we ever stand for less than that? But then, maybe what follows someone's first act of kindness is just the beginnings of a learning curve?"

"So, Eleni, when did you go from being a firebrand, to a saint?" Harry asked his wife, who looked like a bright bit of flame sitting there, her red hair flickering in the breeze that stole upon them from the waters in the distance.

"Oh stop it, darlin'. I know I can't be that fair all of the time! But that bit of an understanding that Vassili gave me? It's alive, it breathes and grows. It took awhile, but ... I'll speak for myself again, because Harry, you already are far more open minded, more grounded in calm than I am ... but I do seem to be living a lesson in patience, here. Patience is not a good subject for me and I'm a horrible student anyway, but I do think that now, with a better understanding of their past I'm able to have a bit more compassion for those folks here who piss me off so much. That past doesn't absolve anyone, far from it. But, in knowing more, I can no longer just always allow myself the lazy-ass luxury of expecting that they should know to care for the animals the way I do, or that they even want to! Hallelujah, I am learning a bit of patience!"

"Hallelujah, hallelujah!" Harry winked at Aethna.

"And, I'm learning that probably the best I can do is to try to show what is a kinder way of behaving towards the animals. Right? Try not to tell anyone that they are wrong, just show them a kinder way. You might have to tape my mouth closed, Harry. Like I said, I'm not the best student. But Vassili smartened me up, I think. I'm a little less quick to judge, a little less quick to demonize anyone because now I get that it wasn't so long ago that they really had to struggle just to take care of their own. You know, just to feed their own children! It must be hard for some of them, to see us doting on the animals, carrying on the way we do! But ... you know, there is the glimmer of change all around us, now."

"I know what you're sayin' Eleni, aye. I see it too, I do, when I can find the time to venture out into the village. Change is a'foot, as they say and when I can push all of the heartache aside it does me good to see it! And by the way, we know your Vassili. He's made himself quite useful around here from time to time, helpin' with this 'n that and even buildin' a wee room. We call it 'Maria's Room', it's what he wanted — and it's where we house the orphaned pups. Now he comes up here sometimes with a French woman who is quite good at nursin' the sick ones."

Eleni was tickled by that little peek into Vassili's world. *A woman? What woman?*

"I'm not surprised. He's a good man. And good to the animals. He took in a little kitten that came to us a few years ago. She still lives with him on his boat, and apparently runs the man's life! I think she runs the whole harbor now!"

Harry stood to untangle his limbs. With an "ooff" he stretched his long, lean frame and gazed off over the tops of the pines to the brilliant blue. Vast, full of mystery, the sea seemed to hold all of the world there, within his sight. "This planet is facing a monolithic mess right now, with wars, the erosion of cultures, destruction of the environment. AIDS, hunger, genocide ... I hope these troubles don't develop much further before it's finally seen that there is so much in need of fixing." He smiled at the sight of the cats who had quickly found their way back to laps far more comfortable than tree branches and the tabletop. Eleni and Aethna were covered with them. "And compassion for the animals has to be a part of that whole big picture. Maybe it's the children that will be the tipping point for us all, maybe they will make the difference. I don't know."

Gently peeling a variety of sonorous, napping cats from her lap, Eleni got up, moving to crouch by the old dog Pete, now curled under the table. She laid a hand on his back. "Dear old dog ... dear old Pete." There was a slight thump of bony tail in return. "Won't the children just be too late, Harry? They still have to grow up! If we don't get a move on all of this business, now, those children won't even matter! They will be too late to make their difference. Compassion can't ever come too soon."

The old dog groaned and with some effort rolled onto his back, exposing an expanse of itchy belly where Eleni's hand could be of better service. "Obviously, I have no trouble with compassion for the animals, but I can tell you, I've a long way to go before I can be very compassionate with my own fellow humans. I still don't know why we just don't put the murderers and rapists and child abusers on some uncharted isle, give them some seed to grow food and then just let them have at each other. Or better, lock them into those tiny cages we stick the chimpanzees in! Aethna, in America, chimpanzees — they are our relatives, closer to us in DNA than African Elephants are to Indian Elephants! — they're imprisoned in institutions where they are used, mercilessly, for medical and military research. Why? Because of that very DNA! Researchers are determined to find the answers to some of our greatest medical conundrums by testing new procedures and drugs on them. They inject the poor things with dreaded diseases and then go to work. But, the missing bits of DNA, that 1.4% or something like that, make them just different enough from us that a lot of the research is futile, useless ... but it's conducted anyway. As I said, they are determined. Those innocent creatures, with the intellect of, say, a six year old human child, are stuck, with no thought to their needs, in little bare wire cages where they're forced by soulless, pitiless humans to exist without any of the social interaction and touch they crave, without any comforts at all, not even a blanket. In return for what? Shock treatment, injections of HIV — the poor things don't actually even get AIDS from HIV — — and hepatitis, diseases that they have to then live with in isolation, forever. And liver punch biopsies, without the benefit of pain medications. Oh yeah, I think it would be great ... trade a remorseless, murderous thug for an ape and do the testing on them instead!"

Silence again. Harry, wide-eyed.

But Aethna chuckled, and then burst out in laughter. "Oh now there's a thought, Eleni! Good on 'ye! But I can't say it'll win you many friends!"

"Ah, well, there's already plenty of people who just think I'm a nutcase, Aethna. I have a friend ... I suppose she is still my friend, Harry? ... she lumped me right in there with her born again Christian sister and her Islam fanatic brother in law. We're all militants! Extremists, she said. What? Because I speak out against what I think is wrong? I think it's that I stand for all of those things she just doesn't want to see or think about, those things that might make her neat and even life a little untidy, a bit uncomfortable were she to pay attention to them. But you know, the suffering of the voiceless and innocent caused by the human hand, in my view, is unconscionable, unforgivable, and if we dumb-creatures-that-speak can't stop ignoring the problems and can't figure out how to be play nice with everyone and everything, well then, we <u>deserve</u> to live with all of the concerns Harry was talking about."

Eleni stood up again and groaning herself, shook the numbness from her legs. When she could feel them again she moved over to Aethna, reaching out to take her hands.

"Thank you, Aethna — for all that you do, and for trying to help people understand the importance of kindness. These huge efforts you make, well, they can't be in vain, especially not here, in this heavenly little piece of the world. There is the hope."

Aethna stood and hugged both Eleni and Harry, quite vigorously. "Ah, yes! There's the hope, and that is what we must cling to, isn't it?"

"Come now." She motioned them to follow. "Let's give you a peek."

Touring the ramshackle shelter they stopped first at a small den that had "Maria's Room" painted gracefully over the arched entryway, a room lined with cages filled with soft blankets, a corner of its floor full of dog toys, and watching over it all from the framed portrait that hung on a wall was a vibrant, raven-haired beauty.

Maria.

They passed quickly through the small outbuildings that housed a makeshift surgery and a few cluttered sick rooms, but when Aethna ushered them on to an area that housed two dogs per kennel, Eleni began to hang back, taking the opportunity to get to know each one.

First was Fabio. A small dog who really belonged in someone's lap, not on the cold cement floor of a kennel, Fabio looked to be a cross of beagle and afghan and then perhaps part elf and was obviously a victim of abuse. The poor little fellow cringed and peed the moment Eleni simply spoke to him. Flipping over onto his back to show his soft, pink belly in submission, he rolled his eyes up into his head, perhaps thinking that he was making himself disappear. He trembled.

"Oh, there, hear it breaking? My heart?"

Eleni sat with him, talking softly as she laid her hand lightly upon his chest. The dog began to relax, his breathing evened and the trembling lessened, and in time he opened his eyes and reached tentatively for her hand. Once he realized this woman meant him no further troubles or hurt, the hard edge of his fear softened and in the end he'd allowed himself to sidle as close to her as he could, hugging her legs with his thin body.

Marcos looked like he had to be Margarita's kin. He was obviously very ill, with no will to move at all, belly swollen and tight, and was covered with old scars that, according to Aethna, were caused by being dragged behind a vehicle, a rope attached to the car on one end and to his neck on the other. When he was finally stopped on the road, his abuser said that the dog wouldn't come when he was called, and he was teaching it a lesson.

Eleni could think of several ways to teach that man a lesson.

"We don't really know what is wrong with Marcos and therefore don't quite know how to treat him. Ah, there now Marcos, there now little beast." Aethna bent and cooed softly to the dog, scratching and pulling on his ears a bit while he beat a weak thanks with his frayed tail. "We fear it is a cancer, but until a doctor can visit and examine him, we'll just do our best to keep him comfortable."

A large, lanky German Shorthair Pointer type dog sat obediently at his gate, liquid amber eyes focused intensely upon the approaching party. There was no mistaking this lovely dog's cheery attitude. He just radiated happiness. He wore a smile upon his face, so wide he had to squint, and when he stood, his delight was made even more apparent by the ardent waggling, not of his tail, but of his whole body. But for the goofy smile, there was no other barometer with which he could prove his kind spirit — his tail had been docked short, as is the style with this sort of dog, and the little nub that was left there in its place just couldn't handle the full expression of his emotion all on it's own. Adonis was his name and most likely, Aethna said, he had been brought to the island as a hunting dog. Hunting is popular in Greece, ("But what, in God's name, do they hunt here? Sparrows? The tame swans on the lake?" Aethna sputtered.) and to be in vogue a hunter must be seen with the proper equipment, which includes an expensive hunting-bred dog. Perhaps he was too slow, perhaps he enjoyed chasing the fairy seeds that floated through the air rather than the birds, maybe he wouldn't fetch — whatever the reason, Adonis was found abandoned, tied to the shelter's gate, nothing but a starved sack of bones that was not expected to live.

"He's flyin' it now, though, isn't he? He's actually gettin' a bit fat!" The big dog raised up on his hinds, gracefully planted his forepaws on Aethna's chest and set to licking her face.

Finally, there was Peggy. Peggy had come to the shelter a victim of abuse inflicted by someone with no shame at all. Her ears had been cut off, the pads of her feet burned with some caustic substance and she was so thin that the shelter workers had no idea that she was pregnant until they found her with puppies by her side one morning. Five of the pups were stillborn, mummified, frozen in embryonic time. Those born alive, she had no milk for. Yet there Peggy sat now, begging for attention now with a furiously wagging tail and lips carefully lifted up, exposing her teeth in an astonishingly forgiving grin. By now there were tears streaming down Eleni's cheeks.

"This work is heartbreakin'. We all get attached, we do. We just want to help and it's not often yet that things go the way we'd like. But we had to do somethin', somethin' to shift this current, to change the ways these poor, pitiful creatures are dealt with. You know the greatest payback, besides of course watchin' a dog leave here for its' forever home? It's the look of relief in their eyes when they realize they are safe. To see them drunk, from havin' eaten their fill. And to watch them snorin' away in a deep, restful sleep because they're no longer on the run. Aye, it fills the heart, it does."

Aethna recited her litany of hope, a hope that this shelter might also be able to be of help through education. She explained that regularly through the warm months, shelter volunteers had ventured down into the village to host fund raising luncheons at a taverna friendly to their cause, appealing to locals and tourists alike to donate money or time to the dogs. These gatherings really were educational symposiums of sorts, the volunteers attempting to set straight some of the myths about the animals and to enlighten their guests about humane treatment, as well as trying to get the point across that these flesh and blood beings felt pain and happiness and fear, and even grieved as humans do. They also spoke of the effects of spaying and neutering upon the feral populations and of the great joy a companion animal can bring to a family, or a lonely elder. Always, the volunteers were accompanied by a canine ambassador; a calm and friendly dog who did his or her best to win over the captive audience.

Despite any opposition in the town, the luncheons in that first season had been successful. Donations kept the shelter supplied with many of it's needs well past the end of the tourist season, and rather than ignoring or starving, or chasing them off to fend for themselves, more of the townsfolk were warming to the idea of giving safe harbor to the animals. Hopefully the coming year would see even more success.

"Ah, but we do still have to find a way to convince the island's skeptics that our precious vets are not performin' dastardly deeds up here! Can you believe it, there's a rumor circulatin', it's quite creative actually ... some eejit's been saying that we're harvestin' the organs from the females! We're taking out their bloody organs and sellin' 'em! Instead of sterilizin' the dogs? And the people, well some of 'em believe it! Good Lord, now!" Aethna began to laugh. But when the laughter trailed off, her voice grew soft.

"Well, the children are the future, aren't they? No matter what, they are the future. You know, they're startin' to teach 'em now, about the animals, about kindness and such. I think you may be right, Harry, they will live the changes. They may just be the hope, if we can hold out just that long." said Aethna.

With that, the conversation seemed to drift off and away, over the sea with the breeze, and all three turned their heads to the glistening Aegean in the distance as though watching it take its leave. Here, Eleni finally drew up courage enough to ask about Margarita. She handed a photograph of the dog to Aethna and told a bit of her story.

"Maybe you've seen her, in the town? Really, we're hoping that she's one of the lucky ones who has come through this way."

Aethna studied the photograph carefully, but then shook her head.

"No. I'm so sorry, Eleni, no, we've not seen her here. But I have heard about this little dog, she's quite famous, isn't she? And she's the one with the name tag, yes?"

Eleni nodded, hopes rekindled. But Aethna went on, with the resolve of one who has had to harden up her softer edges.

"She could be well up in the hills, you know. But, quite honestly now, if you've run into no one who's seen her recently, well, you'd best not hold out too much hope that she is still alive. I am sorry, so sorry."

And she handed the picture back to Eleni.

Returning to the shelter just a few more times before they left for home, Eleni and Harry helped the volunteers to clean dog runs, wash the water and feed bowls and feed the dogs, which essentially amounted to being sure that there was an abundance of kibble poured into many large bowls, in long troughs and in random piles. When their bit of work was done, they sat with or walked some of the inmates.

The hike up the hill must have been Fabio's first outing ever on a leash. Vulnerable in the open, away from the safety of the shelter's walls, the sad little thing just sat rooted to the ground for the longest time, white rimmed eyes fixed warily on the human feet in front of him. Eleni stood patiently, ready to wait for however long it might take for him to make a first move, but with soothing pats of encouragement and a bit of her sweet talk it wasn't long before he was trotting, and then running along at her side. He seemed to have thawed from a terrified deep freeze, warming with the realization that he was outside and he was safe, and with great dog-delight he sniffed and rolled, and peed on every bush and tree he could reach, ears and pink tongue flopping with each leap he took.

Adonis, the abandoned hunter now sleek and full of life, took them for a walk, pulling Harry up the hill with huge, joyous bounds and a wild grin that screamed "I'm free, free at last!" Allowed to run, and to dance after the birds on his hinds as if trying to follow them in flight, to smell the bushes and trees and rocks, catching up with all of the scents that told him stories, the big dog was almost unable to contain himself and at one point he lunged so enthusiastically that his collar snapped, and off he went, bounding on minus his human companion, oblivious in his joy, dancing right into the deep of the woods until he was just — gone. Left behind, Harry stood in disbelief, mouth agape and limp leash dangling from his right hand as he watched the big dog disappear ahead of him.

"Oh shit." was all he said. Knowing that this fragile soul could easily dance himself into becoming lost in the wilds, or right into another set of wicked hands he and Eleni both took off at a run up the hill and into the woods after him. Out of breath and certain the big dog was lost for good — "Aethna's going to kill us!" — they were about to turn to their fate, empty leash in hand, when they came upon a young couple sitting on the ground, scratching the happy, drooling beast. Walking another of the shelter's dogs themselves, the graceful Adonis had come flying by and after running circles around them, being quite a social character he stopped for a breather and a bit of a chat and they'd been able to snag him.

Eleni and Harry stood now with Aethna at the shelter's fence, flanked by the many faces and wagging tails of longing and hope. The goodbyes were mercifully quick. They crouched to bid a wistful farewell to the dogs they'd grown so fond of and with promises of a next time, with Lily in tow and more boxes full of blankets and any other supplies they could muster, they hugged dear Aethna and set off down the hill on the rickety old moped, and into the last hours of their search for Margarita.

"Cheers you two!" Aethna called out with a grand wave of her arms as they puttered slowly down the steep drive. "God and Mary be with ye!" From the road below, Eleni looked back to see her still standing under the mulberry tree, the dozens of dogs quiet behind her. There were other visitors milling about now, other animal lovers, each with their own deep wells-full of questions and their own compassion, some wanting to take a dog home, all wanting to help out however they could, and Aethna turned to attend to them now. And on it went.

... the graces

Harry sat on the shore embracing his guitar, picking notes from the sun drenched air ... matching sounds rolling from his throat, trying to find a vowel or consonant to land upon. As he watched Eleni float motionless in the cool, quiet waters he played her sadness, note for note, a poignant melody floating out into the whisper of a breeze and away. He knew the sea was taking the bits of sadness from her, moment after weightless moment in the waters' caress filling her with more peace.

With the early evening they had ventured onto the local beach for one last grasp at their fading hope of finding Margarita. They walked the familiar strand from end to end and back again, calling her name into the trees, stopping at the taverna to show her picture to the men there. "Let's let it go, Eleni. I think it's time to move on." Harry said, his hand firm on her shoulder, an attempt to rein in her resolve to walk the beach just once more. They had done their very best.

On their route back to the main road they always passed through an olive orchard. Later on in the season it would be grazed down by the resident goats and ponies, and filled with cicada song as it shimmered golden in the heat of the summer's sun. But now it was a sea of emerald green, full of the late springtime, and wildflowers of every color were spread out ahead of them as far as they could see. Eleni thought to pick a handful to take up to the old cemetery for Selene.

The cemetery was still and quiet there in its place above the water. They both called weakly for Margarita. There was no reply. They peered over the low wall to the rocky beach below, where a dog had been seen saving a small girl's life. Nothing. After leaving flowers for both the old woman and her fisherman they sat, and surrounded by the silence of resting souls, just stared out to sea.

Her sorrows drawn out by the stillness, Eleni finally spoke.

"So many little graces, Harry. Margarita's little graces." She went quiet again as she wiped away the wet from her cheek, sad, for Margarita, for Lily, for all of the animals she couldn't help, all that she couldn't save. She was trying hard to find the goodness. "The Three Graces - you know about the Three Graces, don't you?"

"Mmmm." Harry hummed, tracing the lines on her palm with his fingers.

"Zeus's daughters. Aglaia. Euphrosyne. And Thalia, I think. They were three sister Goddesses who symbolize the graces of charm, mirth and beauty. Something like that! There you go, that's about it, all I know about Mythology!" She laughed, and Harry looked at her, scanning for the signs of relief. "I'm really not trying to go all sappy here Harry, but I do think our little dog friend gave us all of that, and more. Little graces."

They sat listening to the silence, only the whispering sea caressing the shore below them.

"She charmed us, right? Despite her ruckus, and all of those sleepless nights? She did enchant us, eventually! She gave us a world of happiness. Huge." Silence, again. "And she brought us Minou! Right there was happiness enough for us, and for Vassili!"

"Yes. I am still ... graced ... by the scars, from Minou climbing my legs and using me as her scratching post."

"The things we'll do for love and happiness, eh?" She laughed and brushed salty curls from his eyes. They sat quietly again, watching the fishing caiques pulling out from the harbor for a night on the sea.

"I think that, for us, she symbolizes not only all of the island's strays, that unresolved plight of the voiceless ones ... but also all of our experiences here; like an essence, distilled from the good and the bad, she embodies sadness, frustration, anger and all of the heart and spirit of everything, of everyone we've come to appreciate. That's pretty big — and deep, for such a little thing. Knowing her brought us closer to old Selene, to Popi and Theo ... closer to Takis, Kostas, Mana ... Arianna, everyone! We already knew Vassili, but that summer, the 'summer of the dog', that's when he really became our friend. No. Actually, that's when he became family."

She looked at Harry. "He just burst open, like a morning glory — or maybe a prickly cactus flower — once Lily started spending time with him. Didn't he? She pulled the laughter and joy right out of him, out to where he could see it, too. But I think their connection grew mostly because of her bond with the animals, especially with Margarita. And, unbeknownst to Lily, because of <u>his</u> karmic bond with Margarita! The dog was a bridge from Vassili's heart, through Lily, to us. See what animals can do for us?"

"Hmm." He nodded. "They never really would have talked about all of the animal troubles, if not for Margarita. And her pups. Lily's sadness over all of that really touched him and I think that it provided him with the opportunity to stop dwelling on his own loss. And yeah, without Margarita they wouldn't have been as close. And then ... Lil wouldn't have ever learned to pilot a little boat and catch calamari, to swear in Greek or sing gypsy songs, dance a Syrtaki or pick a bit on the bouzouki ... OR drink ouzo!"

"Oh God ... don't tell my Mom!" Eleni sputtered, in a burst of laughter. "Mmm, yes ... he helped all of us understand some of the hard things a little more, despite the drink and curses! I think Lily helped him understand a lot too, but of something we may never know. Do you remember what he was like, back when we first met him?"

"There's no forgetting Vassili, ever! He was quieter, more serious then. Preoccupied. Maybe even a little grumpy sometimes. No spontaneous song and dance that I can remember. But then, he was still mourning Maria! That is deep. And we didn't know! And, with ouzo being his closest friend, well, how happy can that be? You've said it over and over, and I really do get it — the children and the animals can be lifesavers."

"Well, they were for him. Then again, Margarita nearly caused the untimely death of our relationship with Haroula! Oh god, that poor woman."

"I'm surprised that she still lets us stay with her! I think it's a bit like we're on parole, with a room in the pensione only on promise of exemplary behavior. No harboring of hairy fugitives!"

"I wonder how long we can behave? Stay on the straight and narrow?" she laughed. "Not long I'm sure, once we have Lily here with us again!" The laughter trailed off. "I'm amazed at how many doors that silly little dog opened for us, what, to friendships, history lessons, laughter. Sorrows. The pups, oh, those poor pups. What a nightmare." She shuddered a bit, and wrapped her arms around herself against the hint of a chill coming on the breeze.

"That was a sinister piece, but we wouldn't have light, if not for the dark, right?" Harry ran both hands through his hair, stiff with brine, combing through the matted locks with his fingers before wrapping his arms around her, pulling her closer to his warmth, his heart. "Matia mou." he whispered, and she smiled. Those lovely Greek endearments always touched her. *My eyes, my darling ... how achingly beautiful.* She relaxed in the shelter of his embrace.

"It's been what, almost two years since we've seen her? Even now, that dog graces us with more, with Aethna and Mary, and the dog's shelter." She paused as two crows called to one another through the treetops above. "I know why I've felt so damned compelled to find her. Beyond that we adored her. To me, she symbolizes all that is wrong with how we treat the creatures of the earth, and all that can be right in our relationships to them. She is another example of the need for compassion in our world. A tangible example." Eleni went quiet again, closing her eyes, feeling Harry's heartbeat against her cheek. "The Four Graces, Harry! Ha! Four graces, not three. Aglaia, Euphrosyne, Thalia — and. Margarita! Ah, yes, Zeus also begot the little Margarita, she who grants the grace of Compassion ... and all of the little graces that follow in its wake!"

They just sat then, listening to the song of the evenings' breeze as it began to play around them and through the pines, rustling needles and causing boughs to creak. When the breeze left, and he was alone again with Eleni, Harry spoke.

"So, maybe putting all of this into words — all of the experiences and feelings that have forever connected us to her, to the island, to the people — maybe it will allow us some sort of closure. And we can let her go, Eleni? We can just let her rest now? You think? And then, if we can let her go, what we're left with is just the beauty of it all."

Eleni tried not to think of what might have become of Margarita, tried not to wonder if she suffered at all. Instead, she pictured her basking serenely in the warm, waning light on Margarita's Point.

"Yes, the beauty ... and all the little graces."

"Harry!"

They were passing through the old harbor, scanning for sight of Popi when Eleni gasped and pointed, nudging Harry with her elbow, pulling him to a halt.

Vassili and a lovely older woman were sitting together on Hestia's prow, heads close, legs dangling over the water. Vassili was caressing her arm. Minou was begging vainly from a neighboring fisherman as the two chatted and laughed, totally engrossed in their moment.

Vassili had a girlfriend.

"How could we have missed this? His happiness! Look at that! Oh, why do I always miss these things?" Eleni groaned. But then she smiled. *Is this why we didn't hear from him? He was ... busy?*

They found Popi at one of the new, arty bars just opened along the waterfront.

"Anais!" Popi exclaimed with delight as they settled around the table, revealing further that Anais was a French countrywoman who had fallen in love with the island — and Vassili — sometime in the summer past and had settled right into the hearts of both. Though she had a townhouse of her own and Vassili still lived on Hestia, the word was out around the village that they'd been seen together, taking boards off of the windows of his long abandoned cottage, sweeping verandas and working in the gardens there. "And Eleni mou ... you will like this, darling ... she tends to many of the town's animals."

Eleni and Harry had been so engaged in their search that they hadn't even noticed.

They made their way, arm in arm, toward Kosta's taverna. "We can drown the dumb away, Harry. How about a big carafe of white wine, Cretan maybe? Will that help us feel better about being so clueless?"

"Absolutely. We'll splurge, let's share a big fish, too. I saw barbouni at the market this morning, so Kostas will be serving it tonight. That'll help, having to digest it will take the blood away from our brains. So we'll just forget."

"Mmmm, perfect. With Mana's spicy horta, just swimming in oil and lemon! And salad, with sheep feta, maybe some pistachios and oregano sprinkled about? With caper flowers! It's our last supper, Harry, let's do it up ... God, I'm starving!"

But as they closed in on the taverna, Vassili, calling out with arms waving wildly jumped from Hestia to the quay.

"Yia sou! My friends!"

Changing course, they veered from taverna to caique. Vassili waited with hands clasped behind his back, his signature smoke hanging from pursed lips. *Oh, way too nonchalant!* He looked a bit like a child about to spill a secret. Eleni marveled at his neatly combed hair, and the smart Italian shoes on his feet.

He asked how their search for the missing dog had gone. Eleni stood with her arms out to him, empty palms up.

"Empty-handed, Vassili. We'll go home without her."

"Ah. I am so sorry, but no, do not think the worst. The little brown one, she was a survivor from her first day on this earth, you know. She always seemed to find what she needed. But, if she has not found herself a better life here, you must to know that she is in that other place ... and by my Maria's side."

Locking eyes with Eleni, he smiled, his half smoked cigarette clenched tightly between bared teeth, then nodded once with a certainty as though bringing a full stop to that long and difficult chapter. Turning, he offered his hand to the woman standing on the boat behind him, a short, elegant woman with an open face and a long gray braid that draped her shoulder and coursed down her chest. She was smiling broadly, beautifully, her laughing eyes dancing, and Vassili gently pulled her to his side. With his customary élan, and a lovely softness in his voice he introduced Anais Gillette to them, a flawless French accent rolling her name off of his tongue like warm, golden honey.

"Lipon. Filous mou ... Now then. My friends, the Gods, they have smiled upon me! They honor me, with one of their own, a Goddess in the flesh, in the life." He brushed the woman's hand with his lips. "I want to introduce you to my true heart, my soul ... Ah nah ees' Jhee lett'."

Anais Gillette's melodic "Bon jour, 'allo!" bathed Eleni and Harry with a lover's bliss as she stepped from Vassili's side to take both their hands in hers, and at once a great happiness danced around them all, taking up the space between the smiles and 'what a pleasure to meet you' and 'such joy!" and the cheek kisses and "Vassili! You didn't tell us!"

Vassili's delight was a welcome relief from the week's disappointments. *Maybe this will ease the letdown for Lily.* Eleni took several photos of he and his lovely Anais, and of course, the now rather portly Minou, all together on the red caique, evidence for Lily of their friend's happiness and of little Minou's great good fortune.

She had taken pictures every step of their week; pictures of the lovely caiques proudly displaying their fresh, new season's multi colored coats, and of the hillsides, awash in the vivid springtime's graces — as many water pictures as she could capture and of course, photos of the new dog shelter, of Aethna and Mary and many the four legged inmates there.

She also had taken several of Mo, one of Lily's former street kittens now living happily as the resident "greeter" at Arianna's villa. Mo had grown into a very handsome cat, a mischievous joker who demanded attention from everyone he met. He would bat pens from the guests' hands as they were filling out arrivals forms, or he would just dismiss any foreplay altogether and plop his behind down on the papers, right in front of them so that they would have to acknowledge him by looking him squarely in the eye. Arianna was forever apologizing to her guests for his behaviors until she realized that Mo actually was the best receptionist she could hope to have, for soon her villa was renowned as the 'villa of the cat' and while drawing in the cat lovers of the world, Mo became the poster child for stray cats of the Greek islands.

And those who didn't want the attentions of the personable cat? They were kindly shown to lodging elsewhere.

At night Mo prowled the villa grounds carrying a strange toy in his mouth, a wiry pipe cleaner wound into a spring that would bounce wildly in every direction when given a toss. As he made his rounds, with many doors left open to the warm evenings he was able to wander in and out of the rooms as he pleased, charming guests with his attentions and antics. He loved to feign the skill of the hunt and leap in mad pursuit of his toy when those who were willing would give it a toss, but like all great retrievers, each time he captured the silly thing he would bring it back and drop it at the thrower's feet for another go. When he took a liking to someone, someone with a particularly calm touch or who would throw the spring for a lengthy game of fetch, he left the toy just outside their door — their talisman, the undeniable indication that they were his chosen ones — and he would spend the night curled purring at the foot of their bed.

And so, the word was out. And as Aethna had said, change was afoot.

Eleni and Harry enjoyed their lovely meal and finished off the day by watching the promenade over more wine as darkness descended. They never tired of watching the evening volta. It seemed that the whole village was out walking tonight; the lovers, engaged as though no one existed in the world but them, and children set free to run, screaming their delight, some flying along the quay on their bikes, zipping through the crowd like bats with sonar engaged — and the little groups of old women wobbling along hand in hand, the youth within them all still so alive, betraying their ancient façades as they tittered like young girls over the latest gossip.

And they always loved to watch the men, philosophizing, pontificating, politicizing as they strode four or five abreast, colorful komboloi dangling from hands clasped behind their backs, a strangely percussive music, a cacophonic clicking pushing them along as each gave a flip to his string of beads with every several steps.

But best of all was the sight of the old men who were walking very slowly, or sitting quietly ... with a small, contented dog by their sides.

When the last drop of wine was gone Eleni took Harry's arm and they joined the flow themselves, as lovers will, and when their second pass of the harbor came to it's end at the steps that led to their quiet world in the neighborhood above the town, they disappeared into the night.

Early morning found them sleepwalking their way to the harbor to meet the ferry. Vassili, waiting, stepped from the Hestia to bid them farewell, opening his arms to them as they neared.

"Kalimera sas, my dear friends! Eleni, Harry, kalo taxidi, I wish you a good journey." He spoke quietly, in deference to the early morning's calm. "But, before you go, there is something that I must say to you."

It took him a moment. He fidgeted. He took off his cap and clutching it to his heart, arranged his hair, ruffling back and forth through it several times with his free hand. Finally, with his wild, ruffian's eyebrows raised high, he held his hand out as though holding Eleni and Harry still, keeping them in place until, lifting his wide palm up toward the sun, as if invoking some decree from the Gods, he began.

"Please. Now, my friends, you see, it seems that my heart, it has finally found its place to rest, it is no longer adrift. I have been given the very best of goodness, of beauty, of love. And one thing, well, it leads to another. So, I very happily make the request that you ..." He paused, feigning menace with the shaking of a finger as he leaned in towards Eleni, "... but only if you bring with you, my little Kokinoula! ... I very happily request that you must return next year for my wedding, God willing, to my heart of hearts, to my Anais. We both would be very happy to have you here for our celebration."

"Vassili!"

In the quiet, he took Eleni's hands into his own, "So you will come? No? Yes? No?" but she threw her arms around him and held on tightly, whispering,

"We would be honored, Vassili. Of course! And yes, yes, your Lily will be here." She stepped back with a smile and thought she saw a bit of damp hanging in the corners of his happy eyes.

"Bravo, bravo!" Harry took his friend's calloused hand into his own and pulled him close. "This is beautiful, man, this is just beautiful."

"You see? I had to find something more than the little dog to draw you here again, didn't I?" he chuckled, wiping his eyes with his shirtsleeve. "Until then, be well my friends, and please, all my love to that little red haired beauty. Endaxi?"

With an allegiance to the future affirmed and bittersweet farewells exchanged, Eleni and Harry continued on towards the ferry dock. The lumbering old slow-boat was just pulling in. There would be no quick exit today, no reprieve from the torture of watching the island and Margarita's ghostly shadows slowly disappearing into their past. But it really didn't matter, they both were filled with Vassili's happiness, and holding hands they turned to catch a last glimpse of their town, awakened now and bustling with the early season's visitors. The ferries had just begun to bring the first of what would be almost more people than the island could handle — and took a very few away with them when they departed port. Vassili would have a busy season.

"My friends! Yia hara!"

Halfway down the quay now, Eleni and Harry could hear him calling out to them again. He stood on Hestia's prow, holding his arms out to them.

"Magic! Beauty! Happiness! What more do we need, eh?

1993
THE WEDDING

matters of the heart

They sat on a veranda of smooth gray stone, sipping morning coffee, blinking the weariness of long days of travel from their eyes.

Lily was sprawled on the last of the steps with the sand at her feet, the languid sea stretched out before her, a blue carpet of satin reflecting the still weak sun. A cat, thin and yellow with great green eyes circled 'round her legs, eyeing her intently, whispering for more attention.

Eleni just gazed out over the water, her sparse thoughts buoyed by the quiet, syncopated waves of rhythm Harry played on his guitar.

Vassili had arranged this house for the family. A small, whitewashed villa trimmed in the blue common of many of the Aegean islands, it sat just at the edge of the shore. Large white urns and hand painted tins surrounded its sprawling veranda, all spilling over with geranium and herbs. Softly billowing gauze hung from ceiling beams, shade from the heat of the day's sun. Encircling the house, trellises supported gnarled climbing vines of bougainvillea and jasmine, the old plants converging upon the veranda in an impressionistic embrace of scattered color and heady scent, and from there three stone steps led down to a narrow, yellow stretch of sand that they shared only with Vassili's little white and blue caique, beached at its far end and ready for water passage to the village.

Three small bedrooms opened onto the generous veranda, each with a wide view of the tranquil water and diaphanous mosquito netting had been draped, ceiling to floor, over the beds, all fluttering now in the slight breeze washing through the house while the wind chimes, echoing the breeze, called through each triad of notes —

'you are here…
you are here…
you are here…'

It was perfect.

Quiet, simple, otherworldly and decidedly Greek, it was perfect.

Mother and daughter were on their feet now, moving slowly as they made feeble attempts to ready for a trip into the town. Lily brushed sand from her toes before entering the kitchen.

"When do we see Popi?" She was looking forward to seeing their flamboyant friend, slated to arrive on the late morning ferry from Piraeus for she was coming home to the island for Vassili's wedding.

"Soon, Lily." her mother murmured, pouring herself another cup of coffee. Cradling the precious cup in her hands she leaned back against the wood counter and faced the doors, open to the sea, where Lily now sat on the floor with the yellow cat. There was an autumn chill to

317

the air. She grabbed a blanket from a chair and pulled it close around her.

"We'll take the little caique to town." Miles away by road, the town was just twenty gentle minutes or so away by sea. "The ferry comes in around eleven, Harry?" Harry looked up from his guitar, disoriented, as though pulled from the depths of a dream.

"The ferry, darlin'? Eleven?"

He nodded and then dove back into the notes that seemed one with the breath of the morning sea. Already, something new was coming to him.

"We'll have time enough for a little stroll and some shopping before we meet her." She walked over Lily, draping the blanket over the girl's shoulders as she sank cross-legged next to her. They listened to Harry and the sea, and the morning sun rose and strengthened and eventually reached them, thawing the fog of sleep and chasing away the bit of chill.

Warmed and awake enough now, Eleni and Lily quietly set to putting the house in order. They laid out towels and found pitchers for water and wine and as the resident cat's bowl was being restocked with kibble, Harry wandered through with an armload of the wood used for cooking on the outdoor stove.

"Scooters. We'll get a few in town, we'll need them to get up to the shelter. I'll get Makis or Pavlos to ride one back out with me. You girls can come home by yourselves in the caique, can't you?" He dropped the wood by the stove and continued on, down the steps to the beach and toward the boat.

Before they could make the pilgrimage to the dog shelter, which Lily had yet to see, there was Vassili's wedding to attend. Tomorrow was the big day and as they neatened the house now, Eleni told Lily of women in the

318

village, already busy preparing the makings of a traditional feast, the men readying fire pits and the spits that would be used for the roasting of kid goat and lamb.

"For our sweet fisherman." Eleni added with a smile.

Lily, a confirmed vegetarian, wrinkled her nose.

"Yes, but how can anyone kill a cute little baby goat?"

Harry fiddled with ropes and pondered the small engine, rekindling his memory of their workings. The girls were taking their time, meandering down the thin strand in apparent conversation with the yellow cat winding her way around and through their legs.

"Hey!" he called out as he jumped back to the sand to pick up the mooring rope. "Come on girls ... the ferry will be in soon! Let's go!" He leaned his weight back against the rope, pulling the boat just a bit further up onto dry shore where it settled securely and as Eleni and Lily approached, he held out his hand to help them both board.

With Lily at the helm Harry pushed the little caique off of the sand, splashed through the chill blue water and sprung lithely aboard — in a moment they were turned around and heading seaward. The girl was quite adept at handling the small craft, thanks to the many mornings she had accompanied Vassili along the island's coast in search of calamari or some delectable fish. He had often left her at the rudder while he plied his lines and there was no better way to learn than to just be in command and try one's best not to run aground! He'd been a patient teacher, and she had fun memories of those mornings, left in charge while he sang at the top of his lungs, paying his attention only to feeding his lines out to the shallows in the hopes of a lucky catch.

Their little boat moved elegantly over the calm water. With the rocky, green coast port side, an endless sea to her right, Eleni sat on the bow humming, on watch, alert for submerged rocks as they rolled softly along, following the contours of the island shore. Suddenly, shading her eyes with one hand, she pointed out to sea.

"Dolphins! Oh look! Dolphins, Lily!"

Fifty feet away was the unmistakable silhouette of two dolphins, moving as one, breaking surface now and again, sliding slowly through the clear blue water. Harry reached back to cut the engine. Stilled, the little boat bobbed obediently in place while they watched the creatures continue their foraging, blowing softly as they took in air before sinking back to their world below the transparent surface. Lily's eyes were wide as she watched the pair dip and glide, slowly making way closer to the caique.

"They're smiling at us!" she whispered, breathless, leaning over the side of the low lying boat, reaching out as one of the dolphins, hovering on her side to better see, looked directly up at the girl with what appeared to be a smile upon her face. She lingered as Lily traced her smooth, gray speckled skin with gentle fingers.

And then they were gone.

"Well, that was a gift from the Gods and Goddesses." Harry chuckled quietly. "Remember Vassili telling us about the dolphins? They don't hang around here much. I think they came to see you, Lily."

Vassili told them that dolphins weren't seen as often as they once had been, as some areas of the Aegean was getting a bit too polluted and warm for the sensitive creatures. Though it was still a lovely sea in most places, sewage and fertilizers were being dumped into it from the mainland in alarming quantities and it was thought that many of the dolphins had left to find a better environment. "But!" he had said, waving one finger in the air as he always did when he wanted to emphasize a point, "There now are these kids, they are called the 'environmentalists' ... they are working on solving this terrible puzzle of our beautiful sea."

"To see those two is a good sign." Harry said.

"I think it means good luck for Vassili!" Lily replied, scanning the sea for any last signs of the magical creatures.

Lily and her mother chattered on, like excited children certain they had seen the likes of elves or fairies, until Harry started up the engine and gliding once again over the deep blue waters they all fell into a potent stillness. The calm of the sea swallowed them whole, hushed everything around them, the purring of the caique's petite engine the only sound, a mantra left in their wake. But once the boat rounded the promontory the beautiful hush was shattered by a greedy flock of seagulls, noisy shepherds guiding them home to port, crying out loudly for handouts as they circled above the small fishing craft recognized as an occasional source of their breakfast. Lily howled with laughter, ducking each time Harry threw bits of bread up to the birds that swooped and dove to snatch the morsels out of the air just above her head.

When they'd reached the moorings, Lily handed the boat over to her father who dropped anchor and carefully slipped the small craft in place right next to Vassili's Hestia. Upon stepping foot onto the quay she walked a few tentative steps up the red caique's plank to peer over the bow.

There — as she had so hoped — under a bench, curled tightly with one paw over her head in the cozy old bed, lay Minou.

"Minou, ghata!" Lily called breathlessly as she stepped aboard the boat. She squatted, her arms wrapped around her legs. "Minou, come here kitty girl." The cat looked up through half open eyes, seeming to take note of a familiar tone. She sat up, yawned widely and paused a moment as though translating the girl's appeal, licked a paw and swept it over her head in a graceful pass from behind an ear and over an eye, and down across her whiskers and then, just stopped and stared. After another big yawn, and stretching indulgently and completely as only cats can, she shook herself off and padded surely up to the girl.

"Oh! Ghataki mou!" Lily stroked the soft coat and cooed to the fat little cat rubbing furiously now upon her legs, and wondered to herself if many of her other foundlings had survived the last few years.

Minou turned and, standing upon her hind legs, placed her front feet on Lily's chest, gazing intently into the familiar face. Reaching up with a paw, claws carefully sheathed, she touched the girl's cheek and opened her mouth wide. "Aaack!" Lily, laughing, scratched the cat's chin and stroked her firmly from her crown to the tip of the tail that pointed now to the heavens.

"Aaack, aaaaaack!" Minou, drooling with pleasure, arched her back and danced on little tiptoes, back and forth, from side to side, meeting Lily's hand with each turn. Pure bliss — a rich, loud and rattling purr — poured from the little cat. The girl and her foundling disappeared into this happiness for several minutes, reawakening a blending of spirits until Lily finally picked up the rumbling Minou and just held her close, the cat's eloquent toning and Lily's smile further brightening the harbor's already vibrant morning.

322

Finally, she set Minou down and with one last kiss to the top of her downy head left her sitting sentry like some odd, misplaced Egyptian figurehead on Hestia's bow and joined her parents to continue on to the harbor platia, the small, shaded square where they came upon Haroula and her cronies taking respite from their never ending chores. When the old women realized that the tall redheaded girl standing there with the Americans was Lily, they popped to their feet and exclaimed, all at once, in an ascending glissando, "Ooooohhh?", and then erupted in a chorus of "Po po! Koritzi mou! Lily mou!", chittering and clucking loudly like a flock of proud hens. Never mind that Lily now stood at least an inch taller than the tallest of the old ones, they patted her cheeks and hugged her to their ample bosoms as though she were still just a little girl.

Up the long, familiar flight of steps and past Haroula's house, they continued to walk the quiet lane to the town's high hill where they were met by the raspy barking of elder men, echoing off of the hard walls. Turning towards Takis' market, they saw him standing outside his shop, taking in the morning with the old men of the town who spent their days migrating from shop to kaffenion to taverna for coffee and conversation, their laughter and shouting reverberating now off the old stone of surrounding buildings. Genuinely surprised to see his America friends, Takis was especially pleased to see Lily.

"You've grown like my tree here, Lily. How will your kittens ever recognize you? And your Greek lessons, how do they go? Are you ready now, to work for me?" he laughed, shaking the girl's hand.

"Next year Mr. Takis! Tou hronou! When I come back I really want to work at the new dog shelter but I'll work for you too!"

Takis ushered them into his small, dark shop where anything they could possibly need would somehow always be found. "Eleni," Harry called from the depths, "Mana's cheese, fresh!" and after choosing a few fragrant hunks the girls went on to pilfer bins filled with the last of the season's vegetables that had come straight from Takis' wife's fruitful garden. Eleni selected large, deep purple eggplants, perfect for grilling ... and bunches of spicy greens, ripe tomatoes, lemons, and oregano hanging in dried bunches from a rafter, and after some poking around in the dusty corners they found a cache of Takis' own home grown olives and small tins of his oil. Harry found his own personal treasure, a barrel of the locally made wine, and Takis poured it into plastic jugs for transport back to the little villa. There would be a feast tonight!

Silently, with a smile and a wink the kind Takis handed Lily a complimentary bag of cat food, and the two shook hands over their tender bond of caring for the needy animals.

Outside, the small, bespectacled and suspendered old men were still barking opinions as they put on their caps and coats.

"Neh, neh, neh. Kalimera sas Dimitri. Giorgo, Theodorou. Yia sas." Takis' voice echoed in the alley as he bid a good day to his elders, leaving now to carry on with their daily migration. He untied the tidy, white apron wrapped around his waist and motioned to the family to sit with him there in the cool of the autumn morning, and proceeded to catch them up on the talk of the town — until the moist, buttery aroma of warm bread all but lifted them from their seats. It beckoned from the bakery across the lane, where loaves fresh from the stone oven had been set out on the sill to cool, so Eleni, Harry and Lily thanked

Takis for his kindness and hurried off to snatch up several warm bundles of the delicious bread before it all disappeared quickly into the hands and mouths of the others lured in by its scent.

The backpacks and totes were filling quickly. All left missing amongst the fresh cheeses and produce and breads was fish from Vassili's market and as it was early enough yet that there would be plenty still to choose from, they wandered back down to the harbor for this last bit of business.

Neatly laid out on ice and stacked in wooden boxes, the fish was dutifully guarded by an army of polite harbor cats and hopeful seagulls. Eleni snapped photos of the montage — the cats, weary fishermen carrying pallets of fish from their small boats, and her own family queued up with villagers and taverna owners and tourists on the steps of the open air market, all choosing dinner fare from the freshest of the catch which today was a choice of many different kinds and sizes. Harry chose several kilos of the mikros gavros, the delicious tiny fish that he planned to grill for their sunset picnic, and then turned and smiled at Eleni and Lily as he held up two plastic bags full for them to see.

"She's here!" Lily spied the old ferry chugging and heaving around the point, Margarita's point, towards the newer harbor where the larger ships always docked. A bag of cat food flopping over her shoulder, she ran ahead, down the paralia.

Eleni watched her daughter as she sprinted to the boat — at fourteen ("and a half", Lily would surely add) years, that bit of the child left in her still revealed itself now and again. A vision of a younger Lily, running along with little Margarita at her heels, sneaked into Eleni's thoughts. *Does she ever think about the little dog?* Eleni knew

325

that it really was just a matter of time before they chanced upon one of Margarita's kin, a pup or grand-pup, on one of their walks through the town. *We're here for other reasons, now.* Inhaling a great breath of happiness for Vassili, she breathed out her thoughts of the ghost of a dog.

Popi eventually emerged from the smoky bowels of the belching ferry, a sparkly prism reflecting the colors of the Aegean over the relatively plain sea of humanity that boiled out of the boat around her. After the requisite flurry of greetings the group wandered to Kosta's, to nurse frappes and friendships, and in fifteen minutes Popi and Lily were well engaged in their own world of color and laughter while Eleni and Harry sat quietly, wearing relaxed smiles. Being this easily altered was evidence of the effect of Greece's exceptional light, the music of foreign language and the habit time had, of moving counter to the fast pace of their own native culture. Once again, they'd been snared by the magic. It happened more quickly with each visit they made.

An old friend, Makis, joined the table as well, and yet another hour of food and conversation passed. Given to easy laughter, the handsome Makis always kept them well entertained, now spinning the tales of his time, long past, spent living in Florida — the hysterical misadventures of a gorgeous young stranger in a strange land that were capped with "Yes. Once I had twelve girlfriends ... yes, at one time, twelve! ... no, none of them knew! I was young! Young, and very happy - and always so exhausted! And then very much in big trouble, when they all found out!" —before looking up at Harry through the laughter and pointing to his watch, the singular thing reminding them all that time indeed still existed.

"Pahme, Hahree. Let's go and get the bikes. We will be too drunk to ride if we wait too much longer!"

Bags and food were loaded onto the caique while Lily sat on the quay and scratched the flabby belly of the old Queen of the harbor, a graying old-lady dog who lay upon her back in the midst of everything, four paws to the sky and oblivious to the slow-ups she sometimes caused. She groaned with pleasure at Lily's every touch, flapping a rapturous hind leg whenever Lily would hit upon a particularly itchy spot. "This dog actually lives here? She can just hang out here? And no one bothers her? A catch in her breath, she looked up suddenly ... perhaps with a hope of catching sight of a little brown dog in the shadows. *No. Just her ghost. It's everywhere here.*

Harry and Makis went off in one direction, while Popi and Eleni pulled Lilly up off the cement and into the other, into a wandering through the maze of shaded, narrow shop lined streets. This part of the town was a precious, loyal relic of real island life, steadfast and solid as the rock it was built with, while the tacky tourist shops and generic hotels went in and out of fashion all around it. Here there were the old shops, the ones filled with delicate handmade linens and pottery turned by local hands, and others filled with boating and fishing gear; the town Ouzerie was a delicious dark and cavernous room lit only by ambient light reflecting from the glittering bottles full of ouzos and wines and liqueurs from all of Greece, vivid colors packed tightly into shelves that lined the walls from floor to ceiling. A few blue checkered tables were set in the middle of the room, each set with a single candle that flickered in green and blue and burgundy reflection, and wild aromas called out from the kitchen. At the kaffenion next door, old warriors and retired butchers and fishermen sat together under a single garish lightbulb, reliving glories past or intent upon their tavli games at a table littered with butts and bottles and spent cups of coffee. And the gyros stand, where meat sizzled on the spit and the long line of hungry folk waited for a taste of the town's best fast food, was like the local living room, the place where locals were sure to meet up with someone they knew and catch up on the news.

The girls wandered into the Chemist's shop, much like the small, local drug stores in the states, relics that were quickly disappearing from small town America as big box mega-stores made them obsolete. Here though, herbal and homeopathic remedies and over the counter modern medicines were all of equal import and sat side by side upon the shops' shelves.

"What a bounty! This always amazes me. It's so hard for us to find many of these at home." Eleni said, inspecting the jars of natural remedies. She turned to Popi. "Actually, most people there are very suspicious of herbs and all, and hold some strange belief that they belong to the Dark Ages ... well, at least not to the modern world! We can only find them at special shops called herb shops or health food stores."

"What then? The herbs grow from the earth! The earth! She offers them to us, they are a gift, a blessing! Smart people, a long, long time ago figured out that that they heal! And they belong only to the Dark Ages? Oh please, you must be joking!"

"Oh, no! Not joking." Eleni took a quick photo of an incredulous Popi, a bit ruffled, hand upon her hip and dark eyes flashing. "At home, remedies like these are equated with hairy-armpited, pot-smoking and brown-rice-eating Hippies! And maybe even voodoo, or walking barefoot upon hot coals, Popi! In other words, not with what is considered ... there ... to be 'normal', or the civilized world!"

She laughed. "We're taught to trust only in 'modern' medicine, you know. Things such as these?" she shook a packet of tablets used for relaxing and sleeping, gentle and safe, made from valerian root, "At home, these are equated with the burning times ... the days of the witches when people, mostly women of course, were bound and burned alive at the stake because they helped to heal people and animals with the things of the earth! Oh yeah, they belong to the witches ... even though these, right here, are made with valerian, the same herb that is now the basis of a sanctioned, modern drug. A very strong one ... oh much stronger than these little tablets! It's used far too often, by far too many people, to deaden some anxiety, to numb themselves in order to relieve, I don't know ... what? A boredom with their lives? And then, they get addicted to them! So, they're addicted to a life void of feeling! It is amazing, isn't it? Deadening and tranquilizing with lethal modern drugs is OK, but helping a body with herbs to relax and regenerate so that it can heal naturally, is not!"

"Truly now ... now you really are kidding me Eleni?" Popi asked of her friend who shrugged and mouthed an apologetic "No." and laughed again as she took another picture.

Arm in arm they stepped out the door and found Lily across the lane, peering through a window of the building there.

"A pet shop, Mama! Come here, look, there's even dog toys ... and a bird in a cage! And travel thingies! I can't believe it!"

Eleni and Popi, shading their eyes from the sun's glare, looked inside and saw the travel crates and bags of dog and cat foods piled in corners of the mostly empty room. There were bowls and leashes and even wormers and flea prevention products for sale upon its few shelves, a meager offering — but they were there.

"Popi? Is this just for the tourists' animals?"

"I've heard of this place. Yes, a doctor from the mainland moved here a few months ago, he opened this store, Eleni. It will be open all the year, he says, but now I hear from my Yia Yia that the man is seen in the Ouzerie more than he is seen in here! I don't know. But she also says that when it is open, he sits there behind his little desk and will help if you have a sick animal. Every bit helps, no?"

Lily straightened and turned to her mother and Popi, thrust her arms into the air and let go a victorious cry. Here were obvious signs of a caring for the animals.

"There is a VET'S office? Oh ... my ... gosh!" With a spin she leapt away and did a happy dance, shaking and shimmying — the poise of her budding woman-ness again overwhelmed suddenly by that wild child still percolating within her. Popi laughed and floated along right behind the girl, snapping her fingers. They chanted and snapped in rhythm as they fell into a mambo down the lane.

"Yes ... yes, yes." Snap — the snap, accentuated by pointed toes and thrust hips. Eleni was barely able to keep pace with them, she was laughing so hard. She was shooting pictures of the wiggling bums and prancing legs and snapping fingers when two stern faced old women out doing their shopping feigned terror and plastered themselves, wide eyed, to the alley walls as the noisy, happy procession passed them by. "Po po po po!" they hissed, eyes narrowed, shaking their heads after the dancers — but as they turned away, they poked one another and burst into howls and hoots.

The trio eventually danced their way back to the borrowed caique. Breathless, they climbed aboard, and with Lily at the helm it carried them surely away, over the calm blue and back to the quiet of the lovely little house by the sea.

The evening was spent as most always were, there, in laughter and in good company, and with plentiful food and drink. A distant tinkling of bells and the calls of goats coming in from the hills for their milking floated through on the occasional breath of wind — the evening's harmony, gently filling the spaces between words in compliment to quiet conversation, as the friends gathering on the terrace to view the spectacle of the Aegean sunset. Arianna had driven in with Theo, just off of the evening boat from Athens, and once they arrived the wine was passed, and as everyone settled to watch the show Harry stoked the fire at the grill and began to consider his plan for the fish.

The light left behind by the sinking sun was transforming the sky to liquid amber just as the rumblings of an approaching caique ruffled the quiet. Vassili's good friend Mikhalis sailed around the break, waving and singing as he appeared to emerge from that fire set upon the lapis sea. He skillfully ran his dark blue boat aground upon the beach and before Eleni and Lily could begin to walk the length of the small bay to greet the fisherman, he had secured his boat, crossed the strand, bounded up the terrace steps and was hovering over the huge plateful of gavros, crying out "Ohee, ohee!".

Laughing and shaking his finger, Mikhalis turned to Harry. "Oh no, NO, no ... let Mikey cook the lovely little fishes! Hah-rry, you will watch and ... hopefully ... you will learn! Lipon!" He took command of the open-air kitchen, booming orders, get him this and get him that and after meticulously washing his thick hands, he tied an apron around his waist and set to work grilling the small fish to perfection over the old fire fed stove. First tossing them lightly in olive oil, he set them on a grill over the fire, and with a generous flourish of salt, just a dab of butter and a sprinkle of fresh oregano, surely saved the dinner from their inexperience.

The terrace they all now stood upon as they watched the maestro at work had been laid, stone by stone, by his late father, Giorgos Kantizakis. The house itself was built in the late 1940's, on the outer cusp of the big war and the German occupation of Greece. Before that it been a tiny kalivi — just one room, a tile roofed shelter built to withstand the weather, a place to stay while one was grazing his, or her flock in the lush fields that ran from the hills to the sea. The building of the rock sea wall that extended from the promontory in front of the kalivi was arduous work, and only with the muscle and sweat of Giorgos and many of his friends was it accomplished. It afforded the land safe harbor with perfect access to the water and over time, Giorgos enlarged the kalivi to accommodate his growing family. Mikhalis grew up here learning his sea trade.

He now lived in the town with his wife and mother and rented the house by the sea to tourists. Though a spare accommodation by most standards, it was obvious that he had cared for it lovingly over the years, most recently fitting new windows and glass doors with blue shutters that kept out the wind and weather. With the final flourish, a fresh coating of whitewash, the house sparkled in the light against a deep blue sky.

There was only one feeble line that supplied a sometimes tentative stream of power from the main cables snaking the length of the island from the town. But there was little need for electricity, here. Gas powered the refrigerator and indoor cooking stove and the sun's energy provided hot water to bathe with. Light came either from the sun streaming through windows and skylights, or from candles and lanterns that cast their warm yellow glow far into the night.

And now, as the night slowly drew itself around them all, oil lanterns were lit, flaming torchieres were driven into the sand and the villa was swathed in that golden calm. The darker the night grew, the more rarefied the atmosphere, ... the water reflecting only the dancing lights hovering over the shore.

After dinner everyone sat at the edge of the water, just within range of the flickering light, drinking retsina or soda from old glass jars and talking of the magic of the Aegean. Mikhalis held court, telling tales of his trade and of the magical delfines, the magical dolphin ... of days at sea and of her myths, and from talk of the watery mysteries the conversation eventually drifted to matters of the heart. The wine and conversation flowed easily and when the four corners of love had been sufficiently explored and poeticized to great detail, the talk moved on to politics. The older local men, Mikhalis no exception, all loved to debate politics, always with a great passion and especially with people from distant lands — those who either could be ensnared easily by their own ignorance, or those who were equally confounded by the state of the world and, well informed, could hold their own in a good argument. Most of the local men had traveled extensively in the maritime trades in their youth, travels that gave them a broad view of the world outside of their own borders, and having seen politics — and many wars — within those very borders turn their country inside out, they knew what governments were capable of. Not at all loath to voice his opinion of how easily the stupidity of man could turn the tides of history, Mikhalis was in his element here.

While politics and philosophy kept the conversation lively at the house, Popi and Lily had retreated and lay flat out on the beach under a warming blanket, heads close together, eyes starward. Popi, not so far herself from her own metamorphosis from child to woman, listened as Lily spoke in the hushed tones that always seem to barely shield teenage girls' innermost thoughts — of the stars and Gods and Goddesses, hopes and dreams, the animals. In direct alliance, they whispered together of these things that join artists' souls while the yellow cat, now named Ouranos (That's a masculine name, Lily! – Well, I don't care, 'Heaven' fits her, don't you think?) lounged on the rock wall just behind them, their keeper, watching over them slit eyed, but alert.

Talk and laughter and Mikhalis' sudden and frequent fits of song filled the night to full before the captain rose abruptly, bid them all a lovely kalinikta, set off down the darkened sands and climbed back aboard his beautiful boat. Just as the wonderings came — "How can he possibly make his way home in the dark of the moon?" Eleni asked — the veteran captain switched on the boat's running lights and pulled away and into the night. The ability to navigate these waters, in the light as well as in the dark, was deeply etched into the souls of all of the seafarers.

With Mikhalis gone and the evening done, sleep came easily. The quiet sea was alone again with the sky, only the cat stirred, trembling with anticipation as she sat on the wall listening for stirrings in the night.

the wedding

The lazy autumn sun rose to find Harry already up, making coffee while Eleni and Lily fussed around the house. The day of Vassili's wedding was upon them.

The afternoon's ceremony would be held at the cottage Vassili shared years ago with his first love, Maria, but the day's festivities were set to begin with a mid day gathering at Kostas and Mana's taverna. Lily nudged their guests awake and, wrapping herself in a blanket, walked down to join her mother who had wandered off, coffee in hand, and sat sleepily now with Ouranos on the sand.

Eleni placed her hand on the girl's knee when she'd settled, and they sat watching the horizon fill with pinks and golds and reds above the sunrise's own purple sea.

"The greatest show on earth," Eleni always said of the sun's magnificent rising, "a constant as sure as anything in this life." She took a sip of her coffee and turned to Lily.

"Vassili's big day, Lily. Should we get started?"

"We have time, Mama. Lets just sit here."

So they sat, Eleni, Lily and Ouranos, staring out to sea until the colors bled and faded to morning blue.

Harry, already dressed in his finery, waited patiently on the terrace with his guitar, willing the notes to come to him from the lapping waves while Eleni and Lily debated what to wear. When they finally emerged from a back room dressed befitting their Greek fisher-king's wedding in layers of gauzy, floating fabric and colorful shawls, their red hair tied up in knotted scarves, Popi clapped her approval.

"Bravo, bravo! Poli omorfi! So beautiful, both of you!" she cried, and in a sudden burst everyone was moving at once, readying to leave.

Lily was lit up, dancing around the terrace in animated anticipation while her parents closed the house to the day, stopping only to wave her shawl at the car as it sped off towards the village with Popi's orange scarf floating from a rear window like a flame, and billows of dust in it's wake.

Ouranos trailed them down the beach to the boat. It seemed to Lily that the little cat was willing them, with her intense green eyes and cat magic, to return. Maybe she was hoping that they, her present source of abundance, wouldn't forget to come back. Sitting on the sand, Ouranos watched intently as they put out to sea. Perhaps this evening, in sacrifice for the blessing of the return of her good fortune, she would catch a mouse and leave them its bits in their honor, as she had this morning in gratitude for the bowl of perfectly cooked gavros she'd been given for her dinner.

Little mouse feet, the tail and an unrecognizable glob of inner mouse part were all laid out neatly and in orderly fashion on a mat just inside the kitchen's door, and the little cat even sang a special song for them as she sat by her gift. Eleni had almost stepped in it with naked toes, but used to these tributes from the feline clan at home, had praised the generous little cat, then gingerly scooped up the bits and flung them to the crows, far into the field next to the house.

Lily giggled now, watching the ginger cat grow smaller and smaller as they set off.

The boat trip gave time enough for the three to come fully awake and by the time they set foot on the quay they were ready to face the fray. Kosta's taverna was filled with excitement. It looked as though the whole population of the harbor was in attendance, overflowing into the lane and along the quay and while laughter and song — essential elements here, like air and water — echoed over the water. Babies squeaked and squealed, and children dressed in their Sunday best darted between tables chasing after the taverna cats, busy old women scolding halfheartedly as they herded them about.

Quite suddenly the festive group dispersed. Time came for a bit of a rest, the mid day's siesta before the real party began, and with it came a quiet over the waterfront as impressive as the merriment that so recently had filled it. The family retired to the Hestia to relax and play cards on her bow in the sun for a time, missing little Minou's resonant purr ... she had been taken away to Vassili's cottage, to her new life as resident mouse catcher. "I wonder how she'll like life as a land lubber? We will see her later, won't we?" Lily asked with a bit of worry to her tone.

Eleni glanced up at the sound of a caique approaching the sleepy harbor and stood to stretch. The shadows had begun to make their long, autumn reach over the quay, "Let's walk." she said quietly, holding her hand out to the girl, and they left Harry to the attentions of his guitar to haunt the old part of the town just behind the frontage of boats and tavernas. It was a special day, Vassili's day and at this time of year locals could afford to close up shop to join in the celebration, so with only a few tavernas and shops open it was eerily, beautifully quiet, showing a genuine nature that was much harder to see when the tourist season was in full sail.

Two hungry dogs crept furtively through the quiet streets, evidence that Aethna's shelter had not yet quite cured the island of its ills.

"Oh shoot. Mama! We forgot food." Lily moaned. Eleni immediately turned her daughter around and they retraced their steps, back to the open gyros stand where they bought a plateful of meat, and after letting it cool just enough, Lily doled it out behind bushes and in dark corners to the hungry ones who still lingered while the island went through its growing pains. There was no way that neither she nor her mother could have continued on through this day of such great joy had they not taken the moment to reach out to those just beyond it's grasp.

With the afternoon in its wane and the dusk creeping closer they wandered back to Harry and Hestia and another game of cards ... but soon Vassili's wedding party could be heard in the distance. Led along by boisterous musicians who had already and quite apparently been at the ouzo, it came dancing along the beach toward the boats and just behind the drunken band of roisterers walked a glowing, freshly shaven and beautifully dressed Vassili, a delicate, raven-haired woman on his arm.

"His daughter Kaiti." Popi whispered as they joined the procession, a colorful river winding through village back streets and then out of town along the stone donkey path that led into the hills towards the old cottage.

Oh my ... He walked proudly towards his future with his once-estranged daughter at his side. Eleni's eyes began to fill. *Here, the sad story ends, he's made his peace ...* Margarita came to mind as she recalled the role the little dog had played in Vassili's drama from it's very beginnings, *from being her angel of death to being one of her champions in life. He even made that one right.* She dabbed at her eyes and smiled, *another one of Margarita's little graces,* and then turned away from the ghost of the little dog. Now, with his daughter and Anais in his life, Vassili was starting anew, with love and happiness and his beloved sea. Eleni thought of his words, "What more does one need?"

As the entourage drew near to the old cottage, a bent old woman could be seen standing in the doorway. Eleni looked to Popi.

"This is the mother of Vassili's first wife, Eleni. This is Melina, who has stayed close to him since his Maria's death. You see, this is a country wedding, obviously not an Orthodox church wedding and here, in a very, very loose Greek custom, Melina is taking the role of Vassili's own mother who has been gone a long time now. Melina will welcome the couple into the matrimonial home. It is just symbolic. But beautifully symbolic." The wedding would be part Greek country tradition, part Anais' own creative musings, and as Eleni explained this to Harry and Lily the music suddenly stopped, and with a hush, the two parties converged.

With the radiant Anais seated sidesaddle on the back of a stout white donkey adorned with flowers and garlands and bells, the bride's group had walked to the cottage along the dusty paths that led from her apartment deep in the town, through the orchards that blanketed the north side of the hill. The donkey stood dutifully now while Vassili walked over to take Anais' hand and help her gently to the ground. Tears traced his weathered cheeks. "My angel of life", he whispered to his beloved, a vision in her long blue gown, shoulders wrapped in a white linen shawl, sprigs of autumn wildflowers woven into the long graying braids encircling her head and framing a face that could in no way conceal her happiness. They embraced and turned and, each taking one of Melina's hands, walked into their home.

Inside the house, overlooking the once-forsaken land that now again held the huge promise of a future, they faced one another and spoke of their love and good fortune, and of their hopes of productive and peaceful lives together. With the new young Mayor officiating and only the closest of family and friends surrounding the couple exchanged golden rings in a very modern ceremony, drank together from a hand wrought cup engraved with their names and in the eyes of anyone who mattered to them, Vassili and Anais were wed.

Hearty calls of "Hronia Polla, many good years!" rose from the crowd waiting just outside as they crossed the threshold, and in an instant the sodden band of musicians came to life and the dancing began. Vassili spotted Lily standing at the edge of the fray, danced Anais to her side and swept the girl up into his joyous embrace, twirled her about once or twice and when he set her back to earth, with hands folded over his heart he began to speak.

"I must tell you now, my little one, with my bride as my witness. You are the spark that lit up all of this, all of this, all my happiness! Did you know this? It was you, yes, so curious, not at all afraid to speak your mind ... and not afraid to feel, ah, so deeply about things that mattered to you. It was you who helped me to climb out from under the weight of a sad, drunken man's darkness. You and your happy dancing, your courage to speak your beautiful passion for your animal friends, and your trust – – in me! It all brought me back, from my exile from life. Yes! I had no choice then, I had to come back to where there is happiness and laughing all around me, to where I could feel again my heart, pounding in my chest and the air aching in my lungs."

Vassili pounded his chest and laughed to the heavens, a challenge to God, someone's God. "I could taste the salt of the tears upon my cheek, no longer able to pretend that it was only the spray from the sea. And I could finally feel again that I must live, that I must laugh! See? What a difference you can make in one person's life?"

Then, quietly, "For that, which you may not yet understand but must always remember, Kokinoula mou ... I can never thank you enough. "

He took Lily's head gently in his two large hands to kiss her on the forehead, and stepped back with a sweeping bow to introduce his new bride. "And so Lily, now, I present to you my angel, my good friend and now my wife, Anais. And Anais, this is Lily, my little red-haired spark of life!"

"Bonjour, bonjour, Lily, mon chéri. I am so pleased to finally meet you ... and I see that your light is as bright as Vassili has always boasted it was!" Anais took Lily deep into her gentle heart, held the girl's hands firmly in her own and while they chatted Lily marveled at how like an angel the woman really did seem, such a gentle way about her, eyes so kind and her voice so soft, so rich. Lily especially liked that despite all of her softness, she had the worn and hardened hands of someone who worked the earth and handled ropes and milked goats ... *Perfect*, she thought, *her hands match Vassili's!*

When the newly wedded couple was finally swept away by the tide of friends, Vassili's daughter, Kaiti, took the opportunity to approach.

"You must be Lily, yes? You know, my father has told me how he thinks that you are so much like my mother, in heart and spirit. And yes ... I think I can see now why he says this. Yes, I can."

Immediately comfortable, the two unearthed common bonds as they spoke of their love of color and paint, for the animals — and of Vassili. Kaiti smiled at Lily as she handed her a card. "You know, in a way I feel that you are like a little sister to me, Lily. We must stay in touch. Please, take this, let me know when you are coming back to our island. Call me. I will be here — we will kidnap Popi! We will all paint here, together, on this terrace, where she and I used to paint with my mother, OK? God willing, we will meet again."

Lily suddenly felt quite huge in the small space she inhabited, like Alice in her Wonderland. Alone now in the shadows of the terrace she breathed in all of the feelings stirred up with the night, seeing quite suddenly that she was a young woman who mattered in the world — not just the cute little girl who was loved deeply by her parents and her grandma and friends, but a young woman who was loved and respected by others, far from her home.

With the perfect timing cats will have, Minou came out from a hiding spot in a stand of bushes, mewing quietly as she rubbed on the girl's legs. "Oh Minou! You <u>are</u> here!" Lily crouched to greet her purry friend, a much-needed connection to the earth pulling her back from the heady ethers. Still deeply moved, and not quite ready to step back into the light, Lily gathered the pliant little cat into her arms and watched the flow of gaiety from the shelter of the shadows — the singing and dancing, her parents doubled in laughter as they stumbled over quickened steps, Vassili and Anais in their happiness. *Oh yeah ... This is goodness!*

She would never forget this day — the light, even the colors, and how she felt when Vassili thanked her, or when Anais kissed her so sweetly, and some years later she would remember that it was in this moment she knew that somehow along her own life's path she would spread the wealth of all of this love and kindness and encouragement. She basked in this wonder a bit longer with little Minou held close to her heart before Harry walked through the firelight and took her hand, pulling her into the circle where her weighty thoughts were quickly carried away by their laughter as they tried in vain to mimic the steps of the lively kalamatianos, its dancers swirling though the veil of wood-smoke.

Food was everywhere. The cooks had outdone themselves, as was custom for these special events, and hungry people hovered around all of the tables, over the cauldrons of soup and the pots of pastitsio and platters filled to overflowing with beautifully grilled fish of all sizes. There were stuffed peppers and plates of pungent meatballs and men offered up chunks of crisp but perfectly moist bar-b-qued chicken and of course, the pit roasted lamb and goat — bowls filled with the last of the season's tomatoes and cucumbers, cut up and garnished with red onion and olives from local trees and sprinkled with oregano harvested from the local hills, were flanked by plates heaped with hunks of fresh feta cheese made from goat and sheep's milk, and baskets of warm bread.

Of course there were the pitchers of wines fresh from the barrel to wash it all down with and to fuel the evening's dance. They'd never seen so much food in one place, and Eleni and Lily took little samples of everything, Lily, of course, abstaining from the bits of animal, while Harry hovered by the table of desserts a'drip with honey and flecked with coconut, smiling at his girls as he patted his stomach.

From a pause in the festivities a man slipped into the center of the circle formed by dancers and tables. He raised his arms up and a hush fell, and then, slowly snapping his fingers in the sudden quiet he started to dance, alone in the glow of the fire's light. A young man, a friend, kneeled at his feet, staring up into the face that was lost in the passion of the dance, clapping solid time as though doing so might be able to keep the dancer tethered to the earth. It was a sadly breathtaking zeymbekiko, a solo dance, and as others kneeled in a circle to join in the clapping, the musicians were finding their way into the mournful piece. Eleni could not help but recall a quote, by Plato, she thought, one that her favorite English teacher had cited long ago as evidence that art was a balm for one's being —

"The dance, of all the arts, is the one that most influences the soul. Dancing is divine in its nature and is the gift of the Gods." *Surely he had been speaking about this dance ... pure soul ...*

Just as the lonely dancer left the circle, his face twisted with emotion, one of the old ones, a woman dressed in the traditional clothing of the island, stood up. Unaccompanied, her eyes closed, she began to sing and as the words came, Arianna whispered their translation to Eleni and Harry. "There is nothing of my home but what is in my heart and what is in my dreams," The eerie sound of the clarinet, a stirring, a weeping, wove through the woman's plaintive, haunting melody like the flames shimmering now through the dark of the night. "but with my heart, I can sing for you, and with it's fire I can warm you ... with my arms, I will shelter you, and when I dance, you fall into my eyes ... this is all the home I need ..." Her rasping contralto made every hair on Eleni's arms stand on end. Harry stood with tears in his eyes. The song was well known by almost everyone there, and by its end a host of voices had joined the singer and the weeping klarino.

Following the last of those notes lingering in the chilling air there was a long silence, and from within its stillness the smaller and sleepier of the children were ushered away, taken to be bedded down all together like a little herd of goat kids in nests of pillows and soft blankets. A fire glowed in the warm quiet of the potters studio at the back end of the cottage, and they would sleep in peace there under the watchful eyes of several of the Yia Yias, though it wouldn't be long before the old women would be snoring right alongside the children.

Taking Lily by the hand, Eleni and Popi stole her away to help Anais' friends decorate the couple's bedroom, dressing the bed with new French linens strewn with rose petals and placing pots of flowers all around the room, lighting lamps and candles. On the bed stand, the women left a plate of sweet baklava and a big pitcher of wine.

"What do you do this for?" Lily asked.

"Oh, to be sure to sweeten the first moments of the rest of their nights together, my flower." Popi said to the girl, neglecting to explain the part about the sweetening traditionally symbolizing the awakening of sexual passion and fertility. "Wine is the Nectar of the

Gods, you know, it fortifies the spirit! And the sweets, well, the honey is symbolic of all that is delectable in love. We're giving good blessings, here, for the rest of their lives to come!" The other women rolled their eyes and snickered, but the answer was good enough for Lily. "This all is a small part of a big tradition, Lily. Though the marriage itself was not the church's way, this is nevertheless one of the traditions of some of the people."

Old Melina slowly made her way to front of the group of women gathered about the bed, and in the tradition of some distant time flung drachmae coins upon the fresh linens. "For the young lovers" she giggled, like a little girl, as other bent elders filed into the room to do the same.

The considerable breadth of the day had begun to take it's toll and exhausted revelers started to make way to Vassili and Anais to offer their good wishes and blessings and then wander off into the dark one by one, two by two. A young friend, Yiorgo, had kindly offered a ride home and was motioning to Harry that it was time to leave.

"Let me gather up my girls, Yiorgo!" Harry called, breathless from the dance. He found Lily in the cottage and coaxed her from the clutch of women, all singing now, to look around for Eleni who had disappeared into the darkness.

They found her sitting on the veranda that looked out over the village to the sea, the lights from town sparkling like gems in the distance. "You know, this is where that little dog was born! Did I ever tell you that?" Eleni, drunk with emotion and a bit too much of the ouzo she still held in her hand, started to cry and laugh at once. "I'd forgotten that! How sweet, that such a sad story about such a sad little creature would lead to this much happiness!"

"Our Margarita? No Mama, I think you're being silly."

"Oh, no, no, no!" Eleni crooned. "Vassili told me a story one day ... about his wife ... well, his wife THEN ... and about all of the dogs and all of the cats and then she died and her dog had puppies and Margarita was one of them and, oh, then everything was just lost in all of that sadness. Just lost. And Vassili got lost too. But he found himself, didn't he? He found his happiness again. Right here ... with Anais. One day, I will tell you that story." Harry helped her to her feet and put his arm around her while Lily wiped the mascara smudging under her eyes, "My crazy little Mama ... let's forget all of those sad stories, OK? There are happy ones here now."

They slipped away into the night with the others, leaving Vassili and Anais to their bliss. Yiorgo was waiting by his car. The little boat left moored in the harbor would wait to be collected another day.

Harry and Eleni had come to know Yiorgo on their first visit to Greece, meeting him by chance in a vegetarian restaurant hidden deep in the maze of the Plaka's alleyways. They had taken great pains to find the place, for it was one of the very first of its kind in Athens where the utterance of the word 'vegetarian' was usually the cause of great consternation amongst people for whom the diet staples consisted of lamb or pork! It was over a beautiful vegetarian, Mediterranean meal that they met Yiorgo, the co-owner of a small company that specialized in what was just now coming to be known as 'organics', and from there the connection of kindred souls blossomed wildly.

Yiorgo lived in the sprawling city with his mother now, but had been raised on a small farm, on an island. He told Eleni and Harry of its exceptional green beauty, its beaches and hidden ruins and soulful people — just when they were trying to find passage somewhere, anywhere, during the busy Easter season those many years ago.

And that is how they came to know of this, their beloved island-home.

After completing his mandatory two-year service in the Greek military, like many of his countrymen, Yiorgo spent a few years in the Merchant Marines. He didn't mind the hard work and had enjoyed learning of other cultures and lands while traveling the world aboard the huge cargo ships, but farming was in his blood — as soon as he was able to come home with money in his pocket he went to University to study agriculture, and then started a farming cooperative just outside of Athens' scrappy southern suburbs.

His father, and his father before him had worked the land, and in the same ways Yiorgo paid homage to his roots. Besides working the fertile soil mindfully, he traversed the local countryside encouraging the farmers not to give up their old, more natural ways. He helped them avoid the use of chemicals and insecticides by planting vegetation that encouraged the busy birds and beneficial insects to visit, and taught them how to better make use of their animals' manure to make a loamy compost, a natural, wholesome fertilizer that would make the soil healthy for their crops.

His older brother, Christos, did the same for the farmers who raised animals for meats, teaching them how to keep up with so-called 'progress' by growing healthy animals while shunning the new ways, those time cutting factory farming methods of the West — the feeding of antibiotics in a misguided attempt to keep sickness at bay, injections of hormones to get the animals to grow more meat in less time, and the mass confinement of too many animals in too little space, all considered by many to be not only unhealthy for human and beast alike, but also quite inhumane.

Together, the brothers helped this small group of forward-thinking farmers market their healthier products. And these were some of the 'new ways' that Eleni felt were good, those that gave back to the past, back to the land from which they'd sprung.

Yiorgo chatted on about the family business while navigating the winding roads that led back to the villa.

"I don't eat meat." Lily quite matter-of-factly stated her position from the back seat.

He laughed. "You, and Christos, my friend - you are two of a kind! My brother may work with the meat famers, but he won't eat the animals they grow!" He then told a story of the farmers, who, at the end of the growing season turned their pigs out into their gardens and fields, along with their chickens, to eat the rotting leftovers. Naturally fertilizing the soil as they rooted and dug, the pigs aerated the ground with their nose discs, and the chickens, in between delightful dust baths, rid the soil of pests that were unearthed. In the rear view mirror Lily could see the kindness in his face, illuminated by the soft glow of the dash lights.

"And what Christos loves to do more than anything ... even more than fishing on the boat? It is just sitting quietly, watching the pigs and chickens, running and playing free in the fields! That is it! Have you ever seen pigs turned out into fields, Lily? They can run like the wind! They race, like little horses. And they play just like little puppies, biting and rolling over one another! They scoot around, they leap and twist in the air, they even bark in joy, and this is something that many people do not know about them!"

Dancing pigs! Lily smiled at the vision as she snuggled sleepily into the warmth of her mother's side.

They all fell into their beds when they reached the quiet little house, asleep almost before they closed their eyes and hushed further to deep slumber by the sea's gentle lullaby. Ouranos the cat uncurled from her warm slumber vertebrae by vertebrae, stretched, and with a final shiver of the tip of her tail walked to her bowl of kibble. When she'd eaten her fill, she gave herself a bit of a bath and then, gracefully scaled the terrace wall to sit silently at her post, holding the calm in its place for the night.

to open to the mystery

It was almost mid-day before there were any stirrings. One by one, the bleary eyed made their way to the table for a breakfast of yogurt and fruit set out by the admirably energetic Harry, while Eleni brewed fresh pots of coffee in her sleep.

Autumn was making its show and kept them inside around the heavy wooden table while the coffee did it's warming and waking, all bundled with shawls and blankets against the chill. Lily told Popi about her conversation with Kaiti,, and the invitation to paint on the cottage terrace and as she shared Yiorgo's tale of the dancing pigs the laughter seemed to break the chill. Eleni threw the French doors open to the day and tendrils of sun filled air streamed in and grabbed them all, willing them out into the open where they stretched in the sunlight, all but Lily groaning a bit against the indulgences of the night. Theo and Harry, ready to take some advantage of the day agreed to take a moped to town in search of aspirin for sore heads and aching muscles. Harry would bring the abandoned caique home.

There were two boxes in the trunk of Yiorgo's car — supplies for the dog shelter that Eleni had sent to Theo, who then had handed them off to Yiorgo for passage to the island. He wrestled them out now and presented them ceremoniously to Lily.

"For she who only loves ... and does not eat ... the animals." Lily grinned and thought to thank him "for helping the Earth", and with that he hopped into his car and sped after the moped and down the dirt roads to the town to catch the car ferry back home to the mainland.

The three girls spent the next hours shelling on the little beach, and skinny-dipping in its silken waters. Though the season, just an arms length from winter, had cooled the sea considerably, it was still remarkable to dip and float in once one had gotten used to its bite. Wrapped in colorful pareos against the bit of breeze, they wandered the beach searching for shells and finally sitting under the weakened sun, picnicked on bread they soaked in olive oil and then topped with feta and tomatoes sprinkled with oregano, groaning in pleasure as they licked their fingers when there was none left.

In this solitary company of women, they talked at great length of many things, but mostly of this extraordinary respite from the ordinary.

"I know there is good in this world." Eleni said as she rubbed sunscreen lotion over her daughter's shoulders, "We all try to do what we can to add to it and not take away, but sometimes all of the craziness out there just seems too big to me. The hunger, the sadness, the violence ... I get stuck, I forget to try, and my hope just gets away from me. But I'm a mom. I have to maintain hope! This place ... it helps me do that."

"I paint my hope and fear, Eleni." Popi said. "It all comes out in colors and form, and hopefully my fear can be recognized by someone else, "Oh, I am not alone" they might think, and then the hope, perhaps it can inspire."

Eleni began to braid Lily's long red hair, stiffened by the salty water. "I come here and it fills me up with all that is good. It's as if my soul needs something here to thrive, some mysterious, hidden element that cannot be found anywhere else. It's found only in long walks along this sea, swimming in its waters or wanderings through ancient ruins that otherwise only seem real in the pages of picture books! It feeds me. It feed my soul. It quenches my thirst, I write and the words just flow. And the photos I'm able to take here seem to emanate that mystery. I know, Popi, the hope and fear, it all becomes something else, more tangible, more manageable. And for me, the troubles seem to empty away, I get filled instead with a renewal, freshness ... and then, I feel like I can conquer mountains of madness!"

Lily had moved away to make a sand sculpture, one of a small dog lying curled in the sun. Eleni and Popi were quiet now, focused on the bit of warmth that had washed in on the breeze, eyes closed, taking every bit of it in as they might the sound of a goat bell off in the distance or a fisherman's song coming in on aural waves from a boat on the water.

"Mama, look. It's Margarita. I thought that she should be here with us now, somehow, even if she is just made of sand." She forced their hand and brought the conversation around, from the foreign lands of grownup thought to talk of the dog's shelter where she looked forward to taking the furry residents out for walks in the quiet, sun drenched cypress woods, "I want to help the dogs to just be happy. That would make me happy." And what happiness that would bring the dogs, indeed, given time with pads to the dirt and nose to the ground to stretch their legs and catch the meaning in mysterious scents carried in the wind, time to just be happy dogs.

Eleni reminded her that the situation for the animals there had indeed gotten better.

"It's not perfect, but many people have become much more willing to treat them kindly and learn more about them, and take them in as pets instead of just leaving them to the streets. A redemption of sorts."

"Redemshun? What is redemshun?" Lily asked.

"Well," Eleni searched for the words that would make sense to Lily, something she would remember. "it's something good, very good, that has come out of something that has been very bad."

Lily nodded as she sculpted a sand nose on the recumbent Margarita. "When do we get to go to the dogs' shelter?"

"Tomorrow. We'll take the scooters up. And then ... we must head for home."

They all groaned in unison.

"So will there be time to look for kitties?" Lily had been hoping to walk through the neighborhoods to see if she could find any of her foundlings, to see Manoli's cats who lived by Margarita's point, and for the chance to visit Mo, who had become quite the celebrity in his time with Arianna.

"Yes, we'll go to town later, Lil ... dinner at Kosta's, so we'll make our rounds before that. We have the kitty food that Takis gave you, but from what Arianna has told us, we know that there will be no need to feed Mo!"

Mo was very well known now as the greeter and resident bed warmer at Arianna's hotel — he and his mistress had recently been written up in several English newspapers as examples of how a change in attitudes was making a difference for some of the animals in Greece. The articles referenced Arianna's own change of heart, and how Mo had come into her life from the streets. Arianna was quoted as saying that "a little American girl, through her own love and concern for the street cats showed me how to change and instead of fearing the creatures, how to love and care for them myself." The fact that Mo now had been featured as playing such a leading role in the business of the villa drew animal lovers from far and wide to the island, specifically to Arianna's villa for the opportunity to meet the celebrity, and it was becoming increasingly more difficult to secure a booking there.

The men returned in the early afternoon, Theo on the moped and Harry in the caique, armed with the aspirin that was no longer needed as the hours of clear air and sun and sea with fine friends had already chased any aches and pains away.

There was a sudden rush about the little house, as Theo and Popi had a ferry to catch. Bags were collected up while Harry refueled the little boat and they all jumped aboard for the return trip to town with the afternoon's sun and touch of wind turning the deep blue of the sea into shimmering sapphires all around them.

Eleni and Lily left their clan sitting at Kosta's taverna while they took a brisk walk through the neighborhood to Arianna's villa. As they passed the grassy lot where a passel of Lily's street kitties had once lived, the girl suddenly hesitated.

"MOM ..." she whispered, grabbing Eleni's hand. There amidst the rich aromas of garlic and rosemary and something heavenly stewing on her stove, the woman sat in a chair in her blue framed stoop across from the lot — an old woman, swathed in black from head to toe. Two kittens climbed her long skirts in play, and she cradled another, a fat ginger ball of fluff, in her lap. The old one gave them a wave and a toothless grin.

"That's her!" Lily gasped as they turned into Arianna's alley. "That is the old woman who screamed at me, the one who tried to sweep me and the kitties away! Remember? That's her!"

Eleni laughed. "Oh my! And look at her ... covered in kittens! You know what Lily, that is Arianna's old grandma! She must have been watching all along. See how things can change? From her accosting you, to you teaching Arianna about the cats, and now, well ... a lapful of kitties! Right there, it's change we've hoped for. That is just amazing! Now let's find more change ... let's go and find Mo."

And there he sat, at his post as Arianna's 'greeter' as expected, busily batting pens from the desktop and rearranging her paperwork. He must have weighed in at close to fourteen pounds now, a strapping fellow with huge feet and a healthy glow to his coat. Lily couldn't believe that it was her Mo.

"No, this can not be my bony little cat with the big eyes and elephant ears! No way!" she would repeat over and over with a shake of her head as Mo smiled at her from his station, purring, his slowly waving tail further signaling his pleasure. A soft, gentlemanly 'meow meow' was all he had to say.

Arianna walked them down the steps to her breakfast terrace to introduce the plump little herd of street foundlings that she now cared for, all recently spayed or neutered thanks to Manoli, who had taken this band of urchins along on his yearly pilgrimage to the vet clinic on the mainland.

But time was slipping away. Eleni and Lily left Arianna to continue their quest, down the familiar cobbles and past the old pine tree, haunted by the ghosts of puppies, to the stairs at Margarita's Point where they saw several of Manoli's wards, including the friendly black kitty with the perpetual Cheshire Cat grin, now also a sleek, grown cat.

Lily didn't see any of the others she had looked after. Life here was still very hard for a street cat, and it was left unspoken that a clandestine end of season's poisoning may have occurred just before they had arrived for Vassili's wedding. The new mandate, that such cruelty was indeed a punishable offense, had still not been voiced nor acted upon publicly but instead of dwelling on that sadness, Lily and her mother talked again about the hopeful fact that there were very few street dogs left in the town, and of how many more dogs they saw now that were happy pets. The dog shelter women's attempts to educate and illuminate appeared to have paid off. It was heartening to see well-fed dogs wearing collars, and the sight of an old man caressing the head of the loyal companion sitting at his side was priceless.

Down along the waterfront Lily again spied the old Queen of the Quay, the saggy old bitch with a grizzled and graying muzzle who sported her own collar — the name 'Monica' was engraved upon the tag.

"I've heard that she belongs to the young new Mayor!" Eleni said with a chuckle as they watched scooters move carefully around the old lady who was again flat on her back in the afternoon sun right there in the middle of it all, absolutely oblivious to any reason for fear. "No one would dare hurt the Mayor's pet! Apparently the

357

man's a dog lover, a much better model than the old Mayor. Popi told me that he got this old beauty from the shelter!"

They knelt next to the dog who sneezed a hello and gave them an upside down smile. "When I was here last time, well, I know this sweet old dog wouldn't have been right here, making all of these old guys go around her! Someone would have chased her away. And she wouldn't have been such a fattie, that's for sure." Lily was amazed by the changes that seemed to have come about. She fingered the old dog's soft curls. "I can't believe this, Mama ... it makes me sad that it couldn't have been like this for Margarita. It's just kind of not fair."

Eleni looked around, noticing the long shadows and the clarity in the faintly dimming light. Autumn. Wood smoke was starting to curl over the harbor from the stove pipes on the back streets and she imagined families sitting by their fires for warmth. The chill was creeping in earlier today, and she wrapped her shawl tighter around her shoulders. "Me too, darlin'. But after knowing how hard life was for her and all of the others ... doesn't that just make the changes we're seeing now so much sweeter? You know, there probably is some other sad little dog that we could take home with us, Lil. Harry and I talked about it. We think that, if you agree, it is something we can do, you know, in honor of Margarita. Aethna wrote, telling us about how getting papers for passage only takes about a week, now — and then the dogs can be flown to their new homes. We're going up to the shelter tomorrow. Taking a dog from our island home might just be a happy end ... at least for us, and whoever you pick ... to Margarita's sad story. Goddess knows there are plenty of dogs to choose from."

"Oh Ma! Oh yeah!" Lily got up, grabbed her mother and sloppy kissed her on the cheeks, and did her happy dance.

"Wooooo." said the upside down old lady dog, wagging her tail as if seconding the motion.

They met up with the rest of the group for an early dinner at Kosta's but all too soon the ferry was pulling into the harbor. Sad goodbyes were mercifully cut short, for the boat's crew had already ushered in the last of the vehicles and in some furious rush were starting to pull the planks just as they arrived. Once Theo and Popi appeared, waving from the upper deck, and the engines churned the peaceful waters, Lily, Harry and Eleni hurried off themselves to be certain they could reach the villa before darkness set in.

They were readying their own little boat when Vassili and Anais happened by.

"Kalispera my friends! Kapitan Lily! Mana, Baba! Is my grandfather's little old barka treating you well? She is a good little boat, she could probably take you back to your little house all by herself!" He jumped aboard Hestia, rummaging around a bit before holding the raggedy old cat nest up for them to see. "Bravo, lipon — see now, we've come for little Minou's bed! In all of my own excitement I forgot this, her greatest pleasure, and for that, she is not happy with me!"

"What, no honeymoon Vassili?" Eleni called out to their friend.

He laughed loudly. "Ah, Eleni, all of life is a honeymoon ... when you have the love of your dreams by your side, and a fat ghataki to keep your lap warm! And, with the sea at my fingertips," he stood with his hands to the air, facing the southern sea, "dancing over the little waves on my Hestia, the best of the best? No honeymoon? No problem! Ola kala, life, all of it, it is good!"

As was the custom, the family filed aboard Hestia for a visit, Vassili pulling food wrapped up like presents from a bag. As he sliced cheese and bread freshly baked by Anais, she poured them all, including Lily, small glasses of tsipouro so they could make a proper toast.

"... to new beginnings and the long life of great friendships." Harry offered.

Vassili cleared his throat and, facing his wife and friends, thrust his glass towards them with his offering of an old blessing.

"We have shared the bread, and the salt. Yamas!"

"Yamas!" All of the glasses were raised to the sky. The tsipouro went down easily, warming in the cool of the afternoon.

"Lily mou, sit, please sit. Lipon. Please ... you tell this old man your hopes and your dreams. We have a little tiny bit of time here before the night, she starts to come and you all must hurry back to your house. So ... tell me." He offered her a cushion for the portside bench, sat down himself, lit a smoke and leaned back against Hestia's railing, ready to listen.

Lily sat with him, nodding slowly as she looked around for Minou to hold, her grounding comfort and then remembered that the cat was no longer living on the boat. She was on her own.

"Well ..." She took a deep breath. "Well ... hmmm. My hopes and dreams?"

He just closed his eyes and nodded. There was no way out.

"Vassili!" she whined. He nodded. "Ok, OK, well ... Let's see ... um, I want to travel. I want to live here. I want to paint with Kaiti at your house ... I want to start a

360

rescue shelter for old horses at home. I want to take African dance classes."

"Po po, wait, wait! Oh my gosh, little one, of course, of course you do. But, if you could pick just one thing, not that you must ever only have one dream, no of course not ... but just the one thing to pour your heart and your soul into, one thing that might change the world, well, what could that be?"

She was quiet. And then it came.

"I love animals. I just want to help them. When I grow up, I really think I want to study this thing called 'Humane Education'. It's something new, I think, and it will help me teach people to care for everything that lives, to be good to the earth, to other people but most especially, to the animals ... I mean, they share this planet with us. It's theirs too."

"Ah, my darling, this, you would be very good at. See, here? You and your mother? In your actions, you have already changed the minds of half of the people of this island! Soon, all of these old men that you see?" He tipped his cap up a bit with the tip of his finger and with a sweep of his thick hand, gestured to the walkers on the paralia. "Not a wife at their sides, but a dog, a little, fat dog! And so ... what gave you this idea of saving us stupid human beings from ourselves, eh? Why this 'Human' Education?"

"<u>Humane</u> Education, Vassili!" She giggled. "I grew up with them all around me, dogs and cats, ponies, even an old cow that my Mom brought home. It was totally fun, kind of like I had tons of brothers and sisters, you know? Only, they were furry! They are as much a part of our family as any of us big people are. Me and my friends play with them, probably even more than if they really were my real brothers and sisters. Anyway, I learned

... from them ... that they felt things like we do, and that they were very smart and really, really funny, and just knew that we had to respect them. And love them. Just like I learned that about my human family, and my friends. I just don't know how anyone couldn't love them! Then I watched a television show with my Mom, I think I was about eight years old then maybe? It was about this woman named Jane Goodall? She has studied chimpanzees in Africa all her life. They are <u>such</u> incredible animals, Vassili. You know, they are our closest relatives, I think that they have almost exactly the same DNA genes that we do? I would love to be able to live in Africa with them, to help them! Anyway, Jane Goodall is really amazing, kind of like a hero to me. She's super cool! She's kind of old now, but she still goes all over the world, helping people see how important our environment is. Not just to us, but to everything that is alive, and she shows how we are ruining the places the chimpanzees and other amazing animals live in. Sounds bad, I know, but actually, by teaching about all of this stuff, she mostly helps people to learn how to help, and to have hope for the future."

The large ferry's passage away from the island always sent waves coursing to shore, and they came now, causing the well moored Hestia to nod wildly as if she and the sea were in agreement with all Lily had to say. Lily laughed as the boat bobbled, but Vassili urged her to go on.

"That show ... I don't know, it just made me want to do what she does. Anyway, so not too long ago my Dad heard about this new college course called 'Humane Education' that pretty much teaches about all those things Jane Goodall talks about. It's so new that not many people even know about it. It really interested me, but

362

then I kind of forgot about it. But now, for some reason, I know that is what I want to do. I just know. So when I am old enough to go to college, that is what I want to study."

Vassili sat rapt, bushy eyebrows raised in his wonder.

"Bravo, I am impressed, my Lily ... though, am I surprised? No! You have so much intelligence, so much passion and with all that and your great and caring heart, you will be able to do anything you want to do with your life. Anything! And it will be good!"

He slapped his thighs and nodded.

"My Kaiti, she is a bigwig, you know ... a big artist in the city of New York in your states. But now, it seems she has grown very tired of the crazy, fast life, it does not hold her in its magic spell anymore. So, she thinks she will come here, back home, to spend the next years here on the island, painting its beauty and teaching art to the cute little kids. Ah, opening up the young souls to light, and to beauty, and to mystery ... just like you! It is good!"

Vassili was perched on the edge of the bench with his elbows on his knees, resting his head in his hands, but suddenly sat straight and flicked the ash from his smoke over the side of the boat. They both heard it sizzle as it hit the water before he shook his head and leaned in close to Lily again, his worn palms held together, offering her his gentle prayer.

"With both of you at work," he said, "what a wonderful world we will have."

The light was just beginning to fade and he bent back and looked past the edge of the boat's awning to the sky and then the sea, as if measuring what was left of it.

"Lipon. It is time to go, my Kokinoula. Pahme." Vassili stood, and holding his hand out to the girl he called to Harry and Eleni on the other side of the boat, "You just have time, my friends. You will go now." And the next moments swirled like they were caught up in a sudden wind as Eleni took photographs of Vassili and Harry hugging, and Anais hand feeding a slice of cheese to Lily in the brilliant, last light. Belongings were collected and plates and glasses were gathered up and then Vassili quickly ushered them over to the smaller caique, untying the mooring lines and throwing them to Harry once they were all aboard. As the little engine purred to life, he stood with Anais by his side, waving his cap high above his head.

Harry took the helm now and Eleni and Lily huddled together for warmth as they set off upon the glassy water into the orange of the setting sun and back to their last nights at their villa by the sea.

there's the hope

Once Harry figured out how to secure the unwieldy boxes to the equally unstable scooters, they set off. With Lily behind him on his bike, Eleni riding the other they puttered off towards a few last hours on a favorite beach to scan for shells and feed the begging fish, and to burn a fresh image of the familiar sea into their memories.

After that they were off, up into the hills.

They arrived in the middle of siesta, which the multitudes of dogs there even seemed to recognize. It was quiet, with just a whisper of a wind in the tall cypress and the dogs were laying about, snuggled deep in their sheltered dreams. Lily and Eleni crouched quietly by the chain link fence, observing sleepy inmates while Harry carried the boxes to the office. They could hear him chatting a bit to Aethna, whose voice was raised with the pleasure of seeing him again. One by one, dogs awoke and ventured over to the fence to see if they might possibly solicit a scratch behind an ear and eventually the quiet gave way to all of their stirrings, rising to a fevered pitch of excited barking.

There were about ninety dogs in all, really too many to count as they milled about. Lily pointed to a few of them with the thought of taking one home in mind — a shaggy, cream-colored terrier of sorts that looked like one of their own sweet dogs at home, and the lumbering, sloppy, smiling dog that looked to be half Labrador. Most, though, were small and wiry, fit for a life 'on the run', with little bulk to have to keep nourished. Perfect island mutts.

Lily stood at the wire, peering over the fray to the dogs who had hung back, older dogs with little energy left to them — or those with perhaps not such pleasant memories of human strangers — and then pointed out a brown dog curled on a chair behind them all.

"Mama … I can see one that looks like it's maybe part Margarita. Can you see it? Maybe it's one of her grandchildren!"

Eleni looked up. Lily hadn't mentioned much of their lost friend. Maybe this dog was one of Margarita's kin, maybe this would be the one they would take home with them? Suddenly there was commotion amongst the dogs in the back of the group. *Aethna's coming*, Eleni thought as she scanned the crowd for other prospective family members. *Or someone's bickering over a bone?*

She heard it then, the strangled rasp morphing to a grating howl, and she struggled to grasp the familiar sound. Confused, she looked over at Lily, whose face had drained of all color and who just stared back at her, speechless.

Lily already knew. And after just one more uncertain moment, Eleni knew too. She knew that it was a voice calling out to them from the depths of memory, a voice that was shrilling now in its own knowing. A blur of brown swept across the courtyard towards them and as they both freed the breath they'd been holding in, Lily finally let out a sound.

"Margarita! Mama! Oh! ... Margarita ..."

The little brown dog jumped and strained against the fence, stretching her short legs up as far as she could, trying desperately to touch them both with her paws and her nose and her tongue, shrieking now with the same heartrending joy and sorrow and pain and elation as they were.

There was a moment of panic, they yet were outside the fence and she was within — the only thoughts, how to get her out and into their arms, out and away from the lost years, the sadness and fear, the abandonment.

"Please! Get her out, get her OUT, GET HER OUT!" Lily shouted.

Aethna, alarmed by the commotion in the dog's yard, came running as fast as she could. Eleni was still crouched, stunned, clinging silently to the wire fence, but Harry had seen the astonishing reunion unfold from the office veranda and was laughing as he ran to catch hold of his hysterical daughter.

"Lily, it's OK! Oh, she's OK!" he said into her ear, enveloping her in calm. Finally springing to her feet, Eleni levitated over to her daughter, held safely together now by Harry's embrace. They all had tears running down their faces, even Aethna who was inside the enclosure trying to pry the screaming Margarita away from the fence so that she could carry her out to her loved ones, out to freedom.

In moments the little dog, much grayer and thinner, more worn than they remembered her, was at their feet, singing and leaping and smiling, all wiggles and wagging tail and they could barely get their hands on her for all of her joy. But Lily swooped her up, holding her close in her arms while the dog licked her tears away, her raspy shrieks giving way to soft whines and soon she just seemed to melt in exhaustion, the years of yearning and waiting and searching taking their toll, and now that she had found them she could finally relax.

They carried her to the tree-draped-with-cats, and sat with Aethna as she gave them her account of how this dog had come to the shelter.

"She's not been here long, I must say. A kind young man brought her in, he said that his mother had taken the dog in some years before. The woman was a goatherd, lived far up in the hills, she did, and had found the little doggie one stormy night, layin' in a terrified and hungry heap under a tree in her orchard. She first thought the wee thing was dead. But she took her in and brought her back to life, and the loyal dog never left. Apparently she tended the goats with the old woman, sat in the shade of the olive trees with her at siesta, ate at her table, slept in her bed. But the lad said his mother had died recently and the little dog just seemed to give up. He couldn't get her to eat, and she was so forlorn ... her spirit seemed to be in another place, he said. He couldn't make her thrive no matter what he did, but he just couldn't bear to do away with her either, the dear soul. So he brought her to us. He said that maybe she would revive under the care of women, and either be able to live out her days here or find another person who she could live for. You gotta love him for all that, now."

"Oh my god. Oh my god." was all Eleni could say as she watched Margarita panting in Lily's arms. The old dog looked like she was smiling.

"He called her Nana." Aethna said. "She perked up a bit in the companionship of the other dogs here, yes, she did, maybe she even knew some of them from her town days. But the poor dear, she's never really warmed to people and she usually just keeps to herself. She claimed that old wicker chair in the back, there, as her own ... rarely does she ever move from it, other than for food and drink and to do her business. She would perk up at the sight of children, is all. Many of the dogs here seem to always be watchin', for someone, for somethin', but not this old girl. She just seemed to have given up, to be waitin' her time out. And at this point, I never would've thought that this was your wee Margarita, the famous little heroine! Never in a million years. Jesus, Mary and Joseph!"

Aethna told them that they could take her home, nothing would stand in their way now, nothing but a bit of time. Though there was blood-work and paperwork to be done, everything could be taken care of right there and Margarita could have her papers for passage within the week.

"We do have a new mayor now, just a lad he is, but a good boy and though he's not been very effective for us, at least doesn't get in our way. He likes the animals, he does. Oh, thank God for that! And our vets can get your papers drawn up quite quickly, now."

"A week?" Lily grew anxious. "A week? We have to go home tomorrow, how can we leave her now? We just found her! If we go, she'll just think that we left her again! She'll die of a broken heart! We can't leave her!"

Lily was right and so it was quickly agreed that she and Harry would leave the island as planned and Eleni would stay, accompanying Margarita home once the papers were in order. Aethna offered to provide a travel crate, and a collar and leash.

"It's OK, Lily. It will be fine! Harry has work, you have school ... but I can stay here. I'll find somewhere to stay in town with Margarita ... maybe with Popi's grandmother. And we have friends who offered to help us before. Someone will get us to the airport in Athens when we're ready and I'll fly home with her. I'm sure it all will work, it all will work perfectly. It all couldn't BE more perfect!"

It was quiet, now. The dogs had settled and were back to their siesta. All that could be heard was the last of the season's cicadas humming weakly in the old tree, and the breeze, up from the sea, whispering through its colorful, drying leaves — and Aethna, who sat straight, looking out to the water in the distance, soft sighs coming from deep within her as she worked to regain her composure. Eleni and Harry just held one another's hands very tightly as they watched over Lily, with Margarita, the lost one, in her arms. The little dog was fast asleep.

TESTAMENT

testament

Blinking in the early light, she raised her nose and drank in the scent of the morning.

She gently pushed away the fat, snoring orange cat and stood stiffly, stretched, and moaning in great pleasure, scratched behind her right ear. The door was open to the balmy air and she moved a few feet closer to the big screen, as though closer would bring the finer points to her in more delicious detail.

She smelled the new summer's warmth, the fresh scent of green that cloaked these early hours. She could smell the scent of the horses in the barn as they shifted and blew softly in happy anticipation of their morning hay and she could smell cunning in the palpable shadows left by coyotes who had passed so stealthily through in the dark of the night. She took in all she could of more of the delicious telling, until she'd drunk her fill.

The old brown dog turned with a bit of a shuffle and shook off the last bits of sleep before nuzzling the large, black Labrador who slept so close by her side each night. She headed for an open door.

Stopping first to kiss the hand that draped over the side of the bed, she then made way down the hall to check to see that her sleeping girl had made it through the night without harm. The dog's eyes had begun to fail her, she could no longer tell so easily that all was well with just a quick glance — with some effort she stood upon her hind legs, to closely smell safety in the warm skin of the one she truly adored.

Satisfied, the plump, wizened little dog pushed off, planted all fours back upon the ground with a grunt and a sigh and continued on her rounds — through the kitchen, past the Siamese sleeping sprawled over an arm of the chair, past the dish of food, full at all times. She lingered at the water bowl, replenishing her waking cells while a long-haired black and white cat purred wildly and rubbed the length of her body in familiar greeting.

With a stifled hop she squeezed through the dogs' door, to find herself in the open, bathed in the glorious, shimmering warmth of the rising sun.

She stood at the head of the driveway and barked, that raspy hack of a bark, each effort lifting her front paws off the ground — aiii yii yii, yak ack ack! — warning all that may not belong to beware, be gone, stay clear and after her morning chorus, convinced now that all was well in her world, she sat heavily on her behind, nose up to the slight breeze, and finished her reading of the news of the day. It was all good.

Her senses filled, she groaned to her feet and felt her way surely along the path she had worn across the grass, on to her very own nest of dirt and leaves at the foot of a huge grandmother oak that stood on a knoll, drenched now in the dawn's widening light. The old dog scratched the earth there a bit, to fluff it all up just right and turned 'round two or three times before finding just the right spot to lay her body down and with an 'oooomph', she settled, heavily, and stretched out in the welcomed warmth.

In moments, at peace and awash in love, she was snoring.

The tag dangling from her collar glistened in a ray of sunlight, a coppery testament …

It read:

My name is Margarita

I am loved …

I am home

AFTERWORD

A percentage of the proceeds from sales of this e-book will be donated to a few animal charities; a rescue and/or no-kill shelter in Grass Valley, California (yet to be determined) ... and to the Skiathos Dog Shelter, the sanctuary run by living, breathing angels, on the island of Skiathos, Greece.

I have been traveling to Greece since 1986. I remember well the street dogs we came across in Athens that first spring, especially the happy few that accompanied us on walks to the Acropolis or Agora through the back streets of Plaka and the whitewashed Anafiotican quarter. There were dogs all over the city ... napping on stoops just two feet from the onrush of traffic, in the doorways of shops, under benches in parks. Friendly, intelligent dogs, most begged for their food in the street-side tavernas and they all seemed to know to safely cross the busy streets with the flow of people when the stop lights turned from red to green! On that, our virgin journey deep into the heart of Greece's magic, they were just a part of the charm of it all.

That trip sparked a life-long love affair with a people and a place, but it wasn't until our next visit a few years later ... when we met up with little loud Margarita ... that I really began to learn of the sorrowful plight of the dogs and cats of the streets of Athens and the islands. At that time there was no sterilization available unless one lived on the mainland where one might find the services of a vet who, miraculously, actually performed the operations

... spays were most common, if only because there was a lot of alter-ego attached to one's male dog or cat's balls (as there still is, and is here in the U.S. as well!). "Cut THEM off? What do you mean, cut them off?" However, the most common means of curbing the population of the strays, or of dealing with any animal that was deemed a pest, was exactly as you have read in this story.

Though there have been laws against animal cruelty on the books in Greece for years, they still — in 2012 — are not enforced. Animals continue to suffer. Thankfully, over time many things *have* changed ... in some ways, dramatically. Sterilization surgeries are more readily available and people can take advantage of low cost clinics to have their pet spayed or neutered, as well as vaccinated against diseases that can run rampant if not checked. Shelters are more prevalent on the mainland and some of the islands now, though most often they are conceived and built by concerned foreigners and supported by tourists' euro — and while most of these shelters are quite rudimentary and still served only on occasion by visiting veterinarians, the dogs are given sanctuary and comfort, are well fed and have their needs attended to by humans with an amazing capacity to care, despite the great heartache that by nature accompanies the work they do. Eventually many of these lucky ones are adopted, taken to another country by visitors who provide them with comfortable lives, free of fear and filled with the kindness they deserve.

It took a good long while for things to begin to change for the cats, but now there seem to be organizations that focus on helping them as well. They round up colonies of street cats in order to vaccinate and sterilize them, and then take them to an area deemed protected feeding grounds where they can live in relative comfort without hunger. Some of the cats are even taken back to the neighborhoods in which they were found. The problems have not disappeared, and things are still incredibly tight for those who are doing the work to help the animals on a daily basis — but there has been improvement.

That said, now that the hard times are again set upon Greece, the animals will surely suffer. When people struggle to pay bills and feed families, pets tend to be neglected or abandoned; this is something we are seeing here in the U.S. Many will be cast to the streets and the times will reflect on them poorly, I fear.

It is my hope is that wherever we may be in the world, if we love the animals we will be their advocate. They are voiceless. We are not. If we see abuse or neglect we must speak up, and act. We can be sure that our own companions are sterilized, and if able we can help out at our local animal shelters by donating foods, walking dogs, cuddling cats and donating to their sterilization programs. Shelters across the U.S. are filled with lovely dogs and cats, most who once were a families' loving pet; pups, adults, even sweet elders who have been dumped by people who just can't deal with the infirmities of their old age. Some of these places have a 'no-kill' policy, some have animals waiting out their fate in measured days on death row, but what they have in common is that all of their animals need homes. We can make the choice to choose to adopt a loving companion from a shelter rather than supporting the business of a backyard breeder, or a puppymill.

When you travel, please cast your eyes to the streets once in awhile. If you don't like how the animals are being treated, don't continue to support that country with your tourist dollars. Or — be of help. Do what you can to ease the plight of the animals there, and if there is a shelter or organization doing some good, please help them do their job. Donate generously to their coffers. One can usually find kibble at a local market, so it is easy to help by leaving food out for the hungry ones. No, it will not really help them in the long term, and yes, it may make them dependent upon humans — but if we can make their miserable existence even just a wee bit more comfortable, in the moment, I'm all for it. There is so much we can do to ease the plight of these silently suffering, sentient beings.

Margarita, my little stray, and all of the feral but so willing cats and dogs of the Greek isles are simply archetypes for all creatures in need of compassion. Like Lily and Eleni, I happen to feel that the animals are much kinder, better beings than we humans and helping them has become my path ... my great wish is that All The Little Graces will join the ranks of advocacy for the needy animals of the world, helping to bring the plight of the voiceless creatures we humans domesticated so long ago more to the fore. Perhaps it will encourage readers to do what they can, wherever they may be.

Unless we humans can figure out how to treat the voiceless with dignity and caring, we'll never truly be able to figure out how to treat one another with the same ... and we will surly never come know peace.

Thank you for caring.

ABOUT THE AUTHOR

Eleanore MacDonald is a California native ... a musician, an animal advocate, a writer ... who lives in the foothills of the Sierra Nevada Mountains on a small farm graced with a host of furred and hooved creatures. She is also part of an award winning songwriting team with her husband Paul Kamm and has been a performing artist for 32 years.

You are invited to visit their music site - Paul Kamm and Eleanore MacDonald, at http://www.kammmac.com as well as Eleanore's blog - 'Notes From an Endless Sea' at http://www.eleanoremacdonald.wordpress.com.
Please contact her at eleanoremacdonald@gmail.com.

She is presently working on her 2nd novel.

Made in the USA
Charleston, SC
19 April 2013